Next in Line

A native of Dundee, Marion Todd studied music with the Open University and worked for many years as a piano teacher and jobbing accompanist. A spell as a hotel lounge pianist provided rich fodder for her writing and she began experimenting with a variety of genres. Early success saw her winning first prize in the *Family Circle Magazine* short story for children national competition and she followed this up by writing short stories and articles for her local newspaper.

Life (and children) intervened and, for a few years, Marion's writing was put on hold. During this time, she worked as a college lecturer, plantswoman and candle-maker. But, as a keen reader of crime fiction, the lure of the genre was strong, and she began writing her debut crime novel. Now a full-time writer, Marion lives in North-east Fife, overlooking the River Tay. She can often be found working out plots for her novels while tussling with her jungle-like garden and walking her daughter's unruly but lovable dog.

Also by Marion Todd

Detective Clare Mackay

MARION TODD
Next in line

First published in the United Kingdom in 2021 by

Canelo
Unit 9, 5th Floor
Cargo Works, 1–2 Hatfields
London SE1 9PG
United Kingdom

A CIP catalogue record for this book is available from the British Library.

Print ISBN 978 1 80032 454 1
Ebook ISBN 978 1 80032 103 8

Look for more great books at www.canelo.co

Printed and bound in Great Britain by Clays Ltd, Elcograf S.p.A.

3

*To Peter, who is my soulmate, my helpmate
and the most incredible support.*

*Except if we're playing chess
when he's a complete jerk!*

August

Day 1: Saturday

Prologue

It was a quarter to six when Russell stepped out of the back door of Lamond Lodge. The air was still, only the dawn chorus breaking the quiet morning. He closed the door softly, not that it was likely to wake the rest of them. Not after last night.

Out to the east the sky grew lighter and he quickened his step, anxious not to miss the sunrise. He crunched across the gravel, stepping lightly onto the manicured grass. Something caught his eye – a movement through the trees – and then it was gone. A fox, or a deer maybe? He should have brought binoculars. There was bound to be a pair somewhere in the house. It seemed to have everything else.

He reached the wooden steps that led to the treetop walk and began to climb, taking them two at a time. As he gained height the scaly brown bark of the Scots pines became orange and he drew level with the flat-topped branches, admiring their blue-green needles. The elevated walk didn't quite clear the crown of the trees but there were enough gaps to afford him a panoramic view in every direction. He looked first to the south-west, admiring the Lomond Hills, their ancient volcanic plugs the highest

3

points in Fife. Far below he spotted a young deer, grazing on the long grass beyond the trees and he watched it for a moment. Then he swept his gaze round, admiring the steep gable roof of Lamond Lodge, and across the Eden Estuary, north, towards Dundee. The university town of St Andrews sat in the foreground bound by its two beaches, and he completed the circle, turning east to look out over the North Sea.

And then he watched as the light on the horizon became a glint of gold, spreading out across the sky. Best time of the day. They didn't know what they were missing, back in the house. Down on the ground the deer stopped suddenly, raised its head for a moment then, with a kick and a flash of its white tail, it bolted across the field. Something had startled it but he couldn't see what.

He didn't see the gun, didn't hear the shot. The sunrise exploded in his head and he spun round, falling like a stone to the floor of the walkway, a trickle of blood at his temple.

Chapter 1

'Therefore, if anyone can show just cause why this man and this woman may not be joined together in marriage let him speak now or forever hold his peace.'

A shaft of sunlight streamed through the stained glass of the old church, casting a warm light across the congregation. DI Clare Mackay stiffened in the short silence that followed the minister's words and she smiled nervously at the man beside her, DCI Alastair Gibson. He reached across and took her hand, giving it a slight squeeze. Clare swallowed, feeling her mouth dry, and ran her tongue round her lips.

The minister beamed round at the congregation. 'Always a nervous moment,' she said, and a ripple of laughter ran round the church. Then she turned back to the couple standing before her. 'Tom and Gillian...'

From her seat halfway down the nave, Clare craned her neck to see Tom. He was in a morning suit. She had thought he might be in a kilt. But then Gillian didn't strike her as a kilt kind of person. The morning suit with the rose-pink tie was much more her style. Clare could only see the back of his head but as she watched him, glancing at his bride, she couldn't help thinking it might have been her standing there in ivory silk. Her and Tom. A couple for so long, until Tom's role as a solicitor had brought him into conflict with Clare. It had been the beginning of the end and the catalyst for her move from Glasgow to St Andrews. They had both moved on, of course, Clare initially with the sculpture expert, Geoffrey Dark. She had thought he might be *the one* but then he'd moved to Boston and their attempts to keep a long-distance relationship alive had foundered.

And then, after a hesitant start, she had found herself drawn to her boss, DCI Alastair Gibson. She counted back mentally as Tom and Gillian delivered their vows. It was almost seven months now – seven months since they'd decided to give their relationship a go. *And we're still here*, she thought. She glanced at him, and thoughts of Tom and what might have been faded to grey.

'It's my great pleasure to pronounce you husband and wife,' the minister said, and a ripple of applause spread across the church as the happy couple locked lips.

And there it was. Tom was married. Tom who Clare had decided she could no longer be with, despite his best efforts. Tom who had wanted her long after she had stopped wanting him. And she hadn't wanted him any longer. She was sure about that. But a niggling voice in the back of her mind told her she would miss *him* wanting her. She flushed at this and felt the DCI squeeze her hand again.

'Okay?' he mouthed, and she nodded, hoping he hadn't read her thoughts.

The happy couple were heading for the vestry now to sign the register and the congregation prepared to listen to a cellist who had set up his instrument below the pulpit. As he began playing Clare thought the melody sounded familiar. She looked down at her order of service.

Can You Feel the Love Tonight
Elton John

'Is this from *The Lion King*?' the DCI whispered, and she nodded again. Suddenly there was movement from the front of the church and around twenty teenage girls began assembling behind the cellist.

'Oh God,' Clare whispered. 'They're going to sing.'

The DCI suppressed a smile as the girls launched into the chorus and Clare sank back in her pew. It was going to be a long day.

–

'Gaby,' the glamorous woman said, extending a hand across the table. 'And this is Luke.' She indicated a tall man to her left. Clare took him in. His hair was dark, swept back over his forehead, his features swarthy, and she wondered if he was Italian. Mediterranean, certainly. He was immaculately dressed in a beautifully cut suit with a high waistcoat. His tie, which seemed to be of an abstract design, was tightly knotted, a tiny jewelled tie pin catching the light as he moved. Clare felt she'd seen him before but she couldn't place him. Gaby, on the other hand, was a face familiar to anyone who followed daytime TV – her introduction patently unnecessary. *Daytime With Gaby* was riding high in the ratings. She was slimmer than she looked on screen. Maybe it was true about the camera adding ten pounds. Slender features too. Her outfit, a sleeveless lemon shift dress, hung simply, accentuating her figure, and Clare involuntarily drew in her stomach as she took a seat opposite. She could see necks craning at the other tables and she wondered if Gaby was in danger of eclipsing the bride on her special day.

'Al,' the DCI said, adding, 'and this is Clare.'

Gaby smiled broadly. 'Bride or groom?'

7

'Tom's an... an old friend,' Clare said, and Gaby nodded.

'Gillian teaches our daughter.' Gaby looked across to another table around which sat some of the girls who had sung in the church.

'Lovely singing,' Clare said, wondering if Gillian had invited all the girls' parents, or just the glamorous, celebrity ones.

Luke Gasparini reached across the table for a bottle of wine. 'Red, anyone?'

Clare shoved her glass across the white linen cloth in response. This reception, she decided, was not to be faced sober.

She was just finishing a slice of leek tart when the red-jacketed maître d' appeared at their table. He bent and said a few words to Gaby and indicated she should follow him. Clare watched as she threaded her way through the tables, all eyes on her. The maître d' opened the door to the reception area and Gaby passed through. As the door began to close slowly, Clare craned her neck and saw Gaby take up the receiver of a telephone on the reception desk. Then the door was opened again for a waiter bearing a tray of plates. Clare leaned over in time to see Gaby's free hand go to her mouth. She was looking round wildly and the maître d' who had been standing a little way off approached her once more. Minutes later he was back in the room, heading for their table. Luke rose to greet him and, after a few words, he turned back to retrieve Gaby's clutch bag and cream stole. He glanced at them, muttered something that sounded like *apologies* and then he too followed the maître d' out of the room. The door was wedged open now as a procession of waiting staff went to and fro with their trays. Clare saw Luke approach the reception desk and take a clearly distressed Gaby in his arms. She made to rise from her seat but the DCI put a warning hand on her knee.

'Leave them to it,' he said, his voice low. 'You're not on duty today.'

Clare relaxed back into her chair again, feeling a little as if she'd missed a chance to duck out of the reception. The starter plates were being cleared now and there were four more courses to go. And then the speeches. The day was growing longer by the minute.

–

'On behalf of my wife and myself...'

Tom paused for a minute to let the applause and cheers die down then he continued. 'Seriously, folks, Gillian and I are thrilled so many of you could be with us for our special day.'

Clare hadn't appreciated just how loud her mobile ring tone was until it cut through the middle of Tom's speech. She felt her face grow warm as she snapped open her bag and tried to find the mute button. She felt the eyes of the room on her and heard Tom making a joke about *Clare never changing*. She didn't dare look at Gillian's face. She had her phone now but her fingers seemed to have turned into thumbs as she struggled with the buttons. The DCI took the phone from her, flicked the mute button and the ringing ceased. The phone still buzzed in his hands, though, and Clare saw from the display it was Chris, Chris West, her detective sergeant. He knew they would be at the wedding. It was her weekend off. So why was he calling? Ignoring the DCI's frown, she took back her phone and rose from her seat.

'Sorry,' she said to the other guests at the table. 'Better take this.' Smiling an apology to Tom, she walked swiftly through the tables. The call had gone to voicemail by the time she reached the reception area. Without waiting to hear the message she redialled Chris's number.

'Sorry, Clare,' he said, 'interrupting your wedding. I thought it would go straight to voicemail.'

'What's up?'

'We've had a shooting.'

'You're joking?'

'Nope. Country house south of the town.'

'ID'd the victim?'

'Not yet. I'm heading over there now. Thought you'd want to know.'

'I'll leave now,' Clare said. 'Two hours at most.'

'No,' Chris said. 'It's fine. There's no point in you rushing back. Don't spoil your day.'

'Pfft,' Clare said. 'It's the wedding from hell. And the only interesting guests have just left.'

'Seriously,' Chris said. 'If you head back now the DCI will kill me. You know he will.'

'You leave him to me,' Clare said.

A burst of applause told Clare that Tom's speech was over and she moved across to the function room door and peered in. She caught the DCI's eye and motioned to him to follow her out. 'We have to go back,' she said as he appeared.

'Eh?'

'There's been a shooting.'

He drew her over to a corner of the foyer and indicated a small table with two armchairs. 'Tell me,' he said.

Clare stood her ground. 'I'll explain on the way. I'll just let Reception know we're checking out.'

He put a hand on her arm. 'Clare, will you just stop for a minute and tell me what's happened.'

She looked pointedly at his hand and he withdrew it.

'Please?' he said. 'At least sit down.'

She sat, perching on the edge of the chair. 'That phone call. It was Chris.'

'That's your work phone,' the DCI said. 'Why didn't you switch it off?'

Clare shrugged. 'Do you want to know or not?'

'Go on, then.'

'Like I said, there's been a shooting.' She paused to let this sink in. 'Some big house outside St Andrews. So obviously I have to go back.'

'Hold on,' the DCI said. 'You're not the only DI in Fife. Dundee can send someone, for that matter. And anyway, neither of us is fit to drive.'

'Dammit.' She hadn't thought of that. There had been champagne when they'd arrived at the hotel – she'd had two glasses of that. Then the wine with their meal. She recalled the DCI topping her glass up a few times. 'How much have you had?'

He shook his head. 'Too much. There's no way either of us can drive back.'

'Taxi?'

'Clare! It's the best part of seventy miles.'

'But a shooting, Al.'

'Listen, you have a good team back there. They know what to do and we'll head back in the morning. If it makes you feel better, give Chris a call back and remind him of the Standard Operating Procedures.'

She let her shoulders droop. 'Yeah, I suppose. He knows all that, anyway.'

'Well then. Look, Clare, we have a lovely room right here in the hotel. We can enjoy the rest of the reception, have a dance tonight and start fresh in the morning.' He reached across and took her hand. 'Okay?'

She made an effort to smile. 'Doesn't look like I've much option.' She glanced back towards the function room door. 'Suppose we have to go back in.'

He smiled. 'Not really. Let's just say we're too polite to interrupt the speeches again. We'll stay out here and have a drink instead.'

'We could hide in our room for a bit.'

He laughed. 'That might be pushing it.'

She nodded. 'Suppose you're right.'

He squeezed her hand. 'So, what do you want from the bar?'

Chapter 2

Clare moved her seat back towards the wall as Tom and Gillian sank down beside them. The band had struck up a waltz and the more enthusiastic ceilidh dancers were drifting back to their tables for a rest.

'I'm so sorry about my phone,' Clare said, but Gillian waved this away.

'Tom says you're never off duty,' she said, taking his hand. 'I think that's why he married a teacher – for the holidays!'

'I'm sure they're well-earned,' DCI Gibson said.

'I'll say,' Gillian beamed.

'I hope it wasn't anything important,' Tom said.

Clare forced a smile. 'Nothing that can't wait until morning.'

'We're staying here tonight,' Tom said. 'Maybe we could all meet for breakfast?'

'Oh, I think we'd better make an early start,' Clare said quickly. She smiled at the pair. 'You know how it is.'

The band announced an Eightsome Reel and Gillian rose.

'Come on,' she said, pulling her husband to his feet. 'I'm determined to teach you how to do this properly.'

Clare watched the pair head off to join the dancers.

'Fancy it?' the DCI said.

She shook her head. 'I'd hate to make a mistake in front of the teacher.'

He laughed. 'Come on, then. We've done our bit. Let's go and hide in the room.'

They elected to climb the thickly carpeted stairs rather than take the lift. 'I'll tell you this much,' Clare said, stepping out of her heels and stopping to pick them up. 'I am not having breakfast with Bridezilla down there.'

'I'm with you on that,' the DCI said. 'Let's have it sent to the room.'

'DCI Gibson! We are not made of money.'

'I'll pay. Anything other than watching you glaring at the bride over your granola.'

'To hell with granola. I'm having the full Scottish.'

They reached their room and the DCI retrieved the key from his sporran. The bed had been turned down and the lamps lit. An ice bucket with a bottle of champagne sat on a side table.

'Oh, Al,' she said. 'How lovely of you.' The door swung closed behind them and the DCI took Clare in his arms. 'I've been wanting to do this all day.'

She allowed herself to sink in, smelling his cologne, and feeling his hand in her hair. They stood for a minute and then she raised her face to meet his and found his lips.

Day 2: Sunday

Chapter 3

She was awake long before breakfast arrived. The DCI found her in the en suite, texting Chris.

'Seriously?' he said, rubbing his forehead. 'You couldn't wait a few hours?'

Clare shrugged. 'Couldn't sleep.'

'Any particular reason?'

'Just wondered what's happening.'

He hesitated. Then he said, 'Clare, why did we come here? To this wedding, I mean.'

She looked at him. 'I dunno. Because they invited us, I suppose.'

'You could have pleaded work, or said we'd booked a holiday.'

She nodded. 'Yeah. Probably should have.'

'So, Tom – you are over him, aren't you?'

She stared.

'It's just that, well, you seemed on edge all day yesterday, even before Chris called. I couldn't help wondering...'

She rose from her perch on the bidet. 'Come on. Let's get back into bed for a couple of hours. It's going to be a long day.'

He stood back to let her out of the bathroom and watched her move towards the bed. 'So you're not struggling with Tom marrying Gillian?'

She glanced at him. 'I dunno, Al. It's not that I wish I was still with Tom. I, well, I find it hard he's married someone so different to me. It makes me wonder if he thinks our years together were a waste.'

The DCI climbed into bed beside her and pulled her close. 'I'm sure he doesn't. Nothing is ever wasted. It's what makes us who we are.'

She forced a smile. 'Why are you always so bloody sensible, Al?'

'I told you. It comes with being a DCI,' he said. 'It's a condition of accepting the promotion.'

'There's no hope for me, then,' she said.

'Nope. Not a chance.'

–

In spite of her hurry to return to St Andrews they lingered over breakfast, Clare declaring it to be *awesome*.

'It is pretty fab,' the DCI admitted, putting down his fork. 'Coffee's excellent, too.'

She glanced at her watch. 'We'd better get a move on, though.'

'Tell you what,' he said, 'you slip out the side door while I check the bill. Save bumping into the happy couple.'

'We said we'd split the bill.'

'And we will. We can sort it out later!'

Clare rose, dabbing her mouth with a linen napkin. 'I'm not paying for this, though,' she said, indicating the breakfast tray. 'Far too extravagant.'

'Even if it spared you the breakfast from hell?'

'Even that.'

–

They drove back through glorious countryside, the fields golden with ripening crops.

'I love this time of year,' the DCI said. 'The colours are amazing.'

Clare was glued to her phone. 'Mm, yeah.'

'You're missing some lovely scenery.'

'Al, I have a shooting to deal with.'

He sighed. 'Go on, then. What's happening?'

She squinted at her phone. 'Victim's been ID'd.'

'Yeah?'

'Businessman from Glasgow.'

'Who ID'd him?'

Clare scrolled down the message. 'His sister. Seems they were staying in a country house for a few days. Six of them.'

'Staying with friends?'

She frowned, reading on. 'No. Chris says it's a house that's rented out to holidaymakers. Pretty fancy, apparently.'

'Has he interviewed them?'

'He says so. But I'll want to speak to them myself.' Clare's phone buzzed again and she clicked to open the message. 'SOCO still onsite. Been there since late yesterday.' She glanced at her watch. 'If we hurry we should make it before they pack up and leave.'

'Clare, I am not breaking the speed limit because you don't want to miss anything. Your team will update you. Trust them to do their jobs.'

She made no reply, turning her head away to look out of the window.

A few miles on the DCI slowed the car as they entered Cupar, a small but busy market town. Early on a Sunday morning, the traffic was light and they were soon through the town and heading for St Andrews. 'Where's the house?' he said.

Clare studied her phone. 'Chris says it's along Grange Road. South of the town. Go up North Street and I'll direct you from there.'

Grange Road was one of the quieter routes out of St Andrews, the residential streets soon giving way to fields on one side and trees on the other. A few miles further on Clare saw a line of cars parked along the verge. She recognised a couple of reporters, leaning against a field gate chatting, others still in their cars. She wondered about that. The victim's name hadn't rung a bell with her but he must have been a pretty high profile businessman to attract this amount of attention. A uniformed officer stood at a wide gate, opposite the press pack. The DCI indicated to pull in and the officer stepped forward, his hand raised. When he recognised Clare he waved them in and the DCI turned onto a gravel drive hooded by tall trees on either side. Clare felt the familiar nerves in her stomach as she wondered what awaited her.

Suddenly the drive cleared and she had her first view of Lamond Lodge through a barrier of Heras fencing. The starkness of the grey metal fence was somehow at odds with the opulence of the house beyond and she wondered why it was there. A pair of CCTV cameras covered a gap in the fence and she hoped they'd been switched on. It might just help them find the culprit – if the gunman had come from outside the grounds.

Again, an officer stepped out to intercept them then recognised Clare and stood back to allow them through the gap. The drive curved round towards the house which Clare thought was Edwardian. Or possibly Victorian. It was a three-storey dwelling in honey-coloured stone with two prominent bays either side of the entrance. The third storey was built into the eaves of a steep roof with dormer windows to the front. The roof was flanked at both ends by substantial chimney stacks with six – or was it eight – pots on each. It was clearly a sizeable property. A white painted sign to the side pointed left towards a treetop walk and Clare saw that SOCO's investigations were concentrated in this direction.

The DCI pulled his car into the side and Clare jumped out, not waiting for him to kill the engine. She stood for a minute, taking in the scene until her eyes found Chris, her DS, and she walked smartly towards him.

He looked up at the sound of her feet on the gravel and his face fell. 'Clare,' he said. 'Look, I'm sorry about…'

'Forget it, Chris. I'd have been more annoyed if you hadn't let me know.'

Chris shot a glance at DCI Gibson who was heading their way. 'DCI feel the same, does he?'

Clare ignored this. 'So, tell me.'

'Male, aged forty. Single gunshot wound to the head. Probably killed outright but we'll need the post-mortem to confirm that.'

'From Glasgow, you said?'

He nodded. 'Russell Fox. Part of a house party staying in the Lodge. They rented it to celebrate his fortieth birthday.'

'Witnesses?'

He shook his head. 'None. They reckon it happened early on Saturday morning when the rest of them were still asleep.'

'How are they?'

'All seem pretty shocked. Popular guy, no enemies to speak of.'

Clare considered this. 'Could it have been an accident? Stray bullet from a grouse shoot?'

'Definitely not. There's not a shoot close enough. And SOCO reckon it was a rifle shot.'

'Shit,' Clare said. 'I'm starting to not like the sound of this.'

'Nope.'

Clare's eyes turned to a white SOCO tent at the foot of the treetop walk. 'That where it happened?'

Chris raised his gaze. 'Up on the walk itself. Just about there.' He indicated a stretch between two tall Scots pines.

Clare looked up, squinting against the sun. The walk was made up of several sections, the floor built in solid wood. The sides were more open, dark green netting stretched between the floor and stout wooden handrails. She put a hand up to shade her eyes from the sun but the walkway itself was obscured by the dense netting. Beyond SOCO's tent she could see the steps leading up to one end of the walk, but foliage from the trees prevented her from seeing where it ended. 'Actually up there?' she said.

'Yep.'

'Did he fall?'

'No. The sides are pretty secure. In fact when the rest of the party went to look for him, they didn't realise he was up there until someone had the idea of climbing up to see if they could spot him in the grounds.'

Clare studied the walkway and the trees surrounding it. A white-suited figure stood on a small scissor-lift platform, examining the trees beyond the treetop walk, presumably the ballistics expert. 'Any idea where the shot came from?'

Chris followed her gaze. 'Not yet. But between them, the pathologist and the ballistics folk should have an idea of the trajectory.'

She turned and looked back at the Heras fencing and the security cameras. 'Is all this usually here?'

'No. Apparently the victim's sister asked for it. Said she wanted to make sure they had a nice family time without press photographers.'

'He's that famous?'

'Actually I think it's her. Some TV celeb. Seems photos can go for tens of thousands, and she wasn't having it. Not when it was her brother's birthday.'

'Ah. That explains the press pack at the gate. That it?'

He glanced over towards the house. 'No shortage of money.'

'Noted. Where are they, by the way? I presume you've moved them out of the house.'

He nodded. 'They put up in a hotel last night and they've agreed to stay on so you can speak to them yourself.'

'Thanks. That's helpful.' She stood thinking for a moment then said, 'Next of kin?'

'The sister. Mother died a few years ago. The father's still alive but apparently has dementia.'

Clare was suddenly aware of the DCI hovering. 'Al,' she said, 'just you get away I'll phone you later.'

'I could come back for you – when you're finished here.'

She shook her head. 'Chris can run me home.' She moved a little away from Chris and took the DCI's hand, briefly. 'Thanks, Al. I mean, for yesterday. For coming. I'll… I'll call you later.'

He flicked a glance at Chris then gave her a smile. 'Speak soon.' And, with that, he began walking back to his car.

Clare watched him go for a few seconds then she turned back to Chris. 'Okay. Let's head for the hotel. See what they have to say for themselves.'

Chapter 4

The Brodies was a small chain of boutique Scottish hotels which had grown in popularity over the past ten years. The CEO, Matthew Brodie, was on record stating that he'd wanted to create a group of hotels that wasn't recognisably a chain. He'd sought buildings which were notably quirky and had fitted each out to be unique in character. In a few cases he'd purchased land and erected new buildings and The Brodie St Andrews was one of these. It sat a couple of miles west of the town overlooking rich farmland on the Strathkinness High Road. Chris swung the car round into a tarmacked drive, nosing into a space at the end of the car park.

They emerged from the car and took in the building. The outer walls were a mix of a smooth white render and large picture windows with black frames. But there was little adornment, other than the trademark *Brodie* plaque set into the front wall.

Clare looked up as they walked towards the entrance. The whole building was terraced, giving the two upper storeys balconies running the length of the building. 'It's quite something, isn't it?' she said.

Chris seemed temporarily lost for words. Then he said, 'It's a bit plain, don't you think? Boxy.'

'It's modernist, Detective Sergeant.'

'Is that the same as ugly?'

'Peasant!' She stood as the bronzed glass door slid noiselessly back then walked into the cool interior. The entrance hall was laid in large grey floor tiles, the walls off-white. A huge triptych hung behind a mahogany reception desk depicted a Japanese garden, the only note of colour in an otherwise muted palette. To the right of the desk was a small lounge with high stools arranged round a circular bar, a barman dressed in black standing in the centre. Clare approached the reception desk then remembered she had no idea who they were here to see.

Chris moved forward, flashed his warrant card and spoke to the receptionist keeping his voice low. 'We're here to see Ms Fox. Preferably somewhere private.'

The receptionist moved to a telephone and spoke into it. Then she replaced the receiver. 'You can go up,' she said. 'It's room 232.'

Clare moved towards the lift but Chris shook his head. 'Don't like lifts.'

She stared at him. 'You're joking?'

'Nope.'

'Chris? I've seen you tackling huge guys armed with knives, and you're afraid of lifts?'

'Police training doesn't actually cover plunging to your death in a lift.'

Clare shook her head. 'Just when you think you know someone.'

'Stairs this way,' he said.

As they mounted the stairs Chris ran over the occupants of the Lodge. 'Like I say, victim was Russell Fox.'

'And the rest of the party?'

'His sister and her husband, plus three of Russell's friends.'

'And they're all here?'

They reached the second floor and Chris pushed open a fire door. 'Along here, I guess. Yeah, all staying here. Keen to get away, though.'

'Where do they live?'

'The three men in Glasgow. The sister and her husband, London.'

'At least they're not abroad, then. Oh, here we are. Room 232.' She knocked softly on the door and a few seconds later it was opened by sandy-haired man who Chris introduced as Eamon Ferry. He nodded to Chris and gave Clare a polite smile.

'Friend of Russell,' he said, and Clare smiled back.

Eamon stood aside to let them enter then let the door slam behind him. Clare and Chris moved into a large square room. It was decorated in soft greens and shades of heather. An enormous bed was adorned with scatter cushions in a grey tartan. To the side of the bed, two French doors led to a small balcony and to the right of the doors was a sitting area with a sofa and chairs in the same fabric as the cushions.

Clare's gaze swept the room and came to rest on one of the chairs and its occupant. She stared, and the woman in the chair stared back. Her brow clouded and she seemed confused by Clare's appearance.

It was Gaby Fox.

Clare hadn't particularly noticed Gaby's surname when they'd met at the wedding. She was known to everyone simply as Gaby. But now she remembered seeing the name on the seating plan at the reception and she realised Gaby must be the victim's sister. She thought back to the wedding – the maître d' calling Gaby out to take a phone call then returning minutes later to fetch her husband. The news of her brother's death.

She was more casually dressed than at the wedding, in a Breton top and cropped jeans, but she still exuded an air of glamour. She swung her feet out from under her and slipped them into a pair of mules on the floor. Rising, she said, 'You're a police officer?'

Clare nodded. 'Detective Inspector Clare Mackay,' she said, adding, 'I'm so sorry to trouble you at a time like this. Am I correct in thinking the victim was your brother?'

Gaby's eyes were brimming. 'Yes,' she said, her voice barely audible. 'Russell was my brother.'

Clare indicated the seat she had risen from. 'Please do sit down. I don't want to make this any more difficult for you.' She turned to Chris. 'Perhaps you could ask Reception for some tea?' She smiled back at Gaby. 'Or coffee?'

Eamon Ferry had been hovering near the door and he looked grateful for the suggestion. 'I'll do it.' He smiled at Gaby. 'Tea okay for you, doll?'

She nodded and Eamon looked from Clare to Chris.

'Tea's great for us, too,' Clare said. 'Thank you.'

Gaby resumed her seat and Chris pulled a couple of chairs over.

They sat, then Clare said, 'I know you've already spoken to my colleague here, Miss Fox.'

'Gaby, please.'

Clare acknowledged this with a smile. Then she said, 'I hope it won't distress you too much if I ask you to go through what happened once more?'

She nodded. 'It's fine. You have your job to do, Inspector.'

'Call me Clare.' She smiled again then said, 'Maybe you could tell me how you came to be staying in St Andrews?'

Gaby was silent for a moment then she swallowed. 'It was Russell's birthday,' she said. 'His fortieth, you know? And I thought we'd rent a house, invite his friends, make it a bit of a party.'

'How many of you are there?' Clare asked.

'Just the six. Luke and me, Russell and his three oldest friends. We arrived last Thursday.'

'For how long?'

'Supposed to be a week,' Gaby said. 'But now…'

Chris cleared his throat. 'I have everyone's details.'

Clare gave him a nod then turned back to Gaby. 'And the wedding?'

She shook her head. 'I can't believe I was there when I should have been here. Maybe if I had… I should never have gone.'

'You said your daughter was taught by Gillian?' Clare asked.

'Yes, that's right. She boards at the school, actually. We're down in London so much, you see. Me with my TV show and Luke with his work.'

'What is his line of work?'

'He's in TV as well. He has a production company so we both really need to be there. And we agreed that Sacha, that's our daughter, we agreed she'd be better staying up in Scotland. Her friends are at the school and it's really lovely there. Gillian was her housemistress for a couple of years. So, when she asked Sacha to sing at the ceremony and invited us too, well, we could hardly say no, even if I'd rather have been with Russell…' She tailed off, her eyes bright with tears. 'I can't believe he's gone.'

There was a tap at the door and Chris moved to open it. A young woman in a dark grey dress held a tea tray. Behind her Eamon Ferry stood with another man. Clare glanced at the door and recognised the man from the wedding. Gaby's husband, Luke Gasparini. Chris took the tea tray and thanked the woman. Eamon and Luke followed him into the room, Luke moving to his wife's side. He flicked a glance at Clare. 'Haven't you people upset her enough already?' And then he stared. 'Oh,' he said, 'it's you.'

Clare introduced herself. 'Gaby was just explaining about the party.'

Luke nodded. 'Supposed to be a celebration.'

Eamon began handing out slim white mugs of tea. 'Will you be needing me, Inspector?'

Clare shook her head. 'Not at the moment, thanks. Maybe in a bit, though.'

He nodded. 'I'll be out in the garden. The other two went for a walk and I said I'd meet them there.'

Clare waited until he'd left the room then smiled at Gaby. 'So you arrived at the Lodge on Thursday? Is that correct?'

Gaby sipped her tea. 'Yes, that's right. Thursday afternoon. We had a delicious meal in the evening. Russell's a good cook, you know. He'd made some curries and we had a few beers.' She smiled at the memory. 'It was a lovely night. I'm glad we had that…'

'And when did you leave for the wedding?'

'Friday,' Gaby said. 'Just after lunchtime. We thought it would be easier than rushing through on the Saturday. And I think the lads had something planned for Russell anyway.'

Clare raised an eyebrow. 'Any idea what it was?'

Gaby sighed. 'No. I thought it better not to ask. We did warn them not to damage anything – the deposit's pretty hefty, you know. But I've no idea what they were doing.'

'Some surprise for Russell,' Luke said. 'No doubt the lads will fill you in if you ask.'

Clare wondered about that. Were Gaby and Luke trying to hide something? She couldn't decide. 'That's fine,' she said. 'We can ask them.'

'And then we had the phone call at the wedding.' Gaby glanced at Clare. 'You probably remember.'

'Who called you?'

'Doug, Doug Gerrard, one of Russell's friends.'

'Mr Gerrard was the one who had the idea of going up to the treetop walk to look for Russell,' Chris said, his voice low.

'He said we'd better come back.' Gaby's voice was shaking. 'He said something had happened to Russell.'

Luke moved to perch on the arm of Gaby's chair. He put an arm round her and kissed the top of her head. She clutched his arm and began to cry.

Chris threw Clare a look and she gave a slight nod. 'We'll leave you in peace for now, Gaby. But there's just one thing more.'

Gaby looked up but didn't speak.

'We do believe your brother was deliberately killed.'

'No shit, Sherlock,' Luke Gasparini spat. 'I think we'd worked that out for ourselves.'

Clare decided she didn't much like Luke Gasparini, but she knew from experience that grief affected people in different ways so she acknowledged this with a nod. Turning back to Gaby she said, 'Can you think of anyone who might have wanted to harm Russell? Anyone come to mind?'

Gaby shook her head. 'No,' she whispered. 'Russell – he was just lovely.'

Clare smiled. 'Was Russell your only sibling? Any other relatives? We can contact them for you. Save you a difficult job. If it would help,' she added.

A spasm of pain crossed Gaby's face. 'We lost my brother David.'

'Oh,' Clare said, 'I'm so sorry.'

Gaby's lips thinned and she attempted a smile. 'An accident, you know.'

'When was this?'

'Almost ten years.' She dabbed at her eyes again. 'Ten years next month. And now Russell.'

Clare said, 'I'm sorry we have to ask these questions, Gaby.'

She fished a tissue out of her pocket. 'It's fine,' she said. 'You have your job to do.'

'Thank you.' Clare smiled, then she went on. 'I know you have your daughter but are there any other children? Yours or your brothers?'

She shook her head. 'Luke and I, we only have Sacha. Russell wasn't the marrying kind.'

'And your brother David?' Clare asked, her tone gentle.

Gaby shook her head. 'David didn't have children,' she said. 'Or at least none we know of.'

Clare nodded to Chris and they rose from their seats. 'Thanks, Gaby. I know this wasn't easy for you. We'll leave you in peace now.'

They turned to leave then Gaby said, 'Inspector.'

'Yes?'

'I think we'd all like to go home as soon as possible. We've nothing to stay for now.'

This was tricky. Clare was used to interviewing victims' relatives in their own homes and she didn't relish trying to conduct an investigation with the only witnesses spread between Glasgow and London. 'Your rooms here – how long have you booked for?'

'I was hoping tonight could be our last night,' Gaby said, 'but…'

'If you could remain here in the meantime,' Clare said, 'I'd be grateful. Just until our initial enquiries are concluded. It would be easier for us to keep in touch with you.'

'You'll let us know when we can go, then,' Luke said. It was more a statement than a question.

'Of course.' Clare smiled. 'We won't keep you a moment longer than necessary.'

As they walked back towards the main staircase Chris said, 'You don't like him, do you?'

'Nope. Cheeky bastard.'

'I thought the two of you would get on. So, what now?'

'Let's go and speak to Eamon Ferry. Find out what they were up to on Friday night.'

Chapter 5

They found Eamon Ferry in a small section of garden to the rear of the hotel. He was sitting at a wooden table with another two men and he looked up as Clare and Chris approached. He took a last drag from his cigarette then exhaled and stubbed it out in a metal ashtray. The others followed his gaze and Clare took her first look at the two men who had made up the rest of the house party. They struck her as an ill-matched pair and she wondered what they had in common. Their expressions, unlike Eamon Ferry's practised smile, were guarded, unsmiling even. Was it the shock of what had happened? Or was there something else?

'DI Clare Mackay,' she said. Then she motioned towards Chris. 'I gather you've met DS West.'

The men nodded and Eamon did a quick round of introductions. 'Doug Gerrard,' he said, indicating a round-faced man, his neatly trimmed goatee beard, flecked with grey. 'And Steve,' he went on, nodding towards the other. 'Steve Christie.'

Clare studied them. She thought Steve Christie looked vaguely familiar. His face was thin, pinched even, his curly brown hair spiked up with gel. His cheek was scarred, and Clare wondered if he'd been round the block a few times. He seemed to be avoiding her eye. Did he have cause to be uncomfortable with police officers? Doug Gerrard, by contrast, sat studying Clare and Chris, his eyes lingering far longer on Clare as he took her in, up and down. She met his eye, challenging his overt scrutiny, but he continued staring, a hint of a smile on his lips.

They were casually dressed, Eamon the smartest in a polo shirt and dark linen trousers. The others were in shorts and T-shirts. A bottle of Ambre Solaire sat in the centre of the table, its fragrance mixing with the occasional stale whiff from the ashtray. They were drinking craft beers and, as Clare regarded them, Steve Christie raised a bottle to his lips, swigging from it.

Eamon indicated two empty wooden garden chairs and they sat, Clare dragging hers round so it wasn't facing directly into the sun.

She began by extending her sympathies to the men, watching them carefully. 'I gather you were Russell's oldest friends?'

'Primary school,' Eamon said.

'And you've kept in touch since?'

Doug Gerrard nodded. 'Off and on,' he said. 'When we could, ye know?'

'It's nice you were all able to make this weekend,' Clare said, keeping the conversation light.

'Wouldn't have missed it,' Steve Christie said, flicking a glance at Clare.

'Whose idea was it?'

'Gaby's,' Eamon said. 'Surprise for Russell.' He nodded at the other two. 'We all knew, months back, but she only told Russell a couple of days before. And he didn't know we were coming too.'

Chris cleared his throat and the men turned to look at him. 'Was there no suggestion of wives or girlfriends joining the party?'

The men looked at each other. Eamon, as usual, was the first to find his voice. 'Not this time,' he said.

Clare thought he was choosing his words carefully. 'Any particular reason?'

Only Eamon met Clare's eye. 'Russell – he didn't really seem to have anyone special just now. And we thought it might be a laugh, just the lads.'

Clare nodded. 'So you arrived at the Lodge on Thursday?'

'Aye.' Eamon again.

'And I gather Gaby and Mr Gasparini left on Friday to go to a wedding. So you spent Friday night alone?'

Doug Gerrard regarded Clare. 'Aye.'

'Gaby said you had a surprise organised for Russell.' She watched them as she said this. Steve Christie took another swig from his bottle and the other two shrugged. 'Something special?'

Doug laughed. 'Nah. I was just winding Gaby up. We ordered pizza, plenty of drinks, bit of poker. Boys' night, ye know?' He looked round at the others. 'It was a laugh, wasn't it, lads?'

There were murmurs of *Aye... Oh aye...* and more head-nodding.

Clare smiled. 'Can't beat a good pizza. Was it one in the town?'

The men looked at Doug. He took out his phone and began scrolling. 'Bella Pizza,' he said. 'Market Street.'

Clare noted this down. 'What time did it arrive?'

Doug shrugged. 'Anyone remember?'

'About seven,' Eamon said. 'Or just before.'

'And there were no other callers that night?'

Heads shook. Clare watched them carefully. She couldn't decide if they were hiding something. Drugs, maybe. They wouldn't want to admit to anything like that. She'd have to organise background checks on them. There was something here that didn't add up. 'Okay, thanks gents.' She smiled round then said, 'I'd be grateful if you could remain here in the hotel until tomorrow, at least. In case we need anything clarified.'

The men nodded and Clare rose, scraping back her chair. She saw Steve Christie's shoulders sag as he seemed to relax. 'Just one more thing.'

Eamon smiled again. 'Yes?'

'When did you last see Russell?'

'Friday night,' Doug said. 'He went off to bed just before midnight.'

Chris raised an eyebrow. 'Bit early for a boys' night.'

The men looked at each other then Eamon said, 'He liked to get up early in the mornings, Russell – said he wanted to see the sun come up.'

Clare gave a nod. 'That's fine then. Thanks for your time, gents.'

They walked away round the side of the hotel towards the car park. 'Let's get that pizza delivery checked,' Clare said, her voice low. 'And I want the background on those three.'

'Already in hand,' Chris said. 'You reckon there's anything there?'

'I'm sure of it, Chris. They were far too cagey.'

'Could just be the shock.'

'Yes, it could. But I doubt it. They're hiding something and I'd very much like to know what it is.'

As they crossed the car park Clare remembered the security cameras at the Lodge. 'What about the footage?'

'Eh?'

'From the cameras, dummy. The ones at the Lodge gates.'

'Ah right. Sara's back at the station, going through it now. She'll call if there's anything.'

'I bet she was thrilled to be given that job,' Clare said. 'Good thinking, though.' PC Sara Stapleton, the youngest officer in the station, now engaged to Chris, had a keen pair of eyes. If there was something amiss on the footage, she'd find it. They reached the car and Clare stopped, her hand on the door. 'So, CCTV and a fence. I'm guessing they also had someone on site?'

'Yeah, security guard.'

'And?'

'Not much help, to be honest. Says it was a quiet night and he finished at two in the morning. Wasn't due back until midday on Saturday.'

Clare considered this. 'I think I'd like to speak to him once we have the ballistics info back. The post-mortem might narrow down a time of death too.'

'Fair enough. We have his details. Erm, I could murder a cup of tea.'

Clare looked back at the hotel for a moment. She really needed time to take in what had happened. What they had learned. The search of the Lodge grounds would be under way. Was there much more she could do just now? 'Go on then. But you'd better have some biscuits.'

Chapter 6

'Pizza van arrived just before seven,' PC Sara Stapleton confirmed, indicating an image on her computer screen. She clicked the mouse. 'And here it is leaving, five minutes later.'

'Okay, thanks Sara,' Clare said. 'Chris, could you check with the pizza company please? Find out when they ordered, who phoned it in, anything else they can tell you.' She turned back to Sara. 'Is that it?'

'So far,' Sara said. 'I'm only up to seven forty-five, though.'

Clare smiled. 'Keep at it. Fancy a coffee?'

'Please.'

Clare wandered through to the kitchen and flicked the switch on the kettle. As it came to the boil Chris appeared.

'Spoke to Bella Pizza. Order was phoned in at five, asked for delivery around seven. Name of Gerrard.'

'Doug Gerrard, then,' Clare said.

'Yeah, must be. Funny thing is…'

'Yeah?'

'It was a pretty big order.'

'They're pretty big guys.'

'Twelve large pizzas for four guys? Plus sides.'

'Hmm. So, they had company?'

'Looks like it.'

'Boss.' Sara appeared at the kitchen door.

Clare poured boiling water into mugs and set down the kettle. 'Yeah?'

'Something you should see.'

They followed her through and waited while she sat down in front of the monitor. 'It's just after eight p.m.,' Sara said, moving the mouse. 'Now, watch.'

They stood behind her peering at the screen. And then they saw the security guard appear in front of the gap in the fence. A dark-coloured vehicle approached and the guard moved to the side and spoke to the driver. A few seconds later he stepped back to allow the van to pass through.

'Looks like a Transit van,' Clare said. 'What do you reckon's in it?'

'Judging by the amount of food they ordered,' Chris said, 'I'd guess it's people.'

Clare bent to look more closely at the screen. 'Can you zoom in on the van please, Sara?'

Sara paused the footage and zoomed in. Then she advanced it, frame by frame until the van swung round, following the drive and they had a clear shot of the left side.

'Is it a minibus?' Clare said.

Chris peered at it. 'Converted van, I think. See how the evening sun's caught the windows? It's dark glass but look,' he jabbed the screen, 'definitely figures inside.'

They watched the footage for another few minutes but there was nothing else to be seen.

'Keep on it, Sara,' Clare said. 'We need to know when that van left.'

Sara returned to her task while Clare and Chris took their coffees into her office.

'Did the security guard mention this?' Clare asked.

'Nope. Told me about the pizzas being delivered but nothing about another van. And the three friends said nothing about it either. Want to head back up there? Have it out with them?'

'Let's wait for ballistics first. PM too. See if we have a time of death.'

–

Caroline French's phone was engaged so Clare dialled the number for the pathology lab and asked for Neil Grant. After a short delay he came to the phone.

'Just wondering about our gunshot victim,' Clare said.

'I'm writing it up now, Clare. Full report by tomorrow. But the upshot is he died from the bullet wound, probably somewhere between midnight Friday and midday Saturday. Given he was found outside, I'd guess it happened in daylight. Harder to get a clear shot at night, even with a night vision scope. Mind you, I'm no expert on ballistics.'

'What about the bullet?' Clare asked.

'Passed right through the skull. Fair bit of damage to the bullet, obviously. I gather from Caroline it ended up in a tree.'

'Anything on it?'

'Yes, fortunately. Caroline took samples from where it penetrated the tree. The bark had traces of blood and bone, as did the bullet. I'll run DNA tests but I'll be surprised if it's not a match for the victim.'

'Any idea where the shot came from, Neil?'

'Sorry, Clare, that's Caroline's area of expertise. But I can confirm the trajectory was upwards, as she suggested. It entered just below the temple on the left-hand side and emerged through the top of the skull.'

'So our killer was below the victim?'

'I'd say so.'

Clare ended the call and tried Caroline French's number again. This time it rang out.

'Hi Clare,' Caroline said. 'Chasing up your bullet?'

'Yes please. Anything you can tell me?'

'I think so. You probably know the bullet passed through the victim and lodged in a Scots pine beyond. It went far enough into the trunk for us to know the trajectory was upwards. The PM probably showed that too, yeah?'

'It did.'

'Okay. So we used a laser trajectory kit…'

'Hold on,' Clare said, 'I want to put this on speaker so Chris can hear it.'

Caroline waited a few seconds then carried on. 'We put rods into the entry hole then used the lasers to track back the bullet's journey.'

'How accurate can you be?' Chris asked.

'Pretty close,' Caroline said. 'Anything the bullet comes in contact with can cause it to deviate; but we looked at the entry and exit wounds on the PM report and compared them with the damage to the tree. I'd say it didn't stray much from its original path.'

'Which was?' Clare waited.

'Well, taking into account the likely distance and the angle, I'd say your gunman fired from one of the upper storeys of the house. Probably the top floor, although it's hard to be precise about that. We didn't find evidence of a second bullet so he must have been pretty close; either that or a really cracking shot.'

Clare thanked Caroline and ended the call.

'So?' Chris said.

'We need to find out who, or what, was in that van.'

'And the house?'

'I want SOCO in all the rooms that face the treetop walk – top two storeys.'

'Hold on, though. As soon as Russell Fox was missed those three men would have been all over the house looking for him...'

'Compromising any evidence,' Clare finished. 'Yes, I know. But we're only interested in the windows. And SOCO might find traces of gunshot residue.' She stood thinking for a minute, then said, 'Who's running checks on the men?'

'Janey and Bill from Dundee. They'll be over in the morning.'

Clare nodded. 'See if you can hurry them up, Chris, and get the whole household checked while you're at it. I'll call SOCO then we're going to track down that pizza driver.'

—

Bella Pizza was busy with Sunday afternoon diners, the air thick with mouth-watering aromas. There was a small queue for a table, but Clare side-stepped this and showed her badge to a man in dark trousers and a white shirt. The manager, she guessed. He drew them over to the side, away from the queue of customers and explained both delivery drivers were out on jobs.

'Should be back in the next twenty minutes,' he said. He glanced across to the kitchen, its front open to the restaurant. 'I can squeeze you onto a table if you'd like to wait.'

Chris turned puppy dog eyes on Clare but she ignored this. 'We'll wait outside,' she said, smiling her thanks.

Chris followed her out. 'Not even a slice of pizza?'

'If we wait out here we'll catch the driver before the head waiter can warn him we're looking for him.'

'Suppose.'

'Anyway, it's a lovely day.'

They found a sunny spot to the side of the restaurant and leaned against the stone wall, feeling it warm in the sun. A steady stream of holidaymakers ambled past, some licking ice creams, others dodging cars as they spilled off the pavements onto the cobbled street. Somewhere in the distance a guitarist was strumming a Joni Mitchell song. Clare closed her eyes for a moment, enjoying the sun. It all felt a million miles away from the events at Lamond Lodge.

'Here comes one of them,' Chris said, as a van emblazoned with *Bella Pizza* pulled into one of the parking bays outside the restaurant.

The driver confirmed his name as Ross Gilfeather and admitted he'd delivered an order to Lamond Lodge on Friday night. 'About seven, I think,' he said.

'Who did you see?' Clare asked.

Ross crinkled his brow. 'Dunno. Just a bloke. Beard, I think.'

Clare nodded. Probably Doug Gerrard.

'Then he shouted to someone else to come and help,' Ross went on. 'It was a pretty big order. Must have been having a party.'

'Did you see anyone else?' Clare asked.

Ross shook his head. 'No. He just told me to put the boxes down and they'd carry them in.'

'And that's it?'

'Yeah. I had another two deliveries waiting for me back at the restaurant so I wasn't hanging about.'

'Did you see anyone else at all?' Chris asked.

'Nope. Well, the guy on the gate, of course.'

'No one hanging about at the road?' Chris persisted. 'Anyone near the drive?'

Ross shrugged. 'Sorry, no. Look, what's this about?'

Clare said, 'We're investigating the death of one of the occupants.'

Ross stared. 'Seriously? Someb'dy died?'

'I'm afraid so.' She took a card from her pocket. 'So, if there is anything else you remember will you call me, please?'

He looked from Clare to Chris then back at Clare again. 'Yeah, of course. But I didn't see anyone. Honest.'

Clare smiled. 'That's fine, Ross.'

The manager was hovering at the door and Ross glanced in his direction.

'Looks like you're having a busy day,' Clare said. 'We'll let you get on.'

Ross escaped with evident relief, and they strolled back to the car.

'What do you reckon?' Chris said.

'He seems fine. Let's check he doesn't have any previous, though.'

Chris nodded. 'So, what now?'

'Let's go and talk to the security guard. See if we can jog his memory about dark-coloured vans.'

Chapter 7

'House is in Warrack Street,' Chris said, turning the car off the main road into a residential area. He pulled up outside a cream-painted two-storey house. A patch of grass to the front was dominated by a large, netted trampoline. The house was in need of a fresh coat of paint but the grass around the trampoline was neatly trimmed and there were window boxes filled with Livingstone daisies, their petals open to the warm summer sun.

'Oh good,' Chris said, rolling his eyes at the trampoline. 'He has kids.'

Clare threw him a scathing look. 'Stop being such a grump,' she said. 'You and Sara might have kids yourselves, one day.' She saw his expression change and suddenly she was transported back to the time Sara was stabbed trying to stop a kidnapper escaping. She had recovered but had lost the unborn baby she and Chris had just learned they were expecting. 'Oh Chris, I'm sorry. I didn't mean…'

He smiled. 'It's fine, Clare. Don't worry about it. We probably will, one day. Not for a few years, though.'

Clare patted him on the back as they walked up the path that led to the door. 'I'm sure you'll be wonderful parents.' She moved to ring the bell but the door was opened before she reached it and two small boys tumbled out, running past them to the trampoline. From within the house they could hear a woman's voice shouting at

44

the boys to take their shoes off. Clare touched the bell lightly and a few seconds later the owner of the voice appeared. She was about thirty, Clare thought, with short blonde hair. She wore a pale denim skirt and a pink top, the sleeves rolled up. There was a dusting of something white on her cheek and Clare thought she must be in the middle of baking.

She looked at Clare and Chris. 'Yeah?'

Clare showed her warrant card and asked for Mark Mooney.

'Hold on,' the woman said and she disappeared, leaving the door ajar. Minutes later a man in cargo shorts and a Motörhead vest top appeared, the woman hovering from a door at the end of the hall. Clare studied him. He was clean-shaven, his hair closely cropped, his forearms tattooed. She squinted at the tattoos but she couldn't make out what they depicted.

He stared at them then he seemed to recognise Chris. 'DS… West?' he said.

Chris nodded. 'And my boss, DI Clare Mackay.'

Clare was watching Mark Mooney and she saw a faint flicker in his eyes when Chris introduced her. 'Is there somewhere we could talk?'

He turned without a word and led them up the hall into a cheerful room that bore the detritus of family life. The walls were white, lined with bookshelves, either side of an open fireplace. Through the window, framed by poppy-patterned curtains, Clare could see the two boys bouncing high on the trampoline. She turned back to Mark and smiled. 'Do you mind if we sit down?'

He indicated a red sofa and waited for them to sit. Then he perched on the edge of an easy chair. He looked at Clare again and raised an eyebrow.

'I understand you spoke to DS West, here, following the death of Mr Russell Fox on Saturday morning.'

Mark's hand went to his chin. 'Yeah. Awful thing to happen. I'm not sure what else I can tell you, though.'

Clare said, 'You told DS West there was a pizza delivery, around seven.'

'Yeah, that's right.'

'And you also said there were no other vehicles. Is that correct?'

Mark looked over their shoulders for a moment as if watching the boys on the trampoline. 'Far as I remember.'

Chris glanced at Clare. 'That's not what you said, Mark. If I recall, you were quite definite about it.'

He turned back and met Chris's eye. 'Well, yeah, then. I didn't see another van.'

Clare watched him carefully. 'DS West didn't mention a van.' She decided there was no point in wasting any further time. 'I'd like you to think again about that, Mark. Think carefully. Were there any other vehicles that night, after the pizzas arrived?'

He hesitated.

'It's a murder investigation,' Clare went on. 'And, if you prefer, we can continue this at the station. But I'm sure you'd rather we sorted it out now.' She glanced at the sitting room door, still ajar, and wondered if the woman was listening.

As if he saw what she was thinking Mark rose and closed the door softly. 'I think I do remember another vehicle,' he said, avoiding Clare's eye.

'And?'

'Dark van. Came up the drive about eight, I think.'

'Were you expecting it?'

He nodded.

'Who told you?'

'That was Mr Gerrard. The goatee beard lad.'

'And what exactly did Mr Gerrard say about it?'

Mark thought for a moment then said, 'Something about a van arriving and I was to direct it round the back of the house.'

'You spoke to the driver?'

'Aye. She said they were expecting her.'

'She?'

He nodded. 'Dark-haired woman. Anyway, I asked her what name she'd been given – Mr Gerrard said they'd ask for him. Otherwise I wasn't to let anyone in. She said his name, right enough, so I told her where to take the van and let her through the gate.'

Chris shifted forward in his seat. 'Did she say what was in the van?'

'Not that I recall.'

'Try harder, Mark.'

He rose from his seat and went across to the window. He stood for a moment watching the boys bouncing then turned back to face them. 'It's like this. Mr Gerrard, well, he said it was all to be kept quiet. Didn't want anyone knowing all the comings and goings. Papers and that, ye know? So he slipped me a few quid.' He looked at Chris. 'When you spoke to me after the lad died, well, I didn't think it was my place to say anything. I thought they'd tell you themselves.'

Clare said, 'You didn't think someone being found dead was a good enough reason to break your promise to Mr Gerrard?'

Mark's brow furrowed. 'Yeah, I should have.' He shook his head. 'I know that now. But, after he called you lads in – when he found Mr Fox – he phoned me. I was still at home, ye know? Not due back till midday. And he said I'd better get over to the Lodge. Police wanted to speak to me. Then he said not to mention the other van. He'd handle it and tell you lads everything. I was to stick to my story. Just say I didn't notice anything.'

'And that didn't make you suspicious?' Clare said. 'You didn't think lying to officers investigating a murder was maybe a bad idea?'

He met Clare's eye. 'Now? For sure. But at the time he made it sound okay. And I didn't even know he'd been killed – Mr Fox. I thought maybe he'd just had a heart attack. Too much of the partying, ye know? And, well, I thought they probably had enough to deal with. He said it would be easier for the family if we kept it simple.'

Clare considered this. Then she said, 'Why do you think that was, Mark? Why would he not want the van mentioned?'

Mark shifted in his seat, avoiding Clare's eye.

Chris said, 'Was it girls in the van?'

He exhaled. 'Aye. Pretty sure it was girls.'

'And did the van leave again?'

'Yeah. Not long before I knocked off. Back of one, I think.'

Clare nodded. 'Were there any other callers? Vehicles or on foot? Anyone else at all?'

'Definitely not. Just the pizza lad and the van.'

Clare rose and Chris followed suit. 'Okay, Mark. We may need you to make a statement confirming that but we'll leave it for now. In the meantime, stay away from the Lodge and don't discuss what you've told us with anyone.'

Mark showed them to the front door and they emerged into the sunshine. Outside the two boys were lying on their backs on the trampoline, giggling about something.

Clare watched them, thinking they were just a couple of years older than her nephew, James, and she made a mental note to give her sister a call in the next few days.

'Believe him?' Chris asked, cutting across her thoughts. He clicked the key to unlock the car and they climbed in.

Clare pulled on her seat belt then sat thinking for a moment. 'Think so,' she said. 'You?'

'Probably. All the same, I'm suspicious of anyone who starts off lying to us.' He started the engine. 'Back to the hotel, then?'

Clare nodded. 'Yep. Let's speak to the three partygoers again. Get to the bottom of this van full of girls.'

Chapter 8

They set off for the hotel but a phone call from Janey forestalled them. 'Your victim and his friends,' she said, 'got a bit of background.'

Clare motioned to Chris to pull over and she switched the phone to speaker.

'I've emailed it over,' Janey went on. 'But the victim did a bit of time a few years ago.'

'For?'

'Drunk driving. He knocked down a young woman one night. Put her in hospital for weeks. He was three times over the limit.'

'How long did he serve?'

'Eight months.'

'That all?'

'Yeah. It was a dark road, no pavement. She was walking with her back to traffic, dark clothing. The defence made a pretty good case. He pled guilty so it all helped reduce the sentence.'

'Okay,' Clare said. 'Can you look into who he might have met in prison, please? Was it the Bar-L?'

'Yeah, Barlinnie,' Janey confirmed. 'I'll get onto the prison and see who he shared with.'

Chris leaned forward. 'What's he done since prison, Janey?'

'He's done all right, to be honest. He was a chef by trade so he started working in a steak house in the centre of Glasgow. Then he took over a cafe that was going out of business. Got it cheap and built it up. Sold it and bought another restaurant. Up till a couple of months ago he had two restaurants. But he put them on the market. Word is he's had a few offers.'

'Any idea why?'

'No. He might just be that kind of guy. Buy cheap, build it up then sell for a profit.'

'Yeah, could be. Is that it?'

'Not quite. One of the other lads has a bit of previous too.'

They waited.

'Steve Christie. It's a while ago now but he did a couple of years for firearms offences.'

Clare glanced at Chris. 'What sort of offences?'

'Supplying small arms, mainly. Smuggled in from Eastern Europe and sold around Glasgow – small-time gangsters and the like.'

'How long ago was that?'

'Just over ten years.'

'And since?'

'Nothing, boss. He has an online business now. Buys cheap tat from China and supplies a few market stalls, corner shops. All seems above board. Files a tax return each year. No indication he's involved in anything illegal.'

'All the same,' Clare said.

'What about the other two?' Chris asked.

'Nothing. Both clean. Doug Gerrard owns pubs out the west end of Glasgow. Nice places. No problem with the licence and very little trouble, overall.'

'And Eamon Ferry?'

'Works for Glasgow City Council. Quite high up in the Planning Department.'

Clare considered this. 'Any involvement in planning disputes?'

'No. Squeaky clean.'

Clare thought of Eamon Ferry, his smooth manner, neat clothes, and she reckoned if he was involved in anything dodgy he'd be good at covering his tracks. But maybe she was being unfair. 'What about Gaby and her husband?'

'Still to check them, boss. But I'll be surprised if there is anything. She's in the public eye – splashed all over the papers every other week. If there was anything there the press would be all over it.'

'Fair enough. But check all the same, yeah? And get onto Barlinnie prison. Find out who was in at the same time as Russell Fox and Steve Christie. Especially anyone involved with guns.'

Chris restarted the engine and signalled to pull out again.

'Fancy a coffee at the station, first?' Clare said. 'I'd like to get things straight in my head before we speak to the three men again.'

'Can we stop and get some food? Please?'

'Chris, we're in the middle of a murder investigation.'

He cancelled the signal and jerked on the handbrake. 'I've been on the go since seven this morning. You might have started the day with a hotel breakfast but I had a slice of toast about,' he checked his watch, 'nine hours ago and I've barely stopped since. Right now, I could eat my own head.'

'Okay!' Clare said. 'You've made your point. Leave the car here and we'll walk back to Cromars. I'll treat you to fish and chips.'

–

'You might have brought me some chips,' Sara said, wrinkling her nose as Chris and Clare entered the incident room.

'Nose like a ferret,' Chris muttered.

'Sorry,' Clare said. 'We didn't think. Chris'll go back out again. My treat.'

She tossed her head. 'S'okay. I had a sandwich earlier.' Then she glared at Chris. 'You can make dinner tonight, if we ever get home.'

'Still trawling through the footage?' Clare said.

'Yeah.' Sara stifled a yawn. 'Nothing much, though. Just one thing – about eleven, the security guard walks round to the back of the house. Looks like he's talking to someone then he disappears out of sight. Maybe going for a cup of tea, or slice of pizza.'

'Any sign of anyone slipping in while he was gone?'

Sara shook her head. 'Not so far. But I'll keep at it.'

'Let me know, yeah?' Clare stood thinking for a moment. 'Anything else? Did I miss anything over the weekend?'

Sara leaned back in her chair and began rubbing her neck. 'Oh the usual, you know. Couple of lads drunk and disorderly, a missing dog, stolen car.' She rose from her seat, yawning. 'Think I'll just make a drink. I'm falling asleep looking at that screen.'

Clare followed her to the kitchen. 'I could do with a cup myself. That it – the dog and the car?'

Sara switched the kettle on to boil. 'We had a missing child. It's all sorted out now, though.'

'Oh? What happened?'

'Little boy. Daniel something. I've logged it on the system. Mum was out working and the babysitter stayed the night. But he got up and slipped out before the babysitter wakened. He was found a couple of streets away. Said he was hungry and wanted his breakfast.'

Clare stared. 'Seriously? How the hell did he get out of the house?'

'He's three, boss. Nearly four, actually. Easy enough for a bright child to work out how to open a door.'

'What did you do about it?'

'The mother turned up before we found out who he was. She came home, saw he was missing and she and the babysitter went out looking. Someone told her they'd seen police in the street so she came straight to the station.'

'Did you report it?'

'Social Services? Yeah. Give them their due, they came out straight away. The social worker called into the station a few hours later. All checked out at home. He's well cared for, house clean and tidy, food in the fridge. Just a case of the babysitter oversleeping and Daniel waking up early. Mum's called a locksmith to put a chain and a high bolt on the door.'

'But they're going to keep an eye on the family?'

Sara nodded. 'Just mum and Daniel. I think dad's out of the picture.'

'Where was she?' Clare asked. 'The mum, I mean.'

'Night shift. I was in the middle of dealing with it when we got the call from Lamond Lodge. So I kind of left it with Social Services.'

'Fair enough. Maybe give it a day or two then call them again. Make sure they're on top of it. We don't want to risk a child being in danger.'

Sara smiled. 'Will do. But it does look like a one-off. The mum was horrified. I doubt it'll happen again.'

'Okay.' Clare glanced at her watch. She'd like to have spoken to the three men about the minibus but SOCO would be back at the Lodge now, going over those upstairs rooms. Better to wait until they knew where the shot had come from. She still had Benjy to pick up from her neighbour Moira, and Chris and Sara looked done in. 'I think we'll call it a night, guys,' she said. 'I'll check with Jim to make sure everything's secure up at the Lodge. Back in for a briefing at eight tomorrow. Pass the word round.'

'Want a lift back?' Chris said.

'Please.'

Chris drove while Clare called Moira. 'I'm so sorry,' she said. 'I know I said I'd be back early afternoon.'

'Oh Clare, don't worry,' Moira said. 'I heard there was a death out at Lamond Lodge so I assumed you'd be busy. Why don't I keep Benjy overnight and walk him for you tomorrow? Then I'll drop him back late afternoon.'

Clare thanked Moira and ended the call. As she neared Daisy Cottage she saw a lamp was on in the hall but the rest of the house was in darkness. DCI Gibson's car was missing too. He must have gone back to his own house in Aberdour, in the south of Fife. Not surprising, really. He had a conference coming up so he'd have to pack for that. All the same, she'd liked to have had him waiting in the cottage, maybe with some food, a glass of wine. Run her a bath, even.

She climbed out of Chris's car and thanked him for the lift. It was odd putting her key in the door and not hearing Benjy bark. But she was tired now and glad she wouldn't have to do his evening walk. She closed the door and saw her overnight bag standing in the hall. In the kitchen a portion of homemade curry stood defrosting next to the microwave. A wine bottle was on the kitchen table, corkscrew beside it, a Post-it note on the neck. She peeled it off and read,

> *Hope you're not too late home.*
> *You deserve a glass of this.*
> *Enjoy.*
> *Love A x*

She lifted the note and kissed it softly. Then she began to peel the foil capsule off the cork.

Day 3: Monday

Chapter 9

Without Benjy to waken her, Clare overslept. She squinted at her alarm clock and saw it was just after seven. Breakfast would have to wait. She showered quickly and pulled a work suit out of the wardrobe. Twenty minutes later she was on her way, driving past fields dotted with bales of silage wrapped in black plastic. A few more weeks and it would be autumn and the lush green foliage on the tree-lined road would begin turning to red and gold. She slowed down as she approached the roundabout turning into Bogward Road, a residential street to the west of the town. A young lad wandered languidly between the houses, a sack of newspapers on his shoulder. Up ahead a couple of cyclists rode along, chatting, and Clare pulled out, giving them a wide berth as she passed. Suddenly she heard Russell Fox mentioned and she turned up the radio volume.

'Mr Fox is the brother of daytime TV star Gaby Fox,' the newsreader said. The report went on to say that the party were believed to be staying in St Andrews, pending the outcome of the police investigation.

'Dammit,' Clare muttered, signalling left at the round-about. 'They'll be all over it now.'

Minutes later she drew into the station car park, and she saw that the press were indeed *all over it*. The street outside the station was crammed with cars and a cameraman was setting up a tripod on the pavement. As Clare climbed out of her car a couple of reporters rushed towards her, firing questions.

She stopped for a moment, waited until they were within earshot, then suggested they contact the press office. 'We won't be making any comment at this time,' she added.

As she walked across to the building, Chris and Sara were coming along Tom Morris Drive so she waited for them. They were dressed in work clothes, Chris in his usual dark grey suit, Sara in her uniform. But both had trainers on their feet.

'No car today?' Clare said when they were near enough.

'It's such a lovely morning,' Sara said. 'We thought we'd walk.' She smiled at Chris. 'Didn't we?'

'Oh aye,' Chris said, rolling his eyes. '*We* decided to walk.'

'You'll thank me when you're in your eighties.'

'If you're going to make me walk everywhere, I'm not sure I want to live to my eighties,' Chris said.

Clare laughed. Sometimes Chris and Sara seemed like chalk and cheese but they were so good for each other. 'She's quite right,' she told her DS. 'I thought you were getting a bit porky again.'

Chris did his best to look offended and the three of them entered the station. Jim had worked his usual miracle on the incident room. There were extra desks and laptops, and a few officers were under the desks, plugging cables into sockets on the floor. The blinds were closed against the summer sun and the prying eyes of reporters but the temperature was rising. It was going to be a warm day in the station.

'Any news?' Clare asked.

Jim shook his head. 'It's early, yet. But SOCO finished up at the house last night so they might have something for us this morning.'

Clare thanked Jim and went into her office, clicking on the computer. She checked her emails but there was nothing from SOCO. Time enough to call them after the briefing. Her office door opened and Chris entered. He'd changed his trainers for a pair of brogues.

'No Nikes?'

'Shut up.'

'Ach, it'll do you good. Someone needs to look after you, Chris.'

'When did you last go for a run?' he shot back.

'Friday actually,' she lied.

'Hmm.' He sank down in a chair. 'They're ready when you are.'

She reached into her desk drawer and took out a cereal bar. 'With you in a couple of minutes,' she said. 'I missed breakfast.'

Chris indicated the bar. 'You know those things are full of sugar, don't you?'

Clare tore the wrapper off and dropped it into the bin. 'Yup.' She rose from her desk. 'C'mon, then. Let's make a start.'

She recognised a few faces from past investigations. Bill and Janey, the two plain-clothes officers from Dundee, were there, along with some others from Cupar and Glenrothes. Clare nodded her thanks to them and made her way to the whiteboard at the front of the room. Jim had pinned up a photo of Russell Fox provided by his sister, along with shots of the rest of the party, and Clare took up position to the side of the photos.

'Morning, everyone,' she said, smiling round at the room. 'Thanks for turning out so early. And thanks also to the folks from other stations. We'll keep you as short a time as possible.' She tapped the photo of a smiling Russell Fox. 'Our victim,' she said. 'Russell Fox. Businessman from Glasgow, just turned forty.' She looked round the room again. 'Mr Fox was killed by a single bullet, likely from a rifle but I'm awaiting ballistics info.' She tapped a photo of Lamond Lodge. 'He was found on a treetop walk in the grounds of this property – Lamond Lodge. It's a few miles south of St Andrews. We're not sure when he died but probably Saturday morning.'

'Anything on where the bullet came from?' Bill asked.

'Nothing confirmed yet but they do think it came from the house. SOCO were back there yesterday, going over the rooms facing the treetop walk. Hopefully we'll have some news on that today.'

'Remember his previous,' Chris said.

'Yeah, thanks, Chris.' She glanced back at the photo of Russell Fox. 'Our victim served eight months for drunk driving, a few years back.' She scanned the room until she saw Janey. 'You were checking up on him, I think?'

Janey nodded. 'Not heard back from the prison yet.'

'Okay. Leave it with me,' Clare said. 'I know one of the Senior Management Team through there. I'll give him a call.' She studied the board again, trying to collect her thoughts. 'Where were we?'

'Lamond Lodge,' someone said. 'Is our victim the owner?'

'No. The house was rented by his sister.' She paused for a moment then said, 'You'll have gathered as you came into the station that there's considerable media interest. In case anyone doesn't know, the victim's sister is the TV personality Gaby Fox.'

There was a ripple of interest at this and Clare said, 'Obviously we treat this like any other enquiry but I don't want stray remarks to the press, or even to your family. There's enough buzz about it already so nothing we discuss is to go outside this room. Understood?'

She paused for a moment to let this sink in then went on. 'The house party consisted of Gaby, her husband Luke Gasparini…'

'I've heard of him,' Gary, one of the uniformed officers, said. 'TV producer.'

Clare nodded. 'He is. But Gaby and Luke were not at the property on Friday night. They left that afternoon to attend a wedding on the Saturday.'

'Anyone else?' Gary asked.

'Three of Russell Fox's friends made up the party.'

She tapped the photo of Doug Gerrard. 'Mr Gerrard owns pubs in Glasgow's West End.'

'Any precons?'

Clare looked to see where the question had come from and saw Nita, a plain-clothes officer from Cupar. 'Hi Nita. Good to have you here. And, no. Not Mr Gerrard, at least.' She moved to what seemed to be a publicity photo of Eamon Ferry. He was sharp-suited and smiling. 'Eamon Ferry, quite high up in local government in Glasgow. Again, no convictions. But,' she indicated Steve Christie's photo, 'Mr Christie has a firearms conviction, albeit ten years ago. So he is definitely a person of interest.'

'How do they know each other?' Nita asked.

'School, apparently,' Clare said. 'Friends since they were young boys and no indication they'd fallen out recently. But I need volunteers to look further into their backgrounds. Check out their businesses, see if they had any financial problems, anyone sacked lately, any known troublemakers on the payroll, bad debts. You know the kind of thing.'

Bill and Janey indicated they would carry on with this and Clare went on. 'The Lodge was fenced off while the party were staying there and they had a security guard on the gate. Chris and I spoke to him yesterday and, based on what he told us, we plan to re-interview the three men. They did tell us they had a delivery of pizzas around seven on Friday evening, but they omitted to mention what we believe was a minibus of women who arrived an hour later.'

'Are we looking into the guard too?' Nita asked.

'I think so, Nita. Could you check him out please? He told us Doug Gerrard had asked him to keep quiet about the minibus of women. I'd like to know if he has reason to keep quiet. Might our Mr Gerrard have something on him?'

Nita indicated she would do this. Then she said, 'What about Gaby Fox and her husband?'

Janey raised her hand. 'Already checked out, Nita. No convictions. Nothing iffy either, as far as I can tell. Both doing well in their careers. Luke Gasparini was tweeting about securing a big name for his next documentary series.'

Bill raised a hand. 'Who benefits from the victim's death?'

'I've not checked yet,' Clare said. 'And I'd rather not ask the family if I can avoid it. Maybe you could track down his solicitor?'

Bill scribbled a note on his pad and Clare went on.

'Anyone looked into the pizza delivery guy?'

Jim cleared his throat. 'No convictions, Clare. And I checked his deliveries before and after the Lodge. All fine.'

'Thanks, Jim.' Clare stood thinking for a moment. Had she covered everything? And then she remembered the CCTV footage. 'Sara has been going through footage from two security cameras sited at the top of the drive, just at the Heras fencing. There's a point in the evening,' she scanned the room for Sara, 'about eleven, was it?'

Sara nodded.

'Right. So around eleven on Friday night the security guard goes off towards the back of the house, leaving the gate unmanned. Sara spent hours yesterday going through the footage so I'd like a fresh pair of eyes to look at it this morning, please.'

Mandy, one of Sara's fellow uniformed officers, raised her hand and Clare smiled her thanks.

She glanced across to Chris. 'Have I forgotten anything?'

'Phone records?'

'Good point, Chris, thanks. I need someone to go through Russell Fox's phone records. Check his contacts and calls within the past month. Social media too, the works. Anything iffy, get hold of me.'

A couple of hands went up at the back of the room and Clare acknowledged this. 'Okay,' she continued. 'I want every spare officer going over the grounds at Lamond Lodge again this morning. You're looking for anything that might have been dropped, including the gun cartridge. Chris and I will be out and about but we'll keep in touch.'

She smiled, indicating the briefing was at an end, and they began to drift off, clicking laptops to bring them to life. Sara and Mandy went to load up the CCTV footage.

'I need a coffee,' Clare said to Chris.

'Me too.'

'That's kind of you. Bring them into my office and I'll see if the PM report's up yet.'

'I don't recall offering,' he muttered trailing off to the kitchen.

By the time he returned with two coffees Clare was reading the ballistics report. 'They've identified the bullet,' she said.

Chris set down the coffees and produced a pack of Wagon Wheels but Clare barely glanced at them. 'It's a 7.62mm Russian.'

Chris fished a Wagon Wheel out of the packet and pulled a chair over to peer at the monitor. 'What's that when it's at home?'

'The proper name is a 7.62×54mmR. From a hunting rifle, apparently.'

'Can they tell which one?'

Clare peered at the screen. 'Caroline says it could be a couple of different models but, going on past arms seizures, it's likely a Dragunov.'

'Which is?'

'Semi-automatic sniper rifle. Pretty serious bit of kit.'

Chris gave a low whistle. 'This smacks of a professional hitman. Where would he get a gun like that?'

'Or she.'

'Yeah, of course. But, where?'

'It's a Russian gun. Probably through Eastern Europe. That's where most illegal arms come from.'

Chris bit into his Wagon Wheel and slurped his coffee. 'Anything else?'

Clare scanned the screen, reading paragraphs of text. 'Looks like they've confirmed where it was fired from.'

'They're pretty cool, these lasers.'

'They are. Caroline reckons top storey, south-east aspect.'

'Any sign of the cartridge?'

Clare scrolled through the report again. 'That's a good point, Chris. It doesn't say.'

'If they did recover it, there might be a partial print, or DNA, even.'

'Yeah, there might just. I'll go back to her on that.'

'Have they let SOCO know?'

Clare nodded. 'I'll give Raymond a call. See if he's got anything.' She moved to the contacts on her phone and called up Raymond Curtice, the SOCO officer. While she waited for him to answer she noticed the Wagon Wheels. 'How'd you get these past Sara?'

'Keep 'em in my locker.'

'She'll find out, you know. Oh, Raymond. Hi. Just wondering if you've found any gunshot residue.'

'Yep. Got it. Top storey, as Caroline said. Furthest left window as you look at the house.'

'And?'

'Traces on the sill and on the floorboards beneath the window. And I'd say the window was recently opened. There are paint flakes on the floor. We've taken some prints from around the sill but there's no guarantee they'll match anyone on the database. We'll try, though.'

Clare thanked Raymond and ended the call. 'That's definite, then. The shot came from inside the house.'

'So, one of them?' Chris said.

'Mm, not sure I'd go that far. There's that minibus for starters. Could have been anyone in that vehicle.' She lifted her coffee mug and drained it. 'Come on,' she said, pushing back her chair. 'It's time we found out who was in that house on Friday night.'

Chapter 10

They headed for the station door but before they reached it, the tall figure of Mark Mooney entered. He was more formally dressed than at their first meeting, in dark trousers and a white shirt. He looked round then his eye fell on Clare and Chris. He hesitated then approached them.

'Quite a crew out there,' he said, nodding towards the door. 'TV folk by the looks of the vans.'

Clare frowned. 'Are they causing an obstruction?'

He shook his head. 'No, nothing like that. It's, er, I wondered if I could have a word.'

Clare glanced at Chris then back at the security guard. Then she turned and led him towards one of the small interview rooms. She opened the door and flicked on the light. 'Please,' she said, indicating a chair.

He stood for a moment, regarding it, then slowly sat down.

Clare took a seat opposite, Chris at her side. She smiled at Mark and, when he seemed reluctant to speak, she said, 'Is there something we can help you with?'

He rubbed his chin. 'It's just...'

They waited.

'It's about Friday night,' he said, at last. 'That minibus.'

'Mr Mooney,' Clare began, 'if what you're about to tell us relates to the killing of Mr Fox then I must caution you formally and record this interview.'

He waved this away. 'Oh no, it's nothing like that. You might even have guessed.'

'Go on, then,' Clare said. 'But I will stop you if I feel a formal interview is indicated.'

He forced a smile then went on. 'I knew there were women in that bus,' he said. 'Mr Gerrard – he said it was entertainment for the lads. Told me to keep it quiet, ye know? Said he'd see me right.' Mark Mooney cleared his throat then went on. 'I thought he meant he'd bung me a few quid. But later on, bit after eleven, I saw one of the girls. She was round the side of the house and she, well, she gave me a nod.' He smiled at Chris, as though looking for support. 'I mean, I'm not gonna turn it down if it's offered on a plate, am I?'

Clare ignored this. 'Are you saying you went round the side of the house to have sex with one of the women who'd arrived in the minibus?'

The colour began to rise from Mark Mooney's neck and he avoided Clare's eye. 'Well, yeah. Suppose I did.'

Clare nodded. 'And where exactly did this liaison take place?'

'Round the back.'

'Outside?'

'Yeah. There's a log store just outside the kitchen door. No' so many logs in the summer, obviously. So...'

'Did you pay?'

'Eh?'

'Did you offer the woman any money?'

'No! It wasn't that kind of thing, Inspector. She just – I suppose she just fancied me.'

Clare raised an eyebrow. 'And how long were you away from your post at the gate?'

'Five or ten minutes, I suppose.'

She watched him for a few seconds then said, 'Why didn't you tell us this earlier, Mr Mooney?'

He shrugged. 'Dunno, really. I mean, obviously you've seen how I'm fixed.'

'Wife and kids, you mean?'

His face was scarlet now. 'Yeah. It was just a quickie, though. Meant nothing.'

Chris leaned forward. 'Mr Mooney, when you told us Doug Gerrard asked you to keep quiet about the minibus because of publicity, was that true?'

Mark Mooney drew a hand across his brow and wiped it on his trousers. 'He said I wouldn't want the wife hearing about it.'

Chris's eyes narrowed. 'He blackmailed you into keeping quiet about the women in the minibus?'

'Well, I wouldn't put it quite like that,' he said. 'But he was right. It was stupid. Shouldn't have done it. Definitely not worth risking my marriage for.'

'Indeed,' Clare said, her tone sharper than she meant. She met his eye. 'So, is that it? Or is there more?'

He sank back in his chair. 'No, that's everything, honest.' He shook his head. 'I'm kicking myself for being so stupid.'

Clare sat silent for a moment then said, 'Mr Mooney, we may call you back in to take a formal statement. But, in the meantime, I don't want you to speak to anyone about this. And that includes Mr Gerrard. Got it?'

'Don't worry, Inspector. I won't be taking any more calls from him.'

They watched him leave, as fast as his legs could carry him.

'Believe him?' Chris said.

'I think so. You?'

'Yes. I'd say he's spent a pretty uncomfortable night, worrying about it.'

'Last of the great romantics, eh?' Clare said. 'The question is…'

'Yeah?'

'Did Doug Gerrard send that woman out…'

'…to make sure he had something on Mark Mooney?' Chris finished.

'Exactly.' Clare nodded slowly. 'I'd say our Mr Gerrard doesn't do anything without a reason. And I'd very much like to know what it is.'

Chris rose from his seat. 'Brodie Hotel?'

'Yep. Let's see what they have to say for themselves.'

Chapter 11

Clare was relieved to see there were no reporters outside the Brodie Hotel when they arrived. The grounds to the rear were cleverly designed, with individual sun decks screened from each other by neatly trimmed hedges. They found Gaby Fox and Luke Gasparini sunning themselves in one of these. Luke sat up on his lounger, regarding them through a pair of gold-rimmed sunglasses. 'Back again, officers,' he said unnecessarily.

Gaby swung her tanned legs round and off her lounger, slipping her feet into a pair of sandals. She at least had the grace to remove her sunglasses. She held up a hand to shade her eyes and tried her best to smile. 'Inspector,' she said. 'Erm, can I offer you a drink? Or tea perhaps?'

Clare waved this away. 'We were hoping to speak to Mr Fox's friends, but, as you're here, maybe we could have another chat? If you felt up to it.'

'I'm not sure she is,' Luke Gasparini snapped. 'She has just lost her brother, you know.'

Gaby gave Clare an apologetic smile. 'Luke, darling, why don't you run to the bar and order some cold drinks. I don't mind talking to the officers.'

Luke glared at them and seemed unwilling to leave.

'Go on,' Gaby said. 'I'd like a drink too.'

He glanced at his wife then said, 'I'll be a few minutes, then. If you're sure?'

She nodded and Luke went off towards the hotel.

Gaby spread her hands. 'I'm sorry, Inspector...'

'Clare, please,' Clare reminded her. 'Clare and Chris.'

Gaby acknowledged this. Then she said again, 'I am sorry about Luke. He's rather protective, you see. And losing Russell in such a horrible way.'

Clare smiled. 'I understand. I think you're both being very helpful, in the circumstances.' This seemed to put Gaby at her ease and Clare went on. 'I wondered, if you didn't mind, could you tell us a bit about Russell. If you felt up to it, of course. We'd like to build up a picture of what he was like. And I'm sure you knew him better than anyone.'

Gaby's eyes were bright and for a moment she didn't speak. Then she said, 'Of course.' Her voice was small. 'I'd like to talk about Russell.' She paused for a moment then said, 'I was so proud of him.' She smiled and gave a slight nod. 'People think I'm the one who's achieved so much, but Russell – well you probably know he had a spell in prison. And when he came out, it wasn't easy for him.'

'Can you explain?'

'People,' she began, 'they're so quick to judge. Russell made a mistake and he had to live with it. But Facebook, the keyboard warriors, they don't miss you and hit the wall.'

'It can be pretty nasty,' Clare agreed.

'And he felt guilty, too,' Gaby went on. 'Guilty for that poor woman's injuries. He wrote to her, care of the police, obviously. But he didn't hear back. Maybe she never received it.'

The sun went behind a cloud, casting a shadow on the courtyard. Gaby shivered and reached for a cotton cardigan, pulling it on over her arms. She began rubbing her hands together and Clare noticed her fingers were white.

'Are you cold?' she asked.

Gaby followed Clare's gaze to her fingers. 'Oh this?' she said. Then she shook her head. 'It's nothing. Raynaud's syndrome. Affects the circulation.' She continued rubbing her hands together. 'It'll come back in a minute.'

'We can carry on indoors, if you prefer,' Clare said. Gaby's fingers were very white, compared to the rest of her hands.

'Honestly it's fine. Erm, what were you saying?'

'Did Russell ever speak about the people he met inside prison?' Chris said.

Gaby hesitated and seemed to be choosing her words. 'Not really.'

'Maybe the odd time?' Clare pressed, but Gaby said nothing.

'Perhaps he kept in touch with someone,' Chris persisted. 'Someone he met when he was there.'

Gaby looked at Chris, her brow furrowed. 'You think it's someone from back then? That he fell out with someone in prison and this is what they've…'

The chink of glasses interrupted them as Luke reappeared bearing a tray with four glasses and a tall jug, bobbing with ice. 'I thought you might want something after all,' he said glancing at Clare. He placed the tray down on a wooden garden table and Chris rose to help. The ice cold lemonade was refreshing and Clare sipped at it. Then she smiled at Luke. 'Gaby was telling us Russell found it difficult when he came out of prison.'

'What you'd expect, I suppose.'

'Were you aware of anyone who might have harboured a grudge over the years?' Clare asked.

Luke glanced at Gaby then back at Clare. 'Not sure, really. He went into the restaurant trade when he came out of prison. He's done that for a good few years now. It's not exactly the kind of job where you make enemies – not the sort to come after you with a gun, at least.'

'So business was good?' Clare said.

Luke nodded. 'Yeah, it was. But he'd been talking about getting out. Selling up.'

Gaby stared at him. 'I didn't know that.'

Luke shrugged. 'He mentioned it.'

'Did he say why?'

'Think he'd had enough,' Luke said. 'Told me he'd put the word out a couple of months back and had a bit of interest.' He nodded at this. 'They were busy restaurants, you know? I reckon he'd have got a good price.'

Gaby took a draught of her lemonade. 'I'm sure he would.'

Was there a slight edge to her voice? *She doesn't like being the last to know*, Clare thought. Time for a change of tack. 'Did Russell have anyone special in his life?'

Gaby shook her head. 'I don't think so.' She turned to her husband. 'Unless of course he told you.'

The tone was lost on Luke. 'No,' he said. 'Not that I was aware. Mind you, Inspector, we were down in London and Russell was in Glasgow so he might have had someone.' He looked past Clare towards the trees screening the rest of the garden. 'I think the three lads have gone for a wander. They'd be the ones to ask.'

Clare smiled. 'We'll do that, thanks.' She lifted her glass to drink then her phone rang, cutting through the birdsong. She glanced at the screen then moved away from the sun deck, excusing herself before answering the call. 'Neil,' she said, her voice low, 'what can I do for you?'

'Couple of things,' Neil Grant said. 'The full PM report is up on the system but I thought you'd want to know the DNA on the bullet matches the victim.'

'No real surprise there.'

'No indeed. But something else might be.'

Clare waited.

'Your victim was not a well man. There was an extensive abdominal mass.'

'Cancer?'

'Afraid so. And pretty far gone.'

'Would he have known about it?'

'Oh yes. You'll have to check with his GP but I can't imagine he didn't.'

'Was it operable?'

'In theory, yes. But it would only have bought him time, delayed the inevitable.'

Clare ended the call and stood thinking. From her brief conversation with Gaby and Luke she didn't think they could have known about Russell's illness. But it certainly made sense of his decision to sell the restaurants. Cash in his investments and spend what little time he had left enjoying his life. The sound of conversation cut across her thoughts and she saw Russell's three friends emerge from the trees, strolling in Clare's direction. They saw her and there was a brief, whispered conversation. Clare walked smartly across and they hung back to wait for her.

'Inspector,' Eamon Ferry said when he was near enough, 'sorry to miss you. It's such a lovely day we thought we'd explore the grounds.'

She wondered why Eamon seemed to have appointed himself spokesman for the group and she thought she'd like to speak to them individually. 'Isn't it,' she said, smiling. 'I hope we're not inconveniencing you too much.'

Steve Christie and Doug Gerrard seemed anxious to move away and Clare took her chance. She caught Chris's eye then turned back to the trio. 'I wonder if you could spare me a few minutes, Mr Gerrard?' She looked across the garden and saw a bench seat in front of a deep herbaceous border 'If we could just…'

She led him over to the bench, conscious that Eamon and Steve's eyes were on them as they went. Chris walked briskly across the lawn to join them and Clare indicated the bench. 'Please,' she said to Doug Gerrard, 'do sit.'

He eased himself down then met her eye. 'What's this about?'

'Friday night,' Clare said smoothly. 'I gather you had some visitors.' She watched him, his eyes flicking left and right as he seemed to be deciding what to say.

'Visitors?' he said, at last.

'Yes. A dark-coloured van, or maybe a minibus. It arrived about eight o'clock. I'd like you to tell me who or what was in that van.' She waited for a few moments and when he didn't speak she went on. 'I think it was a party of women. Am I correct?'

He looked at her, his hand rubbing his chin. 'Aye,' he said. 'A few girls. Just to make the night go with a swing, ye know? Bit of a treat for Russell.'

'Were the women sex workers?'

'Oh no,' he said, forcing a laugh. 'Nothing like that, Inspector. Just lassies that liked a party.'

'Friends of yours?'

He shook his head. 'No. Friends of a friend, you might say.'

'You arranged for them to attend?'

'Aye. Kind of.'

'How?'

He glanced at Chris and inclined his head. 'Ye ken how it is. Ye get chatting in the pub. Someb'dy says they know some lassies – the kind that like a laugh and a few drinks.'

'And did any of you have sex with the girls?'

'Oh now, Inspector, I'm not sure that's relevant. I mean I'm no' the kiss and tell kind of guy.'

'In a murder enquiry, Mr Gerrard,' Clare said, her tone icy, 'you have no choice. So, I will ask you again, did any of you have sex with these women?'

'Suppose.'

'And did money change hands?'

He avoided her eye. 'Not from me. Can't speak for the other lads.'

'Let's talk about the security guard then. Mark Mooney.'

He still didn't meet her eye. 'What about him?'

'Did you arrange for one of the women to have sex with him?'

'Me?' He spread his hands in a gesture of mock inno-cence. 'Why would I do that when we're paying him to man the gate?'

'I'd say it was so you could later persuade him to keep quiet about the minibus. Did you threaten to tell his wife he'd been with one of the women?'

'Nope. None of my business what he got up to.'

Clare glanced at Chris. They were getting nowhere. He took the hint.

'How did you arrange for the women to be there?' he asked.

'Cannae remember.'

Chris leaned forward. 'With respect, sir, even I know that's bollocks. You don't just happen to book a busload of women then forget how you managed it.'

He looked at Chris for a moment and Chris held his gaze. Eventually he said, 'I met a lad in a pub one night. Got chatting, told him we were coming through here for the party. Lad says he knows some girls out this way – girls that like a good time – phone numbers were exchanged, I made a call and that was it. We provided the venue, plenty of food and drink and we had ourselves a party.'

'The number?' Clare said.

'Eh?'

'The number you called to invite the women to your… party.'

He looked past them, towards the house where the others were waiting. 'Dunno,' he said. 'Don't think I have it any more.'

'It'll be stored on your phone,' Clare said. 'Can we see it please?'

'Deleted. I like to keep the phone tidy, ye know?'

'We can get it from your phone company.'

A smirk was forming on his face. 'Knock yourself out, Inspector. I've nothing to hide.' He rose from the bench. 'That it?'

'For now.'

He gave a slight nod then ambled off, glancing back at them. 'Adios.'

They watched him go and, when he was out of earshot, Clare said, 'I'll wipe that smirk off his face if it's the last thing I do, Chris. Mark my words.'

Chapter 12

Eamon Ferry and Steve Christie were no more forth-coming on the subject of the minibus women. Yes, there had been girls there on Friday night but, no, they weren't sure who had booked them. Yes they'd had a bit of a party but they were cagey when the subject of sex came up.

'We don't go in for public orgies,' Steve Christie said. 'We're no' like that.'

Eamon Ferry looked appalled when Chris asked if any drugs had been taken and Steve Christie seemed to agree.

'Mug's game, that, Sergeant,' Steve said.

When they had drifted off, Clare said, 'Get anything else out of Gaby and Luke?'

'Nope. What was your phone call?'

Clare's expression was blank for a moment. The conversations with the men had put the call out of her head. 'Oh,' she said, remembering. 'It was Neil. Neil Grant.'

'And?'

'Well, the bullet in the tree was the one that killed Russell Fox. DNA matched.'

Chris nodded. 'We pretty much expected that.'

'But what we didn't know is that Russell Fox wasn't long for this world.'

'Eh?'

'Massive abdominal tumour. Neil reckons he must have known about it.'

Chris looked towards the hotel. 'D'you reckon the rest of them know? The sister and the friends?'

'Doesn't sound like it. But Russell's decision to sell the restaurants makes more sense now.'

'Make the most of the time he had left?' Chris said. 'I'd say so.' He looked towards the sun deck. Luke and Gaby had been joined by the three men and the five of them were deep in conversation. Doug Gerrard glanced across once or twice.

'Getting their stories straight,' Clare said. 'Question is: do we tell them about Russell's illness?'

'No reason we should. It could add to their distress.'

'Fair point.'

'I have my uses. So, what now?'

'Let's head for the Lodge. I'd like to go up to the top floor. See the room the gunman used.'

They walked round the other side of the hotel, avoiding the sun deck and back towards the car.

—

The press pack seem to have divided itself between the station and the Lodge. As Clare and Chris slowed their approach they saw a TV reporter speaking on camera. But as they pulled into the drive every camera turned to follow their progress.

'This is going to get tired, very soon,' Clare said.

'Already is.'

They drew up outside the Heras fence and jumped out of the car. Jim was standing near the steps to the treetop walk and he strode across to meet them.

'Anything?' Clare asked, nodding towards the officers searching the grounds.

He shook his head. 'Nothing so far. I'll keep you posted.'

Clare thanked him and they headed round the other side of the Lodge towards the gardens at the back. 'I want to get the lay of the land,' she said.

As they rounded the house they passed a side door which stood open, leading to a large kitchen. A stone alcove half filled with logs was next to the door, presumably the location of Mark Mooney's 'quickie' with the minibus woman. Two black wheelie bins stood to the side of the log store, the lids resting on an overspill of empty bottles.

'Looks like quite a party,' Chris said, nodding at the bins, and Clare agreed.

Beyond the house the gardens seemed to be extensive, screened here and there by clumps of trees.

'Want a look?' Chris said, but Clare shook her head.

'Not till the search team's finished.' She turned back towards the front of the house. 'Come on, let's see what it's like inside.'

Gary, a uniformed PC, was stationed at the front entrance and he moved aside to let them pass. They stood in a central hallway just inside the door, marvelling at their surroundings. The walls were ochre with deep skirting boards in light oak. A picture rail ran round the walls with plaster cornicing picked out in light cream. On one side of the hall, a fireplace was set into a corner with easy chairs arranged in front of it. Solid oak doors led off in every direction and Clare opened one, peering into a large sunny room. The walls were decorated with brightly coloured wallpaper, a Liberty pattern, she thought, the bay windows in the same light oak with what looked to be the original shutters pulled back to admit the daylight. A rosewood grand piano sat to the side of the room, the rest given over to comfortable-looking sofas in front of thick-pile rugs.

Another door led to a dining room which seemed to have been unused by the party, the table neatly laid with china plates and polished cutlery. They continued exploring the downstairs rooms, Chris marvelling at the kitchen with its pale blue units and enormous refectory table.

'Sara would love this,' he said.

'Wouldn't we all.' Clare turned on her heel. 'Come on. Let's find the room the gunman used.'

A richly carpeted central staircase led from the front hall up to a gallery on the middle storey and they climbed quickly to a broad landing with doors off left and right. Bedrooms, Clare guessed. Straight ahead, down a short passage was a smaller return staircase. The wooden treads were bare and the second flight narrower. As they ascended, Clare wondered if this had been servants' quarters at one time. Or perhaps a nursery.

The stairs led to a smaller hall with coombed ceilings. She stood for a moment, orientating herself, then she turned to her right. 'This way, I think.' She crossed the hall towards three identical doors and moved to open the furthest left. Light flooded out from the room, which was in full sun thanks to a dormer window with no curtains. The room was unfurnished, the floorboards bare, and Clare thought it felt unused. She went to the window and looked out. It afforded a clear view of the treetop walk and she guessed this was the room used by the gunman. She pushed the sash fastener back to unlock it and raised the window up. It grated a little and she saw where the paint had flaked off. She looked out and down the slates to the guttering below. No sign of anything there.

'Reckon this is where the shot came from?' Chris asked.

She squinted into the sun, her gaze fixed on the treetop walk, imagining Russell Fox's last moments. He'd have been a sitting duck, up there. Nowhere to run to, even if he'd noticed the gunman. 'Yeah,' she said, stepping back from the window. 'See for yourself.' She waited while Chris checked the view. Then he, too, stepped back.

'Has to be one of them,' he said.

'What, Gaby and that lot?'

'There's no other explanation.'

'It's a bit obvious,' Clare said. 'Even if one of them did want to do away with Russell, for whatever reason, to do it from the upstairs window of the house they were staying in… it's a huge risk.'

'You want to search the house for a weapon?'

She shook her head. 'If it was one of them, they'd have got rid of the gun long before raising the alarm.'

Chris nodded. 'All the same, the shot did come from the house. And another thing – it would have made a fair bit of noise, even with a suppressor.'

'I know. But you saw those bins full of empties, Chris. They were probably sleeping it off on Saturday morning. Especially if he was killed early on.'

'Suppose.'

They closed the window and left the room.

'What now?' Chris asked as they walked back down the stairs.

'I'd like to speak to my contact at the prison,' Clare said. 'Find out what I can about Russell Fox's time there.'

–

'Clare Mackay, how are you?' Colin Morris said, when the telephonist at Barlinnie prison finally tracked him down. 'Sorry to keep you waiting; I was dealing with something.'

'I'm well, thanks, Colin. You?'

'Oh you know, same old, same old. Too many bodies, not enough cells, not enough time or money to do everything I'd like.'

'Sounds pretty much like police work,' Clare said.

'So, what can I do for you?'

'Information, if possible. Going back a few years now. Russell Fox.'

'Name rings a bell,' Colin said. 'Refresh my memory.'

'Drunk driving. Coming up for eight years ago. Knocked a woman down on a dark road.'

'Oh wait, is he the lad with the famous sister?'

'That's him.'

'I remember him, now. Don't think he came back for another stint. What do you want to know?'

'He was shot dead on Saturday morning. Sniper rifle.'

'Sheesh.'

'Quite. So, I need to know who he associated with when he was inside. Anyone he rubbed up the wrong way, particularly anyone in for firearms offences. Think you can help?'

'Aye. Might take a bit of time but I'll get onto it. If you could send through a formal request?'

'Will do. But if it's possible to rush it, meantime.'

Colin laughed. 'It's always the same with you lot, isn't it? Leave it with me, Clare. I'll see what I can do.'

Chapter 13

Nita looked up as Clare entered the incident room. 'Mark Mooney, your security guard,' she said, 'he checks out. No precons. Fully licensed for security work. Regularly does jobs like this one.'

'Okay, Nita. Thanks. Anything on Russell Fox's social media? Or phone records?'

'Checking them now,' Janey said. 'Nothing much so far.'

Clare thanked them and wandered back out to the front office. She spotted Zoe, the Admin Assistant, at her desk. She'd been so busy earlier she hadn't noticed Zoe, maybe because there was something different about her. But, distracted by the murder investigation, she couldn't think what it was. 'You've had your hair done,' she said, tentatively.

Zoe put a hand up and patted her curls, piled up on top with a couple of clips. 'Time for a change,' she said. Then she glanced across to the incident room door and lowered her voice. 'Fancy a cake?' She reached down under her desk and produced a Tupperware container. 'I made some strawberry blondies last night but I didn't know all these other folk would be here and there's not enough to go round.'

'What's a blondie?'

Zoe rolled her eyes. 'Like a brownie only not chocolate.' She removed the lid and held the tub out for Clare to see. 'I stirred a strawberry compote through the top before baking.'

'Oh Zoe! You are not good for my waistline.'

'Ach, rubbish,' Zoe said. 'As my mum says, it's the belly that keeps the back up.'

'I like the sound of your mum,' Clare said, selecting a sticky piece of strawberry blondie. She took this into her office and sat down at the desk. For some reason she was finding it hard to think clearly about this case. Was it because she'd been away at the wedding? Missed those crucial first few hours? Whatever the reason, she had to get a handle on it.

She bit into the cake, licking her fingers clean. As usual it was utterly delicious. She'd bet money on Zoe winning the Bake Off competition one of these days. Her office door opened and Sara looked in.

'Boss,' she began then her eye fell on the remains of the cake. 'Zoe gave you a blondie then,' she said.

'They are so good, Sara. How does she do it?'

'Beats me. She gave me the recipe. But they never turn out the same when I try them.'

Clare thought of her own attempts at baking – non-existent these days. 'Nor me,' she said. 'Anyway, take a seat.'

Sara hovered by the door. 'Actually I can't stop. Just came to say I was due to follow-up with the mum whose toddler wandered off but there's been a road accident down on North Street.'

'Anyone hurt?'

'Don't think so. But it's partly blocking the road and you know how congested it gets down there so I'd better head over.'

Clare suddenly thought a bit of ordinary police work was just what she needed. 'Tell you what, Sara,' she said, 'give me the toddler mum's details. I'll call in on her myself.'

Sara looked doubtful. 'You sure, boss? She's a nice woman. I wouldn't want her worrying. You being a DI, I mean.'

'Don't worry. I'll not go in heavy-handed. You go and sort out your traffic, and I promise I'll be kind to your toddler woman.'

Sara turned to leave then Clare said, 'Sara.'

'Boss?'

'Was Zoe's hair always purple?'

—

Melanie Fraser lived in a two-bedroomed flat above a hairdressing salon in Bell Street. Clare was pleased to see she only opened the door a few inches, thanks to what seemed to be a shiny new chain. She studied Clare's warrant card before releasing the chain and inviting her in. She led Clare into a small sitting room. It was sparsely furnished but clean and tidy. A TV sat in one corner with a selection of Peppa Pig DVDs. Next to this stood a bookcase filled with toddler board books and chick lit novels, and there was a Duplo train on a rug beneath the window.

Clare's practised eye took it all in and she decided there was nothing to worry about here. She looked round for somewhere to sit and her eye fell on a copy of the local newspaper on a chair. The photo wasn't a recent one, Clare thought, but they'd caught Gaby at a thoughtful moment, her wide smile for once absent. She inclined her head and read,

Daytime Gaby's Tears for Brother

and she sighed inwardly. There would be no holding back the press now. She took the seat Melanie had indicated and gave her a smile. Melanie followed suit, perching on the edge of a chair, twisting a silver ring on her middle finger.

Clare looked round the room. 'It's nice here,' she said. 'Lots of light.'

Melanie nodded. 'I do my best.'

'Is it just you and your little boy?'

'Yeah. Just the two of us. Me and Daniel. He does see his dad sometimes but we mostly manage on our own.' A black cat strolled languidly into the room, brushing past Melanie's legs. Then it saw Clare and stood for a moment, unblinking, taking her in. Melanie moved to pick up the cat but it leapt from her hands and walked up to Clare, sniffing at her legs. 'Sammy,' Melanie said but the cat ignored this. It continued to sniff Clare until she put a hand down to stroke its head. At this, it turned and began rubbing its head against Clare's hand, purring softly. 'He likes you,' Melanie said.

'Probably smelling my dog,' Clare said. And then she remembered she hadn't seen Benjy since Saturday morning. He'd be having a wonderful time with Moira, her nearest neighbour and dog walker, but she'd be so glad to see him later on.

'So,' Melanie said.

Clare smiled. 'It's really nothing to worry about. PC Stapleton who spoke to you on Saturday – she's dealing with something so I said I'd pop in for a quick chat.'

Melanie sighed. 'I don't know what else I can do,' she said. 'I had a reliable babysitter, or I thought she was reliable. She told me later she was on some new pills and they were making her drowsy. I suppose she slept through Daniel waking up.'

'You were on night shift?'

Melanie's eyes flicked away for a moment, a gesture that didn't escape Clare. 'Yeah,' she said.

'Where do you work?' Clare asked, keeping her tone light.

The eyes again. Clare wondered what Melanie was hiding.

'Oh, various places.'

She tried again. 'You're an agency worker?'

'Yeah, something like that.' Melanie checked her watch. 'I need to pick Daniel up soon,' she said. 'From nursery.' She glanced towards the door.

Clare smiled. 'I can give you a lift if it helps. Give us a few more minutes to chat.'

Melanie's shoulders sagged. 'Okay.'

'Can you tell me what kind of work you do, Melanie?'

The cat turned its head away from Clare's fingers and strolled back across to Melanie, jumping up on her lap. She put out a hand to stroke it and it nuzzled her neck in response. Clare waited. She was good at silences.

'Waitressing,' Melanie said at last.

'Must have been quite a distance away.'

Melanie's brow furrowed.

'For you to stay overnight,' Clare said.

'Yes. Quite far.'

'Still in Fife? Or further afield?'

Melanie rubbed the cat under its chin and Clare heard it purring again. 'I really don't know. There were a few of us and we were chatting, you know? And suddenly we were there.'

'Someone picked you up then?'

Melanie nodded. 'Yes. In a kind of minibus. The windows were dark so we couldn't see much.'

Clare was suddenly alert. A minibus with dark windows. 'Are you sure it wasn't a bit closer?' she said. 'Maybe just a few miles out of town?'

She shrugged. 'I honestly can't remember. Does it matter?'

'I'm afraid it might, Melanie. It might matter very much indeed.'

Melanie flushed and she seemed near to tears. Her eyes strayed to the newspaper. Then suddenly she said, 'Look, I read about the man. The one who was shot. And yes, I was there. We were hired to be at the party. But I didn't know anything about it. I swear. And I'd no idea it was that Gaby woman's brother. She wasn't even there.'

The cat leapt down from Melanie's lap and walked back out of the room. With nothing in her hands, Melanie resumed twisting the ring. She glanced at Clare then looked down at her hands. 'Honestly,' she went on, her voice a whisper. 'I didn't know anything until it was on the news last night.' She checked her watch again. 'I have to go,' she said. 'Daniel…'

'Come on,' Clare said, rising from her seat. 'I'll drop you at the nursery. And I can run you back here again. Then I'd like you to come into the station so we can take a proper statement.'

Melanie bent to pick up a brown shoulder bag from the floor. 'I haven't done anything wrong,' she said.

Clare smiled. 'I know. But you might have seen something that could help us.'

She stood for a moment as though unconvinced then she led Clare to the front door and took a set of keys from her bag. Outside she pulled the door closed and turned a key in the mortice lock.

In the car she began directing Clare to the nursery. 'Take a right here.' As Clare swung the car round into Church Street Melanie spoke again. 'Look, I don't suppose it could be tomorrow? When Daniel's at nursery, I mean. Save me getting a sitter.'

Clare considered this. Melanie probably didn't know anything about the shooting. But she had been another pair of eyes inside the house on Friday night. And, judging by the time she'd arrived at the station the next morning looking for Daniel, she'd been there all night. Perhaps still there when Russell Fox had been shot.

They were approaching the nursery now. Melanie clicked off her seat belt. 'Just drop me here if you don't mind,' she said. 'Don't want anyone seeing me getting out of the car. No offence.'

Clare was about to say she'd like Melanie to come straight over to the station, that they'd find someone to keep Daniel occupied when she saw something that changed her mind.

Or rather someone.

Walking towards the nursery building, pushing an empty stroller pram was Susan Clancy. Suddenly Clare was transported back to a missing baby case. Susan had come under scrutiny because her own little girl had been taken into care. But then she had helped Clare track down the real culprits and had proved herself capable of looking after her daughter once more. Clare had helped her find a flat in the town, away from her old contacts, and she'd begun a new life in St Andrews. She racked her brains trying to recall the name of Susan's daughter and then she remembered it was Paige. And now, she guessed, Paige was at the same nursery as Melanie's son Daniel.

Melanie opened the car door. 'So tomorrow morning?' she said. 'I can come about nine fifteen.'

'Erm, yes. That's fine, Melanie. See you then.' She watched as Melanie quickened her step and headed for the nursery door. She overtook Susan and nodded to her. They exchanged a couple of words then Melanie walked ahead of Susan into the building. Clare saw Susan enter behind Melanie. 'I wonder,' she said, starting the car engine.

Chapter 14

Sara was at the front desk dealing with callers when Clare returned. Presumably the traffic accident hadn't taken long to sort out. As she entered her office the phone began to ring. Colin Morris from the prison.

'Colin,' she said. 'Good of you to call so quickly.'

'Ah, no problem, Clare. How's the investigation going?'

'Early days. I'm kind of hoping you might have something.'

'Well, yes and no,' he said. 'So, first of all, our records show Russell Fox had four different cellmates while he was inside. No particular problems with any of them. Seemed to get on okay.'

'Do you know where they are now?' Clare asked.

'Aye. Two of them have since died. One's back inside and the fourth went to an address in England when he was released.'

Clare snatched up a pen. 'Name?'

'John Joseph Alexander, known as Jonjo. And, from what I can see, he's still in England. Birmingham, last I heard. But you might want to check that.'

Clare scribbled the name down. 'Anything else?'

'Yes. Bit of trouble a few weeks before Russell was released.'

'Oh yeah?' This sounded more hopeful.

'One of Russell's cellmates was set upon by another lad: Zac Buchanan. A real bad lot, Zac. He was doing a stretch for an aggravated assault. Don't ask me why it wasn't attempted murder. Anyway, Russell's cellmate must have done something to upset Zac. Next thing Russell knows, Zac's cornered the lad in his cell, giving him a right kicking. Russell tried to intervene but two big lads were barring the door. Zac half kills the lad then the three of them swan off, leaving him in a bloodied heap. Cellmate of course wouldn't say anything but Russell named all three. Next thing they knew Zac and the others were transferred to another wing and Zac had a year added to his sentence. He swore he'd get Russell for it.'

'But surely that was years ago now.'

'It was. But Zac Buchanan was released, just four months ago. Word is he's living near your neck of the woods now, down in Leven.'

Clare considered this. Leven was a busy seaside town, popular with holidaymakers thanks to its sandy beach. And it was just fifteen miles from St Andrews.

'Thanks, Colin. That's worth following up. Erm, the cellmate – the one who was beaten up?'

'Sadly, one of the ones who died, Clare. Nothing to do with Zac, though. He was found in an alley one night, about a year ago. Needle still in his arm.'

Clare shook her head. 'Drugs, eh?'

'Aye. The misery they cause.'

'Anything else, Colin?'

'Nah. That's it. He was no bother as a prisoner, Russell, apart from that one incident. Did his time and hasn't been back. That's how we like them.'

She thanked Colin and headed for the incident room. Bill was ending a call, scoring things off his notepad as

Clare entered. 'Drawing a blank on the three friends, boss,' he said. 'Janey's still looking into Steve Christie but the other two seem fine. No problems in their personal lives, no debts, no indication of drug use or other criminality.'

Clare nodded. 'Thanks, Bill. Could I ask you to look up another one please?'

Bill drew a line under the list on his pad. 'Okay, shoot.'

'Zac Buchanan.'

He looked up. 'Think I jailed him a few years ago. Nasty piece of work.'

'Any connection with firearms?'

He sat back, tapping his pen on the notepad. 'I'm struggling to remember. But he's the kind of guy who, if he can't get hold of a gun himself, he'll know someone who can. He in the frame for this?'

Clare sat down. 'It's possible. He was in Barlinnie the same time as Russell Fox. Russell's cellmate was assaulted by Zac and Russell gave evidence against him. Zac was transferred and had a year added to his sentence.'

Bill nodded. 'He wouldn't like that. From what I remember he's a hot-headed little shit.'

'Could you prioritise him, please?'

'I'll get onto it now.'

Janey caught Clare's eye. 'Been looking into Steve Christie,' she said.

'And?'

'Nothing anyone can pin on him.'

'But you're suspicious?'

Janey shrugged. 'I can't find any involvement with firearms since his conviction. HMRC have investigated him a few times but nothing they could make stick. The officer I spoke to said he was a slippery sucker.'

'Remind me again what he does,' Clare said.

'Imports tat from China. Supplies market stalls, small shops. The kind of stuff you buy, then it falls to bits a couple of weeks later.'

'Okay, thanks Janey. Ask HMRC to keep us informed. Otherwise, move on.' Clare rose and was heading for the door when Chris ambled into the room.

'We going somewhere?'

'I am. You're staying here to help Janey and Bill. Anything of interest get me on my mobile. I have a call to pay.'

Chapter 15

Susan Clancy's flat was on the second floor of a three-storey block on Roundhill Road, less than half a mile from the police station. She stared at Clare for a moment then a smile spread across her face.

'Inspector,' she said, standing back to admit Clare.

'Clare, please,' she said. 'I think we know each other well enough now.'

'Clare, then. Nice to see you.' She closed the door and directed Clare into a sitting room. A little girl of around three sat on the floor surrounded by toy farm animals which she was pretending to walk along the linoleum. If Clare hadn't known this was Paige she'd have guessed from her resemblance to Susan. Paige looked up as they entered the room and Clare saw she had Susan's eyes and the same dark hair. Susan's hair had been dyed blonde when Clare had met her during that missing baby case. But now it was dark, cut in a long bob with a choppy fringe.

'You've changed your hair,' Clare said.

'Gone back to my own colour. Saves a lot of faff with dyes an' that. Coffee?'

'Only if you're making it.'

'Won't be a minute.' Susan disappeared and Clare heard the sound of water being poured into a kettle, cupboard doors opening and closing. She knelt down beside the little girl who was staring at her.

'Hello,' she said. 'I'm Clare.'

The toddler studied Clare for a minute then she held out a tiny chestnut horse. 'This is my hossie,' she said, her face serious.

Clare went to take the horse from Paige but the little girl withdrew her hand, clutching the horse close. She picked up a black and white cow in her other hand and held this out instead. Clare took the offering. 'It's a cow,' she said, smiling.

Paige nodded. 'He says moo.'

Clare made mooing sounds and Paige began to laugh.

'You two getting on then,' Susan said, coming back into the room with two mugs. She put these on a square dining table. 'Better if we have them up here,' she said. 'So Paige can't grab them.'

Over coffee Susan explained she had a part-time job now. 'Just when Paige is at nursery.'

'What's the job?'

'Helping out in a hairdresser's. Mostly manning the phones, sweeping the floor and that. But the owner's been showing me the basics. Says when Paige goes to school she might take me on as a proper trainee.'

Clare sipped her coffee. 'Susan, that's great. Do you enjoy it?'

She beamed. 'Yeah, you've no idea how good it feels to earn some money. And I'm picking it up too.' She nodded at her daughter, now herding her toy animals together with a tiny sheepdog. 'Cut Paige's hair last week.'

Clare looked at the little girl. 'Not bad.' She patted the back of her own hair. 'I'll have to book you in for a trim.'

Susan laughed. 'Mates' rates!' Then she put down her mug. 'So, it's lovely to see you but…'

Clare smiled. 'I'm long overdue a visit and it is good to see you, both of you. But I did want to ask you something.'

'Go on then.'

'I think Paige is at nursery with a little boy called Daniel.'

'Yeah, Daniel. He was there this morning. I heard something about him going missing at the weekend. Seemed okay, though. Is that why you're asking?'

Clare hesitated. She didn't want to be unfair to Melanie but if there was a chance Susan could help... 'Have you any idea what Daniel's mum does for a job?'

Susan looked at her for a moment then said, 'Melanie? Erm why are you asking?'

'It's not that Melanie's in any trouble, nothing like that, but I am concerned there could be something illegal going on – that she might actually be a victim.'

Susan avoided Clare's eye. 'Wouldn't know.'

Clare regarded her then said, 'Susan, is Melanie a sex worker?' The pause was just long enough to tell Clare she was right. She said, 'It won't go any further, Susan. And I'm interviewing Melanie tomorrow morning in any case.'

Susan's face fell. 'You won't charge her, will you? She must need the money otherwise she wouldn't be doing it.'

Clare shook her head. 'No, nothing like that. I just need a bit of information from her.'

'If you're looking for her to tell you who's behind it you'll have a long wait,' Susan said.

'Oh? Why's that, Susan?'

'Not worth anyone's while to talk, is it?'

'You're not involved yourself, are you?'

'Pfft. Not a chance. I've had my fill of being manipulated by folk like that.'

'But they did ask you?'

Susan took a moment before answering. Then she said, 'Word went round. Anyone who fancied it. Frankly, I wouldn't risk losing Paige again for all the money in the world.'

Clare looked back at Paige, playing contentedly on the floor. 'I'm so glad she's back with you.' She drained her cup and rose from the chair. 'Better get on.'

Susan saw her to the door. As she opened it she said, 'Go easy on Mel. She's a nice girl. Like the rest of us; she's just doing her best.'

—

'Any luck with the CCTV footage?' Clare asked Mandy as she entered the incident room.

Mandy shook her head. 'Not that I can see. I've still a few hours to trawl through. I've got your van, though.'

'Yeah?'

She scrolled back through the footage to the point when the van arrived. 'I asked Tech Support if they could enhance the image and they reckon this is the reg.' She held out a Post-it note. 'I've checked it with DVLA and it's a black Ford Transit, converted to what they call a Crew Van with extra seats in the back.'

Clare stared at the Post-it. 'Good work, Mandy. Got the owner?'

'Yep. I'll just jot it down for you.' She checked her notepad and wrote down a name and address. 'It's out Bogward way.'

—

Lawmill Gardens was a quiet residential street that ran off Bogward Road, Clare's main route home to Daisy Cottage.

'What's her name?' Chris said, peering at the paper Clare had handed him. 'I can't make out Mandy's writing.'

'Samantha Reynolds,' Clare said, pulling up next to a low bungalow. 'And there's our vehicle.' A black Ford Transit sat in the drive and Clare checked the registration against the number Mandy had given them. 'Yep. That's it.' She pulled off her seat belt. 'Let's see what she has to say for herself.'

Samantha Reynolds was in her late thirties, Clare thought. She was slim, dressed in skinny white jeans and a checked top. Her hair was scraped back accentuating her bony features. She was heavily made up and looked as if she was about to go out. She stood in the doorway and glanced at Clare's warrant card. 'What's this about?' she said.

'Could we talk inside please?'

She stood back to let them in. 'I'm supposed to be on my way out.'

'We'll be as quick as we can,' Clare said smoothly. 'In here, is it?' She indicated a door just off the hall.

'Suppose.' Samantha followed them in and stood, her arms folded. 'So?'

'You have a black Ford Transit van outside. Is it yours?'

'Yeah.'

'Can I ask what it's used for?'

Samantha nodded at two black bin bags, knotted at the neck. 'Right now, I'm using it to take this lot to the dry cleaners.'

'I'm guessing you use it for more than that,' Chris said.

Samantha straightened her back. 'Yeah. So?'

'Care to tell us what?'

She shrugged. 'This and that.'

Chris gave Clare a look that said *Over to you, boss.*

Clare took the hint. 'Did you use the van last Friday night?'

She hesitated, just enough to alert Clare.

'Erm, yeah,' she said. 'Can't quite remember what, though. I do a lot of stuff in it.'

Clare smiled. 'Take your time, Miss Reynolds.'

Samantha glanced at her watch. 'Look, could this wait?'

'Sorry, it is urgent.'

She gave an exaggerated sigh. 'Okay. I gave a few friends a lift. They were going to a party. Happy?'

'You drove?'

'Yes, I drove.'

'Where was the party?'

Samantha suddenly became interested in her manicured fingernails. 'Can't really remember now. Some country house.'

'It was only three days ago,' Clare said. 'Try to remember.'

'Probably put a postcode into the satnav.' She brightened. 'Yeah, that's what I did. I remember now.'

'So the code will still be in the satnav,' Chris said. 'We could go and check the van now.'

'I probably cleared it. I don't keep addresses if it's just a one-off.'

'I see,' Clare said. 'And did you stay at the party? Or return later to collect your friends?'

'I really can't remember,' Samantha said, with barely concealed impatience. 'Now, if you don't mind.'

Clare decided she'd had enough of Samantha. 'Miss Reynolds, I have reason to believe your vehicle may have been involved in a serious crime and, as such, I need you to give me the keys so I can have a Scene of Crime Team go over it for evidence.'

'Eh? You can't do that.'

'I'm afraid I can. So, the keys if you please?'

'Both sets,' Chris added.

She stood thinking for a moment then said, 'Okay. What do you want to know?'

'If we could perhaps sit down,' Clare said.

'Be my guest.'

Clare and Chris sat while Samantha remained standing, one foot tapping on the laminate floor.

'Can you tell me who was in your van on Friday evening?' Clare said.

'Five women,' she said. 'I didn't know their names. Picked them up from Market Street and drove them to a posh house out of town.'

'Was the house Lamond Lodge?' Clare asked.

'Yeah, I think so.'

'And you didn't know the women?'

She shook her head. 'Nope. I was booked to take them to the house. Stick around then take them home about two in the morning.'

'And did they all return in the minibus?'

Samantha hesitated, just long enough for Clare to know there was something.

'Save us some time, here, Samantha.'

She shrugged. 'Oh, what the hell. Four of them did, one stayed.'

'Sure?'

'Yep.'

'You took them home?'

Samantha shook her head. 'Dropped them in town where I picked them up. Just off Market Street, like I said.'

'Seems a bit harsh,' Chris said. 'That time in the morning. You couldn't have taken them to their doors?'

'Did what I was paid for. I was told to drop them in the town so I did. It's up to them what they did after that.'

Clare regarded Samantha. Surely any normal woman would have seen them home safely, especially at two in the morning. What was going on here? 'Why were the women booked for the party?' she asked.

Samantha avoided Clare's eye and brushed an imaginary speck of dust off her sleeve. Eventually she sighed. 'Why do you think?'

'Were they sex workers, Samantha?'

'Not as far as I'm aware,' she said. 'I take them there and I'm paid for doing it, just like a taxi. Then I take them back and I come home. End of.'

Clare racked her brains. Whoever was paying Samantha had drilled her well. She was giving nothing away. 'Did you enter the Lodge yourself?'

She nodded. 'Yeah. I parked round the back, took the girls in and found the guy organising the party.'

'Can you describe him?'

'Erm… about forty-ish, quite round in the face, goatee beard.'

That fitted with what they'd learned so far. It had clearly been Doug Gerrard who'd organised the party. 'And was he the man who booked you?' Clare asked,

'No. It was a woman. Couple of weeks ago,' she said. 'Phone call one night. Woman says she needs a driver to take some girls to a party, stick around for a few hours then drive them back again. Good money, and she'd heard I had a van.'

'Got the number?' Clare said.

'Eh?'

'The woman who phoned. I'll need her number.'

Samantha took out her phone. 'Dunno,' she said, flicking back through calls. Then she held out her phone for Clare to see.

Clare copied down the number then said, 'How were you paid?'

'Envelope through the door.'

'Cash?'

'Yeah.'

'Do you still have it?'

'The money? No! Paid it into the bank.' Her eyes strayed to her watch again. 'So, if that's all.'

Clare glanced at Chris. Then she said, 'Look, Samantha, I am grateful to you for being honest with us. But I'm afraid we will need the van keys. We won't keep it any longer than necessary. But it's possible someone you took in the van that night is guilty of a serious crime.'

Samantha looked from one to the other, as though struggling to take this in. 'You are joking, aren't you? That van's my livelihood. And right now I have a load of tablecloths to get to a dry cleaners. For a B&B in the town in case you want to know that too.'

Clare said, 'We can give you a lift into town if it helps but I really do want a team to go over the van. So, the keys, if you don't mind.'

They drove Samantha and her two bags of tablecloths into town.

'Just here,' she said, as Clare turned the car into South Street.

She pulled into a parking space and, as Samantha clicked off her seat belt, Clare said, 'Just one thing more…'

'Go on, then.'

'The woman who booked you, did she give you a name?'

'Just a first name.'

'Which was?'

'Val.'

Clare raised an eyebrow. 'That's it? Just Val?'

Samantha shrugged. 'Think one of the girls called her Big Val.'

Clare was suddenly alert. 'Big Val?'

'Think so. Not that I ever set eyes on her. Might have been a joke, though. I honestly don't know.'

Chapter 16

'I think you're getting ahead of yourself,' Chris said, as they walked back into the station.

'It needs checked out,' she said.

'There must be hundreds, no, thousands of women in Scotland called Val.'

'*Big* Val, remember. And how many of them do you think would be capable of organising sex workers for parties?'

'Suppose.'

'Listen, Chris, we've had dealings with Big Val Docherty in the past. We both know she was up to her neck in drugs when we were hunting that missing baby, but she walked away from any charges because she helped us clear the case up. Since then, as far as we know, she's steered clear of drugs. So she must be making her money somehow.'

'Okay so, what do you want to do?'

'I want to find out if she's still in Edinburgh. And then I think we'll pay her a visit.'

'Oh good!' Chris rolled his eyes. 'She's a charmer.'

'She's all that,' Clare agreed. She was about to head for her office when Bill caught her.

'Zac Buchanan, boss.'

'You got something?'

'Think so.'

Clare nodded to Chris to join them and he ambled across.

'Go on, then,' Clare said.

Bill consulted his notepad. 'So Zac spent a few months living in a hostel with another couple of lads, and one of them did time for supply of firearms. I've checked up on the firearms lad and he's actually on remand in Perth prison so we can rule him out. But it's possible Zac had met some of his associates. Could be that's how he got his hands on a gun. If he is our sniper.'

'Great stuff. We might actually be getting somewhere.'

'And he does have a motive,' Bill went on, 'Russell getting a year added to his sentence.'

Clare was silent for a moment, running this through her mind.

Chris gave voice to her thoughts. 'Thing is though, Bill, the shot that killed Russell Fox was a clean one. SOCO didn't find any other stray bullets and the pathologist reckons he died instantly. And a gun like that, well, it's a lot of trouble to go to for a prison spat.'

Clare nodded. 'Yeah, it's a good point. Do we know anything about Zac's previous? I know he did time for an assault but was there anything firearms-related?'

Bill shook his head. 'Sorry, boss. No idea. I can look, though.'

'We're looking for a marksman,' Chris said. 'But it could be Zac supplied the weapon.'

'I think we'll bring him in,' Clare said. 'Chris, can you get onto the cops in Leven please? See if they know where he is.'

'Way ahead of you,' Bill said. 'I've got an address for him. And there's another thing…'

'Go on.'

'Sara said something about a car being nicked at the weekend.'

Clare's brow furrowed.

'I remember that,' Chris said. 'You were away at your posh wedding. A BMW X5, wasn't it?'

'Yeah, that's it,' Bill said. 'Nice car. No sign of it so far but word is Zac's stealing vehicles to order.'

'Bit of a stretch, Bill. Lots of cars go missing.'

'But they don't all pick up a speeding ticket in Leven.'

Clare looked at him. 'You're joking?'

He grinned. 'Nope. Largo Road in Leven. Early hours of Saturday morning.'

'The same one stolen from St Andrews?'

'Yup.'

Clare shook her head. 'I don't get it, Bill. Surely a seasoned thief like Zac would be watching out for speed cameras?'

Bill shrugged. 'Maybe. But chances are a car like that's heading abroad. By the time the ticket arrives at the registered keeper's address it'll be long gone.'

'Shipping container?' Chris asked.

'Either that or broken down for parts then shipped. Easier to manage like that.'

Clare frowned. 'But surely these cars have trackers?'

'They do,' Bill said. 'But the thieves use jamming devices. And you know what policing priorities are these days. Car theft's way down the list.'

'Insurance companies cough up, so problem solved,' Chris added.

Clare shook her head. 'Not right, though, is it?'

'No argument there, boss,' Bill said. 'Want a copy of the speeding photo?'

'Please. Then get on to Leven and tell them to bring him in.'

—

'That phone number Samantha Reynolds gave us,' Chris said, as Clare was packing up for the night.

She looked up. 'Yeah?'

'No luck. Burner phone. No way of tracing it.'

Clare sighed. 'No real surprise there. Any word on Val Docherty's whereabouts?'

'Still in Edinburgh.'

Clare's brow furrowed. 'Was it Barnton?'

'Yeah. The same house. Pretty nice, as I recall. Crime still pays. I spoke to the local cops. She's there just now, but if she is involved in this case she'll be keeping a low profile. She might even take off for a bit.'

Clare nodded. 'I think we'll go down there tomorrow. I've Melanie Fraser coming in at nine fifteen. We'll head for Edinburgh after that.' She stood thinking for a minute. Then she said, 'Any luck with Zac Buchanan?'

'Not so far. They have an address for him but no one home when they checked.'

'What about the photo from the speed camera?'

'I've sent it to the prison to see if they reckon it's him. Should hear by tomorrow.'

Clare stood thinking. Then she said, 'If Zac did come up from Leven to steal the BMW he must have had an accomplice who gave him a lift. Either that or he caught a bus.'

Chris frowned. 'So?'

'There's CCTV around the bus station, isn't there?'

'I'm starting not to like the sound of this.'

'We need someone to go through the footage to check for anyone who might be Zac.'

'Clare! That's a needle in a haystack job. There must be hundreds of men arrive here by bus. It is the height of the tourist season.'

'Get some decent images for him. He'll be on our system and the prison will have their own shots. Check with the cops down in Leven. They might have a more recent photo. And the sooner the better, Chris. If Zac Buchanan is involved in the murder of Russell Fox then we need to find him – and fast.'

–

Benjy was beyond delighted to see Clare and he demonstrated this by running round and round, chasing his tail.

'He's been as good as gold,' Moira told Clare. 'And it got us out walking, too.'

Clare said how grateful she was and handed over a hastily procured bottle of wine as a thank-you. She bent to clip Benjy's lead on but Moira seemed set for a chat.

'I hear your victim's related to Gaby – from the TV.'

Clare smiled. 'Moira, I can't…'

'Yeah, I know. Don't worry, Clare. I'm not fishing. Just that, well, you'll be busy. Lot of pressure on you. So, if you do need Benjy looked after a bit more…'

As she fastened Benjy into his car restraint, Moira's words rang in her head. *Lot of pressure*. It had only been a couple of days. No time at all in a murder investigation. But when the press were all over it that was another matter. And the pressure would only increase.

At Daisy Cottage Benjy ran through the rooms, sniffing everywhere, as though checking his position hadn't been usurped in his absence. Clare busied herself in the kitchen, boiling water for pasta and tipping the contents of a ready-made Bolognese from her favourite deli into a microwave dish. Benjy, having satisfied himself the cottage was still his domain, took up residence below the window where a shaft of sunlight was warming the floor. A *ping* from Clare's phone alerted her to a message and she poured boiling water into a saucepan then swiped to read it.

> How's the investigation?
> I saw it was top item on the news tonight.
> Hope it's going ok.
> Conference is deadly dull.
> Missing you.
> Al x

She found herself smiling as she read the message. She typed back,

> Miss you too, Al.
> Early days for investigation.
> I guess they'll send us a DCI.
> Don't suppose you could come back early?
> Benjy says Wuff
> C x

She waited then saw he was typing a reply. The pasta came to the boil and she stirred it then put the lid on the pan and turned back to her phone. After a few minutes the message appeared.

Hope to be back Wednesday night.
Suspect they'll send you someone
tomorrow.
Can't mess about with a gunman on the
loose, especially when it's all over the
papers.
Better go. Dinner in a few mins then a
speaker: 'The changing nature of policing'
God help me! xxx

She laughed at this. 'Sometimes,' she told Benjy, 'it's quite nice not to be a DCI.'

He was fully stretched out on the floor now and his tail swished back and forth in response. Then he eased himself up to his feet and wandered over, sniffing at Clare's legs. She took the hint and opened the cupboard where his food was kept. The sky outside was turning a warm red as the sun sank lower and she decided to have her meal in the garden.

She carried her plate and glass out and, as she ate, her thoughts returned to Lamond Lodge and to Russell Fox's friends and family, now decamped to the Brodie Hotel. Did one of them know more than they were letting on? Or was Zac Buchanan the key to it all?

In the woods behind the cottage a blackbird began its evening song and her eye was caught by a movement to the side. A bat, darting to and fro, feeding on the insects that hung in the still night air. The sun had dropped behind the trees now and she felt suddenly cold. Gathering up her plate and plastic wine glass she whistled to Benjy and went indoors to wash up.

Day 4: Tuesday

Chapter 17

Clare awoke to another glorious day, although the forecast warned the weather was set to break. She opened her back door and stepped out into the morning sun, Benjy trotting at her heels. 'Better make the most of it,' she told him. 'Rain tomorrow.' He took off down the garden, running round and round as he waited for Clare to unhook the back gate. Then he raced into the woods snuffling in the undergrowth. Clare strolled on behind, contemplating the day ahead. There was a lot to do. No doubt a DCI would appear at some point. She had hoped Al Gibson might have ducked out of his conference to oversee the case but it didn't look like that would happen now. She was more than capable of running the investigation, she knew that; but with what looked like the work of a trained sniper and the victim being the brother of a high-profile TV star, it was likely the bosses would play it by the book. And that meant a DCI at the very least.

And then there was the Lamond Lodge party. Gaby and co now holed up in an expensive hotel and desperate to leave. *I'd like to bury my brother*, Gaby had said and, frankly, Clare couldn't blame her. There was no question of releasing the body. Not until they knew what had happened. But she couldn't really keep the party here in St Andrews much longer, now they'd all been interviewed.

The letting agency was another problem. They'd already been on the phone to the station, pointing out there was a booking from Thursday. But the whole place was still a crime scene and there was no chance they'd clear the investigation up in two days. She had to hope the owner wasn't one of those with friends in high places! Why did these people always claim they knew the Chief Constable?

She checked her watch. Time to head back. Whistling to Benjy, she turned and began to make her way through the woods to Daisy Cottage. It was time to go to work.

–

The incident room seemed busier than ever when Clare entered. A mix of uniformed and plain-clothes officers were chatting, some on the phone, others tapping at laptops. Someone had left a newspaper on one of the desks and Clare couldn't help seeing the headline:

Police Stumped in Search for St Andrews Sniper

That's all we need, she thought, as she weaved her way through the desks to the whiteboard.

'Right,' she said. 'Let's not hang about.' She indicated a photo pinned up on the board. 'Zac Buchanan – ex-con who we know has a grudge against Russell Fox.' She scanned the room for Jim. 'Is this the most recent photo?'

Jim nodded. 'Taken the last time he went inside.'

'Okay, thanks Jim.'

He raised his hand, indicating there was more. 'Interesting thing: his last stretch was for theft of high-end vehicles. Quite an operation he had going. Sheriff said he'd no option but to jail him.'

Clare smiled. It fitted with the theft of the BMW X5. 'Thanks, Jim.' She looked round the room. 'So, Zac, if he was our car thief, he must have arrived in the town somehow. Anything on the bus station CCTV?'

Gary, one of the uniformed officers, raised his hand. 'Couple of images that could be him, boss,' he said. 'There's a shot of two men walking out of the station. One of them does look like Zac. But it's hard to be sure.'

'Can you email your stills to the cops in Leven please?' Clare said. 'They might be able to say if it's him or not. And while you're at it, get onto his bank and see if his card was used on Friday. If so, let's have the location. If they're difficult about it tell them it's a murder investigation.'

Gary indicated he would do this, and Clare went on. 'The camera footage from the Lodge shows a black minibus-type van going through the gates on Friday evening. We've traced the van and, according to the owner, it was booked to run a party of five women to and from the Lodge. The owner picked them up in town and drove them there. Then she waited in a back room and ran them home about two in the morning. But we know that one of the women didn't go back with the others.' Clare waited for this to sink in then went on. 'The mum of our missing toddler was away from home until around ten on Saturday morning. By that time we think Russell Fox was dead.'

'Is she a person of interest?' Nita asked.

Clare considered this. 'On balance, I'd say not. But she's coming in this morning to make a statement so we'll see what she has to say for herself.'

'Anyone else stay the night?' Nita went on.

Clare spread her hands. 'Not according to the owner of the van. But I'll ask the toddler's mum.'

'Could the gunman have been in the van too?' Janey asked.

'It's possible. SOCO are going over it now. I've asked them to swab for DNA plus gunshot residue.'

'Hold on, though,' Chris said. 'If the minibus left the Lodge at two in the morning, and we think Russell was shot after that, there won't be any gunshot residue. The gun wouldn't have been fired by then.'

He had a point. 'Probably not,' Clare conceded. 'But chances are this wasn't a new gun. Most likely been fired in the past so, unless it was thoroughly wiped down, there could be residue from previous use. Either way,' she added, 'it makes sense to check.'

Chris looked doubtful but Clare pressed on.

'We also know the security guard left his post during the evening. His story is he went round the back of the Lodge to have sex with one of the women. So we need to find out who that woman was. Could be she was a diversion to allow someone to climb over the fence, out of sight of the camera.'

'So the gunman could have come from outside,' Nita said.

'Definitely. Unless our minibus driver was involved. Frankly, she doesn't seem the type.'

'Does she know who the other women were?'

Clare shook her head. 'She was pretty vague about it. But she did give us one thing…' Clare paused to make sure they were all attending then said, 'she told us she was hired by a woman called Val, or possibly Big Val.'

'Not Big Val Docherty?' Bill said.

Clare shrugged. 'I've no idea. It wouldn't surprise me. Val's been linked to a lot of criminal activity in the area but we've never been able to nail her. We can't ignore a possible connection so Chris and I will see her today.' She turned back to the board, scanning the information there, then said, 'Anything else on the house party?'

Bill raised his hand. 'Janey and I had a good look into them. Nothing at all to suggest they'd fallen out with Russell. No money worries, none of them suspected of criminal activities.'

'What about Russell Fox's will? Did he leave one?'

'Yep. It all goes to the sister – Gaby.'

Clare sighed. 'Looks like money isn't the motive, then. Gaby and Luke both have an alibi for the time of the murder.' She looked round the room again. 'Anything else?'

Heads shook and Clare smiled. 'Okay, thanks for your efforts. Let's focus on the victim. Word is he was planning to sell his restaurants. We know from the PM he was ill and it's possible his decision to sell was connected to that. But we can't assume that's the case. There could be something else. Money worries, problems with competitors, I don't know, but let's find out.' She glanced at Chris. 'Have I forgotten anything?'

Before he could reply the door opened. A tall figure stood there, taking in the room and Clare's heart sank. It was DCI Tony McAvettie.

–

Clare led Tony through the front office. He stopped briefly at Zoe's desk. 'You're new,' he said.

'No, she's not,' Clare said, opening the door to her office. 'Come on.'

He strolled through, glancing back at Zoe. 'Her hair's purple,' he said.

'And yours is jet black,' Clare shot back. 'But we don't talk about why that is.'

'Ouch. Someone got out of bed the wrong side this morning.'

Clare stepped neatly round the back of her desk before Tony could assume ownership of her chair. 'Please,' she said, indicating the other chair. 'Sit.'

He seemed faintly amused but pulled the chair out and sat down. 'So,' he said, 'here we are again.'

Clare sighed. 'I take it you're our DCI?'

'I have that honour.'

'Then let's get one thing clear, Tony.'

'Go on.'

'You are not to wind Chris up. Got it?'

He smiled. 'Nah, you're okay, Clare. To be honest, the lovely Sara's not my type. But purple-head out there...'

'Who's getting on for twenty years your junior.'

'It worked for Charles and Di.'

'Actually, Tony, I don't think it did. Maybe we should talk about our murdered man.'

'It's what I'm here for. So, what you got?'

Clare relayed the events of the past few days. 'One of the women from the minibus is due in at nine fifteen,' she said, checking her watch.

'What about the other women?'

'At the moment I can't identify them. The minibus driver was booked by message on a burner phone, wad of cash put through the door in payment, the women were picked up and dropped back in town and, from what I can gather, they didn't know each other.'

'Doesn't sound like they've been trafficked, then.'

Clare shook her head. 'No, I agree.'

'What about the three men – anything there?'

'I'm not sure. One does have previous for firearms offences.'

'He has to be in the frame.'

'I dunno. Hell of a risk, with the others in the house.'

'You think it's an outside job, then?'

Clare explained about the CCTV footage. 'The security guard was away for a quickie with one of the girls. The cameras only cover the gap in the fencing. And with the guard out of the way, our sniper could have climbed over the fence further round, out of sight of the cameras.'

'Then lay low till morning,' Tony said.

Clare checked her watch again. 'Look, Tony, the minibus woman will be here any minute.'

'Want me to sit in?'

'I don't think so. She's quite nervous and I want to build up her trust. See if I can get her to relax. If I take a DCI in she might clam up.'

He nodded. 'Suits me. I'll just hang out here for a couple of hours. Use your desk.'

Clare rose. 'Thought you might.' She left him to her office and sought out Chris.

'I can't believe they've sent him again,' he said.

Clare steered him over to the side of the room and indicated two chairs. 'Look, Chris,' she said as they sat down, 'what happened between you and Tony…'

'You mean when he slept with my girlfriend, and I burst his nose?'

'Yeah, that. It's old news. You're with Sara now and, well, he'll basically always be Tony.'

'A philandering arse.'

'Nicely put, but yes. And a lazy one at that. So, if we stay out of his way, he won't bother us.'

Chris shook his head. 'He gets paid all that money.'

'I know.'

'You know what I reckon?' Chris said, getting to his feet, 'I reckon he asked for this job.'

'You think?'

'Yep. He knows you're a bloody good DI and a hard worker to boot. This,' he waved a hand round the incident room, 'this is an easy gig for him. He puts his name to it, turns up every now and then, you do the work and he takes the credit.'

Clare inclined her head. 'Maybe,' she said. 'But it didn't help him get the Superintendent's post, did it?'

Chris laughed. 'No, it didn't. I always wondered why, though. After the missing baby case was cleared up I thought he'd be a shoo-in.'

'So did he,' Clare said. 'But he didn't get it.'

'Please tell me it went to someone he hates.'

'Worse than that – they gave it to a woman!'

Chris started to laugh but Clare's eye was caught by Jim.

'That's your witness in, Clare.'

She nodded her thanks. 'C'mon, Chris. Let's go and see what Melanie has to say for herself.'

Chapter 18

Melanie Fraser stood a little back from the public enquiry desk, her arms clasped across her body. She was neatly dressed in a print summer dress and white deck shoes. Clare wondered if she'd felt obliged to dress up for the interview. She crossed the room quickly and gave Melanie a smile.

'Thank you so much for coming in,' she said. 'Come this way and we'll find somewhere quiet to talk.'

Melanie hesitated then followed Clare across the front office towards one of the interview rooms. Sara was despatched to make her a cup of tea while Clare introduced Chris.

'It's not a formal interview,' Clare explained. 'We just want to take a statement for now.'

Melanie flicked a glance at Clare then nodded and they sat down, Clare making small talk until Sara brought in a mug of tea on a small metal tray. Next to the mug something was wrapped in a green paper towel and Sara laid this on the desk. 'Thought you might like a biscuit,' she said to Melanie, one eye on Chris. The paper towel opened out to reveal one of Chris's Wagon Wheels. He avoided Sara's eye and, as she closed the door, Clare heard her mutter, 'Busted.'

'Chris, here, has a secret stash of biscuits,' she explained to Melanie. 'Looks like he's been rumbled.'

Melanie smiled. 'Just like my Daniel,' she said, adding, 'only he's just three.'

Clare was glad to see her relaxing and she pressed on. 'We'll take a statement today and, if we need anything further, we'll be back in touch.'

Melanie sipped at her tea then she said, 'Outside...'

'Yes?'

'All those reporters. I'm worried...'

'Melanie,' Clare said, cutting across her, 'unless it turns out that the person who killed Mr Fox had some connection to you or the other women in the minibus, none of you will be mentioned. Your identities will not be revealed.'

Melanie flushed and she avoided Clare's eye. 'I was thinking,' she said, 'if it came to a court case... I might have to testify. It's just... I wouldn't want people knowing.'

She broke off and Clare glanced at Chris. It was a good point. There was every chance the truth about the minibus women would come out – if they caught the culprit. 'Let's not look too far ahead,' she said, and she gave Melanie what she hoped was a reassuring smile.

'Perhaps,' Clare went on, 'you could tell us how you came to be booked for Friday night.'

Melanie hesitated. 'I'll try. It's a bit tricky.'

Clare waited, giving her time to sort out her thoughts. Chris sat, ready to note down the statement.

'It was at nursery, you see. One morning when we were waiting to collect the children, someone was handing out bits of paper. So I took one but, before I could read it, Daniel came rushing out. He had a picture he wanted to show me so I put the paper in my jeans pocket to look at later. I didn't find it again until the next day. I was checking in the pockets before I washed the jeans.'

'Who handed it out?'

Melanie shrugged. 'Sorry, I really can't remember. In fact, now I come to think about it…'

'Yes?'

She closed her eyes as if recalling the scene. 'I think they were on a shelf by the door. Someone picked them up and said *What's this about?* I think lots of us took one.'

'What was on the paper?' Clare asked.

'Phone number,' Melanie said. She reached into her pocket and took out her phone, tapping it to unlock. Then she held it out. 'This number.'

Clare noted it down. She was fairly sure it would turn out to be the number Samantha Reynolds had given her. The burner phone. But they could check that later. 'What else did it say?'

Melanie frowned. 'I've been trying to remember. Something like *Girls – want to earn a bit of cash? Easy work, good money*, and the phone number. That sort of thing.'

Clare waited while Chris wrote this down then she said, 'And you called the number?'

'Yeah. It was a woman.'

'Name?'

'She never told me.'

'Did she have an accent at all?'

Melanie considered this for a moment then said, 'No, don't think so. I mean she was Scottish. Not posh, her voice – it was a bit gravelly, you know? Like she was a heavy smoker. But I can't really tell you much more than that.'

'Okay. Please, go on.'

'Well, this woman – she said was I interested in a bit of evening work. Maybe nights. So I said it depended on what it was and the woman said it was easy enough, providing I wasn't fussy about men.'

Chris scribbled this down then Clare said, 'What did you take her to mean by that?'

Melanie avoided Clare's eye. 'She called it waitressing, with added extras. Said she'd pay me a flat rate to go along, mingle with a few men, party a bit, you know… anything else I wanted to earn above that was up to me.'

'Melanie, this next bit is important so please think carefully.'

Melanie stared at Clare but she said nothing.

'Did you understand you would be expected to have sex with the men? Is that what you were being paid for?'

She looked down. 'It wasn't exactly stated. Not like that. But she said…'

Chris stopped writing and they waited.

'She said if the men were pleased with the party there would be more work for me.'

'And did you think having sex with the men would constitute pleasing them?' Clare asked. 'I'm sorry to be so direct here but I'm concerned you're being exploited.'

Melanie nibbled a bit of the Wagon Wheel and took another sip of tea. Then she met Clare's eye. 'I knew what I was getting into, Inspector. No one forced me. I was never forced. Sometimes I liked the men and things went a bit further. Other times I didn't.'

Clare watched her, wondering how it was a young woman like Melanie could value herself so little that she did this kind of work – if you could call it work. 'And, on this occasion?' she said, 'Did you go a bit further?'

'Well obviously you know I didn't come home in the minibus.'

'You stayed overnight with one of the men?'

She nodded.

'Which of the men was it?'

'Steve,' she said. 'Steve Christie, I think.'

Chris stopped writing briefly and glanced at Clare.

'And did you stay in Mr Christie's room all night?' Clare asked.

'Yes,' she said. 'All night. We had breakfast in the kitchen and he called me a taxi about ten. Everyone else was starting to come downstairs and I thought I'd better make myself scarce.' She looked at Chris then back at Clare. 'He was nice, you know? Nice man. I didn't mind staying. Some of my friends,' she said, 'they go out dancing and have one-night stands. I don't see this is much different to that. Except I earn a few quid doing it.'

Clare wasn't so sure, but she didn't want to upset Melanie. So she changed tack. 'Can you think, please, if Mr Christie left the room at all during the night?'

'I'm pretty sure he didn't.'

'What makes you so sure?' Clare asked.

Melanie smiled. 'I take it you don't have kids of your own, Inspector? If Daniel so much as turns over in bed I hear him. And he's in another room.'

Clare laughed. 'Good point. It would take an earth-quake to waken me. So, you believe Mr Christie stayed all night in the room with you?'

'Yeah. There was an en suite off the bedroom so he might have used that, but the main bedroom door creaks. I'd definitely have heard it.'

Chris stopped writing and looked up. 'Melanie, what about the other women – did you know them?'

'No. I've done a few jobs now but never seen anyone I know.'

'So, none of the other nursery mums?'

Melanie shook her head.

'How many were there of you?' Clare asked.

'Five,' she said.

'Anyone else in the minibus?'

'Just the driver. Skinny woman, dark hair, scraped back.'

Samantha Reynolds, Clare thought. 'You're sure there was no one else in the minibus? Behind the back row of seats, perhaps?'

'Definitely not. I was near the back. I'd have noticed.'

'Okay, Melanie. And did any of the others stay the night?'

'Don't think so,' she said. 'I didn't see them at breakfast. We were in Steve's room by the time the minibus was leaving. One of the girls tapped the door but Steve shouted back he'd get me a taxi.'

Clare reached into a folder on the desk and withdrew photos of Russell Fox and his three friends. She laid these out on the table in front of Melanie. 'Do any of these men look familiar?'

Melanie moved each photo in front of her in turn, nodding. 'This is Steve,' she said, indicating the photo of Steve Christie. She looked up. 'He was lovely, you know. Kind.' Then she turned back to the other photos and identified Russell, Eamon and Doug.

Clare put the photos back in the folder. 'Was there anyone else in the house? Apart from you ladies and the four men?'

Melanie sat back thinking. 'No,' she said. 'I don't think so. It's a huge house but I didn't see anyone else. There was a security guard at the gate – I think one of the girls went out to… well, you know, went out to be with him.'

'What time was that?'

She wrinkled her brow then said, 'Eleven-ish, I think.'

'No one else?'

'Nope. I mean nobody doing the cooking or anything like that. There was loads of food but it was all takeaway. Rubbish, really. All fattening stuff. And I'd had my tea with Daniel before I went out.'

'And how did you spend the evening?'

Melanie shrugged. 'Didn't do much, to be honest. Had a few drinks, bit of dancing.'

'And then?'

Melanie's face reddened. 'Steve suggested we take a bottle up to his room.'

'And did you come down again during the evening?'

She shook her head. 'Not till breakfast time.'

Clare glanced at Chris. 'I think we're almost done here, Melanie. Anything you want to ask, Chris?'

He sat forward. 'Just this. Melanie, was there anything in the minibus – like a case, or a long bag?'

She frowned. 'What sort of bag?'

'Like a sports bag but maybe a bit longer.'

She shook her head. 'Not that I noticed. It was still light when I got into the minibus and I didn't see anything like that but I can't be absolutely sure.'

Chris looked at Clare and she nodded.

'Thanks so much for coming in, Melanie.' She scraped back her chair and rose. 'We appreciate your co-operation. And can I suggest you don't—'

'Oh don't worry, Inspector,' Melanie interrupted. 'After what happened last weekend, I'll not be leaving

Daniel with a babysitter any time soon. I'm done with those parties.'

–

'Good news from the bank,' Gary said when Clare had shown Melanie out.

'Tell me?'

'Zac Buchanan used a cash machine in Market Street on Friday.'

'Time?'

'Eight thirty in the evening.'

'So that places him in the town the night before Russell Fox died. What time was the car stolen?'

'Hard to say,' Chris said. 'Owner got home about six and didn't go out again until the next day. He discovered it was missing just after nine on Saturday morning.'

'I don't get how you can steal a car like that these days,' Gary said.

'Keyless,' Chris said. 'He'd need an accomplice and a couple of relay devices, one beside the car and one near the house, close to where they think the key fob is. The device outside the house tricks the fob into sending a signal to the other one, which unlocks the car. Once they're in they can access the car's computer port and programme a blank fob to work as a key. Takes minutes.'

Gary shook his head. 'Just as my well my car's a heap.'

'Any luck finding Zac?' Clare asked.

'Don't think so,' Gary said. 'Leven guys will let us know.'

'Okay, thanks.' She turned to Chris. 'Big Val, then?'

He rolled his eyes. 'Can't wait.'

Chapter 19

'I'll tell you what,' Clare said as Chris accelerated up the slip road to join the M90 towards Edinburgh.

'Yeah?' He raised a hand in thanks to a lorry driver who'd flashed him out.

'Steve Christie...'

'What about him?'

'He's the only one who had a woman stay all night.'

'And?'

'I'm wondering if he wanted an alibi.'

'But Melanie says she'd have wakened up if he'd moved,' Chris said.

'She might, she might not. He could have slipped something into her drink. Or she might actually sleep more soundly than she thinks.' She glanced across at Chris. 'I seem to recall someone falling asleep on night shift, not so long ago.'

'You said you wouldn't mention that again.'

Clare smiled. 'Yeah, I did, didn't I? Just slipped out! But, seriously, Chris, you see my point?'

'It's possible. But it depends when Russell Fox was shot. What time's it light just now?'

'About six, I think. Or just before.'

'Okay,' Chris said. 'So Russell gets up, say, quarter to six. Goes up on the treetop walk to watch the sunrise. Our man — let's say it's Steve — he nips out of bed, up to the next floor. He's posed the gun somewhere, opens the window and shoots Russell. Nips back downstairs into bed with Melanie. Could she really have slept through that? The creaky door? Noise from the gun?'

Clare shrugged. 'It's possible. No one else seems to have heard the shot.'

'Could Melanie be lying? Maybe he slipped her a few quid to say he was there all night.'

Clare considered this. 'On balance, I'd say not. Given Russell Fox is dead, I reckon she'd have been too scared to carry on lying for him. Particularly in the station, with the two of us sitting across the table. But let's keep it in mind.'

They were passing the huge Amazon warehouse now and Clare's gaze drifted to the horizon. She always loved that first glimpse of the Queensferry Crossing, its white towers standing out against the sky. It was a lovely day for a drive and good to be out of the station, especially with Tony in residence.

'Your question to Melanie about the sports bag…'

'Yeah?'

'You're thinking the gun?'

Chris nodded. 'I was, yeah. Must have got in the house somehow. And that minibus was there from eight until two in the morning.'

'You been watching *The Day of the Jackal*?' Clare said.

'Eh?'

She shook her head. 'Oh Chris, you're hopeless! It's a fabulous film. If you want to know how to smuggle a gun across a border, watch it.' She reached into the glove compartment and took out a pair of sunglasses. 'It's a good point, though. The gun was either in the house already or it came in with the gunman.'

An overhead gantry loomed up flashing *30* and Chris eased off the accelerator. 'Does Val know we're coming?'

'No,' Clare said. 'But I've been on to the local cops and they think she's at home. They're keeping an eye on the house in case she decides to go out.'

A queue of traffic lay ahead and Chris slowed the car until they were crawling along at ten miles an hour. 'I don't know how commuters do this journey every day,' he said. 'It'd drive me mad.'

'To be fair,' Clare said, staring out the side window, 'you do have a head start on that.'

'Don't give up the day job, Inspector.'

–

Barnton was a popular suburb in the north-west of Edinburgh, off the busy Queensferry Road. Val Docherty's house was in Barnton Avenue, a quiet curving road with individually designed houses behind mature hedges. A police car was parked discreetly at the end of the road and Chris pulled in behind. As they approached the car an officer jumped out.

'She's at home all right,' he said. 'Postie rang the doorbell half an hour ago. I spoke to him when he came down the drive and he said she took a parcel in.'

Clare thanked the officer, and they made their way up a long gravel drive towards a two-storey house finished in a white render. It was an attractive property with a cross gable roof and a broad corner window on the first floor. The roof, which sloped down low in a concave curve design, was tiled in red with a tall chimney stack at one end.

'How much d'you reckon this would set you back?' Chris asked as they crunched up the drive, which was bordered either side with high laurels.

'Ooft, well over a million,' Clare said. 'Maybe more.'

As they cleared the hedge they heard the sound of running water and Clare turned to see a stone fountain with a cherub in the centre, water pouring from his mouth. 'Ugh,' she said.

'It's a matter of taste, Inspector,' Chris said, laughing at her expression. 'Ey-up, we've been spotted.'

A figure stood at a front window, glaring at them. Clare recognised the brassy blonde hair and leathered face. Valerie Isobel Docherty.

Val seemed unwilling to let them over the threshold. 'A'm busy,' she said, her voice gruff, and Clare thought of Melanie's description of the voice on the phone. Gravelly, she had said. Val's voice was all that.

Val cleared her throat then said, 'If you could come back another day.'

Clare smiled. 'Can't do that, Val. We need some information. But, if you prefer, we could take you back to St Andrews.'

Val exhaled audibly and a whiff of sour breath reached Clare's nostrils. ''Mon, then, if you're coming,' she said, standing back to let them in. 'But you're no' stayin' long, mind.'

A broad hall was patterned in a dark red carpet which continued into a square sitting room. It was a pleasant, airy room with a high ceiling and a bay window, curtained with swags and tails which made Clare think of a tired hotel lounge. It was dominated by an oyster-coloured leather corner settee and Val waved a pudgy hand towards it. 'Take a seat,' she growled, adding, 'I'll no' waste your time with tea or coffee. You'll be busy.'

They sat and Clare said, 'I'll come to the point, Val…' Out of the corner of her eye she saw Chris take out his phone and begin tapping at the screen and she wondered what he was doing. She turned back to Val. 'Do you know a woman called Melanie Fraser?'

Val raised an eyebrow. 'Nope. Never heard of her.'

'Samantha Reynolds?'

'Nope.'

Somewhere distant there was a faint noise, like tinny music. Chris looked up. 'I think your phone's ringing,' he said.

Val regarded him for a few seconds then said, 'Not mine, sonny. My kitchen window's open. It'll be neighbour's kids in the garden.'

Chris tapped at his phone and the ringing stopped. Then he tapped once more and, after a few seconds, the tinny music began again.

Clare realised what he was doing. 'I'm sure that's a phone,' she said to Val.

She scowled. 'You lads got a warrant?'

Clare raised an eyebrow. 'You might want to answer it. Could be urgent.'

Val smiled, showing her teeth, the front ones yellowed with nicotine. 'Like I say – kids.'

Clare nodded. 'Okay. How about this: we believe you are involved with supplying women for parties, that you book people like Samantha Reynolds to drive these women to and from parties and that you are paid for doing so.'

Val shrugged. 'Not me, love.'

'Do you deny recruiting women to attend parties on a sexual or non-sexual basis?'

Clare's phone began to ring but she flicked it to silent.

'Absolutely,' Val said. 'I've no idea what you're talking about.'

Chris's phone began to ring. 'I'll just step into the hall to take this,' he said.

Clare tried again with Val but drew a blank with every question. No, she hadn't arranged any women for a party on Friday night. No, she didn't generally do this. No, she hadn't heard of any of the four men from the Lamond Lodge party and where the fuck was Lamond Lodge anyway?

Chris stepped back into the room and sat down again next to Clare. 'Val,' he began, 'what do you know about a man called Zac Buchanan?'

For the first time since they'd entered the house Val seemed at a loss. Just for a moment. Then she recovered herself. 'Never heard of him.'

'Sure?'

Clare glanced at Chris. What was he driving at?

'You see,' Chris went on, 'our lads back at the station have been doing a bit of digging. And it seems your daughter – Lauren, is it?'

Val's face darkened. 'You leave my Lauren out of it, sonny,' she said, an edge to her voice.

'It seems Zac's son Leo and Lauren – they were a couple. Is that correct?'

Val glared at Chris. 'Why you asking?'

Clare said, 'We're anxious to get hold of Zac. So if you – or Lauren – could tell us where we might find him.'

Val shook her head slowly. 'No dice, lads. Lauren, well, I suppose she might have been seeing Leo, once upon a time. But that's ancient history now. So, if there's nothing else.'

Clare tried one last time. 'Thing is,' she said, 'that party at Lamond Lodge – a man died. And we have reason to believe Zac Buchanan may have been in the area. We also believe there's no love lost between Zac and the victim. If you have evidence of his whereabouts and you withhold it...'

'Like I said. Nothing to do with me. But...'

'Yes?'

'Well, you might find him in Leven. Am no' sayin' I've got an address, mind. But the local polis will know.'

Clare nodded. 'We'll check with them. Just one more thing...'

'Oh aye?'

'What do you know about stolen cars? High-end cars.'

Val raised an eyebrow. 'Zac been up to his old tricks again?'

Clare said, 'It's something we're looking into. So?'

She shrugged again. 'Nothin' to do with me, love. Now, if you don't mind...'

Clare rose from the sofa. 'Thanks for your co-operation.'

As they walked to the door, Chris said, 'Don't forget to check your phone for missed calls.'

The door slammed behind them. 'Well that was a waste of time,' Chris said.

'Not entirely. We now know the burner phone is Val's. Good idea, calling it, by the way.'

'I try.'

'And there's a definite link between Val and Zac Buchanan – their kids knowing each other. What if

Val and Zac are both involved in the killing at Lamond Lodge?'

'Bit tenuous,' Chris said. He clicked to unlock the car and they climbed in. 'I can see Val might have arranged the minibus – and the women.' He started the engine but sat on, letting it idle. 'And, if she did, maybe the gun was hidden in the vehicle. But…'

'Go on.'

'I don't see where Zac fits in. From what Melanie said, it doesn't sound as if he could have been in the minibus.'

Clare pulled on her seat belt. 'Don't forget Zac and Russell have history.'

'Fair point.' He sat considering this then pulled the car out into the road. 'So, back to the station?'

'Yeah, I think so. The Leven lads will let us know if Zac shows up.'

They sat at traffic lights, waiting to emerge onto the busy Queensferry Road.

Clare watched the stream of traffic for a few moments then said, 'Let's recap what we know.'

The lights went green and Chris nosed forward, just making it through the junction as they went to amber again. 'Okay,' he said. 'Gaby Fox arranges a surprise party for her brother.'

'Her brother who,' Clare went on, 'is planning to sell his restaurants – a fact Gaby seemed unaware of.'

'But the husband knew.'

'He did,' Clare agreed. 'So why would that be?'

They'd left the houses behind now and were heading for the Queensferry Crossing.

'Maybe Russell wanted advice from someone he wasn't so close to,' Chris said. 'Fellow businessman – that kind of thing. Who knows?'

'Okay. So Gaby and Luke are away at the wedding.'

'Can you be sure they were there? Early Saturday morning, I mean?' Chris said. 'You've only got their word for it they stayed Friday night at the hotel.'

'Good point, Chris. I'll get someone on to checking that. We can't take anything for granted.'

'Okay, then we have the three friends,' Chris said. 'Steve Christie spends the night with Melanie Fraser and she gives him an alibi. But he is the only one with a link to firearms.'

'Albeit a few years back,' Clare said.

'Once a thug, always a thug.'

'Gawd, I hope not.'

They were approaching the bridge now and Chris slowed to join a queue of cars.

'Doug Gerrard and Eamon Ferry have no precons,' Clare said, 'and, from what we can tell, none of the three has a motive.'

'I'll tell you what we've not considered.'

'Yeah?'

'Who else benefits from Russell Fox's death? We know Gaby inherits the money, but could he have an estranged wife tucked away somewhere? Kids? Anyone who could potentially contest the will?'

Clare nodded. 'Good point.' She fished out her notepad and scribbled this down to check later. 'Then,' she continued, 'we have a minibus with a driver and five women probably booked by Val Docherty. Samantha Reynolds, the driver, remains in the house for the evening.'

'Samantha drives four of them home,' Chris said, 'around two, we think, and Melanie Fraser stays, spending the night in Steve Christie's room.'

'And then there's Mark Mooney,' Clare added. 'He leaves his post around eleven at night for a quickie round the back of the house.'

They had crossed the river Forth now and the sun which had been so bright all day passed behind a cloud. 'Going to rain tonight,' Chris said.

'Yeah, I saw that. Ach, we've had a good run of weather. Anyway, while Mark Mooney is otherwise engaged, an unknown person could have climbed the fence and slipped into the house.'

'We can't be sure about that,' Chris said.

'I know. But it would have been easy enough for someone to wait in the bushes, see him head off round the back then slip into the grounds. And if Russell and co were partying hard he could easily have nipped into the house and up to that room at the top – bide his time until Russell appeared in the morning.'

'So Russell Fox was killed by person or persons unknown,' Chris said.

Clare was silent for a moment. Then she said, 'It looks that way. The question is who? And how did he know Russell would be up on the walkway the next morning?'

Chapter 20

Tony McAvettie was pulling on his jacket when Clare entered her office.

She threw her bag down in the corner. 'Leaving us so soon?'

'Things to do, people to see, Clare,' he said. 'Any luck with Big Val?'

She shook her head. 'Nope. Not surprising, really. She covers her back, that one.'

'And the prossie?'

She glared at him. 'Who?'

'Oh don't go all prissy on me. Your interview this morning.'

'Melanie Fraser? For the record I don't believe she is a sex worker.'

'She was hired to entertain four blokes and spent the night with one of them. What would you call it?'

'I...' Clare found she was lost for words. What was Melanie Fraser? Was it fair to call her a sex worker? Or had she made a good point about her friends and their one-night stands? Whatever the rights or wrongs of it, she wasn't about to let Tony away with badmouthing Melanie. 'Whether she has sex with men for money or not, Tony,' she said, 'we do not use words like prostitute these days.'

'Aye, whatever. Was she any help?'

'Not much, to be honest. But we've found a link between Big Val and a small-time crook called Zac Buchanan.'

He wrinkled his brow. 'Rings a bell. Remind me?'

'Zac did a stretch for serious assault at the same time as Russell Fox. Zac whacked another prisoner and Russell gave evidence against him. Gives him a motive.'

Tony nodded. 'Still, a sniper's pretty far-fetched for a guy like Zac.'

'I agree. It's unlikely he fired it, but he could have supplied it.'

'True. We'll have his DNA on file. Get SOCO to cross-check with any samples from the scene.'

'Gee, thanks, Tony. I hadn't thought about that.'

The sarcasm was lost on him. 'You're welcome, Inspector.' He put a hand on the door then stopped. 'You've seen that lot out there?'

'The press? Hard to avoid.'

'So an early result would be good.'

'We're working flat out.'

'Course you are,' he said. 'Just make sure you're using the resources wisely.' He flashed her a smile. 'And now, I must rush.'

Clare followed him out into the front office, looking for Chris. She noticed Zoe, picking up her bag from under the desk. Tony was striding towards the front door and she saw Zoe give him a slight nod. Clare watched as she fished a lipstick out of her bag. 'Zoe?' she said.

Zoe looked up, running the lipstick over her lips. 'Yeah?'

Clare hesitated. Then she said, 'Tony's a bastard.'

Zoe stared. 'And?'

'He's caused trouble here before. And…' she hesitated, conscious she was straying beyond her role as Zoe's boss, 'I wouldn't want him to treat you badly.'

Zoe rolled her eyes. 'He's offered me a lift home. That's all.' She put the lipstick away in her bag. 'And I can assure you he won't be getting over the threshold.'

Clare nodded. 'All right, Zoe. Just take care, yeah?' She watched her leave then wandered into the kitchen. The sink was full of unwashed mugs and suddenly it seemed an awful lot of effort for a cup of tea. She decided instead to check with SOCO – see if they'd found anything in the minibus. If not, she'd call it a day. And then she remembered the note she'd scribbled on her pad on the way back from Edinburgh.

She found Janey in the incident room. 'Don't suppose you could do something else for me?'

'Sure, boss. Fire away.'

'Gaby Fox and Luke Gasparini were guests at a wedding I attended on Saturday. They were definitely in the church early afternoon and they claim they spent Friday night at the hotel too. I'm pretty sure it's a cast iron alibi but…'

'You want it verified?' Janey said.

'Please. I know she's the victim's sister but we can't assume they're not involved. The hotel's only an hour and a half away. It's perfectly possible one of them could have slipped through to St Andrews for a few hours. They'd have had plenty time to be back for the ceremony.'

Janey scribbled on her notepad. 'Leave it with me.'

Clare thanked Janey and went back to her office. She tried calling SOCO but there was no reply and there was nothing in her emails either. 'Tomorrow then,' she said to herself. She logged off her computer and, picking up her bag, walked through to the front office. 'I'm heading home, Jim,' she said. 'I'll have my mobile if anyone needs me.'

She walked out into the cool evening air. A couple of reporters looked hopefully in her direction but she went straight to her car, head down. The temperature had dropped and the blue sky from earlier was gone. But it would still be mild enough to sit in the garden. There was a cottage pie she could heat from frozen which would give her time to walk Benjy. And she might open that lovely bottle of red Al Gibson had bought the other week. She'd meant to save it for the weekend, but it had been a long day.

There was little traffic as she drove home but the pavements and gardens around the Bogward Estate were busy with children whizzing to and fro on bikes, chalking on the pavement, kicking balls and flipping skateboards. Making the most of the weather, Clare thought, slowing her speed as she passed them. At the roundabout she turned left as usual, taking the country road towards Daisy Cottage. Up ahead a tractor with a hedge flail attached was making slow progress as it cut back the foliage where it encroached on the road. Clare pulled out, giving it a wide berth, and continued on her way.

Minutes later she crunched into the drive in front of Daisy Cottage and came to an abrupt halt. It took her a moment to recognise the car parked in front of the door. And then she realised. It was a blue VW Golf. Her sister's car. And it looked as if Jude was sitting in the driver's seat. As she drew in alongside the Golf and killed the engine Clare saw her sister turn to look at her. She smiled and Jude smiled back. But there was no mistaking her sister's tearstained cheeks.

Chapter 21

'Here,' Clare said, holding out a glass to her sister. 'Drink this.'

Jude waved it away.

'It'll settle your nerves,' Clare persisted.

'No!' Jude was pink in the face now. 'I don't want a bloody glass of wine, Clare.' Then she started to cry again.

'Tea, then,' Clare said, and she flicked the switch on the kettle. She put an arm round her sister and led her to the sofa. 'We'll have a mug of tea together then we can chat.'

Jude nodded and allowed herself to be installed on the sofa. Minutes later, Clare brought through a tray with mugs of tea and a packet of ginger biscuits. She held a mug out to Jude and saw that her hands were shaking.

'Jude, what on earth's wrong? Please tell me.' She suddenly thought of her nephew – Jude and Frank's small son, James. His autism had put a terrific strain on them both but lately Clare had thought Jude was coping better. That she'd come to terms with James's diagnosis and what the future might hold for him. But was there something more? 'It's not James, is it?' she said, a note of urgency in her voice.

Jude shook her head. 'No, nothing like that. James is fine.'

'Frank?'

'No. They're both fine.'

'Then you? You're not ill?'

'Not ill, no,' she said then the tears began coursing down her cheeks again. 'I'm fine,' she said. 'It's just…'

Clare waited, desperate to know what had upset her sister so much.

'I think I'm pregnant again,' Jude blurted out. 'And I don't know what to do.'

–

'A baby's the best news in the world,' Clare said, as they strolled arm and arm up a farm track, Benjy exploring the grass verges. 'And it's not like you've not done it before. You'll know what to expect this time.'

'I dunno,' Jude said. 'It's just, with James…'

'What about him?' Clare said. 'James is more capable than you think. There's an intelligent little boy in there, just waiting to be brought out.'

'But that's just it,' Jude said. 'What if that intelligent boy doesn't come out? James might never be able to live independently.' She stopped and turned to admire the view across the Eden Estuary. Then she said, 'What if this baby's autistic, too?'

'Surely not,' Clare said, trying to think of something comforting to say. 'Surely the odds of having another baby with James's condition aren't high?'

Jude shook her head. 'Depends who you ask. No one knows, really.' She turned back to face Clare. 'But it is a risk.' She shook her head. 'Clare, I love James more than life itself. I'd do anything for him. But I'm not sure I could cope if another baby was autistic.'

'Jude, you cope brilliantly.'

Her sister laughed, a harsh laugh. 'You've not seen me, Clare. I don't have two minutes to myself. James won't leave my side. I can't send him to nursery, to a childminder. I can't even leave him with mum and dad.'

'He stayed with me that one time,' Clare said, remembering a time when James had spent a weekend with Clare – one she wasn't likely to forget when the case she'd been working on had come to a terrifying conclusion.

'Yes,' Jude said, her face softening. 'He loves you. But you have your own life, you have Al, your job – that's not a solution.'

'I know,' Clare admitted. 'But if he's able to come to stay with me, surely you could work on him getting used to other folk?'

Jude began walking again. 'Oh, I don't know. It all seems so difficult just now.'

Clare opened her mouth to say something but her sister went on.

'And what if this baby isn't autistic?'

'That would be good, wouldn't it?' Clare said.

Jude shook her head. 'We'd be condemning the baby to a lifetime of responsibility for James. And that's not fair.'

Clare put her hands on her sister's shoulder. 'Jude, stop. You're getting way ahead of yourself here. You don't even know if you are pregnant yet. And, even if you are, you'll work it out. Mum and Dad don't live too far away. And it might actually help James, having a little brother or sister.'

She nodded. 'I know,' she said, her voice a whisper. 'It just all seems a bit overwhelming at the moment.'

'Baby hormones,' Clare said.

'And you'd know?' Her sister forced a smile.

'Fair point.' She glanced up at the sky. 'Think we should turn back,' she said. 'Looks like rain.'

They began walking back to the cottage, Benjy at their heels.

'How was the wedding?' Jude asked.

'Tom's?'

'Yes. Oh Clare, you didn't duck out of it, did you? Mum said you might.'

'No, I went and I even smiled and said how lovely the bride looked.'

'Did she?'

Clare inclined her head. 'Yeah, she did. She was so... so golden and perfect.' She rolled her eyes. 'So perfect I wanted to tip a bowl of trifle over her head.'

Clare was glad to see her sister laugh at this.

'At least there was trifle.'

'Actually, there wasn't. Dessert was – some tiny crap. Mini-desserts, you know? Three tiny things I wolfed in a mouthful each. Al was so hungry we considered ordering from room service.'

'You should have.'

'We would have done, but there was this murder, you see – kind of got in the way.'

Day 5: Wednesday

Chapter 22

Clare was glad to see her sister looking brighter over breakfast. They sat cradling mugs of coffee while the rain drummed against the kitchen window.

'I slept like a top,' Jude admitted. 'First time for weeks.' She smiled. 'I suppose it was the relief of telling someone.'

Clare lifted the cafetiere and topped up her sister's mug. 'And now?'

'I know,' Jude said. 'Now I have to go home and tell Frank.'

There was a click from the toaster and Clare rose to retrieve the toast. 'And you're really okay about it?'

Jude nodded. 'Yes, I am. I think talking it through, facing my worst fears, I think it helped.' She grabbed Clare's hand across the table and gave it a squeeze. 'Thanks, Clare.'

Clare squeezed her hand back. 'Anytime.' She pushed the butter towards her sister. 'I need to go soon. But stay as long as you like. Just pop the spare key in the box outside.'

–

'I've been looking into Russell Fox,' Chris said, as he followed Clare to the station kitchen.

'And?' She stooped to put her lunch in the fridge.

'Seems the restaurants were doing well. He stood to make a tidy sum from the sale. Plenty of interest, talk of a few offers, just verbal at the moment. But looks like he'd have had no problem selling.'

'And the sister takes the lot.'

'Yep.'

'Hm,' Clare said. 'Maybe we need to look into her. And her husband.'

'I don't see why,' Chris said. 'She's worth a hell of a lot more than Russell was.'

'All the same, I think I'll ask Tony for a warrant to investigate their finances. It's such a high-profile case. I can't risk missing something.'

'Speaking of our DCI,' Chris said, 'he's at it again, you know?'

'At what?' Clare headed for the incident room, Chris in her wake.

'He took Zoe out last night. She texted Sara.'

Clare shook her head. 'I did warn her.' She stopped, thinking for a minute. 'Look, Chris, maybe Zoe thinks I'm coming on a bit strong, being her boss and all that. Could Sara have a word? Set her straight about Tony.'

'She's already tried. But Zoe won't have it. Says she's big enough to look after herself.'

'Oh well. Maybe she is. I mean she's pretty sparky. Maybe she'll finally be the one to break his heart.'

'You're assuming he has one.'

'Sorry,' Clare said. 'Rookie error.' They entered the incident room and the hum of chatter died away.

Clare turned to face them. 'Okay,' she began. 'Lamond Lodge. We've established that a party of five women was driven there on Friday night by a Samantha Reynolds.

Ms Reynolds owns a minibus and was booked by text message from a burner phone. Chris and I believe the phone belongs to Val Docherty but we doubt we can prove it. We also know there's a connection between Val and a small-time crook, Zac Buchanan. We know Zac had a grudge against Russell Fox. But was it enough to get his hands on a sniper rifle, track Russell down then break into the house to shoot him?' She shook her head. 'It seems far-fetched to me.'

Nita's phone buzzed on her desk and she excused herself to take the call.

Clare went on. 'We know Zac was in St Andrews on Friday night. He used a cash machine in the town, and a rather nice BMW was stolen. Zac, as you probably know, has precons for stealing high-end cars. So he might have been in town to nick the car or he could be connected to Russell Fox's death. Or it could even just be a coincidence.'

'Don't forget Val's daughter,' Chris said.

'Thanks, Chris.' She looked round the room again. 'Val's daughter Lauren was the girlfriend of Zac Buchanan's son Leo. According to Val, Lauren and Leo aren't together now but I need someone to check that. It's unlikely to be a factor but we can't ignore it. Val is almost certainly involved with the minibus of women and Zac has a grudge against Russell Fox.'

'They could be in it together,' someone said.

Clare nodded. 'They could indeed. But would someone like Val be interested in a spat between Russell and Zac?' She shook her head. 'From what I know of Val, she's out for only one person – herself. All the same, we have to check it out.'

'What about the hotel?' Chris asked.

'No luck,' Janey said. 'Staff I spoke to weren't on duty at the weekend and they haven't come back to me on the CCTV yet.'

Clare clicked her tongue. 'It is a murder enquiry, Janey.'

'Yeah, I know, boss. I'll get back onto them.'

'If you would.'

The door opened and Nita came back in. 'They've picked up Zac Buchanan,' she said. 'The Leven cops are bringing him up this morning.'

Clare smiled. 'Now we're getting somewhere.' She stood thinking for a moment then said, 'Nita, can you speak to the bank please? See if there's a photo of him at the cash machine. I'd like to see what he's wearing.'

Chris raised an eyebrow at this but Clare ignored it, turning to Bill, whose hand was raised.

'What about the three friends?' he asked. 'Can we rule them out?'

Clare spread her hands. 'At the moment, Bill, the only evidence we have against them is opportunity. They were all in the house when the shot was fired – sleeping, they claim. One of them, Steve Christie, had a companion all night. One of the minibus ladies stayed in his room. She swears he didn't leave the room all night. Says she's a light sleeper.'

'Perfect alibi,' Nita said.

'Exactly.' Clare glanced across at Chris. 'I think we might have another chat with our Mr Christie – by himself, this time. See how he behaves when his friends aren't around.'

'Is it worth doing a formal interview with all three?' Chris said. 'Separately, I mean? Steve's the only one with half an alibi, remember.'

Clare considered this. She was acutely aware the eyes of the press were on them in this case. The papers were running daily features and the reporters outside both the station and the Lodge showed no signs of shifting. If she brought the men into the station it would be all over the news within the hour. 'Tell you what, ask Jim to arrange a room at the hotel and we'll see them there, one at a time. See what they have to say when the others aren't around.'

Bill raised his hand. 'Any word from SOCO, boss?'

'Not yet, Bill. But I'll call them as soon as we're done here.'

The phone in the outer office began to ring and Sara slipped out to answer it.

'Is that it?' Clare said. 'Or have I missed anything?'

Heads shook and Clare ended the briefing. Out in the main office Sara was scribbling on a notepad. As Clare made for her office she ended the call.

'Boss.'

'Yes?'

'They've recovered the car – the stolen BMW.'

'Great,' Clare said. 'I want a SOCO team to go over it for Zac's DNA and prints, please.'

Sara nodded and Zoe caught Clare's eye.

'He's arrived,' Zoe said, nodding in the direction of Clare's office. 'Tony.'

So, Clare thought, they're on first name terms now. She smiled at Zoe but decided to say nothing. After all, it really was none of her business. As long as Zoe wasn't getting in too deep. Even then…

She opened her door and found Tony tapping away at her computer. A slice of cake sat on the desk, wrapped in a blue paper towel. 'Is that yours or mine?' she said.

Tony looked at the cake, a smile playing on his lips. 'You can have it. I'll get mine later.'

She opened her mouth to say something then decided against it. He was only trying to goad her. 'Thanks,' she said, scooping up the cake and putting it on top of her filing cabinet.

She eyed him. 'Comfy?'

Her tone was lost on him. He adjusted his position. 'Yeah, not bad. Chair's seen better days but it'll do.' He picked up a notepad and peered at it. 'Took a phone call for you.'

'Oh?'

'Yeah, SOCO. Seems there's no gunshot residue in the minibus.' He wrinkled his forehead. 'That make sense?'

Clare sighed. 'Unfortunately, yes. It was a long shot anyway. Is that all they said?'

Tony squinted at the note again. 'Loads of prints... multiple DNA. But none on our system.'

Clare shook her head and sank down in a chair. 'Oh well.' Then she brightened. 'Zac Buchanan's on his way up from Leven.'

'The car thief? Good. Want me to sit in?'

'Probably not. Chris and I can handle it. But there is something you could do.'

'Shoot.'

'I'd like a warrant to look into Gaby Fox and Luke Gasparini's finances.'

Tony exhaled. 'You don't want much, Clare. Have you grounds?'

'I believe so. Russell Fox had found out he was terminally ill and was planning to sell his restaurants.'

'Understandable.'

'I agree. But then someone kills him. Now if, and it's only a guess at this stage, if his reason for selling the restaurants was to have a blowout while he still felt well enough to do it there would be less for Gaby and Luke to inherit.'

'Clare! She's a big shot TV presenter. Surely she doesn't need her brother's money?'

Clare shrugged. 'That's what I aim to find out. That shot came from inside the house.'

'And correct me if I'm wrong but they weren't there at the time.'

'I'm checking that too.'

He sat, considering this for a moment, twiddling a pen in his fingers. Then he said, 'Okay. I'll authorise it. But you'd better not be wrong.'

Chapter 23

Zac Buchanan sat slumped on a plastic bucket chair, his hands driven deep into his pockets. He was in his late thirties, Clare thought. Maybe early forties. Slim, wiry even. Fit enough to climb over a Heras fence and wily enough to slip into a house undetected. His criminal record bore witness to that. He was casually dressed in dark tracky bottoms and a lightweight navy Adidas jacket over a white T-shirt. His hair was closely cropped, his skin sallow. He glanced up at Clare and Chris as they entered then looked away again.

Next to him sat an older woman Clare recognised as one of the duty solicitors and she nodded to the woman. When Clare had completed the formalities and cautioned Zac, the woman cleared her throat.

'Mr Buchanan has indicated he will be answering *No comment* to all questions.' She turned to Zac for confirmation of this. He inclined his head as if to say he didn't much care either way.

'That is your right, of course,' Clare said to Zac, 'but it might help shorten the interview if you did answer our questions. Get you out of here a bit sooner.'

He made no response to this and Clare began the interview. 'Perhaps you could tell us where you were on Friday night.'

Zac mumbled, 'No comment.'

Clare opened a folder and withdrew a sheet of paper. She pushed it across the table so Zac and his solicitor could read it. 'This is a printout of a transaction from an ATM in Market Street, St Andrews.' She paused for a moment as Zac's solicitor leaned forward to examine the paper. 'It shows a withdrawal of cash from an account in your name,' she tapped the paper, 'as you'll see just here.'

Zac barely glanced at the paper.

'And, as you did not report your bank card stolen, I think it's reasonable to assume the transaction was carried out by you. In other words, you were in St Andrews on Friday night about half past eight.'

Again, Zac gave his stock reply and Clare went on. 'Can you confirm please you were in the vicinity of Cant Crescent either late on Friday night or early Saturday morning?'

The solicitor looked at Zac but he made no response.

'And that you unlawfully entered and drove away a vehicle without permission of the owner?'

Zac sighed audibly. 'No comment,' he said, flicking a glance at Clare.

There was a tap on the door and Clare paused the interview. Outside the room Sara stood holding two photos. 'Stills from the speeding ticket and the cash machine, boss.'

Clare took the photos from her and nodded to Chris. 'Come on, let's look at these in a better light.'

They found a vacant desk in the incident room and spread the photos out.

Chris moved in to examine the image from the speed camera. 'Well that's just blown your case out of the water,' he said.

'Yup. I'm afraid so.' She squinted at the photo of the driver who had dark curly hair. 'That's certainly not Zac and there's no one in the front passenger seat.' She sat back considering this. 'But we know he was in the town on Friday night.' She tapped the photo taken at the cash machine. 'This along with the printout from the bank proves it. So, if he wasn't here to steal a car, why was he here?'

Chris frowned. 'Did Bill ever get back to you about that photo from the bus station?'

'The one we asked the Leven cops to look at?' Clare looked round the room. 'I kind of forgot about it. Is Bill here?'

'Don't see him,' Chris said. 'Must be out on enquiries. Want me to give Leven a call?'

'Please.'

Chris went to make the call and Clare sat back, thinking. Zac was a known car thief. Usually high-end cars, too. And the speed camera that had clocked the BMW was in Leven. Leven, where Zac had been living since release from prison. But the driver in that photo certainly wasn't Zac. Was she looking for a link that wasn't there?

'We're getting somewhere at last,' Chris said, cutting across her thoughts. He sat back down next to Clare. 'Leven reckon it's Zac, in the bus station photo.'

'Can you call it up please, Chris?'

He pulled a computer keyboard across the desk and tapped in his password. A few clicks later, the photo from the bus station filled the screen. 'That's our Zac, isn't it?'

Clare peered at it. The hair was the same, the dark tracky bottoms too. Not that they were uncommon, but there was no mistaking the Adidas jacket with its distinctive three-stripes pattern on the sleeves. 'Same jacket in the cash machine photo. And I think it's the one he's wearing today.'

'Look at his companion,' Chris said. 'See the hair?' Then he picked up the speed camera photo and held it next to the monitor. 'That's our speed merchant.'

Clare nodded slowly. He was right. 'So Zac and the driver of the stolen car arrived at St Andrews by bus on Friday afternoon.' She squinted at the other man in the photo. 'Do Leven know who he is?'

'Abe McLeod. Another small-time player. Did a stretch for reset of stolen goods around the same time as Zac. They were on the same wing, too.'

'So they'd know each other,' Clare said.

'Definitely.'

'Any sign of Abe?'

Chris shook his head. 'Nope. Warrant out for his arrest for the theft of the car but no luck so far. They reckon he's probably in Edinburgh, now. Easier to slip under the radar in a bigger city. But there would have to be two of them, remember,' he went on. 'That BMW's keyless. They'd need two transmitters to get into the car. One at the car and one outside the house.'

Clare sat back considering this. 'So Zac and Abe get the bus up to St Andrews together on Friday. Zac uses a cash machine. Maybe they go for a few drinks – wait till it's dark. Then they head across to Cant Crescent, find the car they're after and drive it away.'

'And at some point,' Chris said, 'Zac gets out.'

'Somewhere between St Andrews and Leven. Oh wait.' Clare sat thinking. 'Zac could have gone back to Leven with Abe and got out of the car before they reached the speed camera.'

Chris smiled. 'Nope. I checked. Zac's flat is further on from the camera. He'd have still been in the car when Abe picked up the ticket.'

'So where did he drop Zac?'

'You know what I'm thinking?' Chris said.

Clare nodded. 'Lamond Lodge is on the outskirts of St Andrews. Abe could have dropped Zac there and left him to break into the Lodge.' She squinted again at the speed camera photo. 'One fifteen,' she said. 'How far's Leven from here, Chris?'

'Half an hour in a car. Probably a bit less at that time of night.'

'Okay, Abe left St Andrews about quarter to one. Our security guard finished at Lamond Lodge around two. Zac wouldn't have had to hang about for long after nicking the car. Say Abe dropped him at the gate at quarter to one. He makes his way up towards the fencing, probably sees the cameras, and skirts round the side waiting for an opportunity to climb the fence.' Clare picked up the cash machine photo again. 'It's too much of a coincidence, Zac being in St Andrews the night before Russell Fox was shot.'

'Still doesn't help us if he won't say anything,' Chris pointed out.

'No,' Clare admitted, 'but that might.' She jabbed the photo of Zac at the cash machine. 'The jacket. He's sitting in our interview room wearing the same one he wore on Friday night.'

'So?'

'So, I'm gonna have that jacket off him right now. If he was wearing it when he shot Russell Fox it'll be peppered with gunshot residue.' She put down the photos. 'I want you to run it across to the lab in Dundee. Top priority. We'll soon know if Zac Buchanan fired the gun.'

–

Raymond Curtice, Clare's contact at SOCO, agreed to rush through the test for gunshot residue as a favour. 'That is one enormous drink you owe me,' he told her, and she promised to oblige.

With Zac languishing in the interview room, pending the results, Clare sought out Janey. 'Any luck checking out Gaby and Luke?'

Janey nodded. 'I think so. It's hard to be absolutely sure. But they dined in the hotel restaurant on Friday night and judging by their bill they had aperitifs, then a bottle of wine and whiskies to follow. And they were both up for breakfast too – just after eight.'

Clare smiled. 'Not impossible then, but unlikely.'

'I'd say so. Sorry.'

'Ach, it's fine. I didn't really fancy them for it anyway.'

'Bill was saying you've got the lad Buchanan's jacket away to check for gunshot residue.'

'He was in the town on Friday night and I think he might still have been there the next morning.'

'Fingers crossed, eh?' Janey said.

Clare yawned. 'Yep. We could really do with a break.'

–

Chris returned an hour later, having dropped Zac's jacket off at the lab. 'Raymond says he'll phone soon.' He stiffened as Tony appeared at Clare's shoulder, a gesture that didn't escape the DCI's notice.

'Easy, Tiger,' he said to Chris, the hint of a smirk on his face. 'I come in peace.'

'Did you want something?' Clare said, before Chris could respond.

'Aye.' Tony pulled a chair across the floor and eased himself down. 'The Lamond Lodge folk – when can they go home?'

Clare checked her watch. 'Depending on what SOCO say about a jacket we've sent over, it could be later today.'

'How so?'

Clare explained about Zac Buchanan being in St Andrews on Friday. 'We know he arrived with the car thief early evening on Friday, but it looks like he didn't go back with him to Leven that night. And, given he has history with our victim…'

Tony drummed his fingers on the desk. 'Seems pretty serious stuff for a low-life like Zac. I'd have thought a knife in the guts was more his style.'

Clare nodded. 'I agree. But he has a motive and, to an extent, the opportunity.'

'And the means?' Tony said. 'I'm not seeing it. Correct me if I'm wrong but ballistics thought it was a high-powered rifle.'

'They did; and yep. Going on what's been seized lately it's probably a Dragunov.'

Chris shot a glance at Tony. 'It's a good point. Where would Zac get the money for a gun like that?'

'Unless he didn't pay for it,' Clare said. 'If he'd been hired to kill Russell Fox, the gun could have been provided.'

Chris frowned. 'Would you hire the likes of Zac to shoot someone? It was a clean shot, remember.'

'Don't gang up on me, guys,' Clare said. 'It could easily have been Zac. For all we know he could have been practising somewhere. Middle of nowhere.'

Chris shook his head. 'I still don't see it. I mean that Drag…'

'Dragunov?'

'Yeah, that gun – it sounds like a pretty expensive bit of kit.'

'Oh, it is,' Clare said. 'But a lot of guns aren't sold outright. They're hired.'

Chris stared at her. 'Seriously?'

'Think what you'd pay for a weapon like that, Chris? Thousands. But you can hire it for far less. Some guys don't even want to fire it. They just use it for scare tactics. And,' she added, 'it costs less if you hand it back and it's not been fired.'

'Listen to Annie Oakley,' Tony said. 'She knows her guns.'

Clare ignored this reference to her time as a firearms officer. A time when she had shot and killed a young lad who she'd thought was about to shoot her. They'd *all* thought he was about to shoot her. Problem was, the gun turned out to be a replica. Clare was exonerated, even commended, for her actions but it had left a rotten taste; and so she'd applied for a transfer, ending up as the DI in St Andrews. How many years was it now? Three? Nearer four, but still the likes of Tony McAvettie wouldn't let her forget it.

'But remember the CCTV,' Chris went on. 'From the bus station. It's a clear shot of Zac and Abe walking into town. And neither of them's carrying anything that could be a rifle. You don't stick a gun like that down your breeks.'

Clare nodded. 'Good point. The gun must have been waiting for him in the house.'

'So one of the party's involved?' Chris said.

She shook her head. 'Not necessarily. Anyone who knew about Gaby's booking could have posed the gun there, ready for Zac. And it's a holiday house, don't forget. All sorts going in and out: folk from the rental agency, cleaners, other holidaymakers. Or it could have been left somewhere in the grounds.'

Tony rose from his chair. 'Well whoever it is, find him and get him charged. The press are making a huge deal of it and I'm getting pressure from above.'

'Gee, Tony,' Clare snapped. 'I didn't think of that!' She stood quickly, sending her chair flying back. 'C'mon then, Chris. Let's go 'n' solve the case.'

Chapter 24

'You shouldn't let him get to you,' Chris said, as Clare accelerated along the road towards the Brodie Hotel. 'He only does it to wind you up.'

'That's rich coming from you,' she said, taking the corner a bit too fast. 'At least I didn't burst his nose.'

Chris reached for the grab handle above his window. 'You might want to slow down a bit.'

Clare hit the brakes. 'We're here anyway.' She turned the car sharply into the car park and shot nose-first into a vacant space, jerking on the handbrake. Then she snatched the key and clicked off her seatbelt. 'Coming?'

Chris stayed put. 'I'm not going anywhere with you in this mood. You might be the DI and me only a DS but if you go storming in there you'll have more than Tony to worry about.'

Clare sank back in her seat and exhaled noisily. 'I know. Sorry, Chris. It's just…'

'You don't have to tell me. I thumped him, remember?'

She nodded. 'Yeah. I do remember. Sometimes I forget what an arse he is.' Her phone began to ring and she fished it out of her pocket, switching the speaker on. 'Anything doing, Jim?'

'Caroline, the ballistics woman, she's found your cartridge.'

Clare grinned. 'That is good news. Where was it?'

'In the guttering.'

Clare glanced at Chris. 'But we were up there, Jim. I remember looking down at it. I'm sure I'd have seen a cartridge.'

'I think ballistics missed it first time. The gunman too. A professional hitman wouldn't have left anything behind. Caroline reckons the cartridge was ejected out the side of the gun and must have ricocheted off the slates. She found it further along the guttering. You wouldn't have seen it from the window itself and nor would our sniper.'

'Where is it now?'

'Off to SOCO. But she did say the gun's a Dragunov, right enough. Pretty serious bit of kit, apparently.'

Clare nodded. 'It is that.' She saw another call was waiting. 'Jim, I need to go.'

'No worries – that's all I had for you.'

Clare thanked him and clicked to take the other call. 'Raymond, hi,' she said. 'You got the cartridge?'

'Eh? Sorry Clare. No idea what you're talking about.'

'Sorry. There's a cartridge heading your way. Probably from our murder weapon. If you could check it for prints and DNA.'

'Okay, I'll add it to the list. Meantime…'

'The jacket?'

'The jacket.'

'And?'

'Sorry.'

'Oh.' Clare couldn't keep the disappointment out of her voice.

'I can't find it if it's not there.'

'Does that mean he couldn't be our gunman?'

'No,' he said, 'I'm not saying that. That's for you lot to work out. All I'm saying is the person who fired the gun probably wasn't wearing that jacket. He might have taken it off or he might have been wearing some kind of PPE. I don't know, Clare, but there is no residue on that jacket.'

Clare ended the call and sat on, thinking for a minute. Then she came to a decision. 'Change of plan. The clock's ticking on Zac Buchanan. I want to have another go. See if he'll tell us why he stayed on after Abe stole the car.'

Chris looked doubtful. 'Guys like Zac tend not to talk.' He rubbed his chin. 'We could hang onto him until SOCO's examined the cartridge.'

She shook her head. 'That could take a while. I doubt we'll get a result on it today. But if he is our sniper and he knows we have the cartridge, he'll also know it's only a matter of time until we have the forensics on it. He might just talk.' She pulled her seat belt back on. 'I'm convinced he wasn't acting alone and I want the name of whoever's behind this.'

–

'Told ye,' Zac Buchanan said when Clare revealed the absence of gunshot residue on his jacket. 'I told ye it was nothing to do with me.'

But when Clare said she might detain him, pending analysis of the gun cartridge, his demeanour changed.

The solicitor raised a warning finger. 'Perhaps, before we go any further, Mr Buchanan and I could have a private word.'

Five minutes later Clare and Chris resumed their seats and recommenced the interview.

'Mr Buchanan has some information he would like to share with you,' the solicitor said. 'But we wish to make it clear he denies any wrongdoing. He is providing this information in order to exonerate himself.'

Clare smiled. 'Of course.' She turned back to Zac. 'So, what is it you'd like to tell us?'

He shot a glance at Clare then looked away again, examining his fingernails. 'I caught a bus,' he said. 'To St Andrews, like.'

'Why?'

He shrugged. 'Nice day and that. Fancied a walk on the beach. Mebbe an ice cream, ye ken?' He glanced at his solicitor then said, 'So I met a boy on the bus.'

'Name?'

'Abe. Abe McLeod.'

'You knew Abe?'

'Aye. Met him inside.' He looked at Clare. 'Bar-L, ye ken?'

Clare nodded. 'Go on.'

'So, Abe tells me he's going up to St Andrews, too,' Zac went on. 'Said mebbe we could get a drink. Catch up 'n' that.'

Clare decided to get to the point 'Zac, was Abe in town to steal a car?'

Zac avoided her eye. 'Might have been.'

'And you went along to help him?'

He took a moment before answering. Then he said, 'It's no' a crime to look, is it?'

'No,' Clare agreed. 'But if it goes beyond that…'

Zac glanced at his solicitor. 'Abe, he told me about this car. Said the owner had fallen behind on the payments. But he wouldn't hand the keys back. Abe said he was supposed to go and get the car back. Said if I helped him he'd slip me a few quid.'

Clare suppressed a laugh. She had to hand it to Zac – full marks for imagination. 'So, Abe told you he was legally entitled to repossess this car and asked you to assist. Is that correct?'

'Aye.' He avoided her eye.

'In the middle of the night?'

Zac made no reply.

'And did he show you paperwork relating to the repossession?'

He smiled at this. 'Said it wasnae that kind of deal. The boy had bought the car off a lad Abe knows and hadn't kept up the payments. Abe agreed to help the lad out.'

Clare sat back and folded her arms. She decided to keep Zac talking. Eventually he'd trip himself up. 'What time was this?'

'Bit after twelve.'

'The early hours of Saturday morning?'

'Aye.'

Chris said, 'And, after you got into the car?'

Zac rubbed his chin. 'Then I get this message.'

Chris raised an eyebrow. 'Message? Like a text message? WhatsApp? Somebody pass you a note in the street?'

Zac threw him a look. 'Text.'

'From?'

He shrugged. 'Didnae ken the number.'

'We can check your phone records.'

'Whatever.'

'Go on then,' Chris said.

'So the message says could I meet a boy in the morning. Collect a package and take it back to Leven. Said there was a hundred quid in it for me.'

'What was in the package?' Chris asked.

'No idea. Message said to wait inside the gates of the museum, off Doubledykes Road. Said the boy would be along about seven.'

169

Clare sat forward. 'And?'

'And nothing. Boy never showed. Hardly saw anyone all night. Finally went back to the bus station about eight and caught the next bus back to Leven.'

'Did you phone the number?'

He shook his head. 'Nah. Not worth rattling someb'dy's cage.'

'And?'

'And what? That's it. Nothing more to tell.'

Clare watched him for a moment, trying to come to a decision. She really didn't have enough to hold him. Not at the moment. But if he was guilty and she let him go he'd almost certainly disappear. And if the forensics on the cartridge matched him there'd be hell to pay. No, she couldn't afford to let him go. Better to risk his solicitor kicking up a stink while they waited for Raymond to get back to them.

'Sorry, Zac. I'm going to arrest you now and you will be detained until we have the forensic detail from the cartridge.'

Zac flung himself back in his chair. 'Aw, fucksake, Inspector. I've telt ye – I didnae do it.'

Clare smiled. 'Maybe you didn't, Zac,' she said. 'And, if not, then we'll find out.' She ended the interview and left the room.

Tony was waiting for them outside. 'So?'

'Negative on the gunshot residue but SOCO are looking at what's probably the empty cartridge from the gun. If they find his DNA or prints on it, we'll charge him. Meantime, I'm going to detain him overnight.'

'So the Lodge party can go home?'

Clare frowned. 'I'd like them to stay at least until we have the forensics back on the cartridge.'

Tony rolled his eyes and turned on his heel, heading back to Clare's office. Clare saw Zoe smile as he went past but he barely glanced at her. She stared after him then returned to her work, her cheeks pink.

'Trouble ahead, there,' Chris said with a nod at Zoe.

'Yup, looks like it.'

–

By six o'clock Clare stood the team down. 'I'll hand over to the Inspector in Dundee,' she said. 'He'll phone me if anything comes up. Back in sharp tomorrow, though.'

She emerged from the station and crossed the car park. It was still raining and she saw there were fewer reporters now, those who remained mostly sheltering in their cars. For that, at least, she had to be thankful. She suddenly felt tired. They weren't making progress in this case and, if she was being honest, Zac didn't fit the profile of an assassin. He was too small-time for that. If he was involved, he had to be working for someone. Nothing else made sense. She pulled on her seat belt and started the engine. The windscreen wipers flicked into life and the inside of the car began to steam up. She turned up the fan and sat waiting for the windscreen to clear, her mind running over the events of the day. If Raymond did find traces of Zac's DNA or even a fingerprint on the cartridge Zac might talk, in return for a reduced charge. It had to be better than putting him away for a murder he'd committed but hadn't orchestrated.

The windscreen was clear now and she drew out of the car park past the reporters and headed for home. As she drove she thought about her sister and wondered if Jude had broken the news of the baby to Frank, her husband. Would he be pleased? Clare thought he would but she understood her sister's misgivings. The rain grew lighter and the wipers squeaked across the windscreen. She flicked them to the intermittent setting and blinked away the tiredness she felt. By the time she pulled into her drive the rain was off and her heart rose. The DCI's old Ford Focus was parked in front of the door and she could see there were lights on. From inside she heard Benjy's volley of barks and she stepped out of the car, thankful to be home.

Al greeted her with a cool glass of Chablis. 'I've a fish pie in the oven,' he said. 'I'll just put the veg on.'

Over dinner he talked about his conference. 'Some interesting bits,' he said, 'but it could easily have been squeezed into two days.' He speared a prawn. 'How about you? How's the case going?'

'Oh, you know.'

'No, but I know that face. Is it not going well?'

She shook her head. 'I arrested someone today. Still waiting on forensics. He may be our man but, if he is, I reckon someone's paid him to do it.'

'Any idea who?'

'Not a clue. And to make matters worse, Tony McAvettie's installed himself in my office.'

The DCI picked up the wine bottle and topped up Clare's glass. 'Drink up,' he said. 'Sounds like you need it.'

After dinner Clare lay on the sofa, her head in his lap, a companionable silence between them. She said, 'I like this.'

'What?'

'You. Being here. You've no idea how my spirits lifted when I saw your car.'

'Even the old Focus?'

'Even that. Although you really need to do something about it.'

'It's a good runner.'

'Yeah right.'

'I do like it here, though,' he said, looking round the room.

Clare lifted her head and turned to face him. 'You could be here more,' she said.

He put a hand round the back of her head and began stroking her hair. 'I could...'

'Do you want to?'

'I do...'

'Why do I sense a but?'

'Fear, I suppose,' he said. 'Fear of failure.'

She pulled herself up and took hold of his hand. 'What's to fail, Al?' she said. 'We're paying for the upkeep of two houses and you spend half your time here already. I know it's not long since your divorce and I do know how much Alison hurt you. But you could give it a go. Keep your house on, rent it out and move your stuff into Daisy Cottage. There's loads of room here. And if it doesn't work out — if we drive each other mad — then you give the tenants notice and move back out again.'

He inclined his head. 'I suppose. I'd hate to spoil this, though. Maybe if we were actually living together, then nights like this wouldn't be so special.'

'You're right,' Clare said. 'They wouldn't. But do you want to spend your life endlessly dating? Don't you want some permanence? Someone to come home to?'

He smiled. 'I do, Clare, I'm just afraid.'

She squeezed his hand. 'Of course. I get that. But remember I'm here for you to be afraid with. We'll work it out together.'

A bark from Benjy reminded her he was there too. She eased herself up to her feet and stepped into her shoes. 'I'd better take him for a quick walk.'

'I'll come with you,' he said. 'We'll do it together.'

Day 6: Thursday

Chapter 25

'Any word from SOCO?' Clare said as she entered the station.

The search of the grounds at Lamond Lodge had finished and Jim was back at the public enquiry desk. 'Nothing from the Dundee team, Clare,' he said. 'But the Edinburgh lab has confirmed Abe McLeod's prints on the BMW. No sign of Abe himself yet but it's only a matter of time.'

'And Zac?'

'Nothing conclusive. But they're still going over the car so it may yet come.'

Clare thanked Jim and wandered into the kitchen to put her lunch in the fridge. Sara and Zoe were chatting as they waited for the kettle to boil. Clare's eye fell on a tub Zoe was holding.

'More cakes?'

'Not today, boss. I brought one for the DCI, though. He was asking about the recipe.'

Clare and Sara exchanged glances.

'Yeah, I see you two,' Zoe said. 'And I've told you, I'm a big girl now. I can look after myself.'

She opened the tub and took out a slab of fruit cake. It looked rich and dark and Clare's mouth watered. 'Eyes off,' Zoe said. She took a paper towel and wrapped it round the cake. 'Okay if I leave this on your desk for him?'

'Suppose.'

Zoe went back out of the kitchen, humming to herself.

'I can't get through to her,' Sara said. 'He'll leave her high and dry. You know he will.'

Clare sighed. 'I'll have another go at him. But don't get your hopes up.'

—

Tony was unrepentant. 'She's made me a cake,' he said, indicating the paper towel.

Clare sat down. 'Look,' she said, 'Zoe, she's a real sweetie. Good fun and a good worker, too. I don't want her upset.'

He laughed. 'Don't worry. I won't break her heart. I'll be gone in a few days anyway — if you ever wrap this case up.'

'You'll let her down gently?'

He drew the cake across the desk and broke a piece off. 'Already done.'

'Seriously? You've told her.'

'Nothing to tell. I just said I was going to be busy for the rest of my time here.' He shrugged. 'She seemed okay with it.' He popped the cake in his mouth and began to chew. 'Oh, this is fab. Shame she didn't bring you a bit.'

'I hope it chokes you.' She turned to leave but he called her back.

'Executive decision, Clare: I'm letting the house party go.'

Clare frowned. 'I'm not sure…'

'But I am. Look, it's five days since the brother was killed. None of them's in the frame for it, as far as I can

176

see.' He broke off another piece of cake. 'I reckon you're looking for a professional hitman. There's nothing to be gained by keeping them in that hotel.'

Clare sighed. 'Suppose. When did you say they could go?'

'Whenever they like. The sister – Famous Gaby – she was asking about the body. But I told her it wouldn't be released any time soon. On the plus side, got your warrant to investigate their finances.'

Clare nodded. 'Okay.' She rose from her chair. 'I just hope it's not a mistake, letting them leave.'

'Get the team onto checking anyone with precons for gun crime.' He popped another bit of cake in his mouth. 'That's the way ahead.'

Chris was waiting for Clare in the incident room. 'I hear he's letting them go.'

'Tony? Yeah. Afraid so. I can see his point, to be honest. We can't keep them here indefinitely. And we're making zero progress.'

'What about the house?'

'Eh?'

'The agency have been on the phone again. They want to send the cleaners in. The woman who phoned said they've bookings right through to the end of October.'

Clare looked at him. 'Out of the question. We maybe can't keep Gaby and co in that hotel but the Lodge itself is still a crime scene. Surely they realise that?'

'It's probably the owners making a fuss.'

'That's a good point.' Clare was silent for a moment. 'Who are the owners? I mean whoever shot Russell Fox knew where to go for a clear view of the treetop walk. And it's not like he'd have been able to wander all over, looking for the best spot. There was a house party in full swing.'

'You're thinking it's someone who knew the house?'

'Could be. Can you find out who owns it? And when you've done that, get every spare body onto checking anyone with precons for firearms offences. Start with a fifty-mile radius of the Lodge.'

As Chris went off to telephone the rentals agency Clare's phone began to ring. Raymond from SOCO.

'Your gun cartridge,' he said. 'Got a result.'

Clare moved to the nearest desk and sat down. 'Go on,' she said, picking up a pen.

'We were pretty lucky,' he said. 'It landed in a section of guttering sheltered by the chimney stack. So it didn't get wet when it rained the other night.'

'And?'

'DNA.'

'On the system?' She held her breath waiting to hear if it was Zac's.

'Sorry, Clare. There is a clear profile but it's not on the database.'

Clare's heart sank. 'Not even Zac Buchanan?'

'Definitely not Zac's. And I can tell you it's not a relative of the deceased.'

She sat back and exhaled. 'So, no clues at all then?'

'Only that it's male. Sorry.'

She thanked Raymond and ended the call, mulling this over.

'Agency phoning me back with the owners' details,' Chris said, cutting across her thoughts. 'The property manager was in a meeting.'

'Never mind that,' Clare said, 'I've just spoken to Raymond,' and she related the gist of the phone conversation.

'So our gunman isn't known to us.' He rubbed his forehead. 'Not sure where that leaves us.'

Clare got to her feet. 'Nor me, Chris. Come on, we'd better let Gaby know before she leaves.'

Chapter 26

A black Range Rover was parked near the front door of the hotel, the tailgate standing open. Eamon Ferry appeared as Clare drew into a parking space opposite. He was carrying an overnight bag and he waited for them to approach.

'Any news, Inspector?' he asked. His tone was smooth, the smile fixed.

Clare ignored this. 'If you could let Ms Fox know we're here.'

He looked at them for a moment then said, 'Of course.' He loaded the bag into the back of the Range Rover and walked smartly back towards the front door.

Clare and Chris followed him in and stood waiting in the reception area. A few minutes later Gaby came down the main staircase. She was more formally dressed than she had been over the past few days and Clare guessed she was heading back to London. Perhaps to take up the reins of her morning show again.

'Inspector,' she said, a faint crease to her brow. 'Eamon said you were looking for me.'

'Is there somewhere we can talk, please?'

Gaby drew them across to a quiet corner of the cocktail bar and indicated some chairs. She waited for them to sit then she perched on the arm of a sofa.

Clare thought she seemed more in control than she'd been on their last visit. Perhaps it was the clothes. Was she back in work mode already? 'Gaby,' she began, 'we have some news.'

The frown deepened and Clare searched her expression. Was it worry? Distress?

'Yes?' she said.

'We recovered a gun cartridge from the roof of Lamond Lodge.'

Gaby flinched at the mention of the word *gun* but Clare pressed on.

'We believe it's from the weapon used to kill Russell.'

Her face softened and she gave a slight nod. 'Thank you for telling me. It's not easy… hearing these things. But I know you have your job to do.'

Clare went on. 'The cartridge was examined by our forensic scientists and they recovered a DNA profile from it.' She paused, watching Gaby carefully, then said, 'I'm afraid it doesn't match anyone on our system.'

Gaby's shoulders sagged. 'Then you still have no idea who's responsible for Russell's death?'

'I'm afraid not. But our investigation continues and I have every available officer working on it.'

Across the room Clare saw Luke Gasparini looking round and she raised a hand to attract his attention. He walked quickly towards them, his brow creased. 'We're leaving shortly,' he said, moving to stand beside his wife. 'I hope you won't keep Gaby long.'

Something in his manner made Clare hesitate. Then she came to a decision. She took a deep breath and said, 'There is just one last thing – before you all leave.'

'Yes?'

'I'd like to ask for your permission to take DNA samples.'

Gaby's eyes widened and Luke stiffened. Then he found his voice.

'Mind if I ask why?'

Clare sensed Chris sit forward but she avoided his eye. 'We're still carrying out some forensic tests at the Lodge and it's quite likely these tests will include taking swabs from any doors or windows the gunman might have touched. Obviously if any of our swabs match with your DNA we'll know to disregard them.' Clare's tone was light but she watched the pair carefully. She saw Luke weighing this. He looked about to speak then Gaby cut in.

'So we're not under suspicion?' she said.

Clare smiled. 'No. And it would be entirely voluntary.'

'In that case,' Luke said. 'I don't agree. You can't force us.'

Gaby glanced at him then back at Clare. 'And what would happen to our DNA records – once you've found the culprit, I mean?'

'They'd be destroyed. We're required by law to do so.'

'So you say,' Luke snapped.

Clare ignored this, her eyes on Gaby. 'It really would help us,' she said.

Gaby met Clare's eye. 'All right, then. I consent.' She took hold of her husband's hand. 'Why not? If it helps find who did this to Russell.'

He sighed heavily. 'Oh, go on then. But don't forget we're catching the sleeper to London tonight.'

–

Nita arrived half an hour later with the DNA kits and they made their way to Gaby and Luke's room where the five of them were waiting.

A short while later the samples were taken and Clare said her goodbyes. 'We'll be in touch as soon as we have any news.'

Gaby smiled. 'Russell was very dear to me,' she said. 'Please, find whoever did this.'

'I'll run these to the lab now,' Nita said as they walked towards the car park.

'Actually,' Clare stopped for a moment, thinking. 'I should have taken the security guard's DNA as well – Mark Mooney.'

'Want me to head over there now?'

'Give him a call, first,' Clare said. 'Make sure he's there but don't tell him why you want to see him.'

They waited while Nita made the call.

'No answer,' she said. 'I'll try his mobile.' She stood for a minute, the phone clamped to her ear, then she shook her head. 'Straight to voicemail.'

'Okay,' Clare said. 'Keep trying. Meantime, if you could get these over to the lab.'

They waited until Nita had left then climbed into the car. They sat for a moment, watching Doug Gerrard and Steve Christie load their bags into the Range Rover.

'So, riddle me this, Inspector,' Chris said.

'Yeah?'

'What made you decide to take their DNA?'

She sat, silent for a moment. 'I don't know.' She turned to Chris. 'Something about Luke Gasparini's manner. As though being obstructive with us was more important than supporting his wife.' She shrugged. 'Probably a waste of time. But we do need to check none of them match with the DNA on that cartridge.'

'You don't really think it was any of them, do you?'

'Not really. But those three men all had the opportunity.' She started the engine and pulled on her seat belt. 'And don't forget, Chris, the most likely explanation is often the right one.'

Chapter 27

'We'll have to let Zac Buchanan go,' Clare said.

Tony frowned. 'Pity. He was looking like a good fit for it.'

'I know. He could still be our killer. Might have worn gloves when he handled the gun and the ammo. But even if he did kill Russell, and it looks like we'd struggle to prove it, I reckon he's been paid to do it. And by someone with enough money to get their hands on a Dragunov.'

'And you have onward addresses for the Lodge party?'

'Yeah. The three men are heading back to Glasgow. Gaby and Luke, too. Then they're catching the London sleeper tonight.'

'Okay. Keep me posted.'

Out in the main office Zoe was tapping away at her computer.

'You okay?' Clare said.

'Yeah, fine.' She looked towards Clare's office door. 'Did he eat the cake?'

'He said it was delicious. Frankly, it's far more than he deserves.'

'Oh I don't know,' Zoe said, then she turned back to her computer.

Chris was in the kitchen retrieving a tub of salad from the fridge.

'Pass me that duck wrap,' Clare said, pointing to the sandwich she'd bought on her way in to work. She saw Chris look at it with something approaching longing. 'Sara got you on a diet again?'

He shook his head. 'Ever since she found the Wagon Wheels.'

Clare laughed. 'You need to get better at hiding them.'

'I could put them in your filing cabinet.'

'Oh no! You are not bringing me into this. I've enough problems of my own.' She pulled a paper towel from the dispenser. 'Fancy taking these into the incident room?' she said. 'Find a quiet corner?'

Over lunch – Clare took pity on Chris and gave him half the wrap – they discussed the case.

'So, if it wasn't Zac…' Chris began.

'We don't know it wasn't. He was in the area, remember. All night.'

'True.'

'And that gun could have been left in the house for him.'

Chris frowned. 'He doesn't really fit the picture, though, does he? He's never shot and killed anyone.'

'As far as we know.'

'Suppose. He could be a cracking shot, but he's no history with guns.'

'Again, as far as we know.'

Chris speared a forkful of salad. 'Why are you so determined it's him?'

'I'm not. But there's no love lost between him and Russell Fox. We can't ignore that.'

'It's not enough though.'

She nodded. 'Okay, let's consider this: what if someone's trying to frame Zac?'

Chris munched his salad, weighing this up. 'Certainly seems more likely than Zac being the killer.'

'Remember his story about a message on his phone telling him to wait for a package? That made sure he was in the town overnight.'

'If it's true.'

'But, if someone did want to frame him, what better way to guarantee he'd be in the area when Russell was killed?'

'It would have to be someone who knew Russell Fox had crossed Zac,' Chris said.

'Someone who'd been in prison.'

'Steve Christie?'

Clare nodded. 'Could be.'

'You have his DNA now. So we should know soon.'

'It's a long shot, to be honest. But we have to try.' She fell silent for a moment then said, 'I think I'd like to speak to Zac again, if he's not already been released. Could you check? There's something else I want to do.'

Janey was finishing a bowl of soup in the kitchen when Clare found her.

'Could you do me a favour?'

Janey carried her bowl over to the sink. 'Sure.'

'Could you look into a David Fox please? He died coming up for ten years ago – it'll be ten years in September.'

'What do you want to know?'

Clare thought for a moment. 'I'm not sure. Just whatever you can find out. How he died, if he was married, or living with someone. And especially if he could have had any children.'

'He related to the victim?'

'Yeah, brother to Russell and Gaby.' She smiled. 'It probably won't help but I'd like to know, all the same.'

'We're in luck,' Chris said. 'They released him ten minutes ago and he's heading for the bus station. A couple of the lads were running him there so they'll bring him here instead. I've said we'll put him on a bus back to Leven.'

Zac arrived forty minutes later, accompanied by two officers.

'We'll take him from here,' Clare said, thanking them.

'Am I gonnae be needing a solicitor?' Zac said, trailing after Clare to the interview room.

'To be honest, Zac, I doubt it. You'll still be under caution but I just want to check something with you. I'm happy to arrange for the duty solicitor to attend but it will delay things.' She opened the interview room door and stood back for Zac to enter.

'Go on, then,' he said. 'But if it gets heavy, I'm saying nothing.'

Clare began the interview with the usual formalities and started the tape. 'Zac, you have agreed to be interviewed without a solicitor present, but we are happy to stop the interview to wait for one if you prefer.'

'Aye, just get on with it.'

'Okay. You told us previously that you came to St Andrews by bus with Abe McLeod last Friday evening.'

'Aye, so?'

'And that you received a text message asking you to remain in the town to collect a package.'

'Aye.'

'Do you mind telling us how you spent the night?'

He shrugged. 'Suppose. Spent a bit of time with Abe…' He tailed off and Clare guessed he wanted to avoid mentioning the stolen car again.

She chose her words carefully. 'And when you and Abe… parted company, you went to the museum?'

'Aye. Doubledykes Road, like I told you. Message said I was supposed to wait there and the parcel would be dropped off early morning.'

'So you waited all night?' Clare said. 'Just inside the museum gates, off Doubledykes Road?'

He nodded.

'For the tape, please.'

'Aye, I waited where you said.'

'But the person with the package didn't appear?'

'Naw. Waste of a night. Could have been home in my bed.'

'You also said you hardly saw anyone,' Clare continued. 'I'd like you to think carefully about that, please. It might be important. Was there anyone at all? Particularly anyone you think might have noticed you.'

Zac sat back and rubbed his chin. 'A few folk wandered past – Friday night – after closing time.'

'Did you speak to them?' Clare asked.

He shook his head. 'A couple were chatty but I didn't take them on. I was trying to keep my head down.'

'Go on.'

'Pretty quiet after that,' he said. 'Then, early morning, when it started getting light, ye ken, more folk came down the road.'

'What sort of folk?'

Zac thought for a moment. Then he said, 'Like folk heading for work. Couple of lassies in black skirts and white blouses. Hotel staff, I reckoned. That sort of thing.'

'Did any of them look your way? As if they were looking for someone?'

He shook his head. 'Don't think so, although…' he broke off for a moment, then said, 'there was this one boy.'

'Yes?'

'I say boy, not that young. Maybe thirtyish. 'Bout seven in the morning. Maybe a bit after that. Looked a bit rough, if ye get my meaning.'

'Rough in what way?'

'Well, he needed a shave and a wash, for a kick-off,' Zac said. 'Clothes a bit messy, ye ken? I reckon he'd been to a party and that was him just wandering home.'

'What makes you say that?'

'He said, didn't he? About the party. And he had a guitar.'

'He said? You spoke to him?'

'Aye. I wasnae sure who'd be coming with the parcel and he caught my eye, like. So I wandered over. Just in case it was him.'

'And he had a guitar?' Chris asked.

'Aye. Well, guitar case actually. I'm guessing the guitar was inside. Anyway, he said it'd been a wild night and could he bum a fag. I've been there myself, ye ken, desperate for a smoke. So I lit one up, took a couple of drags and gave it to him.'

'And then?'

'Said thanks, said I was a braw lad and went on his way.'

'And that's all you can remember?'

Zac creased his brow. 'There was one thing,' he said. 'Bit odd...'

'Yes?'

'He was wearing gloves.'

'Gloves?'

'Aye. Thick woolly ones. And I remember thinking it was a bit odd. Height of summer and that.'

Clare sat thinking for a moment. Was there some reason this man stopped to ask Zac for a cigarette? Was this part of a plan to set Zac up by making sure he was in the town the morning Russell Fox was shot? Whether it was or not, they couldn't ignore it.

'Would you help us put together a photofit of the man? It might be important.' She sensed Chris shifting in his seat but she ignored this. 'Zac?'

He sat back and folded his arms. 'Strikes me, Inspector, I've been put to a hell of a lot of trouble. If I do your photo thingy I'll probably miss my bus back to Leven.'

Clare raised an eyebrow. 'Strikes me, Zac, we're not charging you in connection with the theft of a rather nice BMW.' She scraped back her chair. 'You help us with the photofit then we'll talk about how to get you back to Leven.'

Outside the room Chris said, 'You want to catch me up?'

Clare stood thinking for a moment. 'Might be nothing. But, what he said about the man with the guitar...'

'Guitar case.'

'That's my point. Quite big, aren't they – guitar cases?'

'And you're thinking the case could actually... contain a gun?' Chris said slowly.

'Chris, it would work. Our sniper has the gun in the guitar case. He knows Zac's been set up so he wanders

191

by to check Zac's there, as per the message. Then he goes on his way, safe in the knowledge Zac was in the town around the time Russell Fox was shot. He probably knows Zac would head for the bus station when the parcel bloke doesn't appear. And we'd see him on the bus station CCTV.'

Chris fell silent for a moment. Then he said, 'I dunno, Clare. It's a bit far-fetched. He could just be a bloke with a guitar.'

'There's only one way to find out. Let's get him working on a photofit and see if we can identify our tramp with the guitar.'

Chapter 28

The photofit officer was tied up on another job. 'I could probably make it in a couple of hours.'

'Soon as you can then,' Clare said.

Zac agreed to hang around in exchange for a mug of tea and a lift home. They left him in the interview room. 'I'm keen to see if the photofit looks anything like Russell's three friends,' Clare said.

'You still think it's one of them?'

She shook her head. 'Probably not. But it's possible. One of them could have shot Russell early morning then nipped into town to check Zac was at the museum. Plenty time to head back to the Lodge before the rest of them surfaced.'

'Sounds a bit far-fetched,' Chris said.

'It does. But there's something about those three I can't put my finger on.'

Chris yawned. 'Fair enough.' He checked his watch. 'Might nip out for an hour if there's nothing much happening.'

'Get me a bag of crisps, please. Cheese and onion.'

'I'm not going to the shops.'

'You're a dreadful liar, Detective Sergeant.'

As Chris left the station Sara appeared. 'Oh, has Chris gone out?'

'Yeah. On enquiries.'

'Wish he'd said. I could murder some chocolate.'

Clare laughed. 'We need to get you out of uniform and into plain clothes, Sara. You're a far better detective than he is.'

—

With Tony still holed up in her office, Clare took a laptop into an empty interview room and was poring over the station budget when Sara put her head round the door.

'Jim's asking about Zac,' she said.

'Has the photofit guy arrived?'

'Yeah. Nearly done.'

'Right,' Clare said. 'When Zac's finished he can go.'

'He's saying you promised him a lift back to Leven.'

Clare swore under her breath. 'See if there's a bus this evening. I can't spare the manpower.' She rose, closing the laptop. 'Let's see this e-fit, then.'

Zac was at the public enquiry counter, waiting for Gary who'd promised to drop him at the bus station. 'I was supposed to get a lift home,' he said, his face set in a scowl.

'Tell you what, Zac,' Clare said, heading for the incident room. 'Next time I pick you up for nicking a car I'll make sure you're escorted all the way.'

The e-fit image was up on a computer screen as they entered the incident room.

'Just printing off copies,' Jim said as Clare sat down to study it.

'Somebody give Tony a shout,' she said. 'He ought to see this.'

Chris came across and Sara peered at the image too. The hair was collar length, dirty blond in colour, the complexion tanned.

'Zac wasn't sure about eye colour,' the e-fit officer said. 'So we've gone for hazel.'

'Height?' Clare asked.

'About the same as himself, he thought. So maybe...'

'Five nine, five ten,' Chris said. He stared at the image. 'Certainly doesn't ring a bell with me.' And it doesn't look like any of the three friends either. He looked round at the others. 'Anyone else?'

Tony wandered over. Then he shook his head. 'Nope.'

Sara was still staring at the screen. 'He's familiar,' she said. 'I just can't place him.'

Clare looked at her. 'Recently?'

'I think so. I just need to remember...'

They waited while she stood, her brow creased. Then it cleared. 'Got it,' she said. 'The homeless shelter – down by the harbour. I'm sure that's where I saw him. Or someone pretty like him. I was checking on a bit of vandalism they'd had and that e-fit's a likeness for one of the residents.'

'That would fit with Zac's description of him, looking a bit rough,' Chris said.

'Did you catch his name, Sara?' Clare asked.

She shook her head. 'No, but the guys at the shelter will know who I mean.' She fished out her phone. 'I'll call them now.'

'If he's there,' Clare said, 'we don't want him alerted. Just find out if he is and if not, when they expect him back.'

They stood, the room silent while Sara made the call. But Clare knew from her face.

'Sorry, boss,' she said putting down the phone. 'He left this morning.'

'As in gone for good?'

'So they say.'

'Don't suppose they know where he was heading?'

'No.'

Clare sat silent for a minute then she said, 'Sara, call the shelter back, please. I want to know if he had a guitar.'

'A guitar?'

'Yes. Now, please. And, while you're at it, see if they noticed him wearing gloves. And anything else you can find out about him.'

Sara stared for a moment then picked up her phone again. They waited and after a short conversation she clicked to end the call. 'You're right, boss. He did have a guitar, or at least a guitar case. They never actually saw inside it. Apparently one of the others asked Willie – that's his name – they asked him for a tune but he said he was too rusty. He kept it in his room most of the time.'

'Room?' Chris said. 'Like a private room? I thought they all bunked down together on mattresses.'

Sara shook her head. 'Some of the men at the shelter can pay a bit extra for a single room. If they pick up work.'

'And this guy, Willie,' Chris said, 'he'd been working?'

She nodded. Then she turned to Clare. 'That's the other thing. They said that Willie and a few of the others had done some work at a country house, clearing a bit of ground for a children's play area.'

'Not Lamond Lodge?' Clare said.

'Yeah.'

'And the gloves?'

'They noticed that too. Willie said he'd some problem with his circulation.'

A smile was spreading across Clare's face. 'Okay, bear with me, guys, while I work this out.' She was silent for a moment then went on. 'Let's assume this homeless guy, Willie, is our gunman, yeah?'

The response wasn't encouraging but she pressed on. 'If no one's actually seen inside the guitar case, he could have anything in there.'

'Like a rifle,' Bill said.

'Exactly. So, let's say, he plans to shoot Russell Fox.'

'Motive?' Chris asked.

'Dunno. Maybe he's a gun-for-hire.'

'Okay,' Chris said. 'Go on.'

'He makes his way to the Lodge, climbs the fence and sneaks inside the house. Then he goes up to the top floor looking for the best view of the treetop walk. He beds down for a few hours then, early next morning, he sees Russell on the walkway. He shoots him, puts the gun back in the guitar case and slips out of the house. He heads for Doubledykes Road where he knows Zac will be waiting and stops to ask for a fag. Maybe thinks if he chats for long enough, anyone passing will remember Zac. Don't forget, Zac's long-standing grudge against Russell – he's the perfect fall-guy.'

She looked round at them but no one spoke. Even Tony, perched on a desk near the door, was frowning. 'What's with the gloves?' he said. 'Why's that relevant?'

'Gaby Fox has a condition called Raynaud's syndrome.'

'The cold hands thing?' Bill asked, and Clare nodded.

'We need to know if it runs in families,' Clare said. 'Could someone...'

Sara was scrolling on her phone. 'Says here there's a 30 per cent chance of having Raynaud's if a close relative also has it.'

'So, it's a connection,' Clare said. 'We can't ignore it.'

Chris shook his head. 'But how would a homeless guy be connected to the Foxes?'

She spread her hands. 'I don't know yet but I'm sure that lot are keeping something back.'

'So…' Chris said, slowly, 'let me get this straight. You reckon this guy Willie was the same one Zac gave a fag to, that he knew his way round the house and grounds because he'd worked there a couple of weeks before. He set Zac up to be a suspect in the shooting of Russell Fox and he had… the *gun* in his guitar case?'

When she heard it out loud, Clare realised how lame it sounded. 'I think…' she began, 'this Willie, if that's his real name, that he could turn out to be a close relative of Gaby and Russell's and, yes, that he shot Russell and tried to frame Zac.' She ran a hand through her hair. 'Look, I get that it sounds unlikely, but I'm convinced our homeless guy's the link.'

'So why would he still be hanging around, days after the shooting?' Chris said. 'Surely he'd want to get as far away as possible.'

Tony shifted off the desk he'd been perching on. 'I agree with DS West. You're clutching at straws, Clare. Let's get back to basics and check anyone with a history of firearms.'

'Already done,' Clare shot back. 'And it's thrown up nothing. Has it?' She scanned the room. 'Well? Anyone found anything?'

No one spoke. 'Didn't think so,' she said. 'I do realise you think I'm making links where there are none but, in the absence of any other bright ideas, this is what we're going with. So, I want that photofit out to every station in Scotland. I want it on social media and I want an alert put out for this Willie. I want SOCO going over his room at the shelter,' she glared at them, 'and if anyone has an issue with that, well, just keep it to yourselves!'

She marched from the room heading for her office, past Zoe who was in the process of shutting down her computer. 'Boss?' Zoe said but Clare ignored her, slamming her office door.

Her desk was covered in Tony's paperwork and she swept this up, dumping it on top of the filing cabinet. Then she sat down in her chair. She could feel her cheeks burning. It was a long time since she'd lost her temper. A tiny voice in the back of her head was saying they were right. They were right and she was wrong.

The door opened a fraction and a hand that looked suspiciously like Chris's waved a white hankie. 'Okay to come in?' he said.

She scowled at him. 'Well, come in if you're coming.'

He pulled a chair over and sat down opposite her.

'Don't say anything,' she said. 'I know what you're all thinking.'

He smiled. 'For what it's worth, I think you might have something. Maybe we should have hashed it out before putting it to the whole team. But I'm not disagreeing with you.'

She flicked a glance at him. 'Okay.'

'So, should we talk about it?'

'We don't have time, Chris. That's the problem. That house party – they've all gone now and...'

'What?'

She looked at him. 'If the person who killed Russell was a family member, is it possible Gaby's also in danger?'

Chapter 29

'They never turned up for the overnight train,' Chris said.

'Dammit.' Clare sat thinking for a moment. 'Okay. Get their address in London. Check the house, the TV studio – see if Gaby's been in touch. They might have decided to fly instead. Check with the three men in Glasgow too. See if Gaby and Luke stayed overnight with one of them. Maybe we delayed them with the DNA tests.'

'I doubt it. There are sleeper trains pretty much up to midnight. There's no way we held them up that long.'

'Check with them anyway,' Clare said. 'They have to be somewhere.'

'Glasgow cops are on it and I've been onto the Met too. They'll check their London home and workplaces.' He glanced at his watch. 'Clare, it's almost nine. There's nothing more we can do tonight.' He jerked his head towards the incident room. 'They're exhausted. Tony went a couple of hours ago, anyway.'

'Hah. Why does that not surprise me?'

'Said he was feeling a bit off.'

'He always has an excuse.' She yawned and rubbed the back of her neck. 'Fair enough, Chris. Let's call it a day. Back in sharp tomorrow, though.'

Chris left and she took out her phone to send a quick text to the DCI.

> Heading home. Pig of a day.

The reply came back a few minutes later.

> I'll have some food ready.

She typed quickly,

> Honestly, Al, it's fine.
> Too tired to eat.

She rose from her desk and saw,

> Drive safely
> X

She put the phone back in her bag and headed out of the station. A solitary reporter stood leaning against his car, smoking. He looked across at Clare and she gave him a noncommittal gesture in return. The sun was low in the sky now, almost setting, and the car lights came on automatically. The roads were quiet and she was soon on her way, blinking away the tiredness. Ten minutes later she turned into the drive at Daisy Cottage and climbed out of the car, bone-weary. The front door opened and Benjy rushed out to greet her. The DCI stood in the door, smiling. He wore a striped apron and had flour on his face.

'You've been cooking,' she said. 'Oh, Al. I'm sorry I'm so late.'

'Don't you apologise for anything,' he said, taking her hand and pulling her towards him. 'You must be worn out.' He took her jacket and hung it on a hook by the door. 'I've run you a bath. Go on up and I'll bring some snack food.'

Clare planted a kiss on his lips then she kicked off her shoes and climbed the stairs. A cloud of steam, fragrant and inviting, hung at the bathroom door and she slipped off her clothes, leaving them where they fell.

Minutes later she was up to her neck in warm water being fed slices of homemade pizza by DCI Alastair Gibson.

'I've never eaten pizza in the bath,' she said, licking tomato sauce off her fingers.

'The way I make it, it's the only safe place,' he said.

'It is very tomatoey,' Clare agreed. 'Absolutely delicious. Did you make this from scratch?'

'Yep. It's one of my few talents. Did a cookery course in Italy a few years back.'

She took another slice of pizza and bit the end off. 'Any time you want to practise…'

He bent forward and kissed her forehead. 'Just going to wash up. I'll bring you a mug of tea and you can tell me about your day.'

Clare watched him go then put the rest of her pizza slice on the side of the bath. She lay back, enjoying the moment, and closed her eyes. Seconds later she was dozing, the cares of the day drifting away.

Day 7: Friday

Chapter 30

'I don't even remember getting to bed,' she said to the DCI over breakfast.

'I found you snoring in the bath.'

'I do not snore.'

'Like a tractor. Anyway, you did wake up long enough to dry yourself and fall into bed.'

She smiled. 'Sorry, Al. Not much of an evening for you.'

He shook his head. 'I've been a DI, remember, Clare. I know what major enquiries are like.' He sipped his coffee. 'So, what do you reckon?'

'The murder? Who knows? I'm fairly sure that man Willie.'

'From the homeless shelter?'

'Yeah, that's him. I reckon he's involved. With luck, SOCO will find his DNA at the shelter and we can compare it with the profile on the gun cartridge.'

'And you think he could be a relative of the Foxes?'

Clare bit into a slice of toast and chewed. 'I might be clutching at straws there. Raymond did say the DNA wasn't from a relative of the deceased. It could just be a coincidence, both he and Gaby having Raynaud's.'

'It's not that uncommon,' the DCI said. 'I know a couple of guys with it.'

Clare shrugged.

'Where's your motive?' he went on.

'Good question. If they are related, there could be some long-standing family feud, although that does sound unlikely. Or maybe he is just a hired gun. If he is, then who knows what the motive is or who hired him? Maybe some connection with Russell Fox's business. Or someone else he upset in prison. I've honestly no idea.'

The DCI lifted the cafetiere and topped up Clare's coffee. 'Maybe you should examine Russell Fox's affairs more closely.' He sat back thinking then said, 'You mentioned he was selling the restaurants.'

Clare nodded. 'He was. But I can't see how that's connected.'

'Nor can I. But it's worth a look.'

—

She mulled this over as she drove into town. Had Russell Fox been killed because he'd planned to sell his restaurants? Ownership would pass to Gaby now. But was it possible there was a relative somewhere who might contest the will? From what Sara had said about Willie he was too old to be David Fox's child so how might he be related to Gaby and Russell?

Across the road from the station a reporter was being filmed, microphone in hand. The camera turned to her car as she drew into the car park which she noted was filling up. She backed into her usual space, an uneasy feeling in her stomach. All these officers, waiting for her to tell them what to do. The same officers who'd stared at her yesterday when she was desperately trying to explain the significance of Willie. Was she on the wrong track? And, if she was, who would be first to tell her? 'Anyone but Tony, please,' she said out loud as she killed the engine.

Jim met her as she walked through the front office. 'DCI McAvettie won't be in today,' he said. 'Seems he's a bit under the weather.'

'Nothing trivial, I hope?' she said, before she could stop herself.

He suppressed a smile. 'Bit of a tummy upset, I gather.'

'Thanks, Jim. Briefing in fifteen minutes.'

–

Her office felt cold when she entered. One of those summer days when it was colder inside than out and she regretted her choice of thin top under the suit jacket. She sat in her chair, glad to have the office back to herself – for today at least. A welcome break from Tony whose sole interest in the investigation was to have it tied up quickly so he could claim the credit. All the same, she'd have welcomed someone to chat it over with.

As if on cue, Chris's head appeared round the door. 'Morning, Clare.'

She waved him in. 'Hi Chris. I'm just taking five. Then I'll be in for the briefing.'

He came into the room and pulled out a chair. 'You okay this morning?'

She smiled. 'Yeah, don't worry. Temper firmly under control.' She rose from her seat, rubbing her arms. 'I'm cold this morning. Let's get a warm drink.'

–

They took their drinks into the incident room which, thanks to its south-facing aspect, was warmer. Clare moved to her usual place in front of the whiteboard and put down her mug. 'Let's make a start then.' She scanned the room. 'Any luck with the e-fit? Anyone recognise Willie?'

There were murmurs of *No, boss* and *Sorry, boss* and Clare went on. 'SOCO? Any word from them?'

Chris raised his hand. 'They finished up at the shelter late last night. Raymond said he'd let us know if he finds any DNA matches.'

Clare nodded. 'What about the DNA we took from the house party yesterday?'

'Negative, Clare. Sorry – no matches with the gun cartridge.'

Across the room a phone began buzzing and Janey picked it up. She put it to her ear and headed out to take the call.

'What about Gaby and Luke?' Clare went on. 'Any sign of them?'

Bill said, 'Nothing. They've not used their passports so we know they're still in the country. The TV studio said they weren't expecting her back for a couple of weeks. Luke's production company said much the same thing. The flat's in...' he squinted at his notepad, 'Belgravia, apparently. There's a kind of caretaker looks after the block and he let the local cops in. No sign anyone's been there for a few days. Post and newspapers behind the door.'

'And he knows to alert us if either of them appears?'

Bill nodded then he said, 'What I don't get is why they disappeared. Why tell us they were catching a train then not turn up?'

It was a good question.

Clare looked round the room. 'Any thoughts?'

'Maybe they just want a bit of time to themselves,' Chris said. 'Time to grieve, and all that.'

'But wouldn't you want to do that at home?' Clare said.

Chris shrugged. 'Not necessarily. Don't forget Gaby's in the public eye. They'd probably have press at the door round the clock.'

'Suppose. Has anyone tried their mobiles?'

Bill raised a hand. 'Straight to voicemail, both of them.'

'Fair enough,' Clare said. 'But keep trying, yeah, Bill?'

Bill indicated he would do and Clare went on. 'What about the three men? Can they shed any light on Gaby and Luke's whereabouts?'

No one spoke then Nita raised a hand. 'I'll get onto that, boss.'

Clare's eye fell on Chris. 'Did you ever find out who owns Lamond Lodge?'

He shook his head. 'I'll try the agency again when it opens.'

Janey came back into the room. 'Boss.'

Clare turned. 'You got something?'

'It's David Fox.'

'Gaby's brother? The one who died?'

Janey nodded. 'Yeah, that's him. I'm not sure if it helps us but there's no actual evidence he is dead.'

'Eh?'

Janey looked at her notepad. 'He was travelling, 2004, his last known location was Thailand. He phoned Gaby from the beach on Christmas Day. She told the inquest they chatted for twenty minutes – everything seemed normal. And she never heard from him again.'

'2004...' Clare said, slowly. Why did it ring a bell?

'The Boxing Day tsunami,' Chris said.

'His body was never recovered,' Janey went on. 'After seven years Gaby applied for a Presumption of Death and it was granted.'

Clare stood thinking. Then she said, 'Did Gaby benefit by David's death?'

'Not really. David Fox himself didn't leave much; and his share of the parents' money is currently being swallowed up by the father's care home fees.'

Clare stood, processing this. Then she said, 'Any thoughts?'

'He has to be dead,' Chris said. 'It's too much of a coincidence, him disappearing at the same time.'

'Unless he wanted to disappear,' Janey said. 'He'd been travelling for years. Maybe he liked the idea of stepping off the radar.'

'It's a long time, though, Janey, 2004. You'd think he'd have surfaced at some point. The mother's funeral, for instance.'

Janey shrugged. 'He may not have known. If he was travelling.'

Clare considered this. 'I think I'd like to find out a bit more about the Foxes. We have a warrant now to investigate their finances so I want someone on that. But we need to look wider. See if we can turn up anything at all: schools, universities, workplaces, neighbours. But discreetly, mind. This is a family grieving Russell's death and Gaby has a high media profile.' She smiled round at them. 'Okay, that's it. Keep in touch, everyone.'

She went back through to her office, Chris trailing behind. She opened the door and shivered. 'God this room's cold, today. Why's it so cold?'

'Seems okay to me,' Chris said. 'Turn up the radiator.'

Clare bent to do this then she looked up again. 'I'm wondering…'

'Yeah?'

'Do you think we should be looking a bit closer at Luke Gasparini? His background, I mean.'

'Wouldn't do any harm. Want me to do that?'

'Hm, maybe.' She pulled her keyboard across the desk. 'Let's see what's available online.' She typed Luke's name into a search box and thousands of results were returned, mostly about his TV work. 'He's busy,' Clare said, angling the monitor so Chris could see.

He peered at it. 'See what you mean. Says here his next series is on gun control in the USA. Press release claims they've secured a household name to present it. Wonder if that'll be put on hold now.'

'Guns again,' Clare said. 'We keep coming back to them.'

Her computer dinged as an email arrived. She glanced at it. 'Oh, it's Raymond.' She clicked to open the email and read it quickly. 'Dammit.'

Chris leaned across and scanned the text.

> Sorry Clare – called out to another job.
>
> Quick message to say multiple DNA profiles in the room at the homeless shelter.
>
> It'll take a while to sort them out.
>
> Sorry – I know this isn't what you wanted to hear.
>
> I'll be in touch if I do find a match.
>
> R

He leaned back again. 'Sorry, Clare.'

She sighed. 'S'okay. I'll just have to find another way to prove Willie's our killer.'

Chris hesitated then said, 'Assuming he is.' He rose and headed for the door. 'I'll try the letting agency again.'

Clare watched him go and she sat on, his words running round her head.

Assuming he is.

But what if he wasn't?

Chapter 31

'I've spoken to the three men,' Nita said.

Clare was in the kitchen, waiting for the kettle to boil. 'Any luck?'

She shook her head. 'Nope. They left the hotel before Gaby and Luke. All travelled back in Eamon's car. As far as they knew Gaby and Luke planned to follow in a hire car. Eamon said it was delivered just as he was setting off. The five of them were supposed to meet for dinner in Glasgow before Gaby and Luke caught the sleeper to London but they didn't show.'

'Hold on,' Clare said, 'we didn't know anything about a hire car. Did Eamon know who they hired it from?'

'No. Want me to ring round?'

'If you would, Nita. And, when you find the hire company, see if there's a tracker fitted. Might help us find them – if they still have the car.'

Nita left and Clare returned to her computer. and typed Gaby's name into Google. Unsurprisingly there were thousands of results, many of them reports of Russell's death. Clare filtered the results by *News* and adjusted the date range. She scrolled down until she saw what she was looking for and clicked on the first headline:

Daytime Star Gaby's Brother Declared Dead

Checking the date she saw it was almost ten years ago. The photo of a smiling David Fox must have been taken in his late teens or early twenties. She could see the family resemblance, to Gaby at least; and there was a similarity to the photo of Russell Fox pinned up in the incident room. Reading on, she saw the three Fox children had been privately educated in Glasgow. Clare knew of Dalgleish Grammar School but she hadn't known anyone who'd gone there. It was an exclusive establishment on Glasgow's south side, popular with the great and the good. Entry was by examination and the school prided itself on its excellent results. It was the place to send your children if you wanted them to get on in life.

She returned to her perusal of the article. Gaby was mentioned, of course, with a brief summary of her career. The paragraph on Russell was shorter, stating simply that he was employed as a chef at a Loch Lomond hotel.

'Obviously before his drink driving conviction,' Clare muttered.

Reading on, she saw David Fox had done some voluntary work after leaving school and had *found his niche as an instructor at Camp Canada*. She sat back and pondered this. Was it one of those places North Americans sent their kids in the summer? According to the article, David had a place to study Engineering at Strathclyde University. His spell at Camp Canada was part of his gap year. The article went on to say,

> But the wanderlust was too strong and David, a keen traveller, never returned to make his home in Scotland.

The rest of the article consisted of quotes from friends and his headmaster at Dalgleish. Then there was one from

Gaby herself saying that, while it was not the news her family had hoped for, they could finally begin making plans for a memorial service.

Chris put his head round the door and Clare glanced up, her mind still on the article. 'Chris, do you know anything about Camp Canada?'

'Eh? Camp what?'

'Canada,' Clare said. 'David Fox worked there after leaving school.'

'Dunno,' he said. 'Google it. But never mind that…'

'You've got something?'

'Oh, and how.' He came in and closed the door, pulling up a chair. 'Lamond Lodge.'

'The owners.'

'Yep. And you're not going to believe this one.'

'Go on.'

'It's a partnership. Glenkirk Properties.'

'And the partners?'

'Val Docherty and Doug Gerrard.'

Clare gaped. 'Big Val and that sleazy Doug Gerrard are business partners?'

'They are.'

'Let me get this straight,' Clare said. 'Doug Gerrard part-owns Lamond Lodge? So he was renting his own house?'

Chris nodded. 'All done through the agency. It was Eamon Ferry who made the booking. Paid just over three grand for the week plus deposit. Card payment in Eamon's name. I'm guessing the others reimbursed him.'

'Hold on, though, Chris. Are you saying Doug Gerrard let Eamon Ferry pay three grand for a house he already half-owns?'

'Yup.'

Clare shook her head. 'I don't get it. He could easily have agreed with Val that the agency would block out the dates they wanted. And if Val wasn't happy he could have given her what she'd have got from the agency after commission. Why pay top dollar when you don't have to?'

'Good point.'

Clare scraped back her chair and stood, pulling her jacket round her. 'You realise what this means, Chris?'

He frowned. 'To be honest, Clare, I'm not sure what to make of it.'

'Think about it. Doug and Val could access the Lodge any time they liked. They would know all the rooms, the layout and the best place to take a shot at someone on the treetop walk. They could even have posed a gun there.'

'Hold on, though, Clare. Doug's DNA wasn't on the cartridge. And Val's is bound to be on our system, with her precons. SOCO said there wasn't a match with anyone on the database.'

'No,' Clare said. 'They're far too clever for that. But Val has the contacts and Doug was on the spot. And he's savvy enough to have worn gloves.' She stooped to pick up her bag. 'Come on. We're heading for Glasgow.'

Chapter 32

'They've taken them to Baird Street station,' Chris said, glancing at his phone. They were approaching the Clackmannanshire Bridge now, a broad crossing sitting low above the Firth of Forth. 'You know it?'

Clare eased the car into the outside lane past a succession of slow-moving lorries. 'Yeah. It's a good choice. Decent size of station and it's this side of the city so we won't get snarled up in traffic.'

Chris glanced across at the water. 'I love how low this bridge sits,' he said. 'You get used to the other bridges being so high.'

Clare ignored this. 'They do know to keep them apart from each other?' she said. 'I don't want them getting together and fixing their stories.'

'If they've not already done it.'

'Fair point.'

They were over the bridge now, onto the M876. 'Half an hour,' Clare said.

'Who do you want to see first?'

'Let's do Eamon Ferry. Get him out of the way. Somehow, I think he's too careful to get mixed up in anything. Too keen to protect his position.'

'Okay. You know, thinking it through,' Chris said, 'it's starting to make sense. Those women, I mean.'

'Melanie and the others?'

'Yeah. Doug and Val. He tells her he's planning to book the house and she says she can arrange for some women to come along. Make the party go with a swing.'

Clare nodded. 'Spot on, Chris.' There were passing under the iconic Castlecary Arches, the nineteenth-century railway viaduct forming part of the Edinburgh to Glasgow railway line. 'Val wouldn't pass up the chance to make a few quid.'

'And exploit young women in the process,' Chris added.

Clare was silent for a moment. Then she said, 'Those women…'

'What about them?'

'Melanie Fraser made a good point, you know.'

'Hm, go on then.'

'She spoke about her friends – the ones without kids. They go on a night out, get drunk and sometimes they have a one-night stand with a bloke they've only just met and who they'll probably never see again.'

'So?'

'Well, Melanie said she really liked Steve Christie. She liked him and it wasn't much of a hardship to spend the night with him. She won't see him again so how is that any different from what her friends are doing?'

'You're not serious?' Chris said. 'Clare, I can't believe you're condoning women being paid for sex. I thought you were a feminist!'

Clare was silent for a moment. Then she said, 'My sister, Judith… she has a wee one.'

'Yeah, James,' Chris said. 'I know.'

'Jude… sometimes she really seems to struggle.'

'What? Financially, you mean?'

'A bit. But it's more than that. I mean, obviously James is autistic and that makes life a bit more challenging. She had planned to go back to work, you know? After her maternity leave. But the cost of childcare, all the running around, what you do when they're not well – all of it. It makes life really difficult for working parents.' She glanced at Chris. 'I hadn't realised how hard it was until James was born.'

'Still not sure where you're going with this, Clare.'

'Nor am I, to be honest,' she said. 'It's just that, well, Jude and Frank, like I say, they struggle at times and there are two of them. Imagine doing it on your own?'

'Like Melanie?'

'Like Melanie. No one to share worries over bills, never mind the cost of shoes for kids. No one to help you get a sense of proportion. To tell you that sleeping with men for money isn't the answer.' She shook her head. 'I just think we shouldn't judge her too harshly.'

'I'm not. But the likes of Doug and Val – I'll judge them for exploiting women like Melanie. Don't tell me you don't feel the same?'

Clare sighed. 'Yeah, I do. Of course I do. All I'm saying is, I get what Melanie means.' She smiled at Chris. 'Probably sounds stupid.'

'Don't be daft. I know what you mean. Sara's friends have a wee one and they're always stuck for money. Oh, hold on – get in the left lane.'

'Junction fifteen?'

'Yeah. Follow signs for Springburn.'

Clare took the slip road off the motorway towards a T-junction. 'Every time I come through here it feels like they've changed the roads.'

'That's age.'

'Shut up.'

'Next left… then right.'

Minutes later Clare drew into a vacant space in front of the red-brick building. 'I've never actually been inside this station,' she said, as they walked to the main entrance.

'Nor me.'

They were buzzed through, past the public enquiry area, and Clare signed them both in.

'Hello stranger,' a voice said.

Clare turned to see Jackie Boland, a friend from her days in Glasgow. In contrast to everyone else in their work suits or police uniforms she was casually dressed in jeans and a long-sleeved T-shirt. She grinned at Clare and nodded to Chris.

'Jackie! What are you doing here?'

Jackie smiled. 'I heard you were coming in today,' she said, 'so I thought I'd hang about.' She indicated her clothes. 'Obviously I'm not on duty. Well, sort of. I'm only in to catch up on paperwork. Officially it's my day off.'

'So this is your station now?'

'For a couple of months, at least,' Jackie said. 'I'm Acting DI, which is why I'm here on my day off. Trying to create a good impression by pretending I'm on top of things.'

Clare laughed. Then she remembered Chris and performed the introductions.

'I hear you have three of our finest in for interview,' Jackie said, leading them towards the interview rooms. 'Reckon you can make anything stick?'

'You sound like you're after them yourself, Jackie.'

'Just the one – Doug Gerrard. We've been trying to nab him for the past year but he always manages to cover his tracks. Car theft to order,' she added. 'High-end. Changes the plates then sells them on. Or he has them broken down for parts and ships them abroad. But we can't get anyone to give a statement against him.' Jackie held a door open for Clare and they passed into another corridor.

'Funnily enough,' Clare said, 'we'd a car stolen at the weekend. But it was recovered pretty quickly. I doubt it made it out of Fife, to be honest.'

Jackie smiled. 'That's something, then. Anyway, we have the three of them in separate interview rooms.'

'How are they?'

'Not bad. One of them looks pretty worried – guy by the name of Ferry.'

Clare nodded. 'I think we'll see him first, Jackie. I'd say he's the one with the most to lose.'

—

Eamon Ferry was perched on the edge of a chair when Clare and Chris entered. He jumped to his feet and attempted a smile.

'Inspector… and Sergeant, erm, I'm at a loss to know how I can help you.'

Clare invited him to sit again. Then she began the tape with the official preamble. In the face of such formality the colour left his face.

'I…' he began, 'I'm not under suspicion here, am I? If so, I'd like a solicitor present.'

Clare smiled. 'Of course, Mr Ferry. That is your legal right and we can wait for your solicitor to attend if you wish. However, you are not a suspect. Nor are you under arrest. We just wish to clarify some information that has recently come to light.'

His shoulders sagged and he relaxed back into his chair. 'Well, as long as that's clear.'

Clare reminded him he could suspend the interview at any point to wait for legal representation and he indicated she could begin.

'First of all, Mr Ferry, I wonder if you can help us find Gaby and Luke. They didn't turn up for their train to London and we haven't been able to contact them since.'

Eamon spread his hands. 'I'm sorry, Inspector. I really don't know where they are.'

'You wouldn't know of anyone they might be staying with?'

'They have so many friends,' he said. 'They're probably somewhere in the city, catching up.'

Clare regarded him for a moment. His response was too glib, too practised. If he knew where they were, he'd been ready for the question. She decided to move on. 'Perhaps you could tell us about the booking you made for Lamond Lodge.'

There was a short pause then he said, 'Well, yes. I booked it. Paid with my credit card and the others reimbursed me for their share.'

Chris said, 'Did everyone contribute to the cost?'

'Yes, of course. Well, not Russell. It was his birthday, you see.'

'So, was that a four-way split?' Chris went on. 'Or five?'

Eamon's eyes were flitting back and forward.

He's trying to work out where we're going with this, Clare thought.

'Er, four,' he said. 'Me, Steve, Doug and Gaby.'

Clare nodded. 'And what made you choose Lamond Lodge?'

He glanced at her then away again. 'Oh, I don't know,' he said. 'I think one of the others found it.'

'Would that be Mr Gerrard?' Clare asked.

'Probably. Yes. I think it was Doug.'

'Any idea why he chose the Lodge?' Chris said.

Eamon shrugged. 'I'd say it was a sound choice, apart from what happened to Russell, obviously. You saw the house. Pretty amazing.'

Clare said, 'So there was no other reason for choosing Lamond Lodge?'

Eamon shifted on his seat.

'It wasn't, perhaps,' Clare went on, 'that Mr Gerrard had an interest in the property?'

There was a pause. Eamon avoided her glance, brushing at his sleeve as though there was dust on it. 'Doug…' he began, 'erm, Doug said he could get us the Lodge at a decent price. Top-notch accommodation, nice and secluded so Gaby wouldn't be bothered. Said he'd even throw in a security guard.' He smiled. 'Seemed like a good deal to me.'

Clare said, 'Was there a reason Mr Gerrard didn't book the Lodge himself?'

Eamon smiled. 'I'm good with paperwork, Inspector. It's what I do. Doug said would I mind, as he was pretty busy with the pubs. So I gave my credit card to my PA and asked her to book it for me.' He took out his mobile phone. 'I can give you her number if you like.'

Chris noted down the number then Clare went on. 'Did any of you visit the Lodge prior to your stay? To check on the accommodation. Anything like that?'

Eamon looked genuinely surprised at this. 'No,' he said. 'I'd have thought – a place like that – well, it'd be booked up in the summer. Wouldn't be easy to have a look round.'

'And, during the time you stayed there, did you have cause to go up to the top storey?'

Eamon stiffened. 'I didn't shoot Russell, if that's what you mean, Inspector. I've never handled a gun in my life.'

Clare shook her head. 'No, not at all, Mr Ferry. I'm not suggesting that. Only that, if you were in the room used to shoot Russell Fox, you might have noticed something.'

'To be honest, Inspector, I couldn't tell you. The house was a maze. Ten bedrooms, you know.'

'Okay, thanks, Mr Ferry. I wonder if I could ask you about Russell, please? You said you were at school together. Is that correct?'

He nodded. 'Yes, that's right. All through primary. Then Russell went off to private school and the rest of us to the local secondary. But we still kept in touch. He wasn't a snob, Russell.'

'And did you know his brother?'

'David? Not really. He was a year or two younger than Russell, you see? Just young enough to be annoying to boys of our age. Obviously it was dreadful what happened – the tsunami. Russell was devastated. Mind you...'

'Yes?'

'I don't think he'd seen David for a few years before he died. He said David could be a bit funny.'

Clare frowned. 'Funny? In what way?'

'Moody,' Eamon said. 'Up one minute, down the next. I tried to suggest to Russell that David should see someone – that it could be a mental health issue. But Russell said that wasn't David's way. He was always a bit of a maverick. I suppose that's why he went off-grid for so many years.'

Clare glanced at Chris. They weren't learning much they didn't already know. Were they done here?

Chris leaned forward. 'Just one last thing, Mr Ferry: what can you tell us about Russell's decision to sell his restaurants?'

Eamon looked relieved at this. 'Not much,' he said. 'Only that he seemed keen to offload them. We spoke about it, you know?'

'When was this?'

'Oh maybe a year ago. It's hard to be precise but probably the end of last summer.'

'Did he say why?'

Eamon shook his head. 'Not exactly. But I got the impression he was finding it all a bit much. Staffing, all the rules and regulations. I think he was looking for something else to do with his money.'

'What sort of thing?' Clare said.

'Not sure. Maybe invest in something. Russell always had ideas.' He smiled at this. 'He'd have found something.'

Chapter 33

'Believe him?' Chris said as they watched Eamon Ferry make his way down the corridor towards the exit.

'Nope. I'd say he knows more than he's letting on, especially about Doug's connection to Lamond Lodge. But is he implicated in Russell's murder? Nah. He's not the type.'

'I agree. Interesting that Russell was talking about selling his restaurants as far back as last summer.'

Clare nodded. 'Yep. So it can't have been anything to do with his illness.'

'So, who next?'

'Let's leave Mr Gerrard to stew a bit longer. Steve Christie next.'

Steve Christie appeared agitated from the minute they entered the room. He watched Clare setting up the tape, drumming his fingers on the table. When she began the interview he burst in. 'Listen, Inspector, I know how it looks. Me with previous for firearms. But I had nothing to do with this.'

Clare smiled. 'Thanks for that. Noted. We just have a few questions. Shouldn't take too long.'

A look of relief crossed his face. 'Happy to help.'

'Can you tell me how the party came to be at Lamond Lodge, please? Why that particular property?'

He seemed surprised by the question. 'Oh,' he said, his brow creased. 'I think it was Eamon. He phoned to say was I interested in coming along for the week. Then he said he'd let me know where we were going and how much...' he tailed off.

'And did he?'

Steve nodded. 'Yeah. About three weeks ago. Told me my share and I transferred the money to his account. Then he said he was taking his car and he could give Doug and me a lift.' He looked from Clare to Chris. 'That's about it.'

Clare said, 'You weren't consulted? Given a choice of properties to look at?'

'Nah. It's coming up to my busy time. Lots of customers looking for their Christmas stock. I told Eamon I'd go anywhere there was plenty of beer.' He laughed at that.

Clare took a moment to frame her next question. 'Mr Christie, did you have any contact or correspondence with the owners of Lamond Lodge?'

Again, he looked surprised. 'No. There's a key box round the back of the house. With a code, ye know? I think Eamon knew it and he opened up.' He wrinkled his brow for a moment then said, 'Him or Doug. I was getting the bags out of the boot. I think...' he went on, 'I think there was a kind of folder on the kitchen table. Emergency numbers and that. But we didn't need it. Nice house,' he added. 'I'd book it again.'

Clare said, 'Would it surprise you to know the house is part-owned by Mr Gerrard?'

There was no doubting Steve Christie's reaction. He sat forward, his eyes wide. 'Eh? That fancy house – *Doug* owns it?'

'Part–owns.'

Steve sat back in his chair, rubbing his chin. He seemed to be turning this over in his mind. Then he said, 'Sneaky bastard. He could have given us it for nothing.' He laughed. 'Always the businessman, that's Doug.'

'So you didn't know?'

'No I did not!' Then he said, 'Who's the other owner?'

Clare smiled. 'I'm sure Mr Gerrard will be happy to tell you. Meantime, we're keen to contact Gaby Fox and her husband. Do you know where they are?'

He shook his head. 'No idea, sorry.'

Clare watched him carefully. Was he hiding something? She decided to wait. See if he would say anything else.

The awkward silence worked. 'I heard they hadn't caught their train. But that's all I know.'

'How did you hear?'

He was quiet for a moment. Then he said, 'Can't remember. Probably Eamon. He usually knows what's going on.'

'Where do you think they might be?' Clare asked.

'No idea. Maybe they wanted a break away, after what happened.'

Clare smiled. 'Okay, Mr Christie. Just a few more questions.'

'Sure. Fire away.'

'How well did you know David Fox?'

His eyes narrowed but he didn't reply.

'Gaby and Russell's brother,' Chris added. 'The one who died.'

'Yeah, of course, I er... I know who you mean. Just surprised you're asking.'

'You remember David?'

He inclined his head. 'Not really. He was that wee bit younger, you see? Obviously tragic what happened.'

'Did you ever meet him? After you left school, I mean?'

'No. We didn't have the same friends. And he was always a bit...'

They waited.

'Well, a bit odd, to be honest.'

'In what way?'

'He... didn't seem to think he needed to get a job. All that travelling, bumming off his mum and dad. Didn't sit right with me.'

Clare thought doing a bit of travelling was a lot better than dealing in guns but she stopped short of saying so.

'There was a memorial, though,' he said.

'Did you go?'

'Ah no, Inspector.' He rolled his eyes. 'I was otherwise engaged, ye know. At Her Majesty's pleasure.'

Clare nodded. She glanced at Chris. 'I think that's everything, Mr Christie. Unless...'

Chris shook his head.

'Thanks for your time,' Clare said. 'Obviously if Gaby or Luke get in touch...'

'Yeah, I'll let you know.' He rose from his chair. 'I can go then, yeah?'

Clare smiled. 'Yes. If you just let us finish up here we'll escort you to the door.'

He laughed. 'I reckon I can find my way, Inspector. Plenty practice.'

They watched him stride out of the station fishing car keys from his pocket.

'You know,' Clare said, as they walked back towards the interview rooms, 'he's the only one of the three who's done time, but I think he's probably the most honest.'

'He's still a convicted criminal,' Chris said.

'He is. But there's something more straightforward about him. That Eamon Ferry is too smooth for my liking. I wouldn't trust him as far as I could chuck him. And as for Doug Gerrard…'

'You ready for him?'

'Am I ever!'

—

Doug Gerrard was casually dressed in faded jeans and a zip-neck sports top. He raised an eyebrow when Clare and Chris entered the room but didn't speak. Clare thanked him for attending, said they would keep him as short a time as possible and reminded him he could have legal representation at any time.

'Am I likely to need it?'

Clare smiled. 'I hope not, Mr Gerrard. This isn't a formal interview and you are here voluntarily.'

He raised an eyebrow. 'It didn't quite sound like that to me.'

She made no reply to this and started the tape. The formalities completed, she began by asking him how the party came to be staying at Lamond Lodge.

There was just the hint of a smile. 'I'm guessing you already know that, Inspector.'

She decided not to waste time. 'You are one of the owners of the property, yes?'

The smile became a smirk. 'Aye. So?'

'And the other owner?'

'Again, I reckon you already know.'

'Val Docherty.'

'Aye.'

'What led to you go into partnership with Val?'

He avoided her eye. 'Can't remember. It's a while back now. I had some money kicking around. Thought I might put it into property. So I put the word out and someb'dy said there was a pretty nice house near St Andrews. So, I'm thinking golfers, students with rich parents an' all that. Made a lot o' sense. But it was pricey, like. So someb'dy put me in touch with Val and we bought it between us.'

'Who was that?'

He shrugged. 'Sorry, Inspector. Can't remember.'

Clare could feel her temper rising but she bit it back. 'How long have you owned Lamond Lodge?'

'Dunno. Four, maybe five years.'

'And have you stayed there before?'

'Couple of times.'

'Recently?'

He shook his head. 'Nah. Last year. Can't remember the date.'

'And since last year?'

'Nope.'

'You didn't pay a visit ahead of your party? To check things were in order, for example?'

'Why would I? Got the agents for that.'

This was like pulling teeth. She tried again. 'Mind if I ask why you charged your friends to stay in a house you own?'

'Business, isn't it?' he said. 'Got bills to pay, council tax is a fortune, insurances… plus it's not all mine. Like you said, I only part-own it.' He shifted on his chair and flexed his fingers, making the knuckles crack. 'And the agency get arsy if you make bookings they don't get commission on.'

You had to hand it to him, Clare thought, *he was well rehearsed*. 'Explain to me again,' she went on, 'how you came to arrange for the group of women to attend the party on Friday night.'

Doug Gerrard exhaled audibly and folded his arms. 'Like I said, I met a lad in a pub.'

'Which pub?'

'Can't remember. Anyway, met a lad, got chatting. Told him it was my mate's fortieth and he said if I needed some girls to make the party go with a swing, he knew who to call.'

'And who was that?' Clare asked.

'Can't remember. So, he makes a call, then he gives me a number. I call. Spoke to someone...'

'Man or woman?'

'Does it matter?'

'It might.'

He shrugged. 'Dunno. Sometimes it's hard to tell. Could have been a woman with a deep voice, or a man with a high one. Anyway, I told them the date, said how many there were of us and whoever it was said to leave it to them.'

Chris leaned forward. 'Did money change hands?'

'Oh sergeant,' Doug said, grinning. 'You'll have to try harder than that.' He looked back at Clare and nodded at Chris. 'No, money did not change hands. That would be *illegal*, wouldn't it?'

Clare decided to change the subject. 'Are you aware Gaby Fox and her husband didn't catch their train to London?'

This seemed to amuse him. 'Nothing to do with me.'

'So you don't know where they are?'

'Er, no! I don't.'

'You've not spoken to them since leaving Lamond Lodge?'

'Nope.'

Clare glanced at Chris, and he took his cue.

'What do you know about the younger brother David?'

'Nothing.'

'You don't remember him?'

'Not really. He wasn't around much. Always heading off somewhere in the world. Russell talked about him sometimes – where he was and so on. I wasn't that interested, to be honest.'

For the first time since the investigation began Clare found herself wondering what sort of man Russell Fox was, and why he'd been friends with someone like Doug Gerrard. A thought struck her and she said, 'Did you know Russell planned to sell his restaurants?'

He nodded. 'Yeah. Matter of fact, I said I might be interested.'

Clare said, 'You were considering buying Russell Fox's restaurants?'

'Yeah. All above board, obviously.'

'Had you made an offer?'

He shook his head. 'Nah. It was early days. But I probably would have. He ran them well. Good investment for somebody.'

Clare glanced at Chris. There was nothing to be learned here. Doug Gerrard was far too well prepared. She ended the interview. 'If you do hear from either Gaby or Luke,' she said, 'I'd like you to contact me immediately.' She withdrew a card from her pocket and held it out.

He looked at the card for a few seconds then said, 'Don't worry. I'll find you.'

Chapter 34

'I really hate that guy,' Clare said, as she accelerated up the slip road to join the M80.

'We're all with you on that,' Chris said.

Clare waved her thanks to the car behind which had flashed her out then she rubbed her temple.

'You got a sore head?'

She grimaced. 'More a thick head. Been fuzzy all day.'

'Too much of the falling-down water?'

'No, actually. Not a drop. I just feel a bit off, today.'

'Pull over if you like,' Chris said. 'I can drive us back.'

She flashed him a smile. 'Thanks, Chris. I'm fine. Tell you what, though, let's get onto Russell Fox's solicitor. See if he knows anything about Russell's plans to sell the restaurants. He might have been in hock to someone. And that could be connected to his death.'

While Chris phoned, Clare drove on trying to ignore her headache. She thought there might be a pack of paracetamol in her drawer back at the station. They'd be there in an hour. She gave herself a shake and focused on the road ahead.

'Solicitor's out seeing a client,' Chris said. 'His secretary said he'd call back in an hour so I gave them your number.'

Clare nodded then said, 'Okay, then, let's think. What did we learn today?'

'I'm not sure, to be honest,' Chris said. 'The more I see of Doug Gerrard the less I like. But nothing he told us points to Russell's murder.'

'Believe him about wanting to buy Russell's restaurants?'

Chris considered this. 'I don't see why not. You?'

'I don't think I believe anything that comes out of that man's mouth.' She glanced to her left as they passed Arria, the huge steel mermaid sculpture. It always caught her eye. Then she dragged her thoughts back to the case. 'What time do you reckon it is in Canada?'

'I've no idea. Why?'

'Remember David Fox went out there to work.'

'But that was years before he died,' Chris said.

'All the same, we might learn something from them. Speak to the police in Canada. See if they can tell us where he worked.'

Chris took out his phone again. 'I'll see what I can do.'

—

The roads were fairly quiet and they managed to reach the station before rush hour. Clare went straight to the kitchen to make herself a mug of tea which she carried to her office. Her drawer was the usual jumble of clutter but she found the paracetamol and swallowed a couple. As she sipped the tea the phone rang. An unfamiliar number.

'Inspector Mackay?'

'Yes?'

'Patrick Meikle, returning your sergeant's call from earlier.'

Clare remembered. Russell Fox's solicitor. 'Thanks so much for calling back, Mr Meikle.'

'Not at all. Under the circumstances, anything I can to do help.'

Clare thanked him and said she was interested in Russell's decision to sell his restaurant business. 'Can you tell me anything about it? Perhaps why he decided to sell and what his future plans were?'

'I'm afraid not,' the solicitor said. 'He spoke to me about it, of course. But I understand it was a decision he made in conjunction with his financial advisor.' He paused for a moment then said, 'I have her details here, if it would help.'

Clare scribbled down the advisor's number and thanked Patrick Meikle for his call. Then she tapped the number into her phone. A recorded message told Clare that Natasha Lynch was on annual leave until Monday, so she left a brief message and rang off.

Chris tapped on the door and came in. 'Phew, Clare,' he said, waving his hand. 'It's like an oven in here.'

She looked at him. Her eyes hurt now. 'Is it?' She shivered. 'I can't seem to get warm today.'

'You need to go home,' he said. 'You're probably coming down with something. Go on, get home. Before you infect the rest of us.'

She shook her head. 'It's nothing, Chris. I'll be fine.' Then she peered at him, forcing her eyes to focus. 'What did you want?'

'Oh, just to say the Mounties are calling me back.'

'It's not really the Mounties, is it?'

'It is, actually. But they'll find out which province he was working in and pass it on Should get a call back later today, or tonight at worst.'

She nodded. 'Okay, anything else happening?'

'Nita's got hold of the hire car company. There's a tracker on the car so they should locate it pretty soon.'

'Good.' She leaned back in her chair. 'Actually, Chris, I really don't feel great. Think I'll go home for an hour or so. See if a nap will sort me out.'

'I'll drive you,' he said. 'Keys.'

'Don't be daft,' she said. 'I'm quite capable.'

'Clare, you're as white as a sheet. Keys!'

She logged off her computer and followed him out to the car, muttering it was a lot of fuss about nothing. Sara followed behind in another car to take Chris back to the station. They arrived at Daisy Cottage just as Moira, Clare's neighbour, was finishing Benjy's walk. She took one look at Clare's face and, after a hurried conversation with Chris, said she'd take Benjy back and keep him overnight.

'You get yourself into bed,' she told Clare.

Clare, who was too tired to argue, thanked them all, told Chris she'd be back in a couple of hours and staggered inside, shutting the door behind her. She let her jacket fall to the floor. Her head was swimming and she climbed the stairs on her hands and knees, fearful she might fall. Then she staggered to her bedroom and kicked off her shoes. She was shivering now and she cursed her summer duvet. The DCI's navy woollen dressing gown hung on the back of the door and she pulled this round her and climbed into bed under the covers.

Day 8: Saturday

Chapter 35

Clare wakened at six o'clock with the sun streaming in through a gap in her bedroom curtains. Her nose was blocked and her throat felt dry. She sneezed and reached for the box of tissues at her bedside. She blew her nose then sat up in bed, putting a hand out to steady herself. Her head was still swimming and she glanced at her phone. She could see messages and missed calls but her eyes were still fuzzy and she put the phone down. It was time she got back to the station. They'd be wondering where she was.

The bedroom door opened and DCI Alastair Gibson appeared with a mug of tea. 'Thought you might want a hot drink,' he said. 'Fancy some breakfast?'

'Breakfast?' She stared at him. 'Don't tell me...'

'You've slept the clock round, Clare. I came home about seven to find you wrapped up in my dressing gown, snorting and snuffling. I popped in to see you a few times during the evening but you were sound.'

'It's morning?'

'Yep.' He set the mug down on a coaster and sat on the bed. 'I slept in the spare room,' he said.

Across the room Clare could see her reflection in the mirror. Yesterday's mascara was smudged down her cheeks

237

and her nose was red. 'I don't blame you,' she said. 'I look like the wreck of the Hesperus.'

He laughed. 'Not quite. But I have seen you look better.'

She reached for her phone and the DCI put out his hand. 'No you don't,' he said. 'You're not fit to go in.'

She sneezed again. 'It's just a cold.'

'And you'll infect the whole team.'

She shook her head. 'I've a killer to find, Al. I need to go in.'

'I phoned Tony. He'll be back today.'

She regarded him. 'That's exactly why I need to go in.' Then she sneezed again.

'Back in your bed, you. Or I'll phone Elaine.'

The mere mention of the Force Welfare Officer was enough for Clare to admit defeat. She sank back on her pillows. 'Okay but I want updates by phone.'

He rose from the bed. 'Just drink your tea.'

—

It was after nine when Clare lifted her head from the pillow again. Where on earth was the time going? The house was quiet and she propped herself up on her elbows and pulled back the bedroom curtain. Al's car was gone. She had the house to herself. She sat up gingerly and was pleased to see her head was no longer spinning. She swung her legs round and out of bed. Her eyes still felt gritty but her head wasn't as sore as it had been. Maybe she could make it into work…

She walked slowly out of the bedroom, her hand on the wall to steady herself. In the bathroom she turned on the shower and eased herself out of her clothes. The water was a shock and she began to shiver again. She gave herself a cursory rub with shower gel then switched the water off. It took another half hour for her to dress and make it downstairs. She felt queasy at the thought of food and wondered if she'd caught whatever had ailed Tony. Hadn't Al said he'd be back in today? Maybe it was a twenty-four-hour thing. She had to hope so. There was simply too much to do.

She poured a glass of water and sat at the dining table to look at her phone. There was a missed call from an unfamiliar number and the voicemail icon was flashing. She clicked to play the message and listened.

'Hello Inspector Mackay. This is Natasha Lynch from Carloway Money returning your call. I'm on holiday for a couple of weeks but, if it's urgent, please feel free to call me back.'

She had to think for a minute. Then she remembered. Russell Fox's financial advisor. Her finger hovered over the icon to call back then she decided against it. Her head simply wasn't clear enough. Maybe she wasn't up to work after all. She tapped out a brief message to Chris asking him to call Natasha then went to find the paracetamol.

–

Clare wasn't sure how long she'd been asleep when she became vaguely aware her phone was ringing. She sat up, rubbing her eyes, and looked round. It was still on the dining table. She got to her feet, steadying herself on the mantelpiece and walked over to answer the call.

'Inspector?' a voice said.

Clare racked her brains. She'd heard the voice some-where before, but where?

'Yes,' she said, surprised at how loud her own voice sounded in her head. She tugged at her earlobe trying to make it pop.

'I need to speak to you. It's really important.'

Who was it? She knew she'd heard it recently. But…
'Who is this?'

'It's Luke,' the voice said. 'Luke Gasparini. Can I come to the station, please? I want to make a statement.'

Chapter 36

Clare had no idea how she managed to drive to the station. She knew if she'd called Chris to ask for a lift he'd have told her to stay in bed. She could bet the DCI would have warned him about letting her come into work. She nosed into her parking space, not trusting herself to reverse the car, and climbed out. There was a bit of a breeze, cool against her cheeks, and she wondered if she was running a temperature. Pulling her jacket close around her she walked across and in the door. The front office was quiet, Zoe's head bent over her typing and Sara at the desk. Clare gave her a wave and pushed open the incident room door.

Tony was sitting on a desk near the front, holding court. He turned to see who had come in and he stared at Clare. 'God help us, it's Typhoid Mary,' he said, putting his hand up to his face in mock horror. 'What the hell do you look like?'

Clare sneezed loudly and felt in her pocket for a tissue.

Chris came across the room towards her. 'Clare, for God's sake.'

Sara opened the door and put her head in.

'Look, everyone,' Clare said, 'I've a bit of a cold but...'

'Bit of a cold?' Chris said. 'It's more than that, Clare. Looks like flu to me.'

She waved this away. 'Something's come up.' She nodded to the door. 'I'm going to my office. I'll explain there.'

Tony and Chris followed her and she sank down behind her desk. The room felt cold again and she bent to adjust the radiator, feeling her head swim. She sat back up, clutching the desk for support and waited for the dizziness to pass. Then she said, 'I had to come in.'

'Why?' Tony said. 'You're not that indispensable, Clare. Trust me!'

Sara opened the door and put a steaming mug down in front of her. 'Lemsip,' she said. 'It'll help.'

Clare smiled at Sara and pulled the mug towards her. The steam rose, hot and lemony, but her stomach lurched as though it didn't agree. All the same, she was glad of the warmth from the mug and clutched her hands round it, making an effort to gather her thoughts. 'Luke,' she said. 'Luke Gasparini... he phoned me a little while ago. He's on his way in to make a statement.' She glanced at her watch. 'We've half an hour to prepare.'

–

Clare's head felt a bit clearer after the Lemsip. She regarded Tony and Chris. 'You two managed not to fall out?'

'Well he's not punched me yet,' Tony said, and Chris had the grace to blush.

'It's a start,' Clare said. 'So, before Luke gets here, fill me in on what's been happening. Did you get Mark Mooney's DNA?'

Chris shook his head. 'Nita called round to the house. Seems he's taken off for a couple of days up the hills. Wife thinks he'll be back late tonight, or tomorrow at worst.'

Clare raised an eyebrow. 'That sounds convenient.'

'Nita thought it seemed okay. The wife said he'd been planning the trip for a few weeks. Weather looked good this weekend so he took off.'

'Okay. I'll be happier when he's back, though. Anything else?'

Chris said, 'I spoke to the police in Ontario and they put me onto the camp organisers. Seems David Fox spent a few seasons out there. He was popular and good with the kids. They were genuinely sorry when he moved on.' He hesitated.

'Go on,' Clare said.

'He was a riflery instructor.'

Clare stared. 'Riflery? As in guns?'

'Yep. So I went back to the school – Dalgleish Grammar. Seems they had a kind of cadet corps the kids could join.'

'Let me guess – they taught them to shoot.'

'They did. And David Fox was apparently one of the best they'd ever had.'

Clare put a hand up to rub her temple, trying to take this in.

'So, our killer,' Tony said, 'is a cracking shot and Gaby's brother is also a cracking shot. And, let's not forget, David Fox's body's never been found.'

Clare looked at the two of them. 'It seems too much of a coincidence, doesn't it? But I can't see what his motive would be.'

'Remember the three men in Glasgow,' Chris said. 'They all said he was a bit of a maverick. Maybe he took against Russell. Long-standing grudge Gaby didn't know about.'

Clare frowned. 'Maybe.' She rubbed her forehead. 'Erm, what else?'

'They've still got the hire car, Luke and Gaby, and the tracker shows it's in Fife.'

'Oh?'

'Looks like they decided to stick around for a bit longer.'

'Explains why they didn't catch their train,' Tony said. 'Maybe they did just want a bit of time before heading home. Away from all the fuss.'

'They could have just stayed on at the hotel,' Chris said. 'That Brodie place.'

Tony shrugged. 'Maybe the press got wind of them.'

'Yeah,' Clare said, yawning. 'Makes sense.' She checked her watch again. 'Well, he'll be here shortly. He can tell us himself.'

'Clare, I don't think you're up to interviewing him,' Tony said. He nodded at Chris. 'The lad and I will do it.'

Clare took out a tissue and blew her nose. 'Nope. It's my case and it's me he phoned. If I start to struggle Chris can take over.' She dropped her tissue in the bin and reached into her drawer for a small bottle of hand sanitiser. 'You're welcome to sit in, of course.'

'I wouldn't go into an interview room with you if you paid me,' he said. 'I don't want a dose of whatever you're carrying.'

She regarded him. 'You feeling better then?'

'Aye. Just a dicky tummy. Must have eaten something.' He glanced at Chris. 'Keep an eye on her, son. I don't want her keeling over.'

'Your concern is touching,' Clare said, her voice heavy with sarcasm.

'Pfft, it's not you I'm concerned about,' he said, getting to his feet. 'I just don't fancy filling in the accident report.'

Chris waited until Tony had left then he turned back to Clare. 'Seriously,' he said, 'I can manage this myself. I'll get Nita or Janey to sit in.'

Clare sniffed. 'And miss all the fun?' she said. 'No chance.' She rose slowly, trying to keep her head level. 'Let's go and prep the interview room.'

—

Clare had insisted on Luke having legal representation and the duty solicitor arrived just before eleven. She began the interview with the usual caution and Luke indicated he understood.

Then he said, 'Erm, are you okay, Inspector? You don't look too well.'

'Just a cold,' Clare said, trying to keep her tone brisk. 'Perhaps I could start by asking where you and Gaby have been since leaving the Brodie Hotel.'

Luke didn't speak for a moment. Then he said, 'A cottage. At a place called Hazelton Walls.'

'Why did you go there?' Clare asked. 'I understood you had a booking on the sleeper to London.'

He sighed. 'Gaby…' He broke off.

'Would you like some water?' Chris asked, and Luke nodded.

Chris left the room for a moment then returned with a plastic cup of water.

Luke took this and sipped. Then he said, 'When Russell's friends left the hotel we sat on for a bit. Just the two of us, you know? The first chance we'd had to be properly alone.' He sipped at the water again then went on. 'Gaby – she said she wasn't ready to go back to London. Not straight away.' He shook his head. 'It's pretty full on, down there. And the press – they'd be waiting for us. I knew what she meant. Or I thought I did.' He glanced at Clare then looked away again. 'So I suggested we stayed another couple of nights in Scotland. See how we felt after that.'

Chris leaned forward. 'Why didn't you just stay on at the Brodie?'

Luke shook his head. 'I'd had a call from my PA. Reporters on the phone. They named the hotel and asked her to confirm we were staying there. She denied it of course but I knew it wouldn't be long before they turned up at the door. She suggested this cottage. Said it was in the middle of nowhere, very quiet.'

Clare nodded at this. 'And how long did you stay there?'

Luke drank again then replaced the cup and Clare saw his hand was shaking. 'Take your time, Mr Gasparini,' she said.

'Luke's fine,' he said. 'Just Luke.' Then he went on. 'I booked it for three nights. I thought we needed that. Gaby began to relax; and we talked properly for the first time since Russell's death.'

'What did you talk about?'

He looked surprised. 'Russell, of course. How we were both going to miss him. Then I said I wondered if we'd ever find out who'd shot him.' He stopped for a minute and took another drink. 'Gaby… she said it didn't much matter. That finding out wouldn't bring him back.' He shrugged. 'She's right about that. I was surprised, though.'

'And after that?'

'Nothing, really. We were both exhausted so we went to bed. I don't know if it was the relief of being on our own, or knowing we weren't going back to work, but I honestly can't remember when I've had such a sound sleep. It was exactly what we needed.'

He broke off for a moment then he took a deep breath and went on. 'Next morning we had breakfast. The sun was out and we took our coffees into the garden. Then Gaby's phone rang. I thought it must be work so I wandered off while she took the call.' His brow creased. 'It wasn't a long call and when it finished she seemed so excited. I asked if it was something about work and she said *No*, it wasn't work but she had a surprise for me – *a really wonderful surprise.*'

Clare and Chris exchanged glances but said nothing.

Luke's shoulders dropped and he shook his head. 'I thought...'

When he didn't continue Clare said, 'What did you think?'

He exhaled heavily. 'I thought maybe Gaby was going to tell me she was pregnant. It's something we've both pretty much given up on. I mean, we have our daughter and we love her to bits. But we'd always wanted another child. Stupidly, I thought that might be what she was going to say.' He shook his head.

'And did she?' Clare asked. 'Is that what she said?'

'No.' His voice was barely a whisper. Then he looked at Clare. 'You have to understand, Inspector, I knew nothing about this.' He turned to his solicitor. 'Nothing at all.'

Clare nodded. 'I understand. Just take your time.'

'David, Gaby's brother, I never knew him. He'd gone off travelling by the time I met Gaby. She sent him an email when we were getting married but he never came.

And then, the tsunami – well, it was dreadful. Gaby was in such a state.' He stopped for a moment, as though reliving the memory. 'To start with, you know, she refused to give up hope. She thought he'd maybe had a knock to the head, lost his memory, something like that. But as time went on she accepted he probably wasn't coming back.' He smiled. 'Having David declared dead was a big step for Gaby. But, in a way, it gave her permission to move on.' He paused for a moment then said, 'We thought he'd been dead since 2004 but Gaby only counts it from the day of the declaration.'

'You say you thought…' Clare said, and Luke gave a slight nod.

'You're very perceptive.'

Clare took her time framing the next question. 'Is David Fox still alive?'

He hesitated, then he said, 'Alive and well, Inspector. And guilty of murder.'

Chris sat forward in his seat. 'Where is David now?'

'I don't know.' He looked from Clare to Chris. 'I honestly don't.' He met Chris's gaze for a few seconds then he carried on. 'Gaby told me that David was alive. Not only was he alive but he was on his way to our cottage. That was the phone call.' He glanced at his solicitor. 'I couldn't believe it. After all these years.'

'When did Gaby find out?' Clare asked.

He shrugged. 'She said she'd known for a few months but David had sworn her to secrecy. It was to be a surprise for Russell's birthday, you know?' He sipped his water again and went on. 'But then she got the news about Russell – that he was ill – and she was upset all over again. She said the doctors couldn't do anything for him. It was only a matter of time. So she decided we'd have a party at Lamond Lodge. Invite his friends, have a last blowout before he became too ill to enjoy it.

'But then she became obsessed.' He nodded as if to reinforce this. 'She's like that, Gaby. Probably why she's so successful. She gets fixated on something and she can't let go.'

'What was she obsessing about?' Clare asked.

'Russell's illness. His tumour. I swear, Inspector, she knew as much as the doctors. And she said the end – for Russell, I mean – that it wouldn't be pleasant. How it would spread, affect him. How he'd be incapacitated, and she cried and cried about it. It got so bad I suggested she see her GP. Get something to calm her down, you know?'

'And did she?'

He nodded again. 'Doc prescribed something, diazepam, I think. But she didn't take them. Said they made her fuzzy and she had to be sharp for her TV show.'

'Go on.'

'So, next thing I know, I'm being introduced to a dead man. David Fox.' He shook his head again.

Clare said, 'Did he explain where he'd been all these years?'

'Sort of. Something about having travelled inland on Christmas Day. Being lucky enough to miss the tsunami. And then he just kept on going.' Luke shook his head. 'I don't think he thought about his family. What they'd be going through.'

'It must have been very emotional,' Chris said. 'For Gaby, at least.'

He smiled. 'Yes, she was so excited.'

'And how did you feel?' Chris asked.

'To be honest, Sergeant, I didn't know what to think. It was such a shock.'

'I can imagine,' Clare said. She rubbed her head, thinking for a minute. 'And did David join the party? No one at the Lodge mentioned him.'

'Not as far as I know. He wasn't at the Lodge when we arrived back from the wedding.' He shook his head. 'I can only guess he changed his plans.'

Clare glanced at Chris. 'Can you explain that please, Luke?'

'I'll try.' He broke off for a moment then said, 'David, I think he's always been a bit of an odd lad but he was so scruffy, dressed like he'd fallen off a flitting. Anyway, he starts talking about where he'd been living for the past few weeks – right here in St Andrews at some homeless shelter.' He nodded again as if to emphasise this. 'So I said was it to be near the Lodge for Russell's party? And he said *something like that.*'

'What did you think he meant?' Clare asked.

'I didn't know. Not straight away. And then he said they had something else to tell me. And I looked at Gaby but she wouldn't look me in the eye. Suddenly she seemed nervous. Not like herself, at all.' Luke's hands were shaking now and he gripped one with the other, as if to steady himself. 'Gaby and I,' he said, 'we've been married all these years and I was starting to wonder if I even knew her.' He swallowed then went on. 'She started to speak but then she broke off so David took over. He told me they'd talked about Russell over the last few weeks and they couldn't bear to think of him suffering, as his illness progressed. Like I said, Gaby had done the research and she knew what was ahead. David said he didn't want his brother's life to end like that. So they'd decided to give him a wonderful party and then...' He broke off.

Clare tapped Chris's ankle gently with her foot. She didn't want Luke interrupted.

'After the party David would... would shoot him dead.' He met Clare's eye. 'I could see Gaby watching me when he said it. Looking to see how I was going to react. Then she said David was an excellent shot; Russell would have known nothing about it. And no one would suspect David because he was already dead.' He shook his head. 'I didn't know what to say. Sitting there, in this lovely cottage garden, watching the birds pecking at the grass – idyllic, you know? And I'm listening to this horrible story. It was utterly surreal.' He glanced at his solicitor again. 'My own wife. I thought she'd gone mad. Lost all sense of reason.' His eyes were swimming now. 'Anyway, Gaby, she said it was done now, that Russell hadn't suffered and we should just enjoy having David there.' He sipped from the water again then went on. 'I've no idea how I got through the rest of the day. It was a nightmare.'

'Did David stay the night at the cottage?'

He nodded. 'Yes. I went to bed early but I couldn't sleep. Then Gaby came to bed and she started all over again, saying it was for the best and that Russell was at peace. And I tried, you know? I really tried to make her see sense. Make her see it wasn't right. But she was way past reasoning with. I couldn't get through to her. Then her mood flipped and she said it was done now and I'd better just get over it.' He shook his head again. 'She's pretty ruthless, Gaby. You have to be to get on in TV.' He paused for a moment. 'For the first time in my life, I was afraid of my own wife.'

Clare glanced at Chris. 'Where are they now – Gaby and David?'

Luke spread his hands. 'I honestly don't know. They'd gone when I wakened up this morning. The hire car too. Gaby – she said David came into the country on a friend's boat. I think he planned to leave again the same way so maybe she took him to a harbour somewhere. I really don't know.'

Clare nodded. 'Okay, Luke. Please go on.'

'I called a taxi,' he said. 'I didn't want to be there when Gaby, or both of them, got back. I wanted to be away – time to think. So I waited in the trees across from the cottage until I heard the car. I wanted to be sure it wasn't Gaby.'

'Where did you go?' Chris asked.

'I came here. To St Andrews. I asked the taxi driver to find a cafe that was open. I needed time to order my thoughts.'

'And then?'

He looked at Clare. 'Then I called you.' He sat back in his chair, as if unburdened by his tale. 'And I still don't know what to do.'

Chapter 37

'Get Nita,' Clare said when they emerged from the interview room. 'Tell her to get back onto the hire company
and find that car. And see who's available to chase up Luke
Gasparini's finances. Personal and his TV company.'

Chris went off to call Nita while Clare updated Tony.

'You're joking?' he said when she'd told him.

'Nope. Sounds like the maverick brother returned, the
sister falls under his spell and, between them, they do away
with Russell.'

'To spare him the pain of a horrible death?'

'So he says.'

'Believe him?'

Clare spread her hands. 'It's pretty bizarre, but I can't
honestly see why he'd make it up. Nita's checking on the
hire car now. It has a tracker so, providing they're still using
it, we should be able to find them.'

'They may know that, of course.'

'Let's hope not.'

Tony regarded her. 'You doing okay?'

She shrugged. 'The Lemsip helped.'

'All the same…'

'You're getting soft in your old age, Tony.'

'Call it fellow feeling, Clare. I wasn't feeling too hot
myself yesterday.'

'Tummy upset, someone said.'

'And how. Anyway, what do you plan to do with him? This Luke guy.'

Clare sat down and rubbed her forehead, trying to clear the dull ache. 'To be honest, Tony, I've no idea. Assuming he's telling the truth, he hasn't committed a crime so I can't charge him. Quite the reverse, actually. He came straight to us to report the crime. He's not an accessory either. And he does seem genuinely afraid for his own safety.'

'We're not running a home for stray TV producers. If he doesn't have any pals he can stay with tell him to book into a hotel in the town. Just till we pick the other two up.'

—

'Nita's waiting on a call back from the car hire folk. Hopefully get the car's location pretty soon.'

'What do we do now?' she asked.

Chris shook his head. 'Sit it out.'

'Tony thinks we should release Luke. Send him to a hotel.'

'He's got a point. Can't really keep him. Unless you're planning to charge him.'

'He's done nothing wrong,' Clare said.

'It is the most bizarre story, though. I mean, think about it: brother coming back from the dead to murder the other brother? And the sister in on it?'

'Positively Shakespearean,' Clare said.

'I was about to say that.'

'Of course you were.'

'So we let him go?'

'Yeah. If you'd do the needful, Chris. I'm just going to shut my eyes for five minutes.'

It was then that she remembered Natasha Lynch, Russell Fox's financial advisor. She scrolled through her phone and found the number but it went to voicemail again. 'She's like the Scarlet Pimpernel,' Clare muttered. She ended the call and wandered through to her office. Tony's jacket was gone and she sank down in her chair, allowing her eyes to close.

—

Clare had no idea she'd fallen asleep until she came to, her head resting on a pile of papers. She was horrified to see she'd drooled on them, smudging the ink. 'Ugh,' she said, dabbing her mouth with a tissue. She gave herself a shake then picked up her phone to check for messages. There was a tap at the door and Chris came in bearing a mug.

'Sara says you're due another Lemsip.' Then he stopped and stared at her. 'What's that on your face?'

Clare put a hand up to her cheek. 'No idea.'

'It's all black.'

She took another tissue from the box on her desk and rubbed at her cheek. Glancing at it she realised it must have been the ink from papers she'd fallen asleep on. 'It's nothing,' she said, too embarrassed to admit the truth.

Chris raised an eyebrow but said nothing, setting the mug down on the desk. He pulled up a chair and sat opposite. 'I don't know what your head's like with that cold,' he said, 'but mine's mince, trying to work this out.'

Clare sipped gingerly at the steaming liquid then she cleared her throat. 'Okay, let's go through it, then. Do we accept that guitar man — the one Zac met early on the Saturday morning — is David Fox? And that he's been staying right here under our noses in the homeless shelter?'

Chris frowned. 'I think so. I know it's a bit far-fetched but then Luke's whole story is pretty far-fetched.'

'Okay. David has previously been in touch with Gaby about Russell's fortieth,' Clare went on. 'Remember, Luke said he'd sworn her to secrecy. Gaby tells David she's booked a house in St Andrews and he sees there's a homeless shelter in the town. He can stay there for a few weeks, under the radar, and slip along to the Lodge whenever he fancies.' Clare reached for another tissue and blew her nose. 'As luck would have it he picks up a bit of work in the grounds of the Lodge.'

'You're assuming that's a coincidence?'

'I can't see how he could contrive it.'

'Me neither. What I can't work out,' Chris went on, 'is whether he had a gun or a guitar in that case.'

Clare dropped the tissue into her bin. 'Doesn't much matter. There's any number of ways that gun could have got into the Lodge. Gaby could even have posed it there.'

'Difficult for her to carry a rifle in from the car without the husband noticing.'

Clare considered this. 'But she could have flown up and visited before the weekend. Asked to have a look round.'

'Would it not have been booked up?' Chris said. 'Fancy house like that.'

'Think who she is, Chris. She's the darling of the daytime telly brigade. If she'd asked to get into the Lodge ahead of the party, I bet the agency would've arranged it.'

'Yeah, I suppose.'

'And then there's Doug Gerrard. Don't forget he part-owns the house.'

Chris shook his head. 'Much as I'd love to think Doug's involved, I can't see it.'

'Why not?'

'He's one of Russell's oldest friends. And I'd say he's pretty cute when it comes to steering clear of trouble. Can you honestly see him agreeing to supply a gun that was going to be used to shoot his friend? And in the grounds of a house where he'd be staying himself?'

'Okay, forget Doug,' Clare said. 'Let's get back to David Fox. We know he's a crack shot, judging by his experience at Camp Canada. Maybe *he* knew where to get his hands on a gun.'

Chris frowned. 'It would cost, though, a gun like that.'

'Maybe. Remember, it's cheaper to hire one.'

'Sometimes, Inspector, I wonder about you.'

'Yeah, me too. So, let's say David gets hold of a gun and, somehow, he sneaks it into the house. Then he has a wander about, finds the best window for a clear shot and he, or someone else, hides the gun in the room.'

'They arrive at the house on the Thursday,' Chris said, taking up the thread, 'and Gaby tells Russell the treetop walk is the best place to see the sun come up.'

'Exactly. Then she and Luke head off for the wedding, knowing David will turn up for the party. Except…'

'Except what?'

'Bill had a point, you know, when he said that none of the three men mentioned David when we interviewed them.'

Chris thought for a moment. 'Maybe David told them he planned to go off-grid again – after the party. As far as they were concerned, he was still dead. If they mentioned him it would just complicate things.'

She lifted the mug and drained it. 'Ugh, I hate this stuff.'

'Helps, though.'

'So you say. Anyway, David turns up at the Lodge, big surprise for Russell – lots of man-hugs and so on. He stays the night. Maybe he even tells the others he'll slip away early in the morning. Some story about the shelter giving his room away if he doesn't go back. He sets an alarm for before sunrise and waits for Russell to go up on the treetop walk.'

Chris nodded. 'He shoots Russell then slips out of the house. Makes his way through the town, checking that Zac's there, then heads back to the shelter.'

'Oh, I forgot about Zac,' Clare said. 'You reckon David Fox set him up?'

Chris frowned. 'I can't see how he would know Zac, unless Val is involved. Remember her daughter was in a relationship with Zac's son. Maybe the son messed her about, broke her heart – that sort of thing. I wouldn't want to get on the wrong side of Val.'

Clare felt a sneeze coming on and reached for a tissue. Then she blew her nose and continued. 'It could just be a coincidence. Zac unlucky enough to be in the wrong place at the wrong time.'

'Yeah, you could be right. It's not like Gaby and David need alibis, is it? One's at a wedding, sitting at the same table as you and the DCI...'

'And the other's dead,' Clare finished.

'So we really need to find David Fox and Gaby.'

Chapter 38

'Got the car,' Nita said. 'It's at Hazelton Walls.'

Clare looked at Chris. 'The cottage Luke and Gaby were staying at?'

'Must be.'

'So they're back then.'

'Well, the car is.'

Clare frowned. 'Where is Hazelton anyway?'

'North of Cupar,' Nita said. She took out her phone and navigated to Google maps. 'It's not actually a village. Just a few houses along a country road.'

'Right,' Clare said. 'Nita, take Gary. Chris and I will follow you. Janey, grab someone and bring another car. Blues and twos until we're two miles away then complete silence.'

They rushed out to the cars. 'I'll drive,' Chris said and Clare nodded. Her head still felt thick and she didn't fancy driving through Fife at speed.

Nita took them through Guardbridge, turning right for Leuchars. Traffic slowed in every direction, leaving the way clear for them. As they passed St Michael's crossroads Nita's car began indicating left and Chris followed her onto a side road.

'Shortcut to the A92,' he said as Clare put out a hand to steady herself. A few miles on they passed Rathillet, a small collection of houses. Nita switched off the blue lights and Chris did likewise. Shortly afterwards she indicated to turn right and a sign marked *Hazelton* came into view. The road narrowed and Nita slowed as they drove past a farm and on through a succession of blind bends. Then the road began to rise up and the trees gave way to a long beech hedge on either side.

'Crossroads up here, I think,' Chris said.

As if on cue, Nita's brake lights came on and she indicated left, pulling into the verge. Clare and Chris did likewise with Janey following behind. Nita got out of her car and Clare jumped out to speak to her.

'This is as close as I can get to the tracker location,' she said. 'There are cottages along to the right but it could be in any direction.'

'Okay,' Clare said. 'What kind of car is it?'

'Vauxhall Insignia. Silver.'

Clare said, 'Janey, park broadside across the junction. Any cars come along – check the occupants. Anyone from the house party – get me on the radio. Nita, you carry on to the right and I'll follow. We'll take the cottages one at a time. Just look for the Insignia. If we don't find the car we can start checking houses.'

They jumped back into their cars and Janey prepared to move hers across the junction. As Chris pulled out to follow Nita, Clare's phone began to ring.

'Inspector Mackay?' a female voice said.

Clare cleared her throat then said, 'Yes?'

'Natasha Lynch from Carloway Money. We keep missing each other.'

At last. Russell Fox's financial advisor. Clare flicked the speaker on so Chris could hear. Nita was out of her car now, running up the drive of a cottage, hidden behind a hedge.

'Thanks so much for phoning back,' Clare said. 'I'm hoping you can give me some information.'

Nita came running back out of the drive, shaking her head. She jumped into her car and pulled away again.

Natasha Lynch began to explain under GDPR she wasn't able to give any confidential information, but Clare cut across her.

'No doubt you saw the news of Mr Fox's death in the papers.'

'Yes. Such a shock.'

'We're treating it as murder I'm afraid and, in such cases, GDPR doesn't apply. I realise you may wish to verify this for yourself but we don't have time for that. We need information urgently.'

'In that case, Inspector, tell me what you wish to know.'

Clare was trying to think clearly. What was it she wanted to know?

'Russell's plans to sell his restaurants,' Chris said, pulling into the verge once more as Nita jumped out to check a drive on the other side of the road.

Clare began repeating what Chris had said but Natasha cut across her.

'I heard, thank you. I'm not in the office just now. I've been on annual leave. But I'll tell you what I can recall. Otherwise I can check the file when I'm back in on Monday, if that helps?'

Clare saw Nita reappear and climb back into the car. They were moving again, Chris accelerating to keep up with her as the road became straight for a few hundred yards. There were trees up ahead and Clare wondered if there might be another cottage behind them. Again, Nita signalled and pulled into the verge, Chris nosing in behind. There was a gap in the trees and Nita disappeared into it. Seconds later she was back, signalling to Chris and Clare. Chris reversed back at speed then pulled ahead of Nita's car so he was blocking the drive. Then he killed the engine and they jumped out to join Nita and Gary.

'Inspector?' Natasha prompted. 'Is this a good time? It sounds like you're busy.'

Clare was tempted to tell Natasha she'd call her back but now she had her on the phone she wasn't keen to let her go. She flicked the speaker off and put the phone to her ear, nodding to Chris to join Nita and Gary. 'I understand Mr Fox had planned to sell his restaurants.' she said, resting against the car for a moment.

'That's right,' Natasha said. 'I'd put the word out and we'd had quite a lot of informal interest already. Obviously everything's on hold now.'

'Do you know why he wanted to sell?'

'Number of factors. I think he felt he'd taken the business as far as he could. Time for a change.'

Clare began walking up the drive, the phone still clamped to her ear. She stopped again, her eyes taking in the cottage. It was a pretty one-storey house built in local sandstone with Velux windows in the pitched roof. A porch had been added to the front door to form a shelter. There was a teak-coloured garden seat against one wall and to the right of the cottage a lean-to served as a log store. But her eyes were drawn to the silver Insignia parked outside the front door and she was glad Chris had the foresight to block off the drive. Nita and Gary were heading round the back while Chris waited outside the front porch.

Clare walked up the drive, her eyes everywhere, ear still glued to the phone. 'Did he say what else he was considering?' she asked Natasha.

'As a matter of fact, he did ask me to look into a couple of ideas.'

'Which were?'

Chris was knocking on the front door now. She heard him say *Police. Open up, please.*

Clare moved the phone away from her ear a little to listen for a response from within the house but the knock was met with silence.

Natasha was still speaking and Clare put the phone to hear ear again.

'I believe he had a business contact in the licensed trade,' her voice said. 'Russell said his contact was interested in acquiring a small chain of pubs in Glasgow's south side.'

'He was moving from restaurants into pubs?'

'Technically, yes.'

Chris was looking in the windows now, shielding the sun with his hands.

'He planned to put up 60 per cent of the capital,' Natasha went on, 'but he told me he'd be a sleeping partner. His contact would run the pubs. Russell would be an investor in name only. I looked into it for him,' she said, 'and it seemed a sound enough investment.'

There was a shout from Nita, and Chris ran round the back of the cottage. Clare followed him, walking briskly. 'And the other investment?'

'Ah, that one was a bit riskier. He wanted to invest in a media company.'

'Clare,' Chris called.

She broke into a run. 'Which company?' she asked Natasha, conscious she only had seconds.

There was a pause then Natasha said, 'Odd name: *It's A Gas Productions.* I think his brother-in-law was involved with it.'

'Luke Gasparini?' Clare said. She was round the back of the house now, Nita trying the door.

Chris was looking round and he darted across to a small wooden shed. He pulled back a bolt securing the door and stepped inside, reappearing moments later with a garden spade.

'Yes, that's him,' Natasha said. 'I did warn him against it. Family investments are rarely the product of clear thinking. But he was set on the idea.'

Chris was at the back door now and he forced the edge of the spade between the door and the frame. The door creaked and finally burst open and they rushed inside.

Clare, still in the garden said, 'Ms Lynch, I have to go now but I will call again to discuss this in more detail.'

'Of course.'

She was about to end the call then a thought struck her. 'The other investment – the chain of pubs – who was Mr Fox's contact? The person he planned to invest with?'

'In here!' Chris called.

Clare dashed in, past the broken door, following the sound of Chris's voice. She moved into a small bedroom at the back of the cottage. It was a bright room, cheerfully decorated with yellow walls and floral curtains. There were watercolours dotted around and a traditional mantelpiece which had been painted a rich cream. It wasn't a large room and was dominated by an oak-framed double bed. And, on top of the bed, fully clothed, her eyes closed, lay Gaby Fox.

Chris had his fingers on her neck, feeling for a pulse. He was shaking his head and then suddenly he said, 'It's there. Faint but it's there.' He turned to Gary. 'Call an ambulance. Tell them east of Hazelton Walls – to look for our cars. And quickly.'

Nita moved to the bedside cabinet where a half empty glass of water stood next to a small cardboard box with a pharmacy label on the outside.

'Don't touch it,' Clare warned.

'Sorry?' Natasha said.

'Sorry, Ms Lynch, not you. I'm afraid I really do have to go.'

'I have that name for you – if you want…'

Clare waited.

'It's a Mr Gerrard. Douglas Gerrard.'

Chapter 39

The paramedics headed off to Ninewells Hospital, siren blaring.

'Go after them,' Clare said to Janey and Bill. 'Stick to her like glue.'

Janey headed off after the ambulance, a photo of the pharmacy box on her phone to show the doctors at A&E.

'Reckon she'll pull through?' Chris said.

Clare shook her head. 'No idea, Chris. She was barely breathing.'

'Pupils sluggish, too.' He frowned. 'Attack of conscience? Or panic, maybe? Realising she'd told Luke everything and he must have come to us?'

Clare's eyes narrowed. 'I'm not so sure.' She tugged at her ear lobe, trying to unblock her ear. 'Where is Luke? We need to get hold of him.'

Chris took out his phone. 'I'll give Jim a call. Get him to put something out on the radio.'

Clare studied the house while Chris made the call.

'Jim's on it,' he said, putting his phone back in his pocket. 'Seems Luke managed to arrange another hire car. Had it dropped off at the station. Jim's ringing round hire companies now to get the details.'

'There's someone else we need to find,' Clare said. 'David Fox.'

'You reckon he's done this? Fed Gaby an overdose?'

'Dunno, Chris. But we have to find him.'

They were walking back to the car now. Gary was on his phone, explaining the location to a locksmith.

'What now, boss?' Nita said.

Clare looked back at the cottage. 'We'd better get in touch with the owners. Can you track them down please, Nita?' She turned to Chris. 'And there's something else doesn't add up.'

They climbed into the car. Chris went to start it but Clare put a hand out to stop him. 'Hold on, I need to think. That phone call…'

'The financial advisor?'

'Yeah. Russell had discussed his plans to sell the restaurants with her. Seems he wanted to invest the money in two other enterprises.'

'Which were?'

'One was a partnership, taking over a small chain of pubs on Glasgow's south side. Russell planned to be a sleeping partner – put up the money but stay out of running them.'

Chris raised an eyebrow. 'Pubs, eh?'

'Uh-huh. Want to guess the other partner?'

'Not Doug Gerrard?'

'Yup.'

Chris sat mulling this over. 'I'm not sure what that means, though.'

'Nor me. Except…'

'What?'

'Well, with Russell dead, that won't happen now. And I'd very much like to know how Doug Gerrard feels about that.'

'Pretty pissed off, I'd imagine,' Chris said. 'He'll have to find another backer now. Unless…'

'Yeah?'

'Well, if Gaby inherits Russell's estate she might have wanted to go along with his wishes. Give Doug the money for the pubs.'

Clare considered this. 'It's possible. It wouldn't be quick, though. There's all the legal stuff. Then the restaurants will have to be sold. It'll take time.'

'So Doug Gerrard doesn't benefit by Russell's death.'

'Nope. Quite the opposite.'

They sat silent for a few moments. Then Chris said, 'What was the other investment?'

Clare smiled. 'A media company.'

'Not Luke.'

'The very same. His production company. So he's also affected by Russell's death, although, again, Gaby could still agree to finance it.'

Chris rubbed his chin. 'I'm struggling to see why anyone would kill Russell Fox. Luke and Doug both lose out by his death. And, as for Luke's story about Gaby and David planning to shoot Russell to spare his suffering – it's a bit far-fetched.'

Clare nodded. 'Mind you, the unknown factor in all this is…'

'David Fox,' Chris finished.

'Absolutely. He had the opportunity and, while we can only guess at his motive, if he really is still alive, I'd say pretending to be dead for seventeen years is pretty bloody weird.'

'You still fancy him for shooting Russell, then?' Chris said.

'You got a better idea?'

'Nope. Let's just hope Gaby recovers.'

Clare's phone began to ring. 'Janey,' she said. 'Hiya. What's happening?'

'She's being assessed now,' Janey said. 'Still alive. Medics plan to get some activated charcoal into her ASAP.'

'Okay, thanks, Janey. Stay with her and keep me posted. I want to know if she recovers consciousness.' Clare ended the call and turned back to Chris.

'Charcoal?' he said.

'Yeah. Apparently it neutralises the effect of the sleeping pills. That's if they can get it into her fast enough.'

'Every day's a school day,' Chris said.

Clare's phone began to ring again. She glanced at the display. Sara.

'Boss... you'd better get back here.'

Chapter 40

Sara was at the front desk when they entered the station.

'Where is he?'

'Interview room one.'

'Has he said anything?'

Sara shook her head. 'Only that he wants to speak to the officer in charge of the Fox case.' She glanced towards the interview rooms. 'I've requested a solicitor – just in case.'

'Good work, Sara. Thanks.'

The PC smiled. 'I'll get you another Lemsip. You're looking pretty white. And the solicitor won't be here for another ten minutes.'

Quarter of an hour later they sat down in front of the man who for the last seventeen years had apparently been dead.

David Fox.

Clare had to hand it to Zac, his description to the photofit officer had been pretty spot on.

'Where's my sister?' was his opening remark.

Clare didn't answer this directly. Instead, she went through the formalities of setting up the tape. She decided, in view of Luke Gasparini's statement, that she would caution him. He seemed frustrated by this and asked again for Gaby.

Again, Clare left the question unanswered. 'I gather you told my officer your name is David Fox. Is that correct?'

'Yes. I am David Fox,' he said, his voice rising. 'It really is me and I'm not dead.' He ran a hand through this hair. 'I just want to know if Gaby's okay. I've been trying to reach her but she's not picking up.'

Clare regarded him. His distress appeared genuine and she took pity on him. 'Gaby is in hospital just now.'

He rose to his feet and the solicitor gently touched his arm. He glanced at her then sat down again. 'In hospital? What's happened to her?'

Clare said, 'At the moment I can't say too much but I have an officer at the hospital. As soon as there's any news I'll let you know.'

He sat for a moment, taking this in then said, 'Is she in danger?'

'I'm sorry, Mr Fox, I don't know any more than that.' She gave him what she hoped was a reassuring smile. 'But she's in the best place.'

He nodded. 'Sorry, it's just, well, I hadn't seen her for so long and now we're back in touch…'

Clare scanned her notes, wondering where to begin with this interview. And then she remembered her boss from CID when she'd been a newly promoted detective sergeant. A crusty old DI. *Always start at the beginning, hen*, he'd say.

'Perhaps we could start with the tsunami, David. Can you tell us about that?'

'It's so long ago now,' he said. 'Not that you forget.'

'Just what you can remember.'

'Well, you probably know I was in Thailand that year. For Christmas. Brilliant time. Met a great crowd. We had

Christmas on the beach. They said *stay a while*. But I'd always planned to head north. So, I thanked them for their company, wished them well and headed off that night.' He looked down for a moment, as if the memory was a painful one. 'Never saw them again.' His voice was husky. 'They probably all died the next day. Someone was definitely looking out for me. No doubt about that.'

'When did you hear about it?'

'A few hours after it happened,' David said. 'It was everywhere. And I kept thinking of all the lovely folk I'd met.' He frowned. 'I just wanted to get away – forget about it, you know?'

Clare nodded. 'And then?'

He spread his hands. 'I dunno, I sort of got used to being off-grid. No responsibilities, no ties. I bummed my way round Asia.' He smiled. 'Have you been? It's the most wonderful continent.'

Chris said, 'Didn't you miss your family? Gaby and Russell?'

A spasm of pain crossed his face at the mention of Russell's name. Then he said, 'Gaby and Russ – they were on different paths to me. They were part of the machine.' He shook his head. 'Wasn't for me. And I thought, if I went back, I'd get sucked in. Responsibilities, you know?'

Clare wondered about this. She couldn't imagine not knowing anything about her loved ones, being out of touch for so many years. Maybe it was true what the three men had said, that David was a bit odd. 'Were you aware you'd been declared dead?'

'No. But I suppose it makes sense.'

'And is this your first time back in the country?'

He nodded. 'Yeah.'

'What made you decide to come home?'

He hesitated for a moment then he met Clare's eye. 'For years after the tsunami, Gaby sent me messages.' He shook his head. 'I never replied. Not sure why. But I liked getting the messages. And then they stopped. It wasn't hard to keep track of Gaby, though. Even thousands of miles away. She's in the papers every few weeks – interviews, gossip, all that. And that's how I found out about my dad.' He broke off for a moment then went on. 'You probably know he's in a care home. Dementia. Gaby spoke about it in an interview, start of the year.' David sighed audibly then went on. 'She said he's not great. Some days he doesn't even know her; and that got me thinking. It didn't seem right, you know, leaving her to do it all. And then Gaby's girl, Sacha, I've never seen her.' He rubbed his chin. 'Maybe you can have enough travelling. Maybe there comes a time when family starts to matter more. So I began to think – about coming back. I knew Russ was forty this year. Suddenly the time seemed right. So one day I phoned Gaby. I still had her number, you know? Anyway, I called her, said it was me and that I was thinking of coming home.'

'How did she react?'

'Pretty shocked. And then she started to cry and said she couldn't wait to tell everyone. But I said no. I wanted it kept quiet. I'd come back for the party, catch up with my dad, meet Sacha and Luke. But I didn't want anything official. None of that *back from the dead* stuff.'

'Mind if I ask why not?' Clare said.

He shrugged, 'I wasn't sure I'd want to stay. And, if folk got to know I wasn't dead, well, maybe I'd get sucked in. Wouldn't be able to go away again. So I told Gaby I'd keep my options open and she was to tell as few folk as possible.'

'Did she agree to that?' Clare asked.

'Didn't give her much option. I said it was my way or not at all. So she agreed. Said she'd get Russ and his pals there on the Thursday and she'd tell them there was a surprise but no more than that.'

'Did you stay at the Lodge?'

'Only the Friday night – after the party, ye know? They don't like you coming into the shelter the worse for drink, and I'd had a few.'

Chris said, 'Mr Fox, why did you stay at the shelter? I'm sure Gaby would have sorted something out for you.'

'Why not? I am homeless, after all. And they're a good bunch of lads. I did some work in the town, earned a few bob for them. I like to give a bit back when I can.'

'You had your own room,' Clare said.

'Yeah. I told Gaby where I'd be staying and she sent me some cash care of the warden. Padded envelope. Meant I had a bit of privacy.' He smiled. 'Nice, after years on the road.'

Clare nodded at this. She felt she was starting to understand David Fox. 'I'd like you to tell us about the party now. On Friday night at the Lodge. Could you start by telling us when you arrived?'

'I turned up about four in the afternoon,' he said. 'Gaby and Luke had already gone to their wedding but I told her I'd see them when they got back on the Sunday. Obviously, that didn't happen.'

'And how did your brother react?' Clare asked.

He smiled at the memory. 'Shuda seen his face. It was a picture.' He looked at Clare. 'I don't mind admitting, we both shed a few tears.' He smiled again at this then went on. 'And I'd taken my guitar along so I gave them a couple of songs.' He stopped for a moment, as if recalling. 'It was a good night.'

'You did have a guitar, then?' Clare said.

He looked surprised. 'Yeah. Any reason I shouldn't?'

'No reason. Just curious.' Clare's throat was becoming dry and she cleared it. 'It's odd,' she went on. 'No one at the Lodge mentioned you when we spoke to them.'

He nodded. 'That's down to me. I asked them not to say anything. And then one of the other lads let slip they'd arranged for some women to make the party go with a swing.' His face darkened. 'I wasn't down for that kind of thing. I don't hold with using women for sex. Saw enough of that on my travels.' He shook his head. 'And, like I said, I wasn't sure how long I'd stick around and I didn't want any of the women asking about me. So, I helped myself to some of the food and drink and went off to my room.'

'You didn't think you were missing out?' Chris said.

He laughed. 'After years on the road, bunking in hostels, no privacy and all that, you've no idea how good it felt to have a room to myself, especially in a house like that. And, like I said, it kind of suits me, being dead.'

Clare's head was thumping now, despite Sara's Lemsip, and she was trying to work out where to go with this interview. Maybe she should have left it to Chris and Tony. She forced herself to concentrate. 'Mr Fox, how did you enter the country without a passport?'

He suppressed a smile 'That would be telling, Inspector.'

'We could charge you.'

'To be honest, I'm past caring. I just want to know my sister's okay.'

Clare studied him. Was he telling the truth? Or was Luke's version of events true? If Luke was to be believed, then the more David Fox talked, the more likely he was to trip himself up. 'Where did you spend Thursday night?' she asked.

'Thursday? Erm, nowhere really. It was a nice night. Rain had cleared up so I walked till dusk. Passed a farm and I found a barn. Dossed down in the corner.' He shrugged. 'Amazing what you get used to.'

'And Friday?'

'Gaby phoned. Said Luke had found a quiet cottage – they planned to stay a few days. Nice place.' He nodded. 'Chance to catch up properly. Without the other lads, you know?'

'Where was this?'

'Hazelton-something, she said. I'd never heard of it but I gave Gaby my location and she sent a taxi.'

'And was it?'

'Was it what?'

'A chance to catch up?'

He looked at them. 'Course it was. I mean she'd been through a hellish time; and we'd a lot of years to make up for.'

'And that was the first time you'd met Gaby's husband?'

'Luke? Yeah. He was there, obviously. But he was pretty good about it. Left us alone for a fair bit so we could talk.' He smiled at this. 'I think Gaby appreciated it. Seems a decent bloke.'

Clare glanced at Chris, wondering what David Fox would have said if he'd heard Luke's statement... was it just yesterday? She closed her eyes for a moment, wishing her head would clear. What was the truth, here? Then she forced herself to concentrate. 'And this morning?'

'Luke and Gaby said they planned to stay in the cottage for a few more days. Before going back down south, you know? I think Luke had some business in Scotland. And he seemed to think Gaby needed the rest.'

'You didn't want to stay on with them? Spend a bit more time with Gaby?'

'Course I did. But I needed to come back here too. I'd missed a couple of guys at the shelter when I left and I wanted to say a proper goodbye.'

'And then?'

He shrugged. 'I wasn't sure, really. Maybe visit my dad. Tell the staff I was a family friend, that sort of thing.' His voice was thick, suddenly, and he cleared his throat. 'I thought, even if he didn't know me, I'd know him.' Then he frowned. 'But then I tried to get hold of Gaby to ask about visiting and she didn't answer. Look, I'm worried about her. Why's she in hospital? What's wrong? Is Luke with her? I don't have his phone number.'

The solicitor cleared her throat. 'I do think Mr Fox has the right to know what's happened to his sister.'

Clare nodded. 'It's possible,' she said, 'that Gaby's taken an overdose. We found her unconscious with an empty box of pills beside her.'

David stared. 'Gaby? An overdose? No. That can't be right. She... she just wouldn't.' He broke off for a moment, then he said, 'There's Sacha. Gaby wouldn't leave her – she just wouldn't. I know Sacha's at boarding school and all that, but Gaby loves her so much. She'd never do anything to hurt her.' He shook his head. 'Whatever you think, Inspector, it's not that. Gaby's just not the type.'

—

They left him to speak with the solicitor.

'What do you reckon?' Chris said.

Clare thought for a moment. 'He seems genuine enough.'

'Yeah, I thought so. But who's telling the truth? David or Luke?'

Clare was frowning. 'What I don't get is… if Gaby knew David would be at the Lodge for the Friday night party, why keep it from Luke? After all, if Russell hadn't died, David would probably have been at the Lodge when Gaby and Luke returned from the wedding. Once the three friends knew about David there would be no reason not to tell him. But Luke said he only found out about David yesterday – at the cottage. So, one of them's lying. And the only other person who knows the truth is in Ninewells Hospital, having charcoal poured into her.' She glanced at the desk and saw Jim poring over a sheaf of papers. 'No news, Jim?'

'Nothing from the hospital, Clare, and no sign of Luke's new hire car yet. But I've got the reg now and the hire company are checking the tracker. There's always the chance he'll ping an ANPR camera, too.'

'Good work, Jim.'

'No bother. Oh, I think Nita was looking for you.'

Clare found Nita in the incident room. 'You wanted me?'

'Yes, boss. About that cottage, the one at Hazelton, it's managed by a letting agency but the owner is Doug Gerrard.'

Clare's expression hardened. 'Get onto Glasgow for me please, Nita. Baird Street. Tell them I want Doug Gerrard again. And this time I want him brought through here.'

Chapter 41

'Any news of Gaby?' David Fox asked as they re-entered the interview room.

Clare shook her head then she restarted the tape. 'Mr Fox, I must remind you that you're still under caution. Do you understand?'

David exhaled audibly and waved this away. 'Yes, of course. I just want to know about my sister.'

Chris said, 'As soon as we have any news we'll let you know.'

David's face softened. 'Sorry. It's… I'm worried, you know?'

Clare said, 'Mr Fox, I am going to ask you a question and I want you to think very carefully before you answer.'

David's eyes widened. 'Erm, okay.'

'Mr Fox, did you kill your brother Russell Fox?'

He stared at her for a moment, as though trying to process this. Then he said, 'Of course I bloody didn't. You think if I'd come all this way to put a bullet in his head I'd still be hanging around? That I'd come voluntarily into the station?' He glanced at his solicitor. 'You guys are unbelievable. You must be even more stupid than you look. I mean… what the actual fuck?' His face was scarlet now and the solicitor put a restraining hand on his arm.

Clare said, 'We recovered some DNA evidence from the murder site which we know has come from a male.'

David's brow creased. 'Can't you tell whose it is? Put out a warrant for him – or whatever you call it?'

The solicitor said, 'What is the evidence, Inspector? And how does it tie the owner of the DNA to the crime scene?'

Clare watched David Fox carefully. 'The DNA was on a gun cartridge which we believe was ejected from the murder weapon when Mr Fox was shot dead. Unfortunately, it doesn't match anyone on our database.'

David's stared. 'And you're telling me because? You surely don't think…'

'As I said, we know it's a man's DNA and we've taken samples from the other guests at the Lodge.'

His eyes blazed. 'Then take my DNA. Take it right now and send it off to your poxy lab. Then we'll see how wrong you are.'

–

Sara was despatched to take David Fox's DNA sample over to the lab in Dundee. Chris watched her go then turned back to Clare. 'So what now?'

She stood thinking. What indeed? 'We can't release him,' she said. 'Not until we have the result back.'

Chris shook his head. 'Even if they rush it through, Clare, it's going to take a good few hours.'

'I know. But—' she was interrupted by a shout from Sara.

'Janey on the phone, boss. Gaby's regained consciousness.'

'Yes!' She took the phone from Sara. 'Janey? How is she?'

'Pretty groggy. A bit hoarse, too. They're keeping her in but the doc's agreed we can speak to her.'

'On my way.'

Chris managed to find a parking space in one of the closer car parks and they headed down the concrete steps towards the main hospital entrance.

'Acute Medical Unit.' Clare indicated the overhead sign.

'Let's take the lift,' Chris said. 'The way your head is I don't trust you on the stairs.'

'Thought you were scared of lifts?'

'I'm more scared of you nosediving two floors, to be honest.'

Clare had to admit she was feeling distinctly wobbly after walking from the car park and she hadn't the energy to argue.

As the enormous lift door trundled back Chris said, 'How do you want to play it?'

'Let's start from Thursday night at the cottage. See whose version her story supports.'

The lift began to descend the two floors to the unit and Clare put out a hand to support herself. Chris gripped her elbow. 'Seriously, Clare, you need to go home.'

'Soon as we've spoken to Gaby.'

The doors trundled open and they emerged onto a landing, following signs for the Unit. It was as busy as Clare had ever seen it, medical staff rushing back and forward A nurse at the reception desk was on the phone and Clare glanced at a whiteboard, studying the list of patient names. Then she saw *G Fox*. 'Looks like they've got her in a side room. At least they've not put her full name on the board.'

'Good idea,' Chris said. 'Publicity and all that.'

They walked round the unit until they saw Janey and Bill standing outside one of the rooms. 'We okay to go in?' Clare said.

Janey nodded. 'Doc said not too long, though. She's a bit hoarse from the tube down her throat so talking might be an issue.'

'Thanks, Janey. Could you radio the station and get a couple of uniforms up here? I don't want her to have any visitors – not even the husband. I need someone outside this room at all times. As soon as the uniforms arrive you can get back to the station.'

Janey took out her phone. 'I'll see if Dundee can help. Be quicker than coming from St Andrews.'

Clare left Janey to her call and pushed open the door to the room. Gaby Fox lay on top of the bed, eyes closed. There was a plaster across the back of her hand, securing a drip, a bruise spreading out from beneath the tape. She was pale and her hair, normally so thick and lustrous, sat flat against her head, almost unrecognisable as the celebrity who graced the nation's TV screens on weekday mornings.

Chris moved to pull two chairs over to the bed and, at this, Gaby opened her eyes. She frowned, as though trying to place them. Then she said, 'Inspector?' Her voice was croaky.

Clare smiled. 'How are you, Gaby?'

Gaby looked down, examining her hand. 'Oh, you know… apparently I'll be fine.' She lifted her gaze to meet Clare's eye. 'I've to see a shrink, though.' She attempted a smile. 'They seem to think I wanted to… well, harm myself.'

Clare took one of the chairs from Chris and sat down next to the bed. 'And did you?' she said, her voice as gentle as she could manage. 'Did you want to harm yourself?'

A tear appeared at the corner of Gaby's eye and she shook her head. 'I don't know what happened,' she said. 'They told me I'd taken too many sleeping pills.'

'You don't remember?'

Gaby's brow creased. 'I don't know,' she said. 'I must have. I suppose. But I hardly ever take them. I didn't even know I had enough to be dangerous. I was tired,' she went on. 'Maybe the strain of what happened... maybe it was catching up with me.' She hoisted herself up the bed on her elbows. Clare leaned across to pull up her pillow and Gaby sank back on it.

'Thanks,' she said, clearing her throat. She looked at Clare. 'I'm not sure what else I can tell you.'

Clare smiled. 'Maybe, if you feel up to it, we could go back to when you left the hotel. I understood you were booked on the sleeper to London.'

She nodded. 'We were. But then Luke said neither of us was fit to go back to work. He'd phoned London and said we'd be staying on a bit.' She paused then said, 'I was surprised he hadn't mentioned it. But then he said he'd kept it quiet because he didn't want anyone to know.' She gave an apologetic smile. 'I know everyone thinks it's a cheek when someone like me complains. But it can be hard to find a bit of privacy, especially at a time like this. So he booked us into a cottage for a few nights.' She flicked a glance at Clare then away again.

Clare looked at Chris then said, 'Gaby, perhaps you could tell us about your brother David.'

Gaby's colour rose and she hesitated.

Clare said, 'It might help if I tell you we've spoken to your brother today.'

'So you know?'

'That he's still alive? Yes, we do.'

'Where is he?' Gaby asked.

'Back at the station. He's helping us piece together what's happened over the past few days. But I'd like to hear your account of it.'

Gaby nodded. 'What would you like to know?'

'The cottage. You said it was Luke's idea, yes?'

'It was. But, when I thought about it, it made sense. It had two bedrooms so there was room for David too. He joined us on the Friday. Gave us a bit more time together.'

Clare's brow creased. 'Just to be clear, Gaby, your husband Luke booked the cottage and said there would be room for David as well?'

'Yes. It was so kind of Luke. David had sworn me to secrecy about him coming back, you know? But once we were on our way to the wedding, I told Luke.'

'How did he react?' Clare asked.

'Oh, shocked, of course,' Gaby said. 'Asking me if I was sure, that it wasn't someone pretending to be David. And then thrilled – once he got over the shock. Excited for me.' She nodded. 'I think he was as pleased as I was.'

Clare wondered about that but she just smiled. 'So, Luke said there was room for David at the cottage?'

Gaby nodded. 'It was so kind of him. I didn't know what David's plans were. He said he wanted to spend some time with Dad, and to get to know Luke and Sacha. But I honestly wasn't sure how long he'd be around. Itchy feet, you know? I just wanted to have a bit of time with him. Time to catch up.'

'And did you?' Clare asked. 'Catch up, I mean?'

'We did. We had a meal together then Luke went out for a walk. It gave David and I time to speak properly.' She smiled. 'Oh, it was so good to be with him again. Especially with what had happened to Russell…' She broke off then said, 'David – he wanted to know all about Russell. About his time in prison, the restaurants and his friends, of course.'

'What was his impression of Russell's friends?'

Gaby frowned. 'I'm not sure. He seemed to think maybe you hadn't investigated them closely enough. He kept saying was I sure the three of them could be trusted.'

'And what did you say?' Clare asked.

Gaby shrugged. 'I said they were Russell's best friends. Of course we trusted them. And then he asked Luke the same question. He seemed fixated on them, as though he really did suspect them of being involved.'

'What did Luke think?'

'Same as me,' Gaby said. 'That they were Russell's oldest friends. All the same.' She broke off for a moment then said, 'It does make you think, something like this.' She raised her eyes to meet Clare's. 'Makes you wonder who you can trust.'

Clare nodded. 'And the next morning?'

'We had breakfast together. Luke mentioned some business he had. Said he'd be gone most of the day.'

'And David?'

Gaby frowned. 'He wanted to go back to St Andrews. Something about saying goodbye to the folk at the homeless shelter.' She smiled. 'He said they'd been so kind. I gave him a bit of money to tide him over and off he went. Luke offered him a lift but he said he'd rather go under his own steam. So we hugged and said we'd meet again once he knew his plans.'

'So David left the cottage,' Clare said. 'What did you do next?'

Gaby wrinkled her brow as if trying to remember. 'Luke went to change. Then he called a taxi. I told him to take the hire car. I wasn't planning to go anywhere. But he said he wanted to leave it for me in case I changed my mind.'

'And then he left?' Clare asked.

Gaby frowned again. 'Actually, we had coffee first. The taxi was going to be half an hour so Luke made a pot and suggested I have a lie down.'

Clare glanced at Chris. 'And did he leave you to drink it?'

'Erm,' Gaby considered this. 'Actually, I think he was still there while I had it. He brought a tray through to the bedroom and we chatted while I drank. I think he topped me up.'

'Do you remember what you chatted about?' Clare asked.

Her face softened then she said, 'We spoke about Dad, you know? Once things are settled with Russell, there will be some money. The restaurants are doing well. They'll sell easily and I don't need the money. I make more than enough. Obviously Russell's will only benefits me – I know that. But it seems fair to share the inheritance with David.'

'How did Luke feel about that?' Clare asked.

'He agreed with me. It's only fair, after all. Then there's my poor dad; he's too ill to be helped now. But I'd like to give some of Russell's money to a dementia charity. I mentioned it to Luke and we're going to check it out.'

Clare seemed about to speak then she stopped.

Chris glanced at her then he turned to Gaby. 'The coffee, Gaby, do you remember taking any tablets with it?'

She shook her head. 'No. But I suppose it must have been all the upset – over Russell, you know? Maybe I was tired and forgot.' She yawned. 'Sorry, I'm just so sleepy...'

Chris smiled. 'We won't keep you much longer.' He glanced at Clare again then he went on. 'Did Luke say where he was going?'

'Sorry, no. I had the feeling it might be Glasgow, though.'

'Any reason for that?'

'He has contacts through there. I just assumed...'

Clare suddenly remembered Gaby and Luke's daughter. The one who'd been part of the singing group at Tom's wedding. 'Maybe visiting your daughter?' she said.

Gaby shook her head. 'No, it wouldn't be that. Sacha's in France just now. A school trip. They left the day after the wedding. Not back till next week.'

The door opened and a nurse came in. 'Just a few more minutes,' she said, 'if you don't mind.'

Clare didn't reply and Chris nudged her. 'Oh, sorry,' she said. Then she smiled at Gaby. 'I think we're done here.' She rose from the chair. 'We'll be in touch, Gaby. Try to get some rest in the meantime.'

Chapter 42

'Something on your mind?' Chris said, as they waited for the lift. An elderly man in a dressing gown shuffled up to wait with them, cigarettes in hand. Going out for a smoke, Clare thought.

'Once we're back in the car,' she said, her voice low.

They emerged from the lift and made their way through the corridors towards the main concourse.

'Rumour is,' Chris said, 'when this hospital was built, one of the doctors drove an MG car down the corridors.'

'I don't believe a word of it.'

'Absolutely true.'

'So you say.'

They were back at the car now. Clare pulled on her seat belt and looked at Chris who was making no effort to start the car. 'Erm, in your own time, Sergeant.'

'Not until you tell me what's going through your mind.'

'Money, Chris. Russell Fox's money.'

'What about it?'

Clare fished in her pocket for a tissue and blew her nose. Then she said, 'Luke Gasparini is lying. Agreed?'

'I reckon so. David and Gaby's statements corroborate each other. Admittedly, if Luke is telling the truth, then their stories would match. But that bit about the two of them hatching a plot to carry out a mercy killing on their brother – Luke fleeing for his life. I don't buy it.'

'Okay,' Clare said. 'Then there's Gaby. She denies taking an overdose.'

'That could be embarrassment,' Chris said. 'It's not uncommon in people who survive overdoses. Maybe she's worried about the publicity – if it gets out. Might harm her career.'

Clare considered this. 'Yeah, that's possible. But she claims Luke made her the pot of coffee and topped up her cup while she was resting in the bedroom. There was no sign of a coffee pot when we got there. Or a cup. There was a glass and the pill box but no cup.'

Chris nodded slowly. 'So he washed it up?'

'Yep. I reckon he drugged Gaby.'

'Motive?'

'That's what we have to work out,' Clare said. 'But the more I think about it, the more I think Luke's trying to frame David for the murder.'

Chris started the engine and pulled on his seat belt. 'I'm not so sure. Remember we took everyone in the house party's DNA.'

'Except David Fox.'

'Of course,' Chris said. 'But we'll have that back from the lab pretty soon; and remember Raymond said it wasn't from a relative of Russell's.' He was about to draw out of the space when Clare put out a hand to stop him.

'Chris.'

'Yeah?'

'There's still one person whose DNA we haven't tested.' She turned to face him. 'We've been so caught up with Luke and David – Gaby's overdose – we forgot about the security guard. We still don't have Mark Mooney's DNA.'

–

'No sign of Doug Gerrard,' Sara said, 'but they'll let us know.'

'I want him brought here, remember,' Clare said. 'If they can't spare someone to drive him through one of you will have to go.' She stood thinking for a moment then said, 'Luke Gasparini?'

Sara shook her head. 'Not yet, boss. Hopefully soon, though.'

Chris was hovering. 'You going to update Tony?' he said, nodding at Clare's office door.

Clare looked at the door but found she hadn't the energy to explain everything to Tony. Instead, she said, 'Has Mark Mooney showed up yet?'

'Sorry, boss. Wife says he's still away.'

Clare stood thinking for a moment. Then she picked up the car keys again. 'Come on. Let's go and speak to the wife.'

–

As they walked up to the front door of the house in Warrack Street they were met with the aroma of barbeque smoke.

'God, but I'm hungry,' Chris said. 'Fancy stopping for some food after this?'

Clare shivered. Food was the last thing on her mind. 'Let's just see how we get on, yeah?'

'Just because you have the lurgy.'

There was no answer from the doorbell so Clare moved to a high wooden side gate and peered over. 'Hello?' she called.

The blonde woman they'd seen on Sunday when they'd questioned Mark was standing bent over a barbeque, rearranging burgers. The two little boys were sitting on a wall a few feet away, clutching pouches of Capri-Sun juice. She looked up at the sound of Clare's voice then glanced back at the boys. 'You two stay put,' she said, raising a warning finger. The boys nodded then whispered and giggled, sharing some private joke. The woman walked over to the gate, tongs still in hand.

'I won't keep you,' Clare said. 'I just wondered if Mark's back yet?'

'Sorry, no. Probably late tonight, or morning at worst. I think he's working tomorrow night.'

'And you don't know where he's gone?' Clare asked.

'I don't. He did mention Glencoe but that wasn't definite.'

Clare smiled. 'We'd like to speak to him as soon as possible,' she said. 'Do you have his mobile number?'

'I do. But he's out of signal, wherever he is. What do you want him for?'

'We've had some information about a car seen near the Lodge,' Clare lied. 'Just wondering if Mark saw it at all.'

She seemed satisfied with this and felt in her jeans for her mobile. She tapped it a few times then held it out for Chris to copy the number.

'Thanks,' he said. 'Got it now.'

The woman indicated the barbeque. 'If there's nothing else…'

'Just one thing,' Chris said, 'Mark was working on Friday night, wasn't he?'

'Yeah.'

'Was it a late one?'

'Think so. Why?'

Chris ignored this. 'Just wondering what time he came home.'

She stared at him for a moment. Then she said, 'Actually, I wasn't here. I'd gone to see my mum. Down near Peebles. Mark said he'd be working most of the weekend so why didn't I take the boys to see her.'

'So you were away on Friday?'

'Yeah, we left about five.'

Chris smiled, keeping his tone light. 'When did you get back?'

'Sunday morning. Why?'

He shrugged. 'No reason. Just being nosey. Comes with the job.'

She laughed and went back to her burgers. Clare and Chris walked slowly to the car.

'So,' Chris said, 'Mark Mooney has no alibi for Saturday morning.'

'He does not! He could have been up there all night. Plenty of time to slip up to the top floor, retrieve the gun. Assuming it was hidden there.'

'Or he could have brought it,' Chris said. 'No one's going to ask the security guard what's in the boot of his car.'

Clare nodded. 'The sooner we get his DNA to the lab the happier I'll be.'

Chapter 43

'Got something, boss,' Janey said, as they entered the incident room.

'Yeah?' Clare wandered over to Janey's desk and sank down in a chair.

'Luke Gasparini's finances. Couple of things come to light.'

'Go on.'

'First of all I called a pal who works for the Met and she spoke to a contact in media circles. Seems Luke has taken a bit of a gamble on his next production.'

Clare frowned. 'Gamble, how?'

'He's signed a big name for a start, half the fee upfront. And word is the production costs are spiralling out of control. So he secured a substantial loan from a third party, just over a month ago. We did see that when we checked initially; it's not that unusual for these companies. But my pal's contact reckons the loan will only keep them afloat for six months, tops. And once something like that gets around investors start pulling out.'

'So he could go bust?' Clare asked.

Janey nodded. 'Quite possibly. Especially if the loan's called in.'

'This guy, Luke,' Chris said, 'strikes me as pretty industry-savvy. This isn't his first big production. He'd surely have known to keep a tight rein on the finances.'

'Could be he was banking on Russell's investment,' Janey said. 'Six months would tide him over until the restaurants were sold.'

'Then Russell died,' Clare said.

Janey nodded. 'Exactly. But he knows Gaby will inherit. My guess is he planned to tell her about the loan and hoped she'd repay it for him.'

'Then Gaby announces she's giving half the money to David and some of her share to charity. That could mean the end for Luke's company.' Clare sat thinking for a minute then she said, 'Janey, who's the lender?'

A smile spread across Janey's face. 'The company's called DG Investments.'

'DG?' Chris said. 'You're joking!'

Clare shook her head slowly. 'Doug Gerrard.' She smiled back at Janey. 'It's him, isn't it?'

'Yep.'

'There's your motive, then,' Chris said.

'There's more,' Janey went on.

'Yeah?'

'That boarding school – they're six months behind with the fees.'

Clare gaped. 'Seriously?'

'Yep.'

Chris frowned. 'I could be wrong, but I reckon Gaby doesn't know that.'

'I'm sure she doesn't,' Clare said. 'She told us she didn't need Russell's money.'

'So Luke's been dipping into the joint account to keep his company afloat,' Chris said.

Clare put a hand on Janey's desk and pulled herself to her feet. 'Come on,' she nodded to Chris. 'Let's update Tony.'

'Just give me the gist of it, then get off home,' Tony said. 'Before you infect the whole damn team.'

Clare sat down and pulled her jacket round her. 'It's freezing in here. Why is this station always so cold?'

'Never mind that. Where are we?'

Clare sneezed and Tony passed a box of tissues across the desk.

'I'll explain,' Chris said. 'Basically we have two different versions of events. Luke Gasparini claims Gaby and David Fox conspired to kill Russell. But David denies this. Says he's no idea who killed Russell.'

'And Gaby?' Tony asked.

Clare shook her head. 'Gaby was still pretty sleepy but her story backs up David's.'

Tony frowned. 'Well it would – if the two of them are in it together.'

Chris looked at Clare. 'But we don't believe they are. We're waiting on DNA results that might help, though.'

'Okay, forget Russell for now,' Tony said. 'What about the overdose?'

Chris said, 'We think the diazepam tablets were fed to Gaby, probably in a pot of coffee Luke made for her.'

Tony frowned. 'Where's your motive?'

'Money.'

'Explain, please.'

Chris looked down for a moment, as though ordering his thoughts. Then he said, 'Russell Fox planned to sell his restaurants and invest the proceeds in two projects: one with Doug Gerrard and one with Luke.'

'So both lose out by Russell's death?' Tony said.

Chris nodded. 'They do. And Luke's in a mess with money. He's behind with the daughter's school fees and he's borrowed heavily for his next TV show.'

Tony sat silent for a moment. 'Who inherits Russell Fox's money?'

'Gaby,' Chris said. 'But she told us she doesn't need it. In fact, she plans to split it with her brother David and to give some of her share to charity.'

'It's still a pretty thin motive for murder,' Tony said. 'If Luke told Gaby he was in a mess, she'd surely have bailed him out. Cut down on the charity donation.'

Chris shrugged. 'She might; but Gaby strikes me as pretty shrewd. I'm not sure she'd pour money into Luke's company if she thought it was badly managed. And they've a pretty expensive lifestyle, don't forget. Never mind the school fees, there's a flat in Belgravia – that won't come cheap. My guess is their income's good but it's matched by their outgoings.'

'Don't forget the loan,' Clare said.

'What loan?' Tony asked.

Chris smiled. 'That's where it gets interesting. He's borrowed from Doug Gerrard. Six-month loan to keep the company afloat.'

'And a guy like Luke's no match for Doug,' Clare said. 'It wouldn't be long before he came asking for his money and then Luke really would be in a mess. But if Gaby was grief-stricken enough at Russell's death to take an overdose...'

'She's probably insured as well,' Chris went on. 'One pot of coffee and all Luke's problems are over. He can repay Doug and still have enough to shore up his company. He might even agree to invest in Doug's pubs as a thanks for helping him out.'

'I'd say Luke and Doug have a pretty strong motive for getting rid of Gaby then,' Tony said.

'And Gaby was found half dead in a house belonging to Doug Gerrard,' Clare added. She sneezed again.

'Right, you,' Tony said. 'Home.' He nodded at Chris. 'The lad and I can deal with anything else that comes up. And I do not want to see you here in the morning unless you're a whole lot better.'

'Aye, right,' Clare said, getting to her feet.

'See she goes,' Tony said to Chris.

Clare waved this away. 'I'm going, I'm going!'

Out in the main office she was surprised to see DCI Alastair Gibson waiting for her. 'Jim called me,' he said. 'Come on. I'm taking you home.'

–

Benjy followed Clare round the house, more subdued than usual.

'He knows you're not right,' the DCI said, bringing her a bowl of soup.

She looked at the soup and her stomach turned over.

'Try a little.'

She smiled. 'You've made me chicken soup.'

'Correction. I've reheated chicken soup. But it is the supermarket posh range.' He handed her a spoon. 'Try a mouthful.'

She took the spoon and sipped at it. It was piping hot and she winced as she swallowed. 'Hurts.'

He nodded. 'The paracetamol should kick in soon. Try a little more.'

She managed half the bowl then lay back on the sofa. Benjy climbed up beside her and put his head on her lap.

She put a hand down to fondle his neck and he nuzzled into her. Minutes later she was fast asleep, snoring like a tractor.

Day 9: Sunday

Chapter 44

'I don't even remember getting to bed,' Clare said nibbling a slice of toast.

'You fell asleep on the sofa,' the DCI said.

'Please tell me you didn't carry me upstairs.'

He laughed. 'No, you wakened up enough for me to walk you up the stairs.' He indicated the toast. 'How's that going down?'

'Doesn't taste of much but I am enjoying it.'

'And your head?'

She smiled. 'Not quite as stuffy today. I'm definitely on the mend.' She took a drink of coffee then said, 'What are your plans?'

'Working from home. Thought I might walk into town and pick up your car.'

'No need. Give me a lift in and I'll drive it home myself, later.'

'Clare...'

'Clare, nothing! I survived yesterday and I'm honestly feeling much better today.'

'Your nose is like a beacon.'

She did her best to smile. 'On the plus side, it's keeping Tony away from me.'

The toaster clicked and the DCI rose to retrieve the toast. 'He pulling his weight?'

'Ach, now and then. He's another pair of ears when I need to go over stuff. But he pretty much rubber stamps what I say.'

'No change there, then. How's he getting on with Chris?'

'They're rubbing along. Better than it was.'

He began buttering toast. 'You can always chat to me about it – if it would help.'

She smiled. 'Yeah, I know, Al. Thanks for that.' She put down her toast. 'Think I've had enough for now. I'll grab something at work.' She rose from the table. 'If you could maybe run me in.'

–

The DCI drew up outside the station door, dropping Clare as close to it as he could. But she couldn't help hearing one reporter call, 'Inspector, why is Gaby Fox in hospital?'

'Where the hell do they get their information?' she said, her voice low.

'In league with the devil.' He smiled. 'Give me a shout if you need a lift home again.'

She touched him lightly on the arm then jumped out of the car and escaped into the station.

She'd phoned ahead, calling a briefing for seven thirty, and the incident room was packed. She declined Sara's offer of a Lemsip but she did accept the mug of tea Jim pressed into her hands.

'Thanks, Jim.'

He frowned. 'Sure you're okay to be here?'

'I am. Much better than yesterday.'

'Okay,' he said. 'Here if you need me.'

'Oh,' she said, remembering Luke Gasparini. 'Any sign of that hire car?'

He shook his head. 'They never came back to us. I'll chase it as soon as they open, though.'

Clare nodded her thanks and moved to the whiteboard to begin the briefing. 'Okay,' she said. 'Thanks for turning out, everyone. I think we're starting to make progress.' She looked at the board for a moment then said, 'First of all, anything come in overnight?'

Chris raised a hand. 'David Fox agreed to remain in custody until his DNA comes back.'

'Dundee?'

'Yeah. They kept him last night and they'll bring him over if he needs to be charged.'

'Thanks, Chris. That it?'

He indicated it was and Clare looked back at the board again. She tapped Gaby's photo. 'Yesterday, as most of you know, we found Gaby in a cottage about half an hour from here. She was comatose and close to death, having ingested a large quantity of diazepam.'

'Suicide?' Gary asked.

Clare shook her head. 'It seems unlikely, although Gaby's recollection is hazy. My thoughts are someone added the tablets to her coffee.'

'How much had she taken?' Bill asked.

'The medics reckon around forty or fifty milligrams. Certainly a toxic dose for someone of Gaby's size. She'd been prescribed five-milligram tablets so we're only talking eight, maybe ten, needed to kill her.'

Nita raised her hand. 'Any idea who's responsible?'

'Possibly,' Clare said. 'We're working on the theory that Luke Gasparini was desperate for money and decided to kill his wife.'

'Bit extreme,' Bill said.

Clare nodded. 'I agree. But he's in one hell of a mess with money. Plus he tried to blame Russell's death on his wife and brother-in-law, an account which we now think is untrue.'

The room fell silent as they considered this. Then Janey spoke.

'Will you release David Fox if the DNA isn't a match?'

Clare hesitated. 'Probably. But I'd like to get hold of Luke Gasparini first. As I said, Luke and David's stories contradict each other so one of them's lying. And then there's Doug Gerrard. He part-owns Lamond Lodge, giving him ample opportunity to scope out likely vantage points for the killer. And he could have posed a weapon there, ahead of their stay. He also owns the cottage where Gaby was found unconscious. So he is now back to being a person of interest.'

Clare looked back at the photos of the house party. Then she remembered the security guard. 'Has Mark Mooney been in touch?'

Chris shook his head.

'Okay. We'll give him till mid-morning then we'll call round again. I'm starting to think he could have a reason for staying away.'

Nita said, 'Is there any indication he's connected to the house party?'

Clare spread her hands. 'Only this: Doug Gerrard told Eamon Ferry he knew of a house they could use and, if they booked it, he'd throw in a security guard for free.' She looked round the room. 'And anyone with a connection to our Mr Gerrard is definitely on my radar.' She stood thinking for a minute. 'Anything else?'

Heads shook. 'Okay,' she said. 'Let's keep checking on Luke and Doug. Money, personal lives, Doug's pubs – anything at all, I want to know about it; and I'd like someone on Mark Mooney too. Dig a bit deeper there. See if you can find any connection to the house party.' She looked round at them. 'We are getting there, guys. Just one last push.'

Jim was waiting when they drifted out of the incident room. 'The lad Mooney's here to see Chris.'

'At last! Thanks, Jim,' Clare said. 'Where is he?'

'Interview room one.'

Mark Mooney looked up as they entered the room.

'Mr Mooney,' Clare said. 'Thanks so much for coming in.'

'Sure, Inspector. Hoping it's just a quick thing. I'm working this evening and I could do with getting my head down for a couple of hours.'

Clare smiled and sat down. 'Might need you to put that off,' she said. 'I'd like your permission to take a sample of DNA from you.'

The colour drained from his face. 'Erm, mind if I ask why?'

'Hopefully just a formality. We suddenly realised we'd tested everyone who'd been at Lamond Lodge over the weekend but we hadn't tested you. In most cases it's to rule someone out, rather than in.' She looked to Chris for support and he nodded on cue.

Mark Mooney was silent for a moment. Then he said, 'I'm no' keen, to be honest, Inspector. Ye hear about mix-ups at labs and all that.' He laughed as if trying to make light of it, but his eyes betrayed him. 'Just be my luck, ye ken?'

'I understand, Mr Mooney,' Clare said. 'But I can tell you these mix-ups are incredibly rare. They almost never happen.'

'Talked up by the papers,' Chris added.

Mark Mooney frowned. 'All the same.'

Clare said, 'Mr Mooney. I'm afraid if you do not agree we'll arrest you which will give us the power to take your DNA with reasonable force, if necessary. But we'd prefer to do it with your consent.'

'Better not to be arrested if you can avoid it,' Chris said.

His gaze dropped as he appeared to be weighing this up. Then he glanced at the door. Chris rose from his seat and moved between Mark and the door. 'I wouldn't if I were you, Mr Mooney.'

He looked at Chris for a moment, hand on his chin. Then he said, 'I'd like a solicitor, please.'

Chapter 45

It was late morning by the time Mark Mooney had consulted with a solicitor and the inevitable DNA sample had been sent to the lab. Raymond agreed to prioritise it.

'Got David Fox's result back,' Sara said. 'Negative for the gun cartridge.'

'Dammit.' Clare couldn't keep the disappointment out of her voice.

'Sorry, boss.'

Clare turned to Chris. 'Any reason we can't release David Fox?'

He shrugged. 'Not that I can think. Want to run it past Tony?'

Tony agreed. 'Yeah. Get rid. We've enough loose ends in this investigation as it is. Phone through and get Dundee to release him.'

Chris went off to make the phone call and Clare sat down.

Tony studied her. 'You don't look quite as grim today.'

'Thank you very much!'

'Seriously. It's good to see you looking a bit brighter. So, where are we now?'

'Good question. We need to bring Luke Gasparini in again. I'm pretty sure his statement yesterday was all lies. Thing is…'

'Yeah?'

She shook her head. 'I can understand Luke trying to kill Gaby if he was desperate enough and he couldn't see any other way to pay Doug back. But I still don't understand why Russell was killed.'

Chris came back into the room. 'That's David Fox released. He wants to see Gaby so I've called ahead to Mandy up at the hospital. Told her it's fine to let him in.'

'No one else, though?' Clare said.

'No. Mandy knows the score. She'll call us if anyone else turns up.'

'So what now?' Tony said.

Clare sighed. 'Bit of a waiting game. Mark Mooney...'

'Who?'

'The security guard. He's in an interview room waiting on his DNA result.'

'That'll take a while, though.'

'Yeah I know. But I'm not keen to let him go until we have it.'

'You think it's his on the cartridge?' Tony said.

Clare shook her head. 'Probably not. He had the opportunity, but I can't see what the motive would be.'

'Bit suspicious, him asking for a solicitor,' Chris said. 'And he wasn't keen to give his DNA, was he?'

Clare nodded. 'True, but there might be another reason for that. Maybe nothing to do with our murder.' She checked her watch. 'Either way, we'll know in a few hours.'

There was a tap at the door and Jim poked his head round. 'Glasgow just been on the phone, Clare. They've picked up Doug Gerrard.'

'Bringing him through?'

'Yeah. Should be here in a couple of hours at worst.'

'Thanks, Jim.' Clare frowned. 'What were we talking about?'

Before anyone could speak Clare's phone began to ring. She didn't recognise the number and she clicked to take the call. 'DI Mackay.'

'Inspector, this is Natasha Lynch again. Carloway Money.'

'Oh yes, Ms Lynch. Russell Fox's financial advisor.'

'That's right.'

'How can I help?'

'Well, look, it's probably nothing. But as it's a murder enquiry I thought I should let you know.'

'Yes?'

'I was going through my emails. I'm back to work tomorrow, you see, and I like to know what I'm going back to. Anyway, there was another email from Russell. Must have been sent a couple of weeks ago. Just after I went off on holiday.'

'Go on…'

'Would you like me to read it out?'

Clare switched the phone to speaker so Tony and Chris could hear. 'Please.'

'Erm, okay. It says,

Hi Natasha,

Hope all's good with you.

Bit of a change of plan, I'm afraid.

Forget those two investments I mentioned – the pubs and the TV thing.

Had a bit of bad news last week.

Doc told me I've a tumour.

No point in operating. Too far gone.

Bit of a kicker, but there you go.

307

I don't want Gaby left to sort out my stuff.

She's enough on her plate with her career and dealing with our dad.

I still want to sell the restaurants as planned – could you arrange for them to be marketed ASAP please?

I might take a bit of a holiday while I'm still fit enough to do it.

But the rest of the money's to go into a trust for Gaby and her daughter Sacha.

Going away for my birthday so I'll call you when I'm back.

Cheers, Russ

Clare thanked Natasha and asked her to forward the email. She put down her phone.

'So now we know,' Chris said. 'But did Luke and Doug know?'

'Good question, Chris. Chances are he did tell them. He wouldn't want them to get too far ahead with their plans if he was pulling out.' She sat thinking for a moment then said, 'It gives them both a clear motive for murdering Russell. With the money going into trust, Luke couldn't repay Doug. Nor could he plough any more into his company. But with Russell dead…'

'Gaby inherits,' Chris said, 'before any trust could be set up.'

'Quite.'

'D'you reckon they hatched it between them? Luke and Doug?'

Clare nodded. 'Wouldn't surprise me. Doug organises a hitman and Luke promises to see him right once Russell's money comes through.'

There was a knock on the door and Jim appeared again. 'The lad you have in the interview room – seems he wants to talk.'

Chapter 46

Clare began the interview by cautioning Mark Mooney but before she could ask what he wanted to say the solicitor spoke.

'Mr Mooney has some information,' she said. 'But he's concerned that, by disclosing this, he may incriminate himself. He would like you to consider a reduced charge, if he divulges this information.'

Clare watched Mark Mooney carefully, but he wouldn't meet her eye. What was it he was about to tell them? 'I can't give any guarantees,' she said. 'But, Mark, if you know something, if you are involved in this crime, you must tell us.'

Chris said, 'Inspector Mackay's right, Mark. It'll come out eventually. It always does. But, if you've helped us, it'll be taken into account.'

He sat staring at the floor for a moment then he lifted his gaze. 'And a reduced charge?'

Clare shook her head. 'No guarantees, I'm afraid. But we'll ensure your co-operation is noted at every stage.'

He looked at Clare then back at his solicitor who gave a slight nod. 'Okay, then.' He cleared his throat then said, 'What I did – you have to understand, I did it under duress. It wasn't my decision. I had no choice.'

Clare said, 'Mark, what is it you want to tell us?'

He took a deep breath then exhaled slowly. Clare and Chris waited then, at last, he spoke.

'It was me,' he said. 'I shot the guy. At that big house, Lamond Lodge. I shot him.'

Clare glanced at Chris. After all the questions, all the forensic investigations, checking the backgrounds of everyone in the house party, and it was the security guard all the time. The obvious person. Why hadn't they seen it? And, more to the point, why was he sitting there in front of them, admitting his guilt?

'Just to be clear,' she said, 'Mark, you are confessing to killing Russell Fox. You are saying you murdered him in the grounds of Lamond Lodge by shooting him?'

'I wouldn't call it murder.'

Clare's eyes widened. 'What would you call it?'

He hesitated, then said, 'I don't know what the charge would be. But you have to believe it wasn't my choice. I did it to protect my family.'

'Okay,' Clare said. 'Perhaps you could explain.'

'Not easy, Inspector. But I'll try.' He took a drink from a cup of water in front of him then he said, 'I like a flutter, ye know?'

'Gambling?'

'Aye. Bit of horses, sometimes a poker game.' He rubbed his chin. 'Anyway, I got this tip one day. Fella said it was a dead cert. Twenty to one, ye ken? One of those races where money had changed hands. The outsider was definitely gonnae win.' His brow furrowed at the memory. 'Didnae win, of course.'

'You'd bet a lot of money on it?'

'Aye. The wife's holiday money.' He shook his head again. 'Florida.'

'Did you tell your wife?'

'Naw. I reckoned if I won it back she'd never know. So I put another few bets on. Lost more.' He glanced at Clare. 'Mug's game.' He fell silent and, after a few moments, Clare prompted him.

'So, you'd lost a lot of money, Mark. What did you do next?'

He seemed to be considering what to say. Then he spoke again. 'You get to hear of folk, folk that'll lend you a few quid.' He shrugged. 'I reckoned if I did some extra shifts, earned some cash I could pay it off.'

'You borrowed money?' Clare said.

'Aye.'

'Who from?'

Again, he took a few moments before speaking. 'Just some guy. In a pub. Said he'd see me every Friday and I'd give him the cash.'

Clare said, 'And did you?'

'For a bit, aye. Then he said the interest rate was going up and I owed him more than when I'd started. Said I'd have to keep paying.'

'How much did you borrow?'

'A grand.'

'You borrowed a thousand pounds from a moneylender?'

'Aye.'

'And… how much did this man say you owed?'

He hesitated then said, 'Eight grand.'

Clare's eyes narrowed. 'You borrowed one thousand pounds and, despite making weekly repayments, you now owe eight thousand pounds?'

'Aye. Or actually I don't. Not now.'

Clare sighed. 'Mark, you could have come to us. We'd have helped.'

He shook his head. 'I doubt it.'

Chris said, 'Was there something preventing you coming to us?'

He looked down. 'Not at first, I suppose. I mean, they've got my SIA card...'

Clare frowned and Mark seemed to notice this.

'Security Industry Authority,' he explained. 'I can't work without it. Took my driving licence, too. Said I'd get one of them back when I'd paid half and the other when I'd paid in full. But the interest...'

Clare's expression hardened. 'These people,' she said. 'They work it so you never pay the debt off.'

He nodded. 'Aye, I know that now.'

Chris leaned forward. 'Mark, you said, *not at first*. Did something change?'

He looked at Chris for a moment then he gave a slight nod. 'Aye.'

'Go on.'

'Got a phone call. Didn't know who. But the guy said he had my SIA card and my licence. Said I'd get them back, debt wiped clean. Just had to do him a favour. Sounded too good to be true.' He shook his head. 'Turns out, it was.'

'What was the favour?' Clare asked.

He took a moment to answer then, with a glance at his solicitor, he said, 'He told me he'd been doing a bit of digging. Found out I used to be a gamekeeper. Thought I'd be a good shot. And he said – he said, if I did a wee job for him we'd call it quits. No more payments.'

Clare watched him carefully. 'And the wee job?'

Mark flicked a glance at his solicitor and she gave a slight nod. He turned back to Clare. 'He wanted someone shot.' Then he sat back, as though relieved to have told them. 'He wanted me to shoot someone. Kill them.'

'What did you say?'

'What you'd expect. Said I wasn't a killer. Wasn't my kind of thing. I'd find a way to get the money.' He picked up the cup and drank again. Then he said, 'But that wasn't an option.'

'What do you think he meant by that?' Clare asked.

He met her eye. 'He said I had two bonny wee boys. The pair of them. Said he'd seen them playing in the garden. Kicking a ball around and playing on the trampoline. Described them. Even knew their names.' His voice was husky now and he cleared his throat. 'Said it'd be an awful shame if something happened.'

Clare said, 'Just to be clear, Mark, this man who asked you to shoot someone dead implied, if you didn't agree, something might happen to your children? Is that correct?'

Mark's hand went to his face and he rubbed his cheek. He blinked a couple of times then said, 'Aye.' He sounded hoarse now and the solicitor was looking at him.

'Are you okay to continue, Mr Mooney?' she said.

'Aye, a'm fine. Better to get it done.'

Clare smiled. 'Thank you. I can see this isn't easy.'

Mark nodded and Clare went on.

'What happened next?'

'The guy on the phone, said he'd get me a job for a week at a posh house in the country. He'd lay on the weapon, show me where to hide myself. Said he'd make sure the lad went up to the treetop walk on the Saturday morning. He'd be a sitting duck. All I had to do was to wait. Even said he'd put some other poor sod in the frame for it. Someb'dy with previous he'd make sure was in the town on the Saturday morning.'

Clare glanced at Chris. Zac. It had to be. That message telling him to wait for a package that never arrived. He'd been telling the truth all along. Whoever had planned this had left nothing to chance. But who was behind it? 'Go on, Mark.'

'So, I said what had the lad done? Why did he want him shot? And he tells me some tale about the lad being ill. Cancer. Said it was one of his oldest friends. Didn't want him suffering. So they'd give him a great party: booze, girls, the works. And in the morning he'd make sure he was up on the walkway. Spin him some yarn about the best place in Scotland to see the sun come up. He said, who wouldn't want to go that way?'

'What did you think about that?' Clare said.

Mark shrugged. 'The way he explained it… I'm a good shot, Inspector. I was a keeper up on Deeside for years. The stags, they get out of hand if you don't cull them. Part of my job, and I never let an animal suffer. Clean shot. That was me.' He nodded to himself then he said, 'My dad, he suffered, you know? Not just the pain. He was like a baby in the end. Had to do everything for him.' He drew a hand across his eyes then said, 'No one deserves to go like that, Inspector. No one.'

The room was deathly silent. Clare felt Chris shift in his seat next to her and she made a small gesture with her hand to give Mark a minute. Then she said, 'So you agreed to carry out what you were told would be a mercy killing in return for wiping your debt clean?'

He was looking down now. 'Aye.'

'And if you refused, your children would be at risk, yes?'

He raised his eyes to meet Clare's and she saw they were bright with tears. 'Aye.'

It was as good a confession as Clare had ever heard. But they still didn't know who the moneylender was. 'And this man?'

Mark's expression clouded. 'So, here's the thing. If I give you a name and you don't nail him, what happens to my wee boys? To my wife? What happens if I'm not there to protect them?'

Clare sighed. He had a point. Whoever was responsible had clearly gone to the trouble of finding out about Mark and his family. And if they didn't manage to find evidence against the moneylender, or if a jury didn't believe Mark's story…

'Mark,' she said, hoping she sounded confident, 'we can protect them. We have people who specialise in this kind of thing. And, if you help us, I'll make sure it's mentioned in court. But, if you don't, he'll just keep on exploiting people like you.'

He sat weighing this for some minutes then he said, 'You can look after them? My family?'

Clare nodded. 'We can arrange for them to be moved, new names if necessary. But it usually doesn't come to that. So, Mark, the name please?'

'Gerrard,' he said. 'Doug Gerrard.'

Chapter 47

'Charged him?' Tony asked.

Clare shook her head. 'Not yet. I want to see what Doug Gerrard has to say for himself.'

'Makes sense, I suppose.'

Chris glanced at his watch. 'Should be here soon.'

'Make sure Jim knows to keep the two of them apart,' Clare said. 'I don't want Doug intimidating Mark Mooney any further.'

Chris nodded. 'Sorted.'

Tony leaned back in his chair. 'So what now?'

Clare frowned. 'We need to find evidence to back up Mark Mooney's story. If it comes to his word against Doug Gerrard's I wouldn't be too sure of a conviction.'

'I agree,' Chris said. 'Problem is finding the evidence.'

'You could lean on the friends,' Tony said. 'See if they know more than they're letting on.'

Clare nodded. 'Yeah, it's the logical place to start. But we've spoken to them twice and I'm not sure they do know about Doug and Mark Mooney. I'll get the Glasgow cops to put out feelers. See if anyone's saying anything.'

'What about overdose woman? Gaby?' Tony asked.

'Gaby... yes.' Clare nodded slowly. 'I do need to speak to her again, in the light of Mark's confession. See if she can shed any light on it.'

'Might want to catch her soon then,' Chris said. 'If the psychiatrist's happy she could be out any time.'

Clare reached for her phone. 'I'll check with Mandy now. She's been up there all morning.'

—

'Doc says she can go home in a couple of hours,' Mandy said. 'Just waiting for the paperwork to be signed off.'

'Is the brother taking her?'

'David? No. He only stayed ten minutes.'

'Eh?' Clare couldn't keep the surprise out of her voice. According to Chris, David Fox had been impatient to see his sister.

'Yeah, I was surprised,' Mandy said. 'He came racing along the corridor desperate to see her. Next thing I know he's out again, heading for the exit.'

'And Gaby?' Clare said. 'Was she okay? Not upset? They hadn't argued?'

'Don't think so, boss. Erm, do you want to speak to her yourself?'

A few minutes later Clare heard Gaby's voice. 'Inspector, is everything okay?'

'Yes, thanks. I just wondered… did you manage to see your brother?'

'Yes I did.' Clare could hear the warmth in Gaby's voice. 'After everything that's happened, you know, it's such a blessing to be in touch with David again. I'm not a religious person, Clare, but it's as if he was sent to help me.'

Clare's mind was racing. Clearly David's rapid departure hadn't been the result of an argument. 'That's lovely,' she said, trying to keep her tone light. 'Did he stay long?'

'No,' she said. 'He'd something to attend to. But he promised to be back soon.' She laughed. 'I tried to tell him I'd be getting out but he said it couldn't wait.'

'Catching up on old times?' Clare said. She was fishing but she hoped Gaby wouldn't realise.

'Not really. It was just a quick visit.'

She was getting nowhere. There was nothing for it but to ask outright. 'Gaby,' she said, 'I hope you don't think I'm being nosey, but can I ask what you talked about with David?'

'Oh, erm I suppose…'

Clare said quickly, 'The more information we have, you see, the more chance there is we'll find the person responsible for Russell's death.'

'Well,' Gaby said, 'if you must know he asked why I'd taken the pills. And I said I didn't think I had really. That I must have been distracted, not thinking. It's been such a strain – the past week. I said to David I must have taken them by accident. But I really don't remember.'

'And is that all you spoke about?'

There was a pause then Gaby said, 'I think I mentioned the cottage. The one at Hazelton.'

'You spoke about the cottage?'

'Yes. I still have my things there. I said to David I'd have to get a car, or a taxi. Pick them up, you know?'

Clare's mind was racing. Was there some connection with this conversation and David's sudden departure? Or was she looking for something that wasn't there? They had Mark Mooney in custody after all, and Doug Gerrard wouldn't be far behind once he'd been interviewed.

'Anything else, Gaby?'

'No, I don't think so. After we spoke about the cottage David said he had a few things to do but he'd be back.

Then I said I'd be discharged soon and he said he'd call me.'

Clare thanked Gaby and asked her to hand the phone back to Mandy.

'Hi boss.'

'Listen, Mandy, I'm not sure what's going on but I don't want Gaby to leave the hospital. I'm sending Gary up to join you. But do not let her leave. Okay?'

Clare ended the call and sought out Gary. 'Get yourself up to Ninewells Hospital and find Mandy. She's outside Gaby Fox's hospital room. Gaby is not to leave until you hear from either me or Chris. Okay?'

As Gary left the station Clare heard Chris shout.

'Car hire company called.'

'Luke's car?'

'Yeah.' He walked into the incident room, Clare following. He went to a map on the wall. 'He's about half an hour away from here. Just gone through a village called Gauldry.'

'Rings a bell,' Clare said.

Chris jabbed the map with his finger. 'That's the back road to Hazelton Walls.' He turned to face Clare. 'He's heading back to the cottage.'

'Where he'll expect to find his wife dead from an overdose,' Clare said. 'And I'd bet my pension the same thing has occurred to David Fox.' She turned towards her office. 'I'll get my jacket. Grab a car and I'll be out in a minute.'

Clare jumped into the car, Janey and Bill rushing after her to take another vehicle. As soon as she'd closed the door Chris sped off.

'How long till we're there?' she asked, tugging on her seatbelt.

'Too long,' he said. 'Luke'll get there first.'

'And David Fox is probably waiting for him.'

Chris pressed his foot down and the car lurched forward, siren wailing.

Clare glanced behind her. 'Dammit. I'm sure that's a press car behind Janey and Bill.'

'We'll lose them,' Chris said.

'Hope so. The last thing we need is an audience.'

They knew where they were going this time and were soon roaring up the narrow country road. As they approached the crossroads he killed the siren and slowed his speed. He drove slowly along, coasting the last couple of hundred yards, cutting the engine as he pulled into the side. Clare jumped out and waited until Bill and Janey appeared. Stationing them at the front door she went round one side of the cottage, directing Chris round the other. She took the grass instead of the gravel, her feet noiseless as she went. Gaby's hire car still stood in the drive, a blue Renault next to it. Luke's other hire car, she guessed. As she reached the back garden she saw a motorbike had been propped up against the shed, out of sight of the main door. Anyone entering the cottage at the front wouldn't have seen it.

'David Fox,' she murmured. Goodness knows where he'd got his hands on a motorbike but she felt sure the bike was his. She caught Chris's eye as he appeared from the other side of the cottage and he nodded to indicate he'd noticed it. Clare was about to approach the back door when a shout from Janey alerted them. They ran round to the front and in through the door which now stood open.

'In here,' Janey called.

They moved into a small sitting room. It was south-facing and the August sun streamed in the windows. The polished floor was oak, possibly the original tongue and groove boards, with a square Persian rug in the centre. A large dark wood coffee table sat in front of a fireplace with two red sofas angled round it. And on the furthest away of these sat a white-faced Luke Gasparini. Behind him, a kitchen knife held against Luke's throat, stood David Fox.

Chapter 48

Bill had moved towards David but Clare waved him back. 'David,' she began.

'Stay exactly where you are, Inspector,' he said. 'Or I'll gut him like a fish.'

Luke Gasparini closed his eyes at this, his lips quivering as he struggled to hold onto his composure.

'Why don't you tell the officers what you did?' David said. 'You sleazy bastard.'

A sob escaped Luke's mouth and he gasped in air. 'N-nothing,' he stammered. 'Nothing.'

'Liar!' David pressed the knife closer to Luke's throat. 'You can't even admit it.'

Luke was weeping now, his face contorted as he tried to control the sobs. 'I… I didn't…'

'Right then,' David said. 'How about I tell the officers for you, eh?'

Clare moved further into the room. 'David, you need to put the knife down. Then we can all talk about this.'

He shook his head, the knife still firmly held against Luke's throat. 'Sorry, Inspector, no can do. You see, I need this piece of scum to tell you what he did. And I have the feeling he might not want to do that without a little bit of… help, from me.'

Tears were coursing down Luke's face and he was gulping for air.

Clare said, 'David, I'm concerned Luke might be having a panic attack. And that knife… well, it does look sharp.'

David smiled. 'Oh it's that, all right. I sharpened it outside on a bit of stone, before *he* arrived.'

'All right, then,' Clare said, 'why don't you tell us, David? Get it all out in the open then we can see where we go from there.'

'Suits me,' David said, his eyes still trained on Luke. 'But, where to start? Oh I know. How about conspiring to murder my brother? I reckon that'll do for starters.'

Clare was watching Luke carefully to see if he reacted to this but his eyes were tight shut again. 'What makes you think that?' she asked David.

He shook his head. 'That lot,' he began, 'they don't take me seriously. Think I'm a bit of an oddball. Pretty careless when I was around. But me? I notice stuff. I've bummed my way round the world for the past seventeen years. I've learned to keep my wits about me and to read people. And this one,' he jerked his head towards Luke, 'I can read his sort like a book. He's the ideas man, you see. Doesn't have the balls to do the mucky jobs. So he makes the bullets for the other lunkhead to fire. Not literally, of course. Neither of them's daft enough for that.'

'Are you saying you heard or saw something while you were at Lamond Lodge?'

'Give the inspector a prize!' He inclined his head so he could see Luke's face. 'You didn't know I was listening when that Gerrard guy took your call, did you? He didn't know either. I was out having a slash when I heard him heading into the hall. Phone going. So I thought I'd just have a listen. Heard him say *Yeah, Luke?* Then a pause. Then Gerrard, he says, *Don't worry. I've told him to get*

himself up to the treetop walk in the morning. It's perfect.'
He shook his head. 'At the time I didn't think much
about it. Thought it was some kind of birthday surprise.
Like a plane towing one of those messages behind. *Happy
Birthday Russell.* That kind of thing. Few drinks later, and
I forgot about it. Next thing it's the morning, still early,
and I hear the red-haired lad, Eamon, he says there's been
an accident. Something happened to Russell. Have to call
the cops.' He glanced at Clare. 'Bearing in mind I was
supposed to be dead, I thought I'd better leg it.'

'But, if you'd heard Doug and Luke talking on the
phone,' Clare said, 'why didn't you come straight to us
and tell us what you'd heard?'

'Couldn't.'

'You mean you'd rather let a murderer go free than
admit to us you hadn't died all these years ago?'

'I don't mean that. At the time, I wasn't even sure what
the phone call had meant. And the lad Eamon, he didn't
say Russell had been shot – nothing like that. So I got
out of the way before you lads arrived.' He paused for a
moment then went on. 'I wondered, ye know, wondered
if there was something in that call. But then your boss said
they could all leave that fancy hotel so I thought I must
have got it wrong. Then Gaby said would I come and stay
with them, here, in this cottage. And this one,' he nodded
down at Luke, 'well, he seemed so normal. I started to
think I was wrong.'

Chris had moved into the room now and he began
edging round the side of the coffee table.

'Not another step, Sergeant,' David said. 'I'll happily
cut his throat and spend the rest of my life behind bars.
Anything to get him away from Gaby.'

Chris held out his hands to indicate he understood, and David went on.

'Then I saw Gaby in that hospital bed. I saw her lying there and I asked her about the pills. *Just between us*, I said. *I won't tell the shrinks. You can tell me.* And she said, *I'm telling them I don't remember, but I know I didn't take them.*' David shook his head. 'And I knew she was telling the truth. I might have been away for seventeen years, Inspector, but I know my sister. She wouldn't have done it. So that only left one option.' He jerked his head down at Luke. 'Tell them why you did it?' He pressed the knife closer to Luke's throat. 'Or, so help me God, I'll finish you right here.'

A dark stain began to appear at Luke's crotch.

'I think,' Clare said, 'Luke's had enough, David. Maybe if you put the knife away?'

David's expression hardened. 'He can piss himself till the cows come home. We're not moving from here until he tells you.' He nudged Luke's shoulder. 'Go on.'

The knife had grazed the skin on Luke's throat and blood began to seep out from the blade. Chris and Bill exchanged glances and Clare tried to remember what she'd learned about the veins and arteries in the neck. Wasn't there something about a large muscle protecting the jugular? The knife, while clearly sharp, seemed to be an ordinary kitchen knife. It would probably take a fair bit of force to inflict a fatal wound. But she couldn't take the chance.

David had noticed the graze on Luke's throat and he held the blade away a little, allowing the blood to trickle down Luke's neck. It wasn't a deep nick, Clare thought, but the sooner they had the knife off David the better. She didn't think Luke knew he was bleeding. But, if he did feel the blood, might he panic?

'Go on,' David said, tugging Luke's hair with his free hand.

Luke winced at this then opened his eyes. He flicked them round the room and found Clare's face. 'It… was Doug,' he began. 'All Doug's idea.'

Clare nodded at this. 'Can you explain, Luke? Help us understand.'

'Doug said Russell was going to die soon.' He took a couple of deep breaths in and out then went on. 'He'd planned to invest in my TV company. Doug's pubs too. But, when he heard he was ill, he told us he'd changed his mind. That he wanted the money for Gaby and Sacha. Some kind of trust.' He lifted his eyes towards David who towered over him. 'Doug said it would be like a mercy killing. Spare Russell the agony of a painful death. But we had to do it before Russell had the trust drawn up. That way, Gaby would inherit Russell's money and I'd persuade her to invest in my TV series. And… I owed Doug a bit of money too. So he said, if he arranged for Russell to die, I'd have to see him right. Interest, he called it.' Luke tried to turn his head to see David's face but David still had a tight grip on his hair.

'Go on,' David said. 'That's not all.'

Luke was shivering now, his voice shaky. 'I… I, er, told Doug I'd be away for the weekend, at that wedding, and he said that was perfect 'cause he didn't trust me not to say something stupid.' He looked back at Clare. 'I was glad to be out of it, Inspector.'

Clare said, 'So you and Mr Gerrard conspired to have Russell Fox murdered.'

Luke's gaze dropped and he didn't speak.

'Say it!' David roared.

'Yes, okay. Doug and I talked about it. But I was away. Inspector, you know I wasn't there.'

'Makes no difference,' David said. 'You still planned it. Conspiracy to murder, isn't it, Inspector?'

'It is,' Clare admitted. 'But there's more, David, isn't there?' She looked at him, holding his gaze, aware that Bill was edging closer to them. Every instinct in her body wanted to glance to the side – see what Bill was doing. She sensed Chris too had moved but she forced her eyes to stare straight ahead. Straight at David Fox. She had to keep talking. Keep him engaged so he didn't see what she knew was about to happen. 'There's Gaby, isn't there?' she said. 'Maybe Luke can tell us about the overdose?'

Luke started to sob at the mention of his wife's name and David bent over him.

'Don't you dare start snivelling,' he yelled. 'You're not fit—'

When Clare thought back to that moment, she remembered the hours of training they'd undergone. Those early Sunday mornings in some deserted warehouse, sometimes in riot gear, sometimes not. Minutes after arriving they'd be given a scenario to take in, then the mock-up of a hostage situation would materialise before them. Yelling, shouting, people rushing in, terrified hostages screaming. And they made split-second decisions which would be pored over later, in great detail. How they'd cursed those Sunday mornings. How many times had she written them off as a waste of time? But now, standing in this charming cottage, less than ten feet from a man who seemed to have nothing to lose, she was thankful for them.

In one seamless movement, Bill, burly, overweight Bill, king of the sweaty armpits, had dashed the knife from

David's hand with a well-aimed fist as Chris grabbed his other hand, forcing it up his back. There was a howl from Luke as a handful of his hair went in David's grasp and he fell forward, weeping and clutching his head. Then he scrambled to his feet and stumbled into Clare, desperate to escape his assailant. Clare scooped him up and held onto him, preventing him from leaving the room while Chris informed David he was under arrest. Clare took Luke through to the kitchen while Janey called for an ambulance and another car to take David back to the station.

'Janey, go in the ambulance with him,' Clare said when the paramedics appeared. 'Bill, are you okay? Need medical attention?'

'Nah, I'm fine,' he said, waving her concern away.

'Then follow the ambulance in your car, please. Once you get to hospital you and Janey are to stay with him at all times. And I want to know when he's fit to be interviewed. Check with the docs before saying a word. And ask him nothing without cautioning him. We play this one by the book.'

Bill went off to follow the ambulance. Nita had appeared with another officer from Cupar and they took David Fox to their car.

'Straight to the station with him,' Clare said.

When they had gone she looked round the room. The red settee Luke had been sitting on was stained where he'd wet himself and the knife which had flown across the room had made a deep score in a side table.

'If this wasn't Doug Gerrard's cottage,' Clare said, 'I'd feel for the owner. As it is, I'm just sorry they didn't make more of a mess.'

They walked slowly out of the cottage. 'Good work,' Clare said to Chris. 'You and Bill.' She nodded. 'I was impressed.'

'Well that's a first,' he said. Then he stopped. 'Clare…'

'Yeah?'

'Look sorry to pick you up on this but, all that stuff Luke told us. You didn't caution him.'

Clare shrugged. 'Doesn't matter. We can't use any of it.'

'What, none of it?'

'Nope. His confession was obtained under duress so it's inadmissible. Our only hope is he sticks by his story, shoving the blame on Doug Gerrard.' She held out her hand. 'Keys, Sergeant. I'm not sure I can face another trip with you at the wheel.'

Chapter 49

It was Jim who reminded Clare she still had Mark Mooney in the interview room. 'Solicitor's getting a bit arsey,' he said. 'I explained you had an emergency and took them some coffees, but I think she'd like to get away soon.'

'Okay, thanks Jim.' She nodded to Chris. 'Let's see him now. There's something else I want to ask.'

Mark Mooney had been slumped in a chair, but he straightened up when Clare and Chris entered. 'Don't suppose I can go home?' he asked.

Clare smiled. 'Sorry, Mark. I'm afraid we'll have to remand you in custody.'

His face clouded. 'But my family.'

'We'll send someone round to explain to your wife.'

'And Gerrard?'

'He's on his way here, under police escort. We'll be interviewing him shortly.'

He nodded at this, seemingly resigned to his fate, and he raised an eyebrow when Clare moved to restart the recording.

She went through the preamble for the tape once more, reminding him he was still under caution. Then she said, 'Mark, there is one further thing I'd like to ask you.' Out of the corner of her eye Clare could see Chris watching her but she carried on. 'I'd like to ask what you did, after you shot Russell Fox.'

He sat thinking for a moment, then he said, 'I, er, well I went to the top of the stairs. Listened, ye know? Guns, they make a hell of a noise. I wanted to make sure there was nobody about. Then, when I thought it was safe enough I went down the stairs and out of the back door.'

'And the gun?'

'There was a black Range Rover, parked just outside. Mr Gerrard – he said if I put the case in the boot of the car he'd see to it.'

'Was the car unlocked?'

'Keys on the kitchen table.'

'Okay. And then?'

He shrugged. 'Then I let myself out of the security gate and headed back into town.'

Clare told Mark he would now be arrested in connection with the murder of Russell Fox and she left him with Nita to complete the formalities.

'So, what now?' Chris asked.

She was prevented from answering by the appearance of Doug Gerrard, accompanied by two uniformed cops from Glasgow. She glanced round and saw Jim at her elbow.

'Interview room two's free,' he said. 'Want me to set it up?'

Clare smiled. 'Please. Oh, and see if he wants a solicitor. I've a phone call to make.'

Clare's friend and colleague Jackie Boland was on duty and the call was put straight through.

'Hi again, Clare. What can I do for you?'

'Jackie, I need a car gone over. Black Range Rover, registered to Eamon Ferry. I interviewed him at your station the other day.'

'Yeah, I remember. Looking for anything special?'

'Gunshot residue. Particularly in the boot.'

'This about your murder last week?'

'Yeah. I think the weapon might have been stored in the boot of the car for a short time.'

'Leave it with me.'

'Thanks, Jackie.'

Chapter 50

'How do you want to play it?' Tony asked.

'Doug Gerrard?' Clare shook her head. 'No idea. Ideally I'd like to have a statement from Luke before interviewing Gerrard but he's not been released from hospital yet.' She checked her watch. 'I can't really hold it up any longer.'

'Want me in?'

She opened her mouth to say she'd be fine but then she thought about Doug Gerrard, so confident, so sure of himself. Maybe the presence of a DCI would rattle him. 'Why not.'

As they entered the room, Doug's solicitor began talking. 'My client is a busy man, officers. I gather you have interviewed him twice already so I'm struggling to see why you've insisted on him being brought eighty miles for a third interview.'

Clare ignored the question and introduced herself and Tony. She thought there was a slight reaction on Doug's face at the mention of Tony's rank but she ignored this and started the tape. She cautioned him and began. 'Mr Gerrard, I would like to ask you again about your involvement in the murder of Russell Fox.'

Doug adjusted his position and crossed one leg over the other. 'Nothing to tell. I was as shocked as anyone.'

She'd been expecting this. 'Perhaps you could tell us how you came to engage Mark Mooney as security guard for the week?'

He began examining his fingernails. 'Someone gave me his number.'

'One of your friends said if they booked your property, Lamond Lodge, you'd throw in a security guard free.'

'Yeah, so?'

'So you already knew about Mr Mooney? You were aware of him?'

'Like I say, someone passed on his name.'

She decided to change tack. 'Mr Gerrard, are you a moneylender?'

He laughed. 'Me? Where would I get money to lend? It's hard enough trying to keep my pubs afloat, never mind shell out to other folk.'

'Do you deny lending money to Mark Mooney?'

He frowned. 'The security guard? Of course I do.'

'Do you currently have possession of Mark Mooney's SIA Licence and Driving Licence?'

There was just the hint of a smirk on his face. 'Now why would I want these? I have my own licences, you know?'

Clare balled her fists under the table, but she managed to keep control of her face. 'Had you met Mr Mooney before engaging him as a security guard?'

'Nope.'

She looked at him for a moment but he met her gaze without flinching. 'Remind me again how you know Valerie Docherty.'

'As I said last time, we jointly own a property.'

'Lamond Lodge.'

'The very same.'

'You were vague on how this came about,' Clare said. 'Maybe you could think again.'

He shrugged. 'I'm always on the lookout, you know, houses to invest in. Like I said, someone put me in touch with Val.'

'As with Mr Mooney, someone passed on her name?'

'Yeah.'

'Mr Gerrard, you are a reasonably successful businessman.' She let this hang in the air for a moment then said, 'I find it hard to believe so many of your contacts are so casual – people you can't remember, men you meet in pubs – this doesn't sound to me like an efficient way to run a business.'

'To be honest, Inspector, that sounds like a you-problem.'

Tony folded his arms. 'And yet, Mr Gerrard, here you are.'

'Not for much longer, *Chief* Inspector.' He glanced at his solicitor.

'Indeed,' the solicitor said. 'Mr Gerrard has answered your questions. I think perhaps we've trespassed on your time long enough, officers.'

'Aye,' Doug Gerrard said, 'trespassed.'

Clare smiled then said, 'Mr Gerrard, you were contemplating the purchase of a chain of pubs on Glasgow's south side. Is that correct?'

A slight frown appeared on the solicitor's face.

Ah, Clare thought, *you weren't expecting that, were you?*

Doug Gerrard said, 'Who told you that?'

'Someone mentioned it,' Clare said, before she could stop herself.

He had the grace to laugh. 'Touché, Inspector.' Then he said, 'I was thinking about it.'

'And were you financing it yourself?'

'Maybe.'

'What was the likely cost?' Clare asked.

'Not sure.'

'Did you have a budget in mind?'

He took a moment to respond. 'It was at an early stage. Nothing set in stone.'

Clare decided it was time to show her hand. 'Were you considering a joint investment with Russell Fox?'

For the first time Clare thought she saw his expression change. The smirk was gone, his eyes steely and she was suddenly glad Tony was sitting next to her.

Then he said, 'Done your homework, Inspector.'

'Just answer the question please.'

'We talked about it.'

'And were you aware of any other plans Mr Fox had? I gather he planned to sell his restaurants and invest the money in one or two projects.'

'I wasn't his keeper, Inspector. I said I had an idea and would he be interested. He said he was. I've no idea what else he was thinking about.'

Clare nodded at this. He'd clearly spent his time on the journey from Glasgow wisely, going over his story. 'You knew Mr Fox had health problems?'

'Yeah, I heard. Poor bastard. Still, he went out on a high, didn't he? Great night on the Friday. Standing looking at the sunrise the next morning. He'd have known nothing about it.'

Clare said quickly, 'What makes you think that?'

There was a flicker in his eyes. *Yes,* she thought, *you've slipped up there, mate.*

'Stands to reason, doesn't it? Bullet like that to the head.'

'You went up on the treetop walk?' She watched him carefully. *He's trying to recall what he said*, she thought. *And he's not sure.*

He put up a hand and rubbed the back of his neck. 'Sorry, can't remember.'

'One of your oldest friends is lying, collapsed on an aerial walkway and you can't remember if you went up or not?'

'I did then,' he snapped back. 'As you say, he was my oldest friend. No wonder I wasn't thinking clearly when I reported it.'

Clare said, 'Mr Gerrard, did you conspire to have Russell Fox killed?'

He did a reasonable job of looking shocked. 'Of course I bloody didn't!'

'Did you arrange for a trained sniper to visit the house and shoot Russell from the top storey?'

He gave a short laugh. 'You guys must be desperate.'

'Just answer the question,' Tony said.

Doug rolled his eyes. 'No, I didn't. I knew nothing about it until I saw Russell lying dead on the walkway.'

'You didn't arrange for a weapon to be concealed in the house prior to your visit?'

'Nope.'

He wasn't making it easy for them. She decided to have one last try. 'Mr Gerrard, you have told us you are not a moneylender. Do you stand by that statement?'

His eyes narrowed and he made no reply.

'Allow me to refresh your memory,' Clare said. 'You recently lent a large sum of money to Luke Gasparini's media company.'

He hesitated then said, 'Not quite the same thing.'

Doug's solicitor glanced at him then said, 'I think, Inspector, I'd like a private word with my client.'

Clare paused the recording and rose from her chair. 'As you wish.'

Out in the main office Tony said, 'He's certainly not going to cough.'

Clare shook her head. 'Nope.' She looked round for Jim. 'Any sign of Luke Gasparini yet?'

'Aye, Clare. He's on his way. Should be here in ten minutes or so.'

'Get a solicitor for him, please; and I'd like a doctor as well. He's had quite an ordeal and I want to be absolutely sure he's fit to be interviewed.'

Doug Gerrard's solicitor indicated they were ready to continue. Clare restarted the tape and reminded Doug he was still under caution.

'My client has a formal business arrangement with Mr Gasparini whereby he advanced the production company a sum of money,' the solicitor said. 'This is a business loan, reflecting Mr Gerrard's interest in the arts.'

Clare smiled. 'Of course. And what was the reason for the loan?'

Doug shrugged. 'Dunno. Luke was having cash-flow problems. I suggested I could help out, short-term. All open and above board.'

'And how did Mr Gasparini propose to resolve his cash-flow problems?' Clare asked.

'You'd have to ask him that.'

'So, if there's nothing else?' The solicitor replaced the cap on his fountain pen and looked from Clare to Tony.

A smirk began forming on Doug Gerrard's face and he sat forward in his chair. 'So how's about a lift back to Glasgow then?'

Tony seemed ready to speak but Clare cut across him. 'Douglas Gerrard, I am arresting you under Section 1 of the Criminal Justice Scotland Act 2016 for conspiracy to commit murder...'

–

Tony began walking back to Clare's office. 'I hope you've done the right thing, arresting him.'

'No option, Tony. He was going to walk.'

'Clock's ticking now, though. And if this Luke guy changes his story, we might struggle to make the charges stick.'

'I know,' Clare said. 'We'll just have to hope he doesn't.'

Chapter 51

'Gaby's being released from hospital,' Chris said. 'Should be out in the next hour.'

Clare nodded. 'She'd better have a police escort, an unmarked car. No point in attracting any more press attention. Ask her to go to a hotel, please. Not the one she stayed at before, though. Try the Kenlybank.'

'Will do. Oh, and Luke's arrived. Doc's with him now.'

'Solicitor?'

'Yeah. Just waiting for the doc to give us the okay.'

'Great,' Clare said. 'Fingers crossed he's fit to be interviewed. And, if he coughs, we can charge Doug Gerrard.'

'Reckon he will?' Tony asked.

Chris shook his head. 'Impossible to say.'

Clare nodded. 'I agree. He was put through hell by David Fox. There's no way of knowing what he'll say.'

Tony rose. 'Only one way to find out.'

The doctor pronounced Luke fit to be interviewed and they left him to consult with his solicitor. Twenty minutes later the three of them crammed into the interview room and sat opposite a clearly nervous Luke and his solicitor. Clare's eye was drawn to a small plaster on his neck where the knife had nicked it, but he seemed otherwise unharmed.

'Before we begin,' the solicitor said, 'Mr Gasparini was the subject of a terrifying attempt on his life. We'd like to be assured the culprit will face the appropriate charges.'

Clare smiled. 'Rest assured, the person concerned is in custody and charges will follow. And, if Mr Gasparini feels unwell at any time, please let us know and we'll suspend the interview.'

'In that case, Mr Gasparini will be happy to co-operate.'

'Actually,' Luke broke in, 'I'd like to explain.'

Clare held up a finger. 'If you'll just wait a moment.' She started the recording and introduced herself, Tony and Chris. Then she cautioned Luke and he spoke to indicate he understood the caution. 'I gather you have something to say,' she began, and Luke nodded.

'And, is this in addition to your statement yesterday? When you accused your wife and her brother David of murdering Russell Fox?'

'Well,' Luke rubbed the back of his neck.

'Or do you wish to recant that statement?' Clare said, her tone brisk.

'Erm, yes.'

'To be absolutely clear, Mr Gasparini, you are now saying the statement you gave yesterday implicating Gabrielle Fox and David Fox in the murder of Russell Fox was false?'

He avoided her eye but gave a slight nod. 'Yes.'

Clare regarded him. 'Can I ask why you gave such an elaborate and completely false statement?'

His head drooped. 'Sorry,' he said after a few moments. 'I… I just panicked.'

Tony sat forward. 'You panicked so you decided to throw your wife under the bus?'

Luke flinched at this, but he said nothing.

Clare glanced at Tony who rolled his eyes. She turned back to Luke. 'Let's move on then. You said there was something you wanted to explain.'

He cleared his throat then said, 'About what I said... at the cottage.'

'In relation to Russell Fox's death?'

'Yes, that. Well, I may, in the past, I may have given Doug Gerrard the impression it would be better if Russell were to die. That's not to say I wanted it to happen, mind you.'

Clare made no reply, allowing an awkward silence to hang in the air.

'Just one of those conversations,' Luke went on. 'One night when we'd had a few too many; and Doug, well, it looks like he took it too far.'

'You are saying Doug Gerrard killed Russell Fox?'

'Oh no! Not that. But he might have, let's say, arranged it.'

'Doug Gerrard hired someone to kill Russell Fox?'

'I believe so.'

'And you conspired in that?'

'No, not as such.' He broke off, as if trying to find the right words. 'As I said, it was spoken about, mostly in jest, but then I think Doug must have thought I wanted it to happen. But I'm not responsible for him taking the law into his own hands, am I?'

Clare watched him. He was like a worm wriggling on the end of a hook. 'Why did you think it might be better if Russell Fox were to die?'

'Well, he was suffering from cancer. It can be a... a difficult death for some.'

'So your support for Russell Fox's murder wasn't motivated by him proposing to withdraw finance from your next TV series?'

'Absolutely not.' Luke shook his head vigorously, to confirm this.

'And your phone conversation with Doug Gerrard on the Friday evening – the one overheard by David Fox.'

Luke spread his hands. 'David only heard one end of the conversation. I think he must have misconstrued what Doug was saying.'

'What was the conversation about?' Clare asked.

'It's so hard to remember now. We were at the hotel, you know. Just about to go into dinner. Doug phoned. I think I asked if Russell was having a good birthday and he said something about him seeing the sunrise from the treetop walk the next morning.'

Clare studied him for a moment but he avoided her eye, smiling instead at Chris and Tony.

Tony leaned back in his seat and crossed one long leg over the other. 'What did you think when you heard about Russell Fox's death?'

There was a flicker in Luke's eyes. Clearly a question he hadn't prepared for. 'Oh, I'm not sure,' he said. 'Shocked, obviously. Yes, shocked. And concerned for Gaby. I mean her brother...'

Clare regarded him with something approaching contempt. She reckoned he was the type who would do anything to wriggle out of trouble. 'So to be absolutely clear, Mr Gasparini,' she said, 'you lay the blame for Russell Fox's death squarely with Doug Gerrard. Is that correct?'

'Yes,' he nodded. 'That's it. All Doug's doing.' He shook his head. 'I never imagined he'd go that far.'

'Thank you.' Clare's tone was brisk. She was keen to give nothing away. And then she said, 'And Gaby, your wife, did you add sleeping pills to her coffee?'

He flicked a glance at his solicitor then away again. 'I added one. Just the one.'

'Just one?'

'Yes.'

'Why?'

'Gaby had been through a traumatic week. It's no surprise she wasn't sleeping. So I found this cottage — peace and quiet, you know? David joined us for a night and I think it did Gaby good to spend some time with him. But, after he went she was tired, you know? She looked washed out and I thought, if I left her, she might sleep. So I told her I had some business to attend to and that I'd be gone for the day. She seemed fine with that so I made her some coffee. I knew she wouldn't take the pills. She always said she didn't like how they made her feel. But she was exhausted. So I added one to her coffee. Just so she'd be able to sleep while I was gone.'

It was all too glib. Too practised. Clare reckoned he'd been going over his statement since he'd been carted off in the ambulance. She saw his shoulders droop as he relaxed, having told his tale. She smiled, pretended to make some notes on her pad. Then suddenly she said, 'Gaby had ingested at least eight of the tablets, Mr Fox. Possibly as many as ten. Not just one.'

He seemed to be ready for this. 'I'm afraid I underestimated how devastated she was by her brother's death.'

'You believe your wife meant to end her life?'

He allowed his head to droop. 'I'm afraid so, Inspector.'

Clare observed him. He wouldn't be picking up an Oscar any time soon. 'Frankly, Mr Gasparini, I doubt your

345

account of events. However, we do have Mr Gerrard in the station so I've no doubt he'll bear out your statement – if it's correct.'

–

'What I don't get,' Chris said, 'is how Eamon Ferry didn't notice the gun in the car. It can't have still been in there when they were packing up.'

They were gathered in the incident room, Tony having pronounced Clare's office *stifling*. 'You and that damn virus,' he said. 'Turning up the radiators in August, for God's sake.'

'Yeah, whatever,' Clare said, pulling her jacket round her front. 'Anyway, Chris has a point. If Mark Mooney's telling the truth he put the gun in the back of Eamon Ferry's car. But, unless Eamon's in on the whole thing, the gun couldn't have been there when they drove back to Glasgow.' She turned to Chris. 'It definitely wasn't in the boot of the Range Rover when we saw them loading their bags.'

'Could be it's hidden somewhere in the Lodge grounds.'

Clare nodded. 'Unless Doug got rid of it before he called 999. But according to what David Fox said, Eamon knew early on that something had happened to Russell. David then left the Lodge early enough to see Zac Buchanan in the museum grounds. So I can't see how Doug would have had time to get rid of the gun.'

'So where is it?' Tony asked. 'You did have the grounds searched, Clare?'

'The area immediately surrounding the house, yes. But there's a lot of land. And I can't honestly see anyone

346

leaving a gun out in the open, to be collected. They're too expensive for that.'

Chris said, 'I think you're right Clare. I reckon he must have posed it somewhere for Val, or someone else, to collect once the fuss had died down.'

'In which case,' Clare said, 'it might still be there. Chris, can you ask Jim to send some cops up there for another look?'

Chris went off to find Jim. Tony watched him go then said, 'What you thinking?'

Clare frowned. 'I'm damned if I'll let Mark Mooney take all the blame for this one. In fact if I was his solicitor I'd be pleading coercion. A clever advocate could do something with that.'

'Yeah,' Tony agreed. 'I'd like to see those two charged.'

'Let's see if they can find the gun,' Clare said. 'Our Mr Gerrard is too damn cocky for his own good. We might just get a print or two off that gun, or the case.'

'And if not?'

Clare's shrugged. 'We can hold onto Doug for a few hours yet before we have to charge him. If necessary we can apply to have his detention extended. But I reckon we have enough to charge the pair of them. Doug with Incitement to Commit Murder and I'll have a bloody good go a Possession of a Firearm, with Intent.'

'And the TV lad?'

'Luke? Conspiracy to Commit. My guess is their defence advocates will turn on each other and sling enough mud so they both go down for it.'

'And druggling the wife?'

Clare frowned. 'That's a toughie. I'm going to speak to her later on. At the very least I can make her aware of our suspicions. It's up to her if she takes it on board or not.'

It was almost seven o'clock when Clare heard the gun had been found.

'There's a kind of old summerhouse,' Chris said. 'Over the hedge from the main part of the grounds. Not been used for years by the look of it. Trees grown up all round. But there's a new padlock and the windows were boarded up.'

'They got in?'

He nodded. 'Bolt cutters but they got in. Gun case was behind a load of old garden furniture. SOCO are going over it now.'

'It's enough,' she said. 'Let's get them charged.'

–

Doug Gerrard assured Clare he would be out of custody by morning.

'Go for it,' Clare said. 'Do your worst!'

Luke Gasparini burst into tears when he was told he'd be remanded in custody.

'They're gonna love him in Perth prison,' Chris said. 'All his airs and graces.'

'Won't they just,' Clare agreed. 'I couldn't care less about those two, but I do feel for Mark Mooney.'

'He's a cold-blooded killer.'

'The lad's right,' Tony agreed. 'Shot Russell Fox with a high-powered rifle. Deserves all he gets.'

Clare inclined her head. 'You're probably right,' she said. 'All the same,, those wee boys.'

'You're getting soft in your old age,' Tony said. 'Must be that virus. It's warped your brain.'

'What about David Fox?' Chris said. 'He's still in custody.'

Clare shook her head. 'Right now, Chris, I have no idea what to do with him.'

'You have to charge him,' Tony said. 'He's another one. Bloody maniac.'

Clare sank down in a chair. She was suddenly dog-tired. 'His brother's just been gunned down, shot by one of his closest friends; and then his brother-in-law tries to kill his sister.' She shook her head. 'You can see how…'

'Charge him with abduction,' Tony said. 'If you don't, I will.'

'Suppose.' She yawned.

'Home, you,' he told her. 'I'll sort out the charges.'

Clare pushed herself out of the chair. She had to admit she felt weary. Clearly whatever virus had assailed her was still in her system. 'Must be a novelty for you,' she said to Tony, 'working late.'

'Don't push it, Inspector.'

Chapter 52

A delicious aroma reached Clare's nostrils when she pushed open the door of Daisy Cottage. Her sinuses must be unblocked.

'I can smell again,' she said, falling into the DCI's arms.

He held her there for a moment then took her hand and led her through to the sitting room where her dining table was laid for two. 'Hungry?'

She pulled out a chair and sat down, kicking off her shoes. 'Surprisingly, yes. What is it?'

'Veg goulash. Rice or pasta?'

'Ooh rice, please. Benjy likes leftover rice.'

At the sound of his name Benjy trotted over and put his head on her lap. Clare ruffled his ears and he responded by licking her hand.

Over dinner, most of which Clare managed to eat, she told the DCI about the case. 'We've got them all in custody. I'm just not sure if the charges will stick.'

He helped himself to more goulash. 'Sometimes it's like that, Clare. You do your best, hand it over to the Fiscal and it's out of your hands from there.'

She nodded. 'Yeah, I know. It just doesn't sit easy. There's Mark Mooney, driven to shoot someone dead to protect his family.'

'So he says.'

'Yes, I know.' She put down her fork, her appetite sated. 'But I do believe him. And he'll serve the heaviest sentence of them all. It just seems unfair.' She pushed her plate away. 'He has such a lovely family, you know? Two smashing wee boys.'

'Clare.'

'Yeah, I know. Leave it at the station door. But sometimes…'

He smiled and took her hand across the table and she thought she'd never tire of his eyes. So piercingly blue.

'Come on,' he said. 'Over to the sofa and I'll give you a shoulder massage.'

As he teased out the knots in her shoulder she asked about his day.

'Interesting.'

'Oh?'

She swung her legs off the sofa and turned to face him. She caught a hint of his cologne, now so familiar and comforting. 'In what way?'

'I've been asked to apply for a promotion. Well, I say promotion, more of a sideways move. But a good one.'

Suddenly Clare was aware of the goulash lying heavy on her stomach and a sense of unease overtook her. 'Oh,' she said. 'That's quite something.' Somewhere, in the far reaches of her mind, she was transported back a couple of years. Sitting in this very house, having a similar conversation with her ex-partner, Geoffrey Dark. He had told her of an opportunity but it had meant him moving away to Boston. He'd assumed Clare would want to go with him and it had been the beginning of the end for their relationship. Was it happening again?

'I don't want to jinx it,' he said. 'Do you mind if we don't talk about it?'

'Oh,' Clare said again, not sure what else to say. 'Erm, of course. If you prefer.'

He wrapped his arms round her and kissed the top of her head. 'Coffee?'

'No,' she said. 'I mean, no thanks.' For some reason she felt like being awkward. 'I might go up and have a soak.'

He smiled. 'Sure you don't mind me not talking about the job?'

'Course not,' she said, but she didn't meet his eye.

'You go on then. I'll clear up down here.'

She knew she should offer to help. He'd made the meal. She ought to clear up. But instead she heard herself say, 'Thanks, I will if you don't mind.' Opening the door she beckoned to Benjy who leapt to his feet and followed her upstairs. She closed the bathroom door and turned on the taps. She poured some of her favourite Jo Malone bath oil in and sat down on the toilet lid, waiting for the bath to fill. Benjy put his front paws up on her legs, as though sensing she was upset and she bent to his face, wrapping her arms around him. 'You'll never leave me, will you Benjy?' And she felt the comfort of his tail beating against her legs.

Day 10: Monday

Chapter 53

Clare was delighted to see the reporters and camera crews had gone from outside the station.

'Press release gone out then?' she said as she entered the staff kitchen.

'Must have,' Chris said. 'We charged them all last night.'

She bent to put her lunchbox in the fridge and she thought back to last night. She'd gone straight to bed after her bath and had lain there next to the DCI, stiff as a board, a thick atmosphere separating them.

Over breakfast he'd asked her if everything was okay and she'd said *yes* that it was *probably just the cold in her head.*

Don't overdo it today, then, he'd said and she'd said *of course she wouldn't* then headed out to the car.

'Any reply to the charges?' she asked Chris.

'Only David Fox. Said prison would be a new experience, that a change was as good as a rest.'

'Hm,' Clare said. 'We'll see what he's saying after a few weeks of prison food.' She slammed the fridge door shut. 'Anything else?'

'Good news on the Range Rover.'

'Eamon Ferry's?'

'Yeah. Traces of gunshot residue. Glasgow cops are interviewing him today but I doubt he knows much about it. Doug Gerrard probably moved the gun out of the car before they called us in.'

Clare nodded. 'Sounds about right.' She switched the kettle on to make a hot drink. 'Pity we can't pin anything on Big Val, though.'

'Yeah. But she's a pro, Clare. Covers her back every time.'

'I'll get her one day. You see if I don't.' She began pouring boiling water into a mug. 'What about Tony?'

Chris shook his head. 'According to Zoe he won't be back today. He left a message. Said as it was all pretty much tied up there was no point in him being here.'

Clare frowned at the mention of Zoe's name. 'She okay about him? Not upset?'

Chris began to smile. 'Oh yeah.'

Clare looked at him. 'What? Come on, spill.'

'Remember the cake? The one she made for him and she wouldn't give anyone else a slice?'

'Yes.'

'And he said it wasn't like anything he'd ever tasted.'

'Yes.'

'Apparently it was a special recipe. Just for Tony.'

Clare began to laugh. 'Oh God. What did she put in it?'

'Half a tin of Pedigree Chum.'

Clare stared. 'The dog food?'

'Yup.'

'Can humans even eat that stuff?' She recalled the smell of some of the tins she'd tried out on Benjy before switching to dried food. 'Oh I feel sick at the thought of it.'

'Apparently it's safe enough,' Chris said, 'but he did have that gastric upset so...'

Clare laughed. 'I suppose the moral of that tale is don't mess with Zoe.'

'What we up to today, then?' Chris asked.

Clare picked up her mug and sipped from it. 'Think I'll pop along to the hotel and have a word with Gaby before she heads off home. We have half the house party in custody so I don't see any need for her to stay on.'

—

Gaby was delighted to see her. 'A friendly face,' she said standing back to admit Clare to her room. Clare had been in a few of the rooms at the Kenlybank Hotel but none so plush as Gaby's. Up on the top floor it had views across the countryside, north towards St Andrews and east to the North Sea. The enormous bed was piled high with pillows and cushions and there was a small sofa in front of a coffee table on which sat a hamper of snacks.

'Nice, isn't it?' Gaby said. 'Compared to London hotels. You really are spoiled here.'

Clare smiled round at the room. 'It certainly is.'

'Can I offer you something?' Gaby said, indicating the snacks. 'Or I could ring for room service.'

Clare waved this away. 'I won't keep you long. I just wanted to update you.'

Gaby listened while she explained that both Luke and Doug were in custody now.

'We do believe they conspired to have Russell shot,' she said.

Gaby put her head in her hands. 'I can almost believe it of Doug,' she said, 'but... Luke? My Luke?'

Clare nodded. 'I know. It's an awful lot to take in.' She hesitated then said, 'I'm not sure how to say this, Gaby, but we also suspect your overdose wasn't accidental.'

Gaby held up her hand. 'You're not telling me anything I don't know.' She shook her head. 'I don't *think* Luke tried to drug me. I *know* he did.'

Clare stared at her.

'I didn't get where I am without being sharp. I've had my rough times – I'm sure you have too. But the one thing I never did was to seek solace in a bottle of any kind, including pills. I only had a few of these pills to start with. I'm guessing Luke phoned for a repeat prescription for me and stashed them away.'

Clare said, 'But that would suggest it was planned.'

'Let's just say I threw a grenade in.'

Clare's brow furrowed.

'It's like this, Clare. You remember me telling you I thought I might give my share of Russell's money to dementia research?'

'Yes.'

'Well, it was only half an idea. I knew Luke was relying on Russell for his next TV series. He's so ambitious, you see? Once he's planning a production nothing gets in the way. And I knew too that he'd be expecting me to step in and fund it when Russell's legacy came through. I thought I'd see how he reacted if I said I was giving the money away.'

Clare looked at her. 'Gaby, you almost died.'

She nodded slowly. 'I know. That went badly wrong. But I have you to thank for saving me.' She rose and moved to the window looking out at the view. 'It changes you,' she said, 'something like this.' Then she turned back to face Clare. 'I'm not the person I was two weeks ago – the person you met at the wedding. I'm changed by what's happened.' She frowned. 'Keep this to yourself for now, but I'm moving back up to Scotland. I want to be near my daughter, and my dad for as long as I have him. David too,' she added. 'He's back in my life and I don't want to lose him again. Oh, I know he'll be in prison but I'll visit and, when he comes out, he'll have us to come out to.'

'But your TV show.'

'I'm cutting down. I'll do three days a week and give someone else the chance to do the other two. I'll fly down or take the sleeper; either way I'll make it work. I've spent far too long putting work before my family.'

'Are you going back to London today?' Clare asked.

Gaby shook her head. 'No. My daughter comes home from her school trip tomorrow. I want to be there to see her. I'll take her out for the day and we'll have a proper chat. She'll be upset, you know, about Luke.'

Clare rose from her seat. 'I've kept you long enough. But I do hope it all goes well for you, and your daughter.'

Gaby moved forward and took hold of Clare's hands. 'You've been such a rock this past week. Would you – will you come and see me when you're next in London? I'd like to see you again.'

–

The incident room was being restored to normal when Clare arrived back at the station. With Tony gone she spent most of the day in her office catching up on emails and outstanding tasks.

By four o'clock she'd had enough. The case was more or less tied up with reports prepared for the Procurator Fiscal and she decided to finish early. She sought out Chris and found him and Sara poring over kitchen brochures. Sara hurriedly shut them and put them in a drawer, but Clare waved this away. 'We've all been working like donkeys this past week. Enjoy a bit of downtime while you have it.'

'You heading off home, boss?' Sara said.

'Yeah. Home to relax. Unless anything else comes up I'll be back in tomorrow morning.'

She left them to their domestic plans and went out to the car. It was a lovely afternoon but the sun was lower in the sky now, summer turning to autumn. As she drove home, her pace more leisurely than usual, she admired the gardens in the Bogward Estate, filled with late summer favourites. The trees on the Craigtoun road were in full leaf and she drove on through dappled shade. At Daisy Cottage she could hear the sounds of Benjy in the garden and, instead of going in through the front door, she pushed open the gate and walked round to the back of the house. DCI Gibson was down on his hands and knees, weeding the border while Benjy chewed a toy rabbit, shaking it from time to time in a misguided attempt to stun it. The DCI rose when he saw her, dusting soil off his hands. She moved forward and held out a hand, taking hold of his muddy one.

'Sorry, Al. I was horrible last night.'

He smiled. 'Of course you weren't. But there is something wrong, isn't there?'

She hesitated. 'Fancy a drink? I've some cloudy lemonade in the fridge.'

She went in the back door and emerged minutes later carrying a tray with two tall glasses. She put it down on the garden table and they sat, enjoying the afternoon sun.

The DCI drank his down in one go. 'I needed that,' he said.

'More?'

He shook his head. 'No that's great, thanks. I want to get back to the weeding before I go off the idea. But… won't you tell me what's on your mind?'

Clare looked down at her glass, watching the bubbles rise to the surface. Her mouth was dry now and she took another sip. Then she said, 'The last thing I ever want to do is to stand in your way, Al.'

He frowned. 'Why would you ever think you'd do that?'

'Your promotion, or whatever it is. I do realise it'll be in Scotland and I know it's not a huge country but…'

He took hold of her hand. 'Clare.'

'I was so hurt when Geoff moved away. I don't think I could do that again.'

'Clare,' he said again, 'I'm not Geoff. And I'm not going anywhere. Not as long as you want me, at least.'

'Aren't you?'

'Of course not, you dope. The promotion – even if I get it, which is unlikely – I can choose my base.'

'Oh.'

'Yes.'

'And where would you go?'

He shrugged. 'I mean Dunfermline's great – friendly staff, I have a good office, handy for my house but it's a bit away from you; and I do seem to be spending more time here.'

She waited. Waited to see what he would say next.

'I thought maybe Dundee. It's a decent size of station, handy for St Andrews… and Daisy Cottage.' He smiled and began tracing a muddy finger across her hand. 'I could even think about renting my house out.' He flicked a glance at her. 'If I wouldn't be in the way here.'

A smile spread across her face. 'I like the sound of that, Al,' she said. 'I like it very much.'

'Good,' he said. ''Cause, frankly, this garden could do with a bit of attention and it gets bugger all from you.'

She laughed. 'None taken!' From within her pocket she felt her phone vibrate and her heart sank.

'Leave it,' he said.

She shook her head. 'You know I can't.' She took it out and a smile spread across her face. She swiped to take the call. 'Jude! Hi,' she said. 'Lovely to hear from you. How's—'

Her sister cut across her. 'Clare,' she said, an odd note to her voice, 'you're on speakerphone. Frank and I have some news…'

Clare realised what her sister was trying to tell her. *Don't ask about the baby. I'm about to tell you. Sound surprised.*

'We're having another baby!' Jude said and Clare heard the sound of Frank cheering in the background.

'Oh Jude,' Clare said, doing her best to sound as if this was news. 'How wonderful! Hold on, I'll pull out a sun lounger and you can tell me all about it.'

Two months later

Chapter 54

DCI Alastair Gibson held open the door and they walked into the building, following the signs for Reception. A smiling woman at the front desk checked their names, issued them with lanyards and said someone would come to collect them shortly.

'Nervous?' the DCI said.

She nodded. 'A bit.'

'You'll be great.'

A young woman in jeans and a red jumper appeared. 'DI Mackay?' she said.

'Clare's fine.'

She smiled. 'I'm Jess. I'll be looking after you this morning.'

They followed Jess through a security barrier, swiping their lanyards across a reader, then through a maze of corridors.

'Like a labyrinth, isn't it?' Jess said. 'Don't worry. Someone'll see you back.'

They passed endless doors labelled with numbers until, eventually, Jess stopped at one and swiped a reader with her lanyard. The door clicked and she pushed it open, leading them into a large room. There were desks dotted round one side with laptops standing open and a collection of low sofas towards the other end. At the top of the room there was a long table with a stack of plates and white china mugs. An urn was plugged in next to a selection of teabags and coffee sachets. Beside this was a large ashet of sandwiches and other savoury snacks. High on the wall were two TV screens showing the current programme, the morning news bulletin.

'Hungry?' Jess said. 'Tea? Coffee? We have bottles of water too, somewhere.' She cast vaguely around. 'I can get you water if you like?'

Clare said a small coffee would be lovely and Jess obliged, bringing a plate of sandwiches. Her stomach was turning somersaults but the DCI tucked into a bacon roll, pronouncing it delicious.

'I wouldn't eat for half an hour before you're on,' Jess advised. 'You don't want to be burping on live TV.'

'What time will I be on?'

'Just after the eleven o'clock news,' Jess said, 'unless anything changes.' She studied Clare then said, 'We'll get you into make-up about ten fifteen. Do a light check then you'll be ready to go. Just before we go to the news desk I'll take you to the studio door. Then one of the producers will escort you onto the set. You'll have a few minutes to get settled then we'll be live.'

Clare thought she might actually vomit from nerves.

The DCI saw this and squeezed her arm. 'You'll be great,' he said again. 'You've done TV stuff before.'

'Yeah, for work. When we're asking the public for help. But this is about me.'

Jess patted her on the shoulder. 'Trust Gaby. She's ace. She'll put you at ease and, honestly, it'll be over before you know it. It's only an eight-minute slot.'

A man Clare vaguely recognised rushed into the room, announcing he was famished. He made his way to the table and began loading a plate with sandwiches.

'Isn't that…' she began to whisper.

Jess smiled. 'Yep. Danny. His new six-parter starts on Sunday night so he's in for a chat.' She scanned a whiteboard across the room. 'Think he's on after you, Clare. You have top billing!'

They were just finished their coffees when Gaby appeared. She was beautifully dressed in an exquisitely cut pale grey outfit. 'Clare!' she said, all smiles. She touched her lightly on the arm. 'Can't kiss you, I'm afraid. Just out of make-up. Hair's like a brick!' She laughed and Clare was glad to see her looking more cheerful than the last time they'd met, in Gaby's hotel room.

'Do you remember Al from the wedding?' Clare said, indicating the DCI.

Gaby made a show of taking him in then winking broadly at Clare. 'Oh, I remember,' she said, and the DCI flushed.

Clare said, 'I'm as nervous as hell, Gaby. Not sure what I've let myself in for.'

Gaby sat down beside them, taking care to smooth her dress under her as she sat. 'Don't be,' she said. 'Just be yourself. It's a short item where I talk about my own recent experience of dealing with the police, then I introduce you and ask you a few questions about living and working in St Andrews – how it differs from bigger cities, how you're forging a career in a world that's still male-dominated, how to set about major enquiries from such a small base – it's a little bit of insight into the work you do. People love to hear behind-the-scenes tales from the emergency services.' She smiled again. 'I gather you inherited your dog during your first major enquiry in the town.'

Clare gaped. 'How on earth…'

'Oh we have very good researchers.' She nodded. 'The best.'

Someone shouted Gaby's name and she rose. 'Better go. Just off to run over a few things. I'll see you on set!' And with that, she swept off leaving Clare even more nervous than before.

Just after ten fifteen she was taken off to the make-up room. A man of about thirty sat her down in front of a brightly lit mirror and scrutinised her from behind.

'I don't want too much,' Clare said.

'Don't worry, love. We won't go *full panto* on you.'

As he worked he chatted away, dropped a few names of celebrities he'd worked with and in no time at all it was finished. He turned Clare round and she was amazed at her reflection. 'See?' he said. 'Told you you'd look fab.'

Clare was moved to another chair where a hairdresser began spraying dry shampoo into her hair, teasing out the layers. 'Just giving it a bit of body,' the woman said. Then she picked up a set of straighteners and set about tidying up loose ends. Finally, she sprayed Clare's hair, patting it to check it was secure. 'You'll do,' she said, and Clare rose from her seat. Jess appeared to take her back to the green room.

The DCI shook his head. 'My God but you scrub up well, Clare Mackay,' he said. 'You look amazing.'

Clare patted her hair nervously. 'It's not too much?'

'Definitely not. A bit OTT for chasing killers but, for TV, I'd say it's pretty much perfect.'

She smiled. 'Thanks, Al.'

At five to eleven Jess took her along a dark corridor towards a heavy door marked *Studio Four*. There was a red light illuminated outside the door and Jess put a finger to her lips. They stood silently for a few minutes until the red light went out. Jess tugged open the door and ushered Clare in. She was immediately struck by how bright the studio was. And how large. She recognised the set where she'd watched Gaby on the odd days she'd spent at home with daytime TV on in the background. But she was struck by how small the set itself was, compared to the rest of the studio. A gantry of lights hung from the ceiling and there were four, or was it five, large cameras on tripods, dotted around, cables trailing everywhere. A TV monitor out of sight of the cameras was showing the news presenter from another studio and, on the set itself, Gaby was having her face dusted with powder.

Another young woman led Clare across the studio and installed her on a sofa. A technician appeared and pinned a microphone to her jacket, tucking a power pack down the back of the sofa.

'You'll be on camera two,' the technician said. 'But try to ignore it. Just focus on Gaby and don't look around.'

Clare gazed at the camera. There was an autocue screen below the lens and she wondered if it was a backup for Gaby.

'Thirty seconds,' someone called.

'Okay?' Gaby mouthed and Clare nodded.

'Five, four…' the voice said then, out of the corner of her eye Clare saw a red light on the front of the camera. They were live.

'Welcome back,' Gaby was saying, and Clare tried to focus on her, making an effort to smile. Gaby explained she had recently suffered a family tragedy while on holiday in St Andrews and it had brought her into contact with police officers from the town. And then they were chatting. Clare began to realise why Gaby was so successful. She had a wonderful way of putting guests at their ease and she felt herself relaxing into the interview. She couldn't quite forget the presence of the cameras, but it really did feel like a conversation between two friends.

And suddenly Gaby was thanking her, saying what a pleasure it was to chat and she hoped Clare would come back again soon. She then turned to another camera and began to talk about the next item. Clare was aware that the red light on the camera had gone off but she sat on, smile fixed until Gaby introduced a short video piece. The technician then appeared at her side to remove the mic and Gaby walked across.

'Clare, you were fab! Well done. Twitter's full of it already, judging by the updates on my phone.'

'Thirty seconds, Gaby,' someone called, and Gaby rolled her eyes.

'Better get back. I'll be in touch.'

Clare was led back across the studio by the technician and through the heavy door. Back in the green room the DCI was full of it. 'You were brilliant,' he said, taking her in his arms and hugging her. 'My phone's buzzing with it.'

Clare felt as if a huge weight had been lifted from her shoulders. 'Was it really okay?'

'More than okay.'

Jess appeared and smiled. 'Bloody brilliant, Clare,' she said. 'Twitter's gone bonkers.'

They collected their coats and Jess led them back through the maze of corridors to the reception desk where they handed back their lanyards. As they approached the front door Clare switched her phone on and it immediately began to buzz. She stood inside the door waiting for her messages to load.

'One from Chris,' she said. She clicked to open it and saw a hyperlink. It took a few seconds for the link to load. 'Oh,' Clare said. 'It's a TikTok video.' She looked at the DCI. 'I've never used it. You?'

He shook his head. 'Let's see then.'

She held out her phone so they could watch then saw herself appear on the screen. She was sitting on the couch speaking to Gaby and had put out her arm, as if explaining something. But Chris had edited the video so her arm went in and out repeatedly, and he'd added an audio clip of *The Hokey Cokey*.

'That's really clever,' the DCI said. 'Look at this bit: *in-out-in-out* – he's matched it to your arm movements.'

'I'm going to kill him.'

'Eight thousand views already,' the DCI said. 'Clare, you're a TikTok sensation!'

'I really am,' she said. 'I'm going to kill him. And I'll get away with it because I know how!'

He took her hand and led her towards the door, which slid back, and they emerged into the autumn sun. The street was busy, cars whizzing back and forward, and he held up his hand to hail a taxi.

'Come on,' he said. 'Gaby's got us a table at The Ivy. Let's go and celebrate your new-found fame.'

Acknowledgements

There are so many lovely people who helped me turn a tangle of ideas into the book you have just read and I'd like to thank a few of them, below.

In the early days of planning *Next in Line* I badgered Ally Todd, Chris Roberts and Chris Smith with questions about guns. Guys, your knowledge was invaluable and, at times, worrying! The lovely Hilary Arsenault of the Leverhulme Research Centre for Forensic Science took such trouble to answer my questions in terms that even I could understand – huge thanks for that, Hilary. My good friend Isabel's medical knowledge made sure I didn't accidentally kill one of my characters and Jonathan Whitelaw so kindly allowed me to pick his brains on media matters. And, as ever, Alan Rankin is on hand to stop me making a fool of Clare and her team. Thank you all for giving your time and knowledge so willingly. I hasten to add that any errors in these matters are entirely mine. Never let it be said that I allowed the truth to get in the way of what I hope is a good story.

As the first draft left my hands a whole team of wonderful humans descended on it and helped turn it into a book I'm now so proud of. To my incredible editors, Louise Cullen and Siân Heap for their skill, patience and ability to tease out all the plot glitches, to the quite brilliant Francesca Riccardi and everyone at Team Canelo, I'm so proud to work with you all and so grateful for the magic touch you bring to my novels. Thank you for all you do. To the trio of folk who polish this novel until it shines, I am eternally grateful: Deborah Blake for her superb copy-editing, Abbie Headon for her eagle-eyed proofreading and James Macey for his glorious cover.

My agent Hannah Weatherill is a constant source of support and I feel so lucky to be one of her clients – thank you, Hannah, for being the absolute best any writer could wish for.

Finally, to the many booksellers, bloggers, reviewers and readers who have helped me to the point where I am publishing my fifth book, a sincere and heartfelt thank-you. I would be nowhere without your unfailing support and I'm so grateful for it.

Marion

CANELOCRIME

Do you love crime fiction and are always on the lookout for brilliant authors?

Canelo Crime is home to some of the most exciting novels around. Thousands of readers are already enjoying our compulsive stories. Are you ready to find your new favourite writer?

Find out more and sign up to our newsletter at canelocrime.com